College life 302;

Advanced Placement

J.B. Vample

Book Six

The College life series

COLLEGE LIFE 302-Advanced Placement

Copyright © 2018 by Jessyca B. Vample

Printed in the United States of America

First Printing, 2018

ISBN-10: 1-7323178-1-X (eBook edition)
ISBN-13: 978-1-7323178-1-9 (eBook edition)

ISBN-10: 1-7323178-0-1 (Paperback edition)
ISBN-13: 978-1-7323178-0-2 (Paperback edition)

For information contact; email: JBVample@yahoo.com

Website: www.jbvample.com

Book cover design by: Najla Qamber Designs

This is a work of fiction. Names, characters, places and incidents are either the product of the author's imagination or are used fictitiously, and any resemblance to actual persons, living or dead, business establishments, events or locales is entirely coincidental.

To all writers; write often, dream big, and always write what you love, no matter what.

Chapter 1

The sound of the heavy rain pounding against the window didn't faze Chasity Parker as she lay across her bed, focused on the television in front of her. She was glad to be relaxing in her room, rather than dragging her belongings from her car.

She'd returned to Paradise Valley University the previous evening, beating the impending storm and heavy traffic. Having unpacked everything in her room the night before, she had been looking forward to a little peace and quiet before her fellow housemates arrived.

The show that she was watching was a welcome distraction. It was nice to focus on the show's dialogue, rather than her own personal life.

The ringtone from her cell phone snapped Chasity out of her thoughts. She grabbed it and rolled her eyes at the screen.

"Yes *Mother*," Chasity answered, voice laced with annoyance.

Trisha Duvall giggled. "Damn girl, what's with the attitude?"

"I just talked to you like twenty minutes ago," Chasity reminded her. "That was *after* you called and woke me up this morning for nothing and *after* you kept me on the phone for my *entire* drive down here from West Chester last night."

She ran a hand through her long hair. "What more could you *possibly* have to say?"

"Is it so wrong that I enjoy talking to you?" Trisha asked.

"Yes, it *is*," Chasity answered bluntly. "Especially when it's irritating me."

Trisha laughed; she knew that it irritated her daughter when she called way too often. "Okay fine, I won't keep you long," she promised. "I just wanted to check in one last time to see if you're okay."

Chasity rolled her eyes as she put her head in her hand. "Don't start this again," she warned. She knew the very topic that Trisha was going to bring up—Jason.

"I just want to know if you saw him yet," Trisha said, confirming what Chasity already knew. "I want this rift between you two to go away, so I can have my future son-in-law back."

Chasity shook her head as she resisted the urge to hang up on Trisha. She had already asked her to stop bringing Jason's name up every five minutes. She hadn't seen him or spoken to him since their last face-to-face confrontation in his home over winter break. After an intense argument, Jason asked Chasity to give him time to be able to forgive her for lying and keeping secrets about her pregnancy and miscarriage. That was over a week ago.

Chasity took a deep breath as she tried to contain her rising temper. "No, I haven't seen him," she replied.

"Oh." There was a pause on the line. "Are you ever going to tell me what the argument is about?" Trisha asked. Even though Chasity told her that she and Jason were having problems, she had never revealed the details.

"Probably not," Chasity answered honestly.

Trisha sighed. "Well fine," she relented. "I'll drop the subject."

"Are you gonna get off the phone now too?" Chasity asked, hopeful.

Trisha sucked her teeth, "You are so damn

disrespectful," she hissed, Chasity smirked, relishing her mother's irritation. "Anyway, yes I'm getting off. Stay safe in that storm on your end."

"I will," Chasity promised before hanging up. She tossed the phone on the bed behind her and went to the kitchen. As soon as she opened the refrigerator to grab her left-over sandwich, she heard the door open. Recognizing the two loud voices, she shook her head.

"Will you hurry up and bring the bags in here?" Malajia Simmons ordered, removing a carry-all bag from her shoulder. "They're getting wet."

Mark Johnson dragged two heavy suitcases into the house. "How did I get stuck doing this shit?" he sneered, tossing the bags on the floor. "Wasn't your dad just out there? Why didn't *he* bring your crap in?"

Malajia looked at him as if he had lost his mind. "Boy, don't throw my shit," she barked.

Mark sucked his teeth. Then he kicked one of the bags with his foot, earning a glove being tossed at him by Malajia.

"Stupid," Malajia bit out, removing her other glove. "Anyway, my dad *was* gonna bring them in here, but then we saw your big ass head walking over to the car all hype and shit, so he figured *you* could bring them in so he could head back home," she answered, removing her coat.

Mark folded his arms, a stern look frozen on his dark face. "Yeah well, I'm not carrying those damn things upstairs," he refused, running his hand over his wet sweatshirt.

"Sure you are," Malajia contradicted confidently. "You may be a complete jackass, but you wouldn't let a girl carry heavy suitcases up a flight of stairs, would you?"

Mark narrowed his eyes at her before turning and walking out the door, much to Malajia's astonishment.

"Wait are you *seriously* not gonna take them up for me?" Malajia fumed, sticking her head out the door.

"Nope. Have fun dragging that shit upstairs, smart ass," Mark laughed, as he took off running in the direction of his house.

Malajia sucked her teeth before slamming the door shut. "Fuckin' *asshole*," she grunted. She looked up as she snatched her scarf from around her neck. She noticed Chasity standing in the kitchen watching. "Hey light-skin," Malajia smiled, referencing Chasity's light-brown complexion.

"You two are beyond stupid," Chasity said, opening a bottle of juice.

"No, it's just *him*," Malajia disagreed, walking in the kitchen. She reached for Chasity's sandwich. "When did you get back?"

Chasity smacked her hand away as she grabbed the plate off the counter. "Last night."

"Oh okay. That was smart," Malajia admitted. "Hell, I was trying to get my dad to bring me back *yesterday morning*, but he was bitchin' about not wanting to miss Dana's indoor track meet or some shit," she sneered, running her hands over her long burgundy-streaked hair. "The chick didn't even win."

Chasity stared at her for several seconds. "You sound like a brat, but I can't say I'm surprised," she smartly commented.

Malajia made a face at her as she tried to grab Chasity's juice from her hand. "Funny," she jeered.

"Stop trying to take my shit," Chasity snapped, moving her juice out of Malajia's reach.

"Is Jason back yet?" Malajia asked, folding her arms. "Have you talked to him?"

"I don't know and no," Chasity answered. "He's still not talking to me."

"Seriously?" Malajia replied. She let out a heavy sigh. "You want me to try—"

"No," Chasity cut in. "It is what it is, so let's not talk about it anymore."

Malajia put her hands up in surrender. "If you wish," she agreed. Even though Chasity was putting on a brave front, Malajia knew how much it was killing her that Jason was still upset with her. She gave Chasity a sympathetic look before giving her arm a slight rub. "I'm sorry though."

Chasity just shrugged slightly.

"You want to hear about my sister's losing ass race to make you feel better?" Malajia joked. Chasity chuckled. "She fell and everything."

"No," Chasity returned.

"Can I dye your hair then?"

Chasity frowned at the unusual request. Then again, she wasn't sure why she was surprised. Most of the things that came out of Malajia's mouth were unusual. "You...you just asked if you could dye my hair?"

Malajia nodded.

"First off, fuck no. Second...*why*?" Chasity fussed.

Malajia shrugged. "I just think you'd look cute with some color," she argued of Chasity's black hair, which fell to her chest. "You've had black hair since freshman year."

"I'm *already* cute," Chasity threw back. "And you've got nerve. You've been sewing that same color in *your* head since freshman year," she hissed. "At least *mine*, color and all, grows out of my head."

Malajia's mouth fell open. "Back to being hateful, I see," she sneered, then a smile crossed her pretty brown face. "We're officially back to normal."

"Yeah, yeah," Chasity mocked, walking into her room. "Move your damn bags before somebody falls over them."

"Can your strong ass help me take them upstairs?" Malajia called after her.

"No," Chasity refused, shutting the door behind her.

Alex Chisolm held her hood on her head as she made a dash for the door, dragging her suitcase behind her. After the bus from Philadelphia dropped her off just outside of campus, she jogged from the bus stop all the way to her house across campus to get out of the pouring rain.

Pushing open the door, she hurried in and collapsed face

first into the cushy sofa.

Malajia, who was struggling to drag one of her suitcases upstairs, sat on the steps and looked at her. "Can you shut the damn door please? The rain is blowing in here," Malajia ground out, shielding her face from water sprays.

Alex sat up, breathing heavily. "Shut up and give me a minute," she bit out, pushing her hood back. "I just ran like ten blocks straight." After catching her breath, she got up and shut the door. She looked at Malajia, who was still sitting on the steps, examining her nails. "How long have you been trying to get that bag upstairs?" Alex chortled.

"About as long as it took your big ass to run across campus from that ghetto bus stop," Malajia spat, eyes not leaving her nails. "They don't even have a place to sit out there."

Annoyed by Malajia's smart mouth, Alex grabbed her suitcase and headed up the stairs past Malajia.

"Wait, can you help me with this bag?" Malajia asked as Alex nudged her with her hips to get by.

"Hell no," Alex sneered. "You just smart-assed your way out of getting any help from me."

Malajia sucked her teeth. "Fine," she mumbled, as Alex opened her room door. "I noticed you finally got a new suitcase with some wheels on it. At least I don't have to see that raggedy duffle bag anymore!" she hollered up the steps.

When Alex didn't respond, Malajia figured she would goad her more. "Hey, since you upgraded your bag, do you think you can upgrade that old ass flip phone you got?"

"Malajia!" Alex shouted, earning a snicker from Malajia. "Don't make me come down there and smack you."

"I'll smack that flip in the garbage disposal if you do," Malajia shot back, then laughed when she heard the door slam shut.

"I can't believe this rain," Emily Harris complained to her father as he pulled into an empty parking space in front of her house.

"I know, it's terrible," Mr. Harris agreed, turning the car off. "Which is why I want to hurry up and get back on the road." He pulled his coat hood up, then opened the door.

Emily stuck her key in her door and smiled. She was excited to be back on campus. Pushing the door open, she hurried in and tripped over a suitcase that was lying near the steps. She let out a scream as she fell to the floor. "Whose bag is this?!" she yelled, rolling over.

Chasity emerged from her room to see Emily sprawled out on the floor; she busted out laughing.

Rolling her eyes, Emily let out a sigh. "Very funny, Chasity," she sneered, struggling to get up.

Still laughing, Chasity walked over and grabbed Emily's outstretched hand, pulling her from the floor. Chasity shook her head as Emily dusted herself off. "Malajia, come get your damn bag!" Chasity shouted up the steps.

"Fuck that bag!" Malajia shouted back through the closed bathroom door.

"I just *tripped* over it!" Emily hollered.

"Who is that?" Malajia shouted down.

Emily removed her coat. "Emily!"

"Fuck Emily," Malajia joked. Chasity snickered as Emily's mouth fell open in shock.

"So rude," Emily muttered.

Mr. Harris entered the house, carrying Emily's bags. "I think I grabbed everything," he announced, making his way up the steps.

"Hey Mr. Harris," Alex greeted on her way down the steps. "What was all the noise?" she asked, hugging Emily.

"Emily busted her ass on Malajia's bag," Chasity informed with amusement.

Emily shook her head as Alex glanced down at said bag.

"That thing is *still* down here?" Alex quibbled. "I've been upstairs for hours."

If anybody had a response, they didn't say it because they were focused on Mr. Harris walking back down the steps. "Okay sweetie, I'm gonna head out," he said, giving Emily a kiss on her cheek. "I want to hit the express way before it gets too crowded."

"Okay, be safe," Emily smiled.

Before walking out, Mr. Harris pointed to the suitcase on the floor. "Do you ladies need me to take that upstairs for you?" he asked.

"Malajia, do you want help with your bag?" Emily bellowed up the steps.

"I said fuck that bag!" Malajia barked, much to Emily's astonishment.

"Hey, you ignorant bitch! Somebody is trying to *help* your stupid ass!" Chasity hurled back.

"Malajia! Emily's father is down here, you fool," Alex added. She then gave Chasity a stiff backhand to her arm.

"Ouch!" Chasity grabbed her arm, shooting Alex a lethal glare in the process.

"Curb your potty mouth, there's a *parent* in here," Alex hissed through clenched teeth,

Mr. Harris put his hand over his face to hide his laughter. Emily once again shook her head.

"Sorry for cussing," Chasity muttered, folding her arms. "She irritates me."

Mr. Harris put his hands up. "It's okay."

Snatching the bathroom door open, Malajia darted out and stormed down the steps. "Why the hell is everybody yelling at me?" she snapped. Stopping in the middle of the stairwell, her eyes widened. "Oooooh," she said, seeing Emily's father. "Sorry."

Mr. Harris smiled. "Is this your bag?" he asked.

Malajia gave a nervous laugh. "Yeah."

He pointed to it. "Would you like me to carry it upstairs for you?"

"Yes please," she replied, a big smile plastered to her face. She skipped down the rest of the stairs and watched as Mr. Harris picked up the heavy suitcase and proceeded to carry it upstairs. As soon as he was out of sight she said,

"You can carry *me* upstairs too you old, sexy, strong ass, light skin, black bastard."

"Malajia come on!" Emily exclaimed as Chasity busted out laughing. "I'm standing right *here!*" Emily was mortified. Her light brown face was nearly flushed red.

"Oh shit, my bad Em," Malajia joked, giving the annoyed Emily a hug.

"Why do you always have to be disrespectful?" Alex chided, folding her arms. "That's her *father* for God sakes."

Malajia sucked her teeth at Alex. "*So?* He's bangable," she teased. Emily put her hands over her ears as she walked into the kitchen. "*Your* dad is bangable *too* Alex," Malajia joked. Alex flagged her with her hand as she sat on the couch. Malajia looked at Chasity. "I haven't seen *your* dad since the ski trip, but from what I remember, *he's* bangable *too.*"

"First off, eww," Chasity scoffed, sitting on the couch. "Second, *I* haven't seen his ass since then *either.*"

"Alright ladies, have a good one and stay dry," Mr. Harris said, trotting down the stairs. "Love you Emily, see you."

"Love you too Daddy," Emily waved as her father walked out the house.

"*I* love you *too* you fine, geriatric son-of-a-bitch," Malajia joked at the closed door. Alex tossed her hands in the air as Chasity shook her head.

Emily couldn't help but snicker at Malajia's silliness. "You know what?" she said, pointing a warning finger at her.

"I'm just messing with you Em," Malajia giggled, sitting on the arm of the couch. "This rain is some bullshit. I'm tryna do something fun," she whined.

"Girl, we *just* got back on campus and you're trying to go act a fool already?" Alex asked, laughter in her voice. "How about you start unpacking all that stuff you have."

Malajia rolled her eyes. "*That's* not fun," she complained, flopping down on the sofa.

After moments of silence, Emily grabbed a bottle of

water from the kitchen counter. Walking back into the living room, she debated if she should bring up what was on her mind. She didn't want to dampen the lighthearted mood, but she felt that it was necessary.

"Um okay…" she began, standing near the couch. "I don't mean to bring up painful stuff…I know how bad this winter break was for you both, Malajia and Chasity."

Malajia and Chasity glanced over at her.

"But…how are you both doing?" Emily asked, concerned. "I know I haven't talked to you much since the incident at the house."

"I'm fine," Malajia returned, though Chasity remained silent.

Alex eyed her with concern. "Are you sure?"

"Yes," Malajia insisted. Malajia understood why they were concerned. Not only did her friends learn of her abusive relationship with Tyrone, they witnessed a brutal fight between Malajia and Chasity, all during a trip to a Virginia lodge during winter break.

Alex reached over and grabbed Malajia's hand, then looked at Chasity. "What about *you*, sis?"

"I'm okay," Chasity answered finally.

"Are *you*, sure?" Emily questioned.

"No," Chasity returned, honest. "But I have no choice *but* to be, so I *will* be."

Alex opened her mouth to give some advice, but decided against it. Chasity had suffered a miscarriage, gotten attacked by Malajia's abusive boyfriend, gotten into a fight with her best friend, and potentially lost her boyfriend all within a short amount of time. It was understandable that she was not okay at that moment.

With her free hand, Alex grabbed Chasity's hand and held it. Chasity looked over at her, eyeing her with skepticism. Alex's intense gaze was creeping her out. "Alex," she called.

"Yeah?"

"You want to stop fondling my goddamn hand?" Chasity

bristled.

"I know right?" Malajia added. "She caressing the *shit* out of my fingers."

Alex busted out laughing. "I was trying to show you both that I'm here for you," she explained.

Chasity moved her hand from Alex's grip. "You looked creepy as shit," she sneered. "You were staring at me like—"

"She wanted to eat you?" Malajia cut in.

"*No*, you freak," Chasity scoffed.

"Why do you always gotta be so damn inappropriate?" Alex followed up, disgusted. Emily was too busy laughing to say anything.

Malajia looked confused. "I was talking about eating as in *cannibalism*," she clarified. "Who's the freak *now*?"

"*Still you*," Alex argued. "That's no *better*."

Malajia waved a dismissive hand as she sat back in her seat. "Whatever, stop being weird and we won't have these types of arguments."

"Malajia, whatever happened to Tyrone?" Emily asked, curious.

"I hope he's dead," Chasity bit out.

"Unfortunately, I'm not that lucky," Malajia grunted. The memory of her ex-boyfriend was filled with hatred. "But just know that that bastard is out of my life for good."

"Did the police ever pick him up?" Alex wondered. "I know you filed charges—"

"Let's talk about something else," Malajia quickly dismissed. She hoped that was the last time that she would ever have to talk about Tyrone. "Em, I heard you got off academic probation. Congratulations."

"Thank you," Emily beamed. "It's a big relief."

"Is academic probation hard to get off of?" Malajia asked, much to the confusion of the other girls. "'Cause I'm about one F away from being put on there my-damn-self."

"Hush up, silly," Alex laughed.

The light chatter was interrupted by the front door opening. It was silent as Sidra Howard walked through the door. Sidra locked eyes with the girls; she smiled.

"Hey...*Alex* and *Emily*," she greeted.

Malajia sucked her teeth. "Oh foreal? It's like *that* now?" she sneered.

Sidra sat her umbrella in a corner behind the door, ignoring Malajia. "Can you believe all this rain?"

Alex and Emily glanced at each other before turning away from the awkward exchange.

Chasity rolled her eyes. "You're really gonna act like we're not here?" she questioned, angry.

"What's your deal, Sid?" Malajia added. "What, are you just *not* gonna talk to us?"

"Oh *now* you want to talk to me?" Sidra hissed, slamming her gloves on the chair.

Malajia shook her head. "You trippin'," she shot back. "I'm your damn roommate, you're gonna *have* to talk to me eventually."

"When Chasity and I were roommates, we went a long time without speaking to each other at first, so I'm sure it can be done again," Sidra spat before walking upstairs, leaving the girls downstairs astonished.

"If she wants to play that silent treatment game, we can play it," Chasity snarled, standing from the couch. "I don't have to deal with her bullshit. I got enough going on."

"Well...*Malajia* does because she has to room with her," Alex pointed out.

Malajia let out a sigh. "Damn it," she whined. "I *can't* be silent. I don't operate like that." She looked over at Chasity's retreating back. "Chasity, can I move in with you?"

"No," Chasity threw over her shoulder.

Malajia turned her attention to Alex. "Alex, you wanna trade rooms back?" she proposed.

Alex rose from the couch. "Nope," she laughed, heading upstairs.

"Come on, I'll take Emily this semester," Malajia begged. She let out a huff when Alex ignored her. "Emily come on, we can be roommates. I'm fun," Malajia directed to

Emily.

Emily shook her head.

"You *know* you don't wanna room with Alex anymore," Malajia harped, slamming her hand on the arm of the couch. "She be having y'all room smelling like feet and shredded cheese."

Emily patted Malajia on the shoulder. "Sorry sis. Good luck," she giggled before darting upstairs. Annoyed, Malajia kicked the chair with her foot.

Chapter 2

Jason Adams adjusted the duffle bag on his shoulder as he walked through his front door. He dragged his suitcase in and let out a deep sigh, shutting the door behind him. The train ride from West Chester back to campus felt longer than usual.

After a bad winter break, Jason was eager to start a new semester. He only hoped that it would be better than the last one. Walking to his room, he stuck his key in the door. Pushing it open, he was shocked to find Mark dancing around the room in nothing but his boxers.

"What the fuck?!" Jason exclaimed, dropping his suitcase to the floor with a loud thud.

Startled, Mark spun around and removed the headphones from his ears "Oh shit!" he panicked, darting to his chair to grab his sweat pants.

Jason's handsome light brown face was masked with disgust. "What the hell were you doing?" he asked.

Mark stepped into his pants. "My bad dawg, I didn't hear the door open," he admitted, pulling his pants up.

"Yeah, no shit," Jason chuckled, sitting his bag on the floor. "You better not have been on my damn bed with just your boxers on."

"Come on, I wouldn't even *do* some shit like that," Mark

laughed, greeting Jason with a hand shake. "How was your trip in?"

Jason kneeled down and unzipped his suitcase. "Too damn long," he grunted, removing several items from the bag. "It's good to be back."

"I hear you man. This break sucked," Mark replied. "I'm surprised you didn't come back yesterday like the *rest* of us."

"I was *going* to, but I had some last-minute running around to do... Naw I'm lying, my family talked me into staying one more day," Jason chortled. "I guess it was for the best, I saw that it was raining pretty bad down here."

"Yeah, it was," Mark confirmed. He tapped his fingers on his desk as Jason began putting clothes in his drawers. "So, the SDC is holding a back to campus night right now. There's supposed to be games and food. We were all talking about heading over there. You wanna come?"

"No, I think I'm just gonna chill and finish unpacking," Jason said. "But thanks though."

"Sure," Mark said, pulling a sweatshirt over his head. Before walking out the door, he turned to Jason. "Yo, it's not gonna be all awkward, is it?"

Jason looked up at Mark, perplexed. "What are you talking about?"

"'Cause, you know, with you and Chaz not speaking right now and shit," Mark clarified. "We just want to make sure that we don't have to walk on sea shells around y'all."

"You mean *egg* shells?" Jason chuckled.

"Yeah man, you know what I meant," Mark snapped. "So, *is* it? I'm not tryna go through that sophomore year shit."

Jason shook his head; it was hilarious how Mark got so worked up when trying to have a normal, serious conversation. "To answer your question...no, it's not going to be," he assured, folding his arms.

"Have you spoken to her?" Mark wondered.

Jason slowly shook his head. "Not since the last time I saw her," he admitted, sorrowfully. "But I *will*...soon."

"Oh...Well good," Mark muttered, walking out the room, leaving Jason to his thoughts.

As Jason continued to unpack his belongings, his mind was racing. He had anticipated the inevitable face-to-face with Chasity the entire train ride back to campus. Having a little more time to reflect and come to terms with his feelings, he'd come to a decision.

Malajia skipped down the steps and headed over to Chasity's bedroom, opening the door.

"Still not practicing the art of knocking on the damn door, huh?" Chasity ground out, sitting on her bed.

Malajia closed the door. "No, and if you *really* wanted to keep me out, you wouldn't keep forgetting to lock it," she teased, leaning up against the door.

"Yeah that *still* doesn't stop you," Chasity calmly pointed out.

"So why are we even having this conversation?" Malajia shrugged.

Chasity rolled her eyes. "What can I do for you Malajia?" she sniped.

"Sooo," Malajia began, looking at her nails. "I talked to Mark a few minutes ago."

Chasity stared at her. "And I should *care* because?"

"He said that Jason is back," Malajia revealed, ignoring Chasity's tart response. "He got in not too long ago."

Chasity successfully hid her anxiety "Oh really?" she replied evenly. "That's nice."

Malajia eyed her skeptically. "So you gonna sit there and act like you don't wanna run over and see him?" she asked, folding her arms.

Chasity's leg started bouncing up and down. "I *don't*," she denied. "When he's ready to see me, he knows where to find me."

Malajia stared at Chasity's leg. "That nervous tick in your leg tells me you're not as calm as you're putting on."

Chasity sucked her teeth; she wasn't even aware that she was doing it. *Damn it!* "Mind your business."

Malajia put her hands up. "Okay fine snappy, I'll drop it," she relented. "Anyway, the real reason why I came down here was to tell you that there is a back-to-school night thing going on in the SDC, and you're coming."

"No, I'm *not*," Chasity refused. "I'd rather stay in my room."

"And do *what*?" Malajia pressed, annoyed. "Sulk?"

"Yup," Chasity bit back.

Malajia stomped her foot on the floor. "Come *on!*" she yelped. "Alex and Emily are corny and Sidra is still being a petty bitch," she complained. "You *gotta* come. Besides, they're gonna have a spades table and I need my partner… It's time for you to have some fun."

"I don't *want* to," Chasity stood firm.

Malajia narrowed her eyes at the stubborn Chasity. "Let me tell you something, heffa," she began, earning a glare from Chasity. "You will *not* hibernate in your damn room all semester because you're trying to avoid running into Jason."

Chasity was shocked. "That's *not* what—"

"You can't lie to me, so don't even try," Malajia interrupted, stern.

Not having anything to say, Chasity shut her mouth.

"Look sweetie, I get that you two are going through something and I get that you're afraid to see him right now," Malajia said. Chasity let out a loud sigh. "But you're *not* gonna be able to avoid him. This campus isn't but so big. So cut this sophomore year shit out Parker and bring your ass to the goddamn game night!"

Chasity glared daggers at her and Malajia stared back, challenging Chasity to say something.

Defeated, Chasity jumped up from her bed. "I don't appreciate the way you're talking to me," she hissed, grabbing her coat.

"Yeah well, I'm not scared of your ass, so let's go," Malajia shot back, pointing to the door.

Chasity snatched the door open. "I liked it better when you *were* scared of me," she sniped, walking out the door with Malajia following.

"Bitch I was *never* scared of you!" Malajia exclaimed, voice filled with laughter, closing the door behind her.

Loud chatter, music, and laughter could be heard even before anyone walked through the doors of the Student Development Center. Inside, returning students of Paradise Valley University were greeted by tables designated for different games, including several card and board games. There was also an area designated for table games, including but not limited to ping-pong, ice hockey and pool. There were buffet tables set up with finger foods, desserts, and plenty of non-alcoholic beverages. The student DJ had many of their fellow students dancing either in their seats or on the floor.

Malajia, having walked in with the other girls, was dancing to the music herself. "It's poppin' in here tonight," she mused, breaking it down further.

Alex looked at her and shook her head. "You look crazy," she teased.

"No, I'm *killin' it* and you're mad," Malajia threw back. "*You* need to dance. You got too much ass to just be standing there."

Alex flagged Malajia with her hand.

Malajia scanned the entire room with her eyes. "Where's the spades table?" she wondered. Looking around some more, she saw Mark and Josh sitting at a small table with two other students across the room.

Mark slammed his final card down on the table. "Ah, beat that joker baby!" he boasted. "Get that ten of club outta here cuz." As Josh Hampton picked up the book and the defeated opponents rose from the table, Mark tossed his hands up. "I told y'all I'm a beast at this game. Who's next?"

Giggling, Malajia pointed to the table. "I'll be over

there," she declared. She grabbed Chasity's hand. "Come on partner, let's go kick his ass."

"Fine," Chasity sighed, allowing herself to be pulled along.

Noticing the two girls walking over, Josh smiled at them. Mark on the other hand, pointed to them, frowning in the process. "Hell no," he barked. "Cheater one and two aren't welcome to play at my table."

"Shut your dumb ass up," Chasity hissed, pulling out her chair.

"Boy stop bitchin' and deal the damn cards," Malajia jeered, sitting down across from Chasity.

Josh laughed as he began to shuffle.

Alex pointed to the table game area. "I have a date with that ping-pong table," she announced, smiling.

Emily craned her neck to see where Alex was pointing. Seeing a familiar face, she glanced at Alex. "Do you see Eric over there?" she asked.

"Sure do, which is why I'm going over," Alex replied. Alex hadn't seen or spoken to her former sex buddy Eric Wendell since she had gone home on break. She found herself thinking about him a lot and was dying to go say hi. "You two coming?" she asked Emily and a sullen looking Sidra.

"I'll be over after I grab something to eat," Emily promised. Alex nodded, then made her way through the crowd to her destination.

Emily looked over at Sidra, who was standing there with her arms folded. "Are you gonna play any games?" she asked.

"I'll play spades with the guys once the liars get up from the table," Sidra spat, examining the dark grey nail polish on her nails.

Emily shook her head at Sidra's reply. "Sidra, Malajia and Chasity didn't *lie* to us," she pointed out, calm.

"They withheld information, it's the same thing," Sidra snapped.

"No, I don't think it *is*," Emily replied slowly, much to Sidra's annoyance.

"I see David over at table tennis, I'll be over there," Sidra dismissed, before quickly sauntering off.

Emily just waved her hand in Sidra's direction then headed for the food table. *She's being ridiculous*, she thought.

"Y'all cheating!" Mark hollered as Chasity picked up their third book. "Where did y'all get all those damn spades from, huh?"

"I swear this is the *last* time I play spades with his loud ass," Chasity bit out, rearranging the cards in her hands.

"We got the spades from the same place you got all those sad ass hearts," Malajia shot back. Chasity snickered.

Mark sucked his teeth and mumbled something incoherently.

"Don't get mad at *us* 'cause you were dealt a bad hand," Malajia goaded. "Get mad at *Josh. He's* the one who shuffled."

Josh tossed a card on the table. "Yeah well, *you* cut the deck," he mumbled of Malajia.

"You just better not throw another spade out," Mark grumbled, studying his cards.

"Or *what?*" Malajia challenged, putting a card out. "You stay talking shit."

"You heard what I said," Mark threw back, tossing out a card.

Chasity quietly threw a spades card on the table, winning yet another book.

Angry, Mark pounded his fist on the table and let out a loud scream. Annoyed by Mark's outburst, Josh threw his cards on the table accompanied with a loud sigh.

"I can't," Chasity barked, slamming her cards down. She

pushed herself away from the table along with Josh.

"Come on, don't leave guys," Malajia pleaded.

"He keeps screaming near my fuckin' ear," Chasity seethed.

"Yeah, I'm with you Chaz. I can't take his loudness anymore," Josh agreed. "Come on, let's go check out that dessert table."

Malajia sucked her teeth as Chasity and Josh walked off. "You always gotta ruin shit," she hurled at Mark, gathering the cards.

"Shut up and be my damn partner," Mark shot back, seeing two other students approaching the table.

"Fine," Malajia huffed, shuffling the deck.

Alex smiled at Eric, watching him lightly tap the ping-pong ball with his paddle. She took a swing at the ball and missed. "I don't even know why I call myself playing this game," she laughed, picking the ball up from the floor. "I'm terrible at this."

"You just need a few lessons, that's all," Eric smiled, setting his paddle on the table before leaning against it.

Alex walked over and stood in front of him. "Are you willing to teach me?" she asked seductively.

Eric looked at her with longing, remembering the intimate moments they had shared last semester. "Sure… You want a lesson *now*?"

Alex tilted her head. "Are we talking about ping-pong or sex?" she questioned, already having an inkling of what his answer would be.

"That depends on *you*," he answered.

She bit her bottom lip and her dark-brown face flushed as she contemplated his proposition; then remembered that she had ended their casual sex relationship months ago because she couldn't handle it. "I think we should stick to the ping-pong Mr. Wendell," she said, reaching around him and grabbing the paddle.

Eric chuckled, watching her walk back to the other side of the table. He tried not to focus on the sway of her voluptuous hips and behind. "Very well Ms. Chisolm," he said, grabbing the ball. "I'll give you a few lessons, and then we'll make a bet."

"And what bet would *that* be?" Alex asked, curious.

"If you can't get the ball past me one time, you have to go out on a date with me," Eric propositioned.

She narrowed her eyes. He knew that she wasn't interesting in dating. "And what if I *do* get it past you?"

He thought for a moment. "You still have to go on a date with me, but I'll let *you* pick the place."

Alex shook her head; he was persistent, she had to give him that. But as much as she found this tall, dark skinned man attractive and enjoyed his company, she was determined to stick to her guns and not date while she was focused on school.

"So? What do you say?" Eric pressed. "You want to make that bet?"

Alex set her paddle on the table in front of her. "How about we just go grab something to eat from one of those tables?" she suggested.

Eric shrugged. "Very well," he said. He left his paddle on the table and put his arm around Alex's shoulder. "We'll revisit this later," he stated confidently.

Sidra grabbed a can of soda and a plastic cup from the refreshment table. She watched David with amusement as he played table tennis against a classmate. "You got this David," she encouraged, opening the can.

"I highly doubt that," David Summers disagreed, missing yet another shot.

Her cheerful demeanor faded when she saw Josh and Chasity approach the table. Rolling her eyes at Chasity, she directed her attention to Josh. "Hey Josh, are you having fun?" she asked.

Noticing the tension between the girls, Josh cleared his throat. "Uh, yeah. It's pretty cool," he replied. "It's nice that the school did this."

"I know right?" Sidra agreed, taking a sip of her drink.

Chasity stood there glaring at Sidra while she spoke with Josh. Irritated with being ignored, she snapped her fingers in front of Sidra's face.

Sidra snapped her head in Chasity's direction.

"Oh *now* you see me?" Chasity hissed.

"Whatever Chasity," Sidra spat out. "What do you want?"

"I *want* you to stop acting petty," Chasity argued.

"I'm not *acting* anything," Sidra shot back, sitting her drink down.

Chasity folded her arms. "Oh? So you really *are* petty then."

Sidra sucked her teeth and turned away.

"What the hell is your problem anyway?" Chasity wondered, angry.

Sidra put her hand up. "I don't *have* a problem okay," she spat. "And even if I *did*, I damn sure wouldn't tell *your* secret keeping ass." Sidra punctuated her retort with a flick of her long ponytail as she stormed off.

Seething, Chasity pointed in Sidra's direction as she looked at Josh. "Josh, I'm two seconds from chopping that fuckin' ponytail off your friend's stuck up head," she warned.

Josh chuckled. "I don't think that'll be necessary," he said.

"I disagree," Chasity returned. "I can choke her with it."

Josh shook his head. "She *is* being a bit dramatic," he agreed. "I don't get why she's annoyed with you and Mel. She should be *supporting* you two."

Chasity just shook her head. "To think, you're actually in *love* with that mess," she scoffed, walking off, leaving Josh standing there.

"Yes, I know," he said to himself.

Chapter 3

Having finished unpacking, Jason relaxed in the living room of his cluster house, watching a movie on the shared forty-two-inch television. After suffering through an hour of a lackluster film, he decided to take a walk. His leisurely stroll through campus took him to the SDC. Removing his hands from his coat pockets, he opened the glass door and walked inside.

Students greeted Jason as he entered the crowded space. He just smiled as he scanned the entire space with his eyes. Not really feeling like being around a crowd of people, he turned and walked out. He planned on heading back to his room to finish his movie. But hearing loud music coming from the girls' house, he stopped. He stared at the door for what seemed like forever, but in reality, it was only a few seconds.

"Just go in," he coaxed himself. Knowing that the girls usually left the front door unlocked while at home, Jason didn't bother knocking. Instead, he twisted the door knob and walked inside. Seeing a few of his friends battling each other's dance moves in the middle of the living room, he shook his head in amusement.

"You can't out dance me cuz," Mark boasted, dancing in Malajia's face.

"Move boy, you just spit in my damn face!" Malajia erupted, giving him a push with her hand. She signaled to Alex. "Alex, get over here and take my place while I disinfect my damn face."

"Gladly," Alex laughed, walking over.

"Whatchu' got bee?" Mark taunted as Alex began dancing.

"He keeps doing the same moves," Josh laughed, before taking a sip of his beer.

"Hey Jase," David waved, seeing him standing by the door. "You see this craziness?"

"It's hard to miss," Jason chuckled, removing his coat and setting it on the arm of the couch.

"Jase, come dance with me," Malajia suggested, walking back into the living room from the kitchen. "I'm sure you've got better moves than *Mark's* two-steppin' ass," Malajia jeered, pointing to Mark. Despite what Malajia said, for being a tall, solid man, Mark had some pretty good dance moves.

"You mad 'cause you lost," Mark taunted. Malajia ignored him and focused her attention on Jason.

"There's no liquor, but Josh bought some of those watery ass beers that he likes," Malajia said, pointing to the refrigerator. She wasn't sure if Jason was staying or not, but Malajia wanted to make sure she stalled him long enough for Chasity to see him.

She got her wish when she heard Chasity and Emily approach the top of the stair case. Malajia saw how Jason glanced up the steps at the sound of Chasity's voice.

"Come on Chaz, please?" Emily laughed.

"Emily, I refuse to tutor you in yet another foreign language," Chasity spat, walking down the steps. "You worked every part of my nerves when I tutored you in Spanish."

"But it's not even *Spanish*," Emily replied, following her down the steps. "It's Chinese."

Chasity looked back at a laughing Emily. "What?" she

exclaimed. "Girl, I don't know how to speak Chinese!"

"Emily, I told you not to choose that shit for your second foreign language requirement," Malajia cut it. "*Nobody* knows that shit. You might as well drop that class, boo."

"I know right?" Chasity agreed. Any other word that she was planning on saying was caught in her throat when she came face-to-face with Jason.

The two of them stared at each other while the commotion continued around them. Chasity had no idea what to say to him, and vice versa.

Fed up with the awkward silence, Jason gently grabbed Chasity's wrist. "We need to talk," he said, pulling her towards her room. Not protesting, Chasity allowed herself to be led out of the noisy living room. Upon entering her room, she walked over to her desk and leaned against it as Jason shut the room door. She folded her arms as she thought about what he would say to her. She'd been anticipating and dreading this at the same time. She was afraid that the time they'd spent apart had made Jason realize that he was better off without her.

Her fear was short-lived when Jason took a step towards Chasity and kissed her. His lips on hers caught her off guard at first, but that too was short-lived. She wrapped her arms around his neck and returned his passionate kiss. After a moment, Jason parted from her and took a step back.

Whoa, Chasity thought as they both caught their breath. "Um…hi."

Jason smiled slightly. He'd forgotten that neither of them had exchanged any pleasantries when they saw each other. "Hi," he returned. He pointed to her bed, directing her to sit down. Once she did, he sat next to her.

Chasity was curious as to what his kiss meant. Was it a make-up kiss? Or was it a goodbye kiss? She wanted to ask, but was afraid of what his answer might be. She didn't know what she would do if he broke up with her.

Jason took a moment to gather his thoughts. It took everything in him not to kiss her again. It had been over a week since he'd last seen her and he missed her. But he knew that they had to talk.

"I missed you," he began.

"Yeah?" she questioned, looking at him.

"Yes," he confirmed. "I know that I asked for space... I *needed* it but...that doesn't mean that it didn't kill me."

"I'm sorry Jason," she blurted out. "I handled the entire situation wrong and I know that... I get why you were upset."

Jason grabbed her hand and held it. "I know that you're sorry," he assured. "And now that I've had time to reflect, in a way I can understand your reasons...but you can't keep things like that from me... We have to deal with things *together*."

"I know," Chasity agreed. "I get it."

Jason took a deep breath. "For *my* part...I shouldn't have shut you out the way that I did," he said, sincerity filling his voice. "That wasn't how I should've handled my issue with you."

Chasity looked at the wall in front of her. "That *did* hurt," she admitted. "I felt like you walked away from me."

Jason looked down at her hand, which was secured in his. "I get it... Given everything that happened...it wasn't the time for me not to be there for you...no matter how I felt." Jason kicked himself for not being there to comfort Chasity through the injuries or through her emotions, given everything that had transpired. "I'm sorry for that."

Chasity looked back at him. "I appreciate that."

"I guess we *both* have some growing to do when it comes to how we handle things," he said. "But...I'll be happy to grow *with* you."

"So you're not breaking up with me?" she asked.

"I'm not crazy," he chuckled. "I *never* wanted that... I'm still in this if *you* are."

Feeling like a weight had been lifted from her shoulders, Chasity threw her arms around Jason, giving him the answer that he sought.

Jason squeezed her slender frame, almost like he was afraid to let her go. When he heard her let out a gasp, he pulled back. "You okay?" he asked, concerned.

"I'm fine," she said, rubbing her side. "Ribs are still a little sore, but its fine."

Jason knew that Chasity had been injured during the attack by Tyrone, but because he hadn't really spoken to her since their fight, he didn't know to what extent. Anger fell over him as the memory of what Tyrone did to her came flooding back. "I should've killed him," he fumed.

"Then you would be locked up," she pointed out. "As much as I hate him, he wasn't worth *your* life."

Despite Chasity's words, Jason still felt that Tyrone shouldn't be allowed to walk the earth after the pain he caused.

Sensing his boiling point approaching, Chasity put her hand on Jason's face. "Look at me," she urged. He complied. "I'm okay…just forget him."

Jason was unable to respond, but just nodded instead. After composing himself, he realized that there was one more thing that he needed to say to her in order for them to completely move past the situation. "Chaz…I need to say this to you," he began.

Chasity could only wonder what else he needed to say. She braced herself. "Okay…say what?"

"I need you to know that I don't blame you for the miscarriage. I never *did*…I'm sorry if I made you feel that way," he said, heartfelt.

"You didn't," she replied. It was the truth. As mad as Jason was, of all the things that he'd said during his period of anger, Chasity never once felt that he blamed her for losing their child. That was more so a blame that she had put on herself.

He hesitated for a moment. "Don't *you* blame yourself *either*," he added finally.

The look on Chasity's face showed Jason that that was exactly how she'd felt. "I'm trying not to," she answered honestly.

"Chaz, seriously," Jason urged. *"Don't*...it wasn't your fault, baby."

"I mean I *know* that but... In the back of my mind I just keep thinking that...my body was supposed to protect it and it *didn't*." She realized that she had never said that out loud. She'd been so busy pushing the loss to the back of her mind that she never expressed how she truly felt about it. "I may have been scared of the thought of becoming a mother but...I *wanted* our baby... Now it's gone and I'm just trying to get past it."

Jason pulled her back into a gentle embrace. "I know," he soothed. "I know it's hard. But we'll get through it together."

She tightened her grip around him. Though her confession lacked tears, she felt better for having gotten it out. Tears she'd shed; her feelings, she hadn't.

"I love you," he said.

"Love you too," she returned.

As Jason moved in for another kiss, they heard a knock at the door. "What is it?" Chasity glared at the door.

"Um...we heard yelling and we just wanna check to see if y'all cool," Mark's muffled voice answered.

"Who was yelling?" Jason asked, confusion mirrored on his and Chasity's faces.

"Can we come in real quick?" Mark requested.

Chasity rolled her eyes. "I swear to God," she muttered to Jason.

"They won't leave if we don't let them in," Jason reasoned. Chasity gave him the go ahead to open the door. Jason got up and upon opening it, found the group huddled in front of the door, staring back at him. He resisted the urge to laugh—they looked silly.

"What's up guys?" he asked.

"Everything good in here?" Malajia questioned, looking around the room.

"Yes," Jason replied.

"Sooo…is everything good wiiiiith…*you two*?" Alex slowly put out.

Jason couldn't help but chuckle as he stepped aside to let them in. "Yes, we're good guys," he confirmed. "We're still together."

There was a collective sigh of relief from the group at that news. "Thank God," Malajia breathed, walking over and sitting on the bed next to Chasity.

"Y'all were stressing us out," Mark said, leaning against the door.

Malajia looked over at Chasity, who looked a little drained. She put her arm around her shoulder. "You okay boo?"

Chasity nodded. "Why do you smell like dish liquid?" she wondered.

"Oh…I was making bubble sculptures in the sink," Malajia explained, nonchalant.

Chasity looked perplexed. "What?"

Malajia quickly put her other arm around Chasity, trying to pull her into a hug. "Shhhh, let's enjoy this bonding moment."

"Get off," Chasity hissed, nudging a laughing Malajia off of her.

"In all seriousness, we're glad that you two worked everything out," Josh said. "It's clear that you two are meant to be together."

Jason glanced over at Chasity and smiled. "Yeah," he agreed.

"Enough of this mushy stuff," Mark scoffed. "The gang is all back together, let's go celebrate."

"What's there for us to do?" Alex wondered. "We just left the game night."

"Yeah 'cause the SDC is the *only* place that we can go," Malajia mocked. "Stupid."

In the midst of all the talking, Jason and Chasity stared at each other with longing in their eyes. The last thing on their minds was hanging out with the group. They had better things to do…couple things.

"Uh, count us out guys," Jason cut in. "We're staying in tonight."

"How you gonna speak for her?" Mark questioned, loud. He pointed to Chasity. "Chaz, you know you wanna go out."

"Get the fuck out," Chasity snapped, inciting a snicker from Jason.

"You heard her," Jason goaded, pointing to the door. "Out."

Malajia sucked her teeth, standing from the bed. "Fine, let's go before they start banging right in front of us," she mocked, walking out the door.

"Aye Mel, speaking of banging, let's head back to my room right quick," Mark teased, grabbing hold of Malajia's arm.

"Boy," Malajia scoffed, jerking her arm away from a laughing Mark. "Those five minutes aren't worth it."

"I could do a *lot* in those five minutes," Mark jeered, walking out of the room behind Malajia who just sucked her teeth.

"Eww," Alex complained, shutting the door on her way out.

Chapter 4

Sidra stood in the hallway of the English building and stared at a text message; smiling.

'Hi sweetheart. I'm in the middle of meetings right now. I just wanted to let you know that I miss you and as soon as I get a break in this case I promise I will come and see you. Have a great first day of classes.'

"Miss you too James," Sidra muttered while texting a response. She hadn't seen her boyfriend James Grant since he'd come to visit her on Christmas. Being a lawyer, he didn't have much free time. But wanting to be a lawyer herself someday, Sidra understood and admired his drive. She ignored the chatter of the students exiting class, while her fingers moved across her phone screen.

"What's got you smiling so bright this early in the morning?" Josh wondered, approaching.

She glanced up at him. "Your class let out early?" she observed.

"Yeah, a whole five minutes," Josh chortled. "Must be my lucky day."

Sidra giggled.

Josh adjusted his bookbag. "So? You gonna tell me what has you grinning so hard?" he smiled. "You can't be excited about this nine o'clock class."

"No, trust me it's not that," Sidra replied, wondering if she should even say what was making her smile. Deciding to just throw caution to the wind and be honest with her best friend, she gestured to her phone. "Just a text message from James."

Josh just nodded. "That's cool," he replied. "Nice to see that he makes you happy."

Sidra looked a little shocked. "Thank you Josh... That means a lot coming from you."

"Why do you look like a deer caught in headlights?" he asked, laughter in his voice.

"I don't know," she shrugged, moving her ponytail over her shoulder. "I guess I—nothing. Thank you."

"Sure," Josh nodded.

Sidra stood there, beaming on the inside. Josh seemed so sincere. She was glad that she and Josh could have a conversation about her boyfriend without an argument happening.

Their relationship had been a little strained ever since Josh declared his love for her last semester and she didn't reciprocate his feelings. After spending weeks not talking to her because of his bruised ego, Josh finally realized that being friends was more important than his pride. But even though they were back on good terms, their relationship wasn't the same.

Sidra tapped him on his arm lightly. "So how is your schedule looking this semester?" she asked. "Anything that's gonna drive you crazy?"

Josh chuckled. "I have mostly business classes this semester and I'm taking Italian as my language requirement."

"No Spanish, huh?" Sidra teased. "I think everyone besides *you* took it."

"Nah, I figured I'd try something different," Josh mused. "How's *your* schedule looking?"

"Mostly business and law courses," Sidra replied, adjusting her purse strap on her arm. "I have Legal Aspects this semester. I will be getting into..." Sidra's words trailed off as her eyes focused on a young woman walking over. She held her gaze as the girl gave Josh a hug.

"Hey Joshua, how are you?" the girl beamed.

"I'm good," Josh replied, smiling from ear to ear. She looked at Sidra. "I'm sorry, I didn't mean to interrupt," she said, polite.

"No, you're fine," Josh assured her. "You just getting back to campus today?"

"Yeah, I had a bit of travel troubles," she answered, rolling her eyes. "Flight got delayed from California… It was a mess."

"Well, at least you're here now," Josh grinned.

Sidra caught herself looking this girl up and down. *Did she just interrupt my damn conversation? And he's okay with that?* She folded her arms as she studied this girl. The slim girl stood nearly as tall as Josh, with black wavy hair flowing past her shoulders. Her skin tone was several shades darker than Josh's brown tone. She was a beauty and certainly seemed to hold Josh's interest.

Her hair is probably weave, Sidra thought. Then quickly checked her own attitude. *Don't be mean, Sidra.* She loudly cleared her throat to grab Josh's attention, because clearly, he'd forgotten that she was standing there.

Josh glanced over at her. "Oh shit, I'm sorry," he apologized. "Sidra, this is December Harley. December, this is my friend Sidra Howard," he introduced.

December offered a cheerful wave.

"Nice to meet you December," Sidra said, face void of a smile.

"Nice eye color," December mused of Sidra's grey eyes. When Sidra's brown face held a perplexed look, December giggled. "Sorry, I'm just fascinated by different eye colors."

"Oh, well thanks," Sidra returned. "That's a unique name you have by the way."

December giggled once again. "Tell me about it," she agreed. "So is *yours*?"

Sidra finally let a smile come through as she nodded in

agreeance.

"I really didn't mean to interrupt your conversation. I just wanted to say hi to him." December clutched her books to her chest then glanced over at Josh. "I'll just see you later Joshua, okay?"

"Um wait a sec," Josh said, halting December's departure. "Have you had breakfast yet?"

December shook her head.

"You want to head to the cafeteria and see what breakfast food they have left?" Josh proposed. "We can catch up."

"I'd like that," December replied, pushing hair behind her ear. "Maybe they'll have those little raspberry pastry things that I like."

Josh chuckled, then turned to Sidra. "See you later," he said to her.

"Um—okay," Sidra returned.

"It was nice meeting you Sidra," December waved.

Sidra didn't get a chance to respond; Josh and December hurried for the building exit. "Yeah, you too," she mumbled to herself as she watched them walk out. Glancing at her watch, she made a beeline for her classroom.

"Anybody want some pizza?" Alex asked Chasity and Malajia, who were sitting at the dining room table. "It's still hot," she informed, setting a large box on the table.

"What kind is it?" Chasity asked as Malajia reached over and opened the box.

"Pepperoni and sausage," Alex informed, removing her coat and sitting it on the arm of the couch.

"Gross," Chasity scoffed, turning her nose up. "I don't eat pork. I don't know why you offered me any."

"Sorry sweetie, I totally forgot," Alex chuckled.

"Since *when* don't you eat it?" Malajia asked, grabbing a slice.

"When have you *ever* seen me eat it?" Chasity

countered.

"You was fuckin' some bacon *up* just *yesterday*," Malajia argued, taking a big bite out of her pizza.

Chasity stared at her. "That was *you*."

Malajia nearly choked on her food as she laughed.

"Ate almost the whole pack too," Alex chimed in. "Greedy."

Malajia shrugged as she continued to devour the slice.

"I take it you're coming in from getting your job back," Chasity assumed, tightening her ponytail.

"Yep, back to slinging pizzas next week," Alex laughed, sitting down at the table.

"Yo, can you start bringing some other shit home besides these dry ass pizzas this semester?" Malajia jeered, wiping her mouth with a napkin. "I mean a cookie, a breadstick, *something*."

Alex narrowed her eyes at her. "You're talking trash about *free* food that *I* brought home, that you're *eating* by the way," she hissed, folding her arms.

Malajia tossed her napkin down before reaching for another slice. "I'm only eating it because I'm starving," she defended, taking a bite. "This shit taste like grease and regret."

Chasity busted out laughing, which only annoyed Alex more.

Malajia pointed at Chasity, smiling. "You liked that one, didn't you?"

"I did," Chasity laughed.

Alex tossed her arms in the air in a huff. "I see that the 'tag-team' is back in affect," she bristled.

"Shut up, greasy boots," Malajia hurled.

Chasity immediately stopped laughing. "No, that was corny. You just lost my respect," she condemned.

Alex snickered at the salty look on Malajia's face.

"I'll get it back, watch," Malajia promised, taking another bite.

Alex leaned back in her seat and ran her hands through

her thick wavy hair just as the front door opened. "Sidra, I'm glad you're back. Your roommate and former roommate are ganging up on me," she chuckled as Sidra walked into the house.

Of course frick and frack are, Sidra thought, setting her books on the couch. "Do any of you know a girl named December?" she asked, not bothering to respond to Alex's comment.

Malajia looked at Chasity. "*Now* she wants to talk to us?" she mumbled; Chasity just shrugged.

"I have a December in my Literary Studies 2 class, but I don't know her per se," Alex revealed. "Why?"

Sidra removed her coat. "Josh introduced me to her today… He seems interested in her," she said, sitting on the arm of the couch. "I was just curious to know if anybody knew her."

"Yeah, he's *interested* in her all right," Malajia commented, picking pepperonis off her pizza.

Sidra looked at her. "What's *that* supposed to mean?"

"That he's interested in her, just like I *said*," Malajia retorted, popping the pepperoni into her mouth.

Sidra made a face at Malajia's snarky tone. "How do you know that? Did he talk to you?" She was curious as to what Malajia knew. "He didn't mention her to *me*."

"He told Mark about her. He started talking to her a little bit before we left for break last semester," Malajia revealed. "He didn't really want to say anything because it's not serious right now," she chuckled. "He asked Mark not to tell anybody, but Mark tells me *everything*. That boy gossips more than a damn woman."

"Yeah, you two are just alike," Alex commented. "You both run your damn mouth about business that isn't *yours*."

"Sure *do*," Malajia quipped.

Sidra examined the blue crystal ring on her finger as her mind wandered. "He started dating her last semester?" she questioned. "I'm surprised he didn't tell me about her."

"Are you *really*?" Chasity bit out, earning a glare from

Sidra.

"Yes Chasity, I *am*," Sidra bit back. "Unlike *you, Josh* shares important stuff with me."

Malajia rolled her eyes at the comment while Chasity just narrowed her hazel eyes at Sidra. "Obviously he *doesn't*," Chasity threw back.

"Whatever," Sidra huffed, standing up. Over the conversation, Sidra headed up the steps without another word.

"The hell is her *problem?*" Malajia asked once she heard the door slam. "This is getting ridiculous. Now she probably mad at *Josh* for no damn reason."

Alex shook her head. "At least she actually engaged you two just now," she pointed out.

"She only did that because she wanted information," Malajia grumbled. "Persnickety hag."

Alex sighed. "I wish she would just talk to you two about what she's feeling and get it over with," she said.

"I give zero fucks about Sidra's whining ass feelings right about now," Chasity snarled.

"I hate this tension," Alex sulked.

"Shit, *you?*" Malajia scoffed, reaching for another slice of pizza. "Try living in the same *room* with that mess. I almost slept down here last night."

Alex watched Malajia. "Damn girl, you wanna save some of that for Emily?" she teased.

"Ain't nobody thinking about no damn Emily," Malajia dismissed with a wave of her hand.

"I'm two seconds from dropping out," Mark complained as he kicked a rock across the path. "Damn it!" he barked, noticing the dirt mark the rock left on his brand-new tan boots.

Josh shook his head. "And what made you say that nonsense?" he asked, evenly. Having just left their first class of the morning, Mark and Josh were headed back to their house.

"It's only been a week and I already have a test in my stupid Tax Auditing class," Mark vented. "This is some straight bullshit."

"No, this is *college*," Josh pointed out. "You should be used to stuff like this. It's our *third* year after all."

Mark shot him a glance. "Nobody asked for your comments," he sneered, earning a snicker from Josh.

As they continued their walk, Josh spotted December standing on the library steps, talking to a group of their peers. They smiled and waved to one another in passing.

Josh was focused on smiling at December while passing; Mark decided to take advantage of his lack of focus.

"Yo watch out!" Mark shouted.

Startled, Josh spun around, stopping suddenly. "What? What is it?" he panicked.

"Nothing," Mark laughed, much to Josh's annoyance. "You excited as shit right now."

Josh backhanded him on the arm. "Shut up," he spat. "I was just waving to her."

Mark twisted his lips to the side. "Uh huh, you about to jizz on yourself and shit."

"You're disgusting, you know that?" Josh bit out. Mark just shrugged. "Anyway, I know you told Malajia what I told you about December. You run your damn mouth too much."

Mark rolled his eyes. "You know me well enough to know that anything you tell me is gonna get out," he joked, in exasperated fashion. He relished the mask of annoyance on Josh's face. "My fault… How did you find out I told anyway?"

"Sidra mentioned it while we were at breakfast the other day," Josh informed. "She said that she felt left out because *I* wasn't the one to tell her."

Mark shook his head. "Sidra's just girlin', don't worry about that," he dismissed. "When are you gonna bring her around and let everyone get to know her?"

"Not for a long time." Josh's reply was instantaneous.

Mark looked insulted. "Why *not*?"

"Would *you* want to bring a girl that you like around *our* girls?" Josh asked. "Hell, the dirty looks *alone* will chase them away. Not to mention their smart mouths... Well except for Emily."

"*I* wouldn't give a damn. If a chick I bring around can't handle them, then I don't want her," Mark chortled. He then gave Josh a pat on his shoulder. "I hear you though. You gotta prep her first."

"Yeah," Josh agreed, running a hand over his low-cut hair. "Don't get me wrong. I love the girls, trust me I do," he assured. "They're like the sisters I always wanted."

"You already *have* a sister," Mark pointed out.

Josh frowned slightly. True, he already had an older sister...Sarah. But he wasn't close to her. At least not anymore. "I said the sisters I always *wanted*," he stressed, stern.

Alex grabbed the apron off the back of her chair and darted out of her room and down the steps.

Sitting on the couch, Malajia saw Alex nearly slip off of the last step. She busted out laughing. "Damn Alex, you hype as shit to go make pizzas," she teased.

"Shut up," Alex spat, reaching for the door knob. "Since you're not doing anything, why don't you wash out your dishes from earlier," she suggested, gesturing to the kitchen.

"No, I think I'll keep my tired ass right on this couch," Malajia refused, flipping through the TV channels with the remote.

Not having the time to argue, Alex just shook her head and walked out the door.

Alex's pace was quick as she made her way through campus. *Ugh, I'm so late!* Needing something to calm herself down, she reached into her bag in search of her MP3 player. She stomped her foot on the ground when she realized that she had forgotten to pack it. "Crap!" she blurted out.

"You okay?" a male voice asked, laughter filling his voice.

Alex spun around, sucking her teeth in the process. "I'm fine—" She paused and smiled when she saw who it was. "Hey Eric."

"Hey your*self*," he replied. "What's the matter? You seem pretty upset."

"What would give you the idea that something is wrong?" Alex asked.

"Um, well yelling to yourself was a big indicator," he teased, adjusting his book bag on his shoulder.

Alex chuckled. "Ha ha," she threw back. "I'm fine though. It's nothing serious. I just forgot my music player...*and* I'm late for work." She glanced at her watch. "Speaking of which, I have to go. I'll see you later okay?"

"Hey, wait up," Eric called as she walked off. He darted to catch up to her.

Alex stopped and turned around. "What's up?"

"How about I walk you?"

"Are you *sure*? It's like twenty minutes from campus," Alex asked, adjusting the hat on her head. "And it's pretty cold out."

"I'm a big boy, Alex," he chortled. "A walk and a little chill never scared me."

That you are. Alex quickly shook her head to dismiss the sexual thoughts that were forming. "Well...I wouldn't mind the company," she said finally.

Eric gave a nod. "Then it's settled," he said, nudging her along. "Now come on. You're already late."

Alex adjusted the scarf around her neck and smiled as she continued her walk with Eric alongside of her.

The twenty-minute walk off campus flew by. Eric's engaging conversation calmed her down and made her forget all about her lack of music or about the fact that she was late for work. Walking into the pizza parlor, Alex removed her coat then stepped behind the counter.

"Thank you for the walk Eric," she said, facing him. "It's always good to see you."

Eric smiled as he leaned on the counter. "I could stick around," he suggested.

"For *four* hours?!" Alex exclaimed. "No, that won't be necessary."

Eric laughed slightly. "No seriously, I could hang out in one of the booths and order a bunch of drink refills."

Alex narrowed her eyes at him as she tried to keep from laughing.

"It's a plus for me, because I can watch you walk past me over and over."

"You are a mess," Alex replied, giving him a playful tap on his arm. "Go home. I'll call you later."

Eric stood up straight as he drummed his fingers on the counter. "I think I like *my* idea better. I'll stick around," he insisted, smiling. "I have some studying to do anyway and it seems pretty quiet in here."

Alex's mouth fell open, watching Eric walk over to the nearest booth and set his book bag in the seat. "Are you serious?" she asked, amazed at his persistence.

"*Very*," he grinned, sitting down in the seat. "Now, Miss beautiful waitress, can you bring me a soda and an order of breadsticks please?"

I would choke you if you weren't so damn cute, Alex thought, shaking her head. She had to admit, she was flattered. "Coming right up."

Chapter 5

"I'm bored as shit cuz," Mark complained, crushing a tortilla chip in his hand. "Let's find something to do." He opened his hand and let the remnants fall on the dining room table.

"Why would you do some dumb shit like that?" Chasity hissed, pointing to the crumbs on their table.

"I just *told* you I'm bored," Mark shot back. He leaned his head on the table. "Come oooonn, it's *Friday*. There has to be *something* for us to do," he grumbled.

Classes over for the week, the gang was sitting around in the girls' house trying to unwind. But Mark's complaining was quickly getting on their nerves.

"Can you shut up please?" Malajia spat to Mark from her seat one on of the accent chairs in the living room. "We've been listening to your grown ass whine for over an hour."

Mark lifted his head up from the table and made a face at Malajia. "It hasn't even *been* that long," he shot back. "You always gotta exaggerate."

Exasperated, Malajia tossed her hands in the air. "Fine, it's been like forty-five minutes," she corrected.

"This campus is *dry*," Mark nagged, flagging Malajia with his hand.

"We could always watch a movie," David suggested, grabbing a chip from a bowl.

"The only movie *I* wanna watch is porn, and I don't think anybody wants to watch it with me," Mark jeered, much to the disgust of his friends.

Malajia scoffed. "Ugh, I just got the grossest image in my head."

Mark was about to fire off a retort when the front door opened. "Alex, your friend is having images of my dick in her head!" Mark bellowed, pointing to an astonished Malajia.

"What? I didn't say that!" Malajia exclaimed, pointing to herself.

Alex stood there baffled. "Umm…O-kay," she said.

"How was work?" Emily asked, pouring herself a cup of juice.

Alex smiled while removing her coat. "It was good." She leaned over the couch. "Eric walked me to work and ended up staying with me through my whole shift."

"Wait. He stayed for the *entire* four hours?" Malajia asked. Alex nodded. "That's weird."

"True," Alex chuckled. "But it was a sweet gesture. Anyway, he just walked me home."

"Why didn't he come in?" Sidra asked, curious.

"Because I didn't want to subject him to *Satan*," Alex spat out.

Chasity looked shocked. "Huh? What did I do?" she asked, pointing to herself.

Alex shook her head. "That's a damn shame that you know to answer to that name," she commented, amused. "Anyway, it's not just *you* Chasity. It's Malajia and Mark *too* with y'all jokes."

"Alex, nobody said anything about your fuck buddy. Stop tryna start shit," Chasity bristled.

Emily nearly choked on her juice. "Oh wow," she coughed.

Malajia busted out laughing at the agitation showing on Alex's face. "Walked right into that with them dogged sneaks," she goaded.

"Whatever," Alex ground out, looking down at her grey sneakers. "And my sneakers are *new*."

"Newly *used*, is not *new* Alex," Chasity snarled, earning laughter from the group. When Alex shot a glower her way, Chasity pointed at her. "You started with me first," Chasity pointed out.

"Walked into that one *too*," Malajia laughed. "When will you learn?"

Alex rolled her eyes. "*Anyway*," she ground out. "There's nothing going on between Eric and I, we're just friends."

"Nobody *mentioned* there was anything going on," Malajia pointed out. "Sidra just asked why he didn't come in." Malajia smiled slyly. "You just wanted to keep talking about him."

"That's not even true," Alex protested, standing up straight.

Malajia stared at Alex. "Alex wants Eric," she crooned, pointing at her.

Alex sucked her teeth as Malajia repeated it. "Cut it out," she spat.

Malajia shook her head. "Nope, you want him. You want to get back with him," she teased. "Alex wants Eric. Alex wants Eric."

Alex's eyes became slits. "Are you really gonna be that immature?" she wondered, putting her hands on her hips. Alex fought the urge to laugh when the rest of her friends joined in on Malajia's chant.

Their chanting became louder when Mark and Jason started making beats on the table with their hands. Josh joined in by making beat box noises with his mouth.

"I hate *all* of you!" Alex laughed over the noise.

"Alex wants Eric and shit," Mark added as the chanting subsided. "I'm still bored though."

Jason threw his head back in exasperation. He was over Mark's complaining. "Then think of something for us to *do* so we don't have to hear you bitch about it anymore."

Mark softy pounded his fist on the table, until a thought popped in his head. "I got it!" he yelped, putting his hands up. "Let's play tag."

Sidra sucked her teeth. "Boy nobody wants to play—"

Before Sidra could finish her sentence, Mark grabbed a handful of chips from the bowl in front of him, then tossed the chips at a shocked David. While David was trying to figure out what was going on, Mark darted for the couch, grabbed a pillow and threw it at David, sending his glasses flying from his face.

"David's it!" Mark shouted before running out the door.

"I'm gonna kill you Mark!" David fumed, grabbing his glasses off the floor. He ran out the door after him in a rage.

The group remained in their seats. Several people fought hard to keep from laughing out loud at what had just taken place. Jason had his hand over his face, quietly laughing. Malajia had her face buried in a pillow, while Josh pulled the collar of his shirt over his face to keep from making eye contact with anyone. Chasity closed her eyes and placed two fingers on the bridge of her nose as she struggled to keep her laughter in.

"What the hell just happened?" Alex asked, confused. The question caused Chasity to bust out laughing. The others followed suit.

"Yo, I hate him so much," Malajia laughed of Mark. "Wait, wait did y'all see David's glasses fly across the room?" She was in tears.

Sidra was not amused. "David should kick his ass," she fussed, folding her arms. "He got chips all over our damn floor."

Before anyone else could comment, the door swung open with Mark running in. "Hide me! Somebody hide me," he panicked, searching for a place to hide. "David's gonna kill me. I think his lens popped out."

"It would serve your butt right," Sidra spat.

Ignoring her, Mark hurried up the steps in search of a

hiding spot.

Not more than a minute later, David came barging in. "Where is he?" he seethed.

Everyone quickly pointed up the steps. Not saying another word, David bolted up in search of Mark.

Downstairs, the others could hear the commotion. "Who told you I was up here?!" Mark yelled.

"You think I can't see you?!" David hollered back. "The damn shower has a *clear* door on it!"

Josh cracked up at the sound of Mark's screams and tussling.

Mark came flying down the stairs and slipped on the bottom step, tumbling to the floor. Taking his opportunity, David grabbed a fallen pillow, stood over him, and with all his strength, hit Mark in his face with it. Annoyed and out of breath, David threw the pillow to the floor then flopped down on the couch.

Mark rolled around on the floor, holding his face and yelling obscenities. "Jason, Josh!" he bellowed, out of breath. "David's glasses lenses just jumped me."

Malajia spat out her drink as she busted out laughing again.

Sidra glared at Mark as David, who was still irritated, shook his head.

Alex stared at the scene, baffled. "And you wonder why I don't bring Eric around." She stepped over Mark. "I'm going to bed," she announced, making her way upstairs.

Chasity stirred her hot cereal in a glass bowl while playing a game on her cell phone. Having to leave for class in less than twenty minutes, she figured she would just kill a little time by trying to beat her high score. "Shit," she mumbled as she lost.

Sidra headed down the steps and made a beeline for the kitchen. She searched in the cabinets, becoming frustrated when she couldn't find what she was looking for.

Chasity looked at her. "What are you looking for?" she asked.

"The instant hot cereal," Sidra muttered, tapping her nails on the counter top.

Without saying a word, Chasity reached for the part of the counter behind her and grabbed the box. "This?" she asked, holding the box up.

"Yes," Sidra confirmed, reaching for the box. Chasity moved it out of Sidra's grasp. "Stop playing Chasity, I don't have time for this."

"Time for *what* Sidra?" Chasity hissed. "Time to open your mouth and *ask* for it? Or to say 'hi' to me at least?"

Sidra rolled her eyes. "Since when do you care about anybody speaking to you?" she sneered. When Chasity just glared at her, Sidra let out a loud sigh. "Fine. Good morning," she spoke, politeness *and* smile phony. "Can I please have the box of cereal that *I helped* pay for?"

"That's real cute," Chasity spat, slamming the box on the counter in front of Sidra.

"Whatever," Sidra grumbled, grabbing a bowl from the cabinet above her.

"So, you're just gonna do this phony shit, huh?" Chasity charged, folding her arms.

"*What's* phony Chasity?" Sidra huffed. "You wanted me to speak, I'm speaking."

"You're full of shit and you know it," Chasity snarled. "*Clearly* you're mad at me and instead of telling me what your *problem* is, you're being fake."

"Don't like it? Go tell your *bestie* about it," Sidra grunted.

Chasity was taken back by Sidra's comment. "What does that even *mean*?"

Appetite now gone, Sidra tossed the packet that she held on the counter. "I gotta get to class." She stormed towards the front door as Malajia came down the steps.

"Bye Sid," Malajia called to her. Sidra ignored her as she walked out of the house, slamming the door behind her.

Malajia sucked her teeth. "Chaz, she's on my last nerve," she complained, heading for the kitchen.

"Yeah, she's tap dancing on mine too," Chasity agreed.

"Forget tap dancing. Her ass is jumping up and down on it with them damn pumps on," Malajia replied, earning a giggle from Chasity. Grabbing two packets of hot cereal from the box, Malajia sighed. "She's either *not* speaking or does that phony nice shit that I can't stand."

"Yeah, she just pulled that bullshit with me too," Chasity replied, taking a spoonful of her cereal from her bowl.

Malajia leaned close to Chasity's bowl. "Ooh let me taste some of that before I make a whole bowl," Malajia proposed.

Chasity pushed the bowl in her hands. "Take it, you fuckin' breathed all on it," she grimaced.

Malajia chuckled, taking a spoonful of the cereal and putting it into her mouth. "Anyway," she began, swallowing her food. "I'm over this, we need to squash whatever this is with her like *now*. I'm two seconds away from tossing all her silk shirts in the shower while she's in it."

Chasity shook her head. "I gotta go," she declared, grabbing her book bag from the floor.

"Later," Malajia said, finishing her food.

Sidra was still seething in silence about her confrontation with Chasity before leaving the house. Her pace was quick as she made her way past several students on her way to class. *Why do they insist on irritating me? Just leave me alone,* she thought. Seeing Josh standing on the library steps several feet in front of her, her pace slowed. "Josh!" she called, causing him to turn around.

He waved to her as she approached. "Morning," he greeted.

"Hey, your nine o'clock is in Pratt Hall, right?" Sidra asked. She already knew the answer to that question, but was curious as to why he was standing around when he should be on his way to class across campus.

"Yeah, it is," he replied, looking at his watch.

"Um, you want to walk with me?" she wondered, voice filled with hope. "Since we have class in the same building, we can go together like we *usually* do."

"Sorry Sid, not today," Josh declined. "I'm waiting for one of my classmates and we're gonna walk together. Since we have to present a project today, it'll give us a chance to go over some last-minute details."

"Oh," Sidra muttered, not hiding her disappointment. "Well okay then. I guess I'll see you later."

"Yeah, I think we're all supposed to meet up for dinner at the cafeteria later," Josh said. "I'll see you then."

Sidra just offered a half-hearted smile before heading off towards her destination. Her smile faded as soon as Josh was out of sight. *He's pulling away again* screamed in her head as she continued a steady pace.

Jason walked up to the gang's usual booth in the cafeteria and set his tray down. "They have a pretty good nacho bar up there," he informed, taking a seat.

Mark pointed to the large pile of nachos on Jason's plate. "Damn bro, did you save anybody *else* any?" he teased.

"Shut up. I'm starving," Jason hissed, grabbing a tortilla chip, loaded with toppings. "I've been in the computer lab all day writing test codes for my Software Development class."

"You almost finished with it?" Chasity asked, squirting ketchup on her sweet potato fries.

"Not even close," Jason said, taking a bite of his food. "I have to get back to it as soon as I finish eating."

"Chaz, why don't you just *help* him?" Malajia cut in, reaching for her glass of soda. "Don't you do computer nerd stuff?"

"I don't do software development, I do *web* development," Chasity pointed out.

Malajia held a blank expression on her face. "What's the

difference?"

"I don't even know," Chasity lied, wanting to avoid a pointless conversation. She knew Malajia wouldn't get it even if she did explain the differences between her and Jason's computer focus.

Malajia shrugged as she drank her soda. Setting the glass down, she eyed Jason's nachos. "I wish I had gotten *that* instead of *this* bullshit," she griped, pointing to her vegetable lasagna.

"It doesn't even look that bad," Alex chuckled.

"It looks like a zucchini threw up in it," Malajia complained, earning snickers from the table.

"Why did you get it if you didn't *want* it?" Alex questioned, dipping one of her chicken strips into some ketchup.

"I thought it had meat in it," Malajia explained, poking at it with her fork.

"I don't know *why*, the sign clearly said *vegetable* lasagna," Sidra mumbled, stirring her clam chowder around in her bowl.

Malajia shot Sidra a glare. "And what did the sign say above *your* food?" she hissed. "Vomit? 'Cause that's what it *looks* like."

Sidra rolled her eyes as she tossed her spoon in her half-eaten chowder. "That was disgusting and uncalled for," she chastised.

"So is that ruffled ass shirt you got on," Malajia bit back, folding her arms.

"So Joshua, how did your presentation go today?" Sidra asked, trying her best to change the subject and ignore Malajia in the process.

Josh looked up from his plate of spaghetti. "Sid, you know I hate being called by my full name," he ground out.

"Oops, he told *you*," Malajia cut in, amused.

Sidra frowned slightly. "Oh, I'm sorry," she apologized. "I thought you didn't mind it now because I heard December call you that the day I met her."

"She did?" Josh questioned.

"Uh yeah, she *did*," Sidra reminded.

Josh shrugged. "Oh well, I guess I didn't notice," he replied, twirling some pasta on his fork.

"Yeah okay. *Sure* you didn't," Mark teased. "You just didn't *care* because you wanna smash."

Josh's face flushed red. "Come on Mark. Chill," he pleaded.

"So anyway *Josh*, how was your presentation?" Sidra asked, moving back to her initial topic.

"It went well," Josh answered, confident. "Can't wait to see that grade."

"That's good. So anyway my Legal Aspects class seems like it's going to be stress—"

"Yo Josh, when are you gonna bring your girlfriend around *us*?" Malajia asked, interrupting Sidra. "You know we're gonna have to meet her eventually."

Sidra gritted her teeth at the interruption.

"She's not my girlfriend, Mel," Josh replied, smiling. "She's just a friend."

"Uh huh. You're cheesin' kinda hard right now Josh," Chasity pointed out, causing Josh to blush.

"Josh said he don't want to bring her around y'all 'cause you're gonna scare her off with your evil faces and ignorant ass comments," Mark blurted out.

Josh nearly choked on his food as the girls' eyes stared daggers at him. "Mark!" Josh seethed.

"What?" Mark asked. "You didn't say that was a secret." He then smiled slyly.

"Josh, you really think we'll scare her off?" Alex charged.

"No, of course not—"

"He lyin' like shit," Mark instigated.

"Shut up," Josh barked at him. "You play too much."

"Okay, I'm sure Josh didn't mean it as bad as it sounds," Emily cut in, trying to diffuse any ill-feelings. She then leaned close to him. "You weren't talking about *me*, right?"

she whispered.

Josh quickly shook his head no. Emily giggled.

"I'm sure when Josh is ready to bring her around, he *will*. Like *why* is this a topic right now?" Sidra huffed.

"'Cause this is what we're *talkin'* about right now," Malajia snapped, fed up with Sidra's attitude. "Don't be rude."

"Excuse me? *You're* the one who cut *me* off when I was trying to talk," Sidra shot back. "And you call *me* rude?"

Malajia sucked her teeth. "Girl, we want to grill Josh about this *chick*, not listen to you whine about your class," she hissed. "We *all* had stressful classes today. Don't nobody wanna hear about *yours*."

Fuming, Sidra grabbed her purse. "I have to go study," she declared, making her way out of the booth.

"Way to go Malajia," Alex commented once Sidra was out of earshot.

"No fuck that," Malajia bit out. "Did y'all *not* hear that smart ass comment she made to me not too long ago?… Tryna say I can't read a food sign and shit."

"You went off on her just now over a comment that she made like fifteen minutes ago?" Alex chided.

"It was *ten* and yup," Malajia boasted, folding her arms.

"Okay, enough of y'all nonsense," Mark cut in. "Back to Josh smashing November."

"Her name is *December*, smart ass," Josh shot back, tossing a balled-up napkin at the laughing Mark.

Chapter 6

Sidra flipped through the pages of her textbook so hard that she ripped one. "Shit!" she blurted out, slamming the book shut. She couldn't seem to calm herself down after her exchange of words with Malajia over dinner.

It didn't help that Malajia walked through the door. Sidra rolled her eyes. *Great, just great.*

"I saw that eye roll," Malajia commented, removing her high-heeled boots.

"Whatever," Sidra mumbled, opening her notebook.

Malajia sat on her bed, letting out a loud sigh in the process. Having homework, she grabbed her books from the floor and prepared to work. After trying for minutes, her concentration was off. Oddly, she was distracted by the silence in the room. Normally both girls would be cracking jokes and laughing in between studying and homework, but the tension in the room was so thick, it could have been cut with a knife.

Malajia couldn't take it anymore. Closing her book, she tossed it on the floor with a thud, grabbing Sidra's attention.

"Can you stop all that noise?" Sidra ground out.

"Can we stop this *bullshit* and get back to normal please?" Malajia shot back, inciting another eye roll from

Sidra. "Now come on Sidra. I'm done with this...I miss my friend."

Sidra glanced up at her. "Can this wait? I have a test to study for, for my *stressful* class."

Narrowing her eyes at Sidra's blatant attempt to avoid the issue, Malajia hopped up from the bed and opened the bedroom door. "Chasity!" she yelled down the stairs.

"What are you doing?" Sidra frowned, closing her notebook.

"What?" Chasity hurled up the steps.

"Can you come up here?" Malajia requested. She then turned to Sidra as Chasity headed upstairs. "We're settling this shit."

"What?" Chasity repeated, poking her head in the room.

Malajia signaled for Chasity to come in. "Come here, this issue with Sidra is getting resolved *tonight*." She sat on her bed.

"I don't *feel* like this tonight Malajia," Sidra protested, angry.

"Yeah, I really don't feel like it either," Chasity agreed. "*Y'all* talk and tell me how it went."

"Get your ass in here and sit down, Chasity," Malajia commanded, pointing to the space next to her on her bed. "Come on, *you're* not okay with how things are either."

Chasity let out a sigh before walking in and sitting down next to Malajia. "Fine."

Sidra turned her chair around and crossed her legs, staring at the two girls. "I don't know what you plan on accomplishing," she began.

"Sidra stop. Just stop," Malajia urged. "Tell us why you're mad at us."

Sidra shook her head. "I'm not mad."

"You're *lying*," Malajia spat out. "It started when everything that happened with me and Chaz came out."

Sidra just sat there in silence, much to Malajia's annoyance.

"I called you *several* times over break, and left messages that you *never* returned… Now that we're back, you're giving us attitude…does that sound like someone who isn't mad?" Malajia threw at her.

Again, Sidra didn't respond, she just offered a nonchalant shrug.

Chasity shook her head. "Sidra, if you really don't want to resolve whatever is going on with you, then I wash my hands of it," she warned.

Sidra rolled her eyes.

"If I walk my ass out this room, I'm done," Chasity added, then looked at Malajia. "*You* can keep kissing her ass if you want to."

"Chaz—" Malajia called as Chasity made a move to get up.

"Nope," Chasity refused.

"Sidra, damn it *talk* to us," Malajia pleaded, exasperated. Malajia's friends meant everything to her and losing even one was something that she was not about to accept. Especially for reasons that were unknown to her. "We can't know what we did wrong if you don't *say* anything."

Sidra watched Chasity walk to the door. "I knew you didn't care," she snarled.

Chasity snapped her head towards her. "Care about *what*, Sidra?!" she yelled, clapping her hands with each word. "*What* am I supposed to care about? What did I *do* to you?!" She folded her arms.

"You keep things from me!" Sidra yelled back. "You…*both* of you."

Malajia's eyes widened as she looked to Chasity, who held a stern gaze on Sidra. "So you're mad that we didn't tell you what *happened* with us?" Chasity questioned.

Malajia looked back at Sidra. "*That's* what this has been about?" she asked. "I thought it was something *serious*."

"It *is* serious!" Sidra erupted, rising from her seat. "You two are *unbelievable* for keeping secrets like that. Malajia, I knew you for *years*, and you couldn't come to me and tell me what was going on between you and Tyrone."

"I didn't even want to tell *her!*" Malajia exclaimed, pointing to Chasity.

"But *she* was the one you *confided* in," Sidra argued, then looked at Chasity.

Malajia was dumbfounded by Sidra's words.

"Chasity, and *you*—"

"I would think *really* hard about what you plan on saying to me, because you're coming off real fuckin' childish right now," Chasity warned, cutting Sidra off.

Sidra let out a huff. "What I'm saying is that you two walk around here like two peas in a damn pod, keeping secrets and shit. Completely forgetting that you have *other* friends that love you and care about what's going on with you. It's not just *you two* in this group."

"You're not the only one who I didn't tell, Sidra," Malajia argued. "My *parents* don't even know what went on…why are *you* so offended?"

"Why is it that you seem more concerned with the fact that we didn't tell you, than the fact of what actually *happened?*" Chasity jumped in.

"*Excuse* me?" Sidra scoffed. "What is *that* supposed to mean?"

"It *means* what I just *said*," Chasity shot back.

"Sidra that *better* not be true," Malajia added, shaking her head in disappointment.

"That couldn't be *further* from the truth!" Sidra yelled. "Of *course* I care about what happened to you."

"Bullshit," Chasity threw back. "You didn't call me *once* to see how I was."

"You wouldn't have answered anyway," Sidra argued.

"Really? *That's* the excuse you went with?" Chasity asked, voice dripping with sarcasm.

"Sidra…if something would've happened to *you*, I would've checked on you," Malajia put in, voice low. "Even if I was mad at you."

Sidra stood there, upset. As much as she wanted to continue to argue the reasons for her behavior, she realized that she had no argument. She had not been supportive like she should have; she wasn't acting like a friend and that wasn't something that sat right with her,

"I'm sorry that I didn't call," she said, tears pricking the back of her eyes. "Excuse me," she sniffled, moving past Chasity to get out of the room.

Malajia, hearing the bathroom door close, sighed. "We shouldn't have ganged up on her," she concluded, standing up.

"*You* called *me* up here," Chasity reminded.

"I know I did. I just wanted us to talk," Malajia explained. "I refuse to believe that she's that selfish," she said. "She *can't* be. I've known her too long, we've been through too much…" she looked at Chasity. "It has to be more to her problem than what she's saying."

"I can *beat* it out of her," Chasity joked.

Malajia narrowed her eyes at Chasity. "Haven't you had *enough* violence?" she returned. Chasity made a face at Malajia in retaliation. "I'm gonna go talk to her," Malajia said.

Chasity nodded, then walked out of the room. As Chasity headed downstairs, Malajia approached the bathroom door. She gave it a soft tap.

"Sidra, can I come in?" Malajia asked, ear to the door. Upon hearing a muffled "Yes," she opened the door to find Sidra sitting on the closed toilet seat, wiping her eyes.

Malajia closed the door and leaned against it. "You okay?" she asked, tone even.

Sidra shook her head. "I feel like shit," she answered honestly.

Malajia just stood there, looking at her.

Sidra tossed her damp tissue in the trash. "I'm sorry that I didn't call you," she said after a moment. "If it's worth anything, I did think about you both every day I just—I guess

I was in my feelings." She let out a sigh. "I didn't mean to be a bad friend."

"I appreciate that," Malajia said, folding her arms. "Listen, I know everybody felt some kind of way when everything came out," she began. "It was a rough time."

"Yeah," Sidra agreed, running a hand over her ponytail. "I guess I just felt...I don't know."

Malajia took a step forward. "You know, Alex asked me why I only told Chasity about what was going on... She asked Chaz the same thing too," Malajia said.

"Yeah, I know," Sidra replied, looking down at her hands. "She told me that your answer was that you were closer with Chasity than you were with the rest of us."

Malajia rubbed her eye with her hand. "I didn't mean it how it sounds," she promised. "All of you mean the world to me, I just..." she glanced at the ceiling while trying to form the rest of her words.

"She's your best friend," Sidra finished when Malajia hesitated.

Malajia sighed; she could tell by Sidra's voice that she was a little hurt by that information. "Sidra—"

"It's fine, I get it," Sidra cut in.

"It doesn't *seem* like you're fine," Malajia contradicted. "Are you... Sidra are you jealous of me and Chasity's friendship?"

Sidra rubbed her face with her hand. "I guess I just thought that since you and I knew each other the longest, that *we* would have a closer bond," she admitted.

"Sweetie, you say all the time that *Josh* is *your* best friend," Malajia pointed out.

"He's a guy, it's different," Sidra said.

Malajia chuckled. "It's *not*, really."

"Yeah, that didn't make too much sense, did it?" Sidra agreed. Malajia shook her head. "I know. I know I'm being petty... You're the first female friend that I had and even though we fell out at one point...you're still like my sister, and I just...I guess I just felt left out."

Malajia walked over to Sidra as Sidra stood up. "Sid… Your friendship—*you* are important to me," she began. "No matter who I'm friends with, *we* will *always* have our own bond. You gotta understand that."

Sidra gave a slight nod. "I guess I do."

"In all honesty, being my best friend is a tough job so you should be glad you dodged that bullet," Malajia commented.

Sidra couldn't help but snicker. She wrapped her arms around Malajia. "I'm sorry," she said.

"I know sweetie. It's okay," Malajia replied, hugging her back. "We're good?"

Sidra nodded. "Always," she promised, parting from Malajia.

"You wanna get matching ponytails?" Malajia teased, giving Sidra's hair a light tug.

"Girl," Sidra sneered, smacking Malajia's hand away. Malajia laughed. "Anyway, I need to go apologize to Chasity too…I'm sure she wants to choke me right now."

Malajia nodded. "She does."

Sidra couldn't help but snicker at Malajia's honesty. "How about I treat you both to some brownies to make amends?"

"Don't we already have a box in the cabinet?" Malajia asked. Sidra nodded. "Then how are you *treating* us?"

Sidra laughed. "Make…I'll *make* you some brownies," she amended.

Chapter 7

"So Chaz, your birthday is coming up," Alex said, shifting her books from one arm to the other. "Do you have anything special that you want to do?"

"Um, no not really," Chasity shrugged, adjusting her book bag on her shoulder. Having just left lunch at the cafeteria, the gang was ambling through campus, making their way to their destinations.

"'No not really' isn't gonna fly," Malajia griped. "You're turning twenty-one in a few days."

"Yes, I am aware of that Malajia," Chasity spat, moving her hair out of her face.

Malajia made a face at Chasity's tone. "Then you should know that we're not gonna let you sit around and not celebrate it...ain't nobody fuckin' around with you."

Alex giggled at the agitated look on Chasity's face. "We'll think of something fun, Chaz," Alex promised. "You girls made *my* twenty-first birthday memorable, so I want to make sure I do the same for yours."

"It's really not that serious," Chasity replied, even toned.

"You know we're not paying you any mind, right?" Sidra chuckled, patting Chasity's arm.

"I could only hope," Chasity sneered.

Josh snapped his fingers as a thought popped into his head. "Ooh! We can take you to this new restaurant that just opened downtown," he suggested.

Malajia stared at him. "That's *it*?" she scoffed. "She's turning *twenty-one* and you wanna just take her to *eat*?" She shook her hand in Josh's direction. "That's some cheap shit. No, we need to get some *drinks* in her. We need to *party*."

"Party *where*?" Chasity wondered. "My birthday is on freakin' *Valentine's* Day. Everywhere and every*thing* is gonna be hearts, bears and...*pink*," she huffed, inciting snickers from her friends.

Jason put his arm around Chasity, laughing. "Still not a fan of all that mushy stuff, huh?" he teased.

"Everything about that day is so...fussy bus," Chasity griped.

Malajia's eyes widened in excitement as she pointed to Chasity. "You said 'fussy bus'!" she exclaimed. "Yes! My made-up term is a thing now."

"That wack ass term will *never* be a thing," Mark grunted.

Malajia flipped her curled hair over her shoulder. "It already *is* and you mad about it," she teased.

"I gotta go guys," Chasity said, glancing at her watch.

"Bye babe," Jason called to her as she headed for the science building.

"I'm not paying her ass no mind, she's gonna have fun even if it *kills* her," Malajia promised once Chasity was out of range.

"And all those shots that she will have to drink probably *will*," Sidra joked, before waving to her friends. "African History awaits me."

"Hold up Sid, I gotta pass that building on my way to the library," Josh said, catching up to her.

One by one, the rest of the group paired off, leaving Malajia and Mark to continue their journey back to the clusters. "Damn, I wish I was done with classes for the day," Malajia complained. "I hate having a late class...fuckin' five o'clock."

"Sucks for you," Mark teased, much to Malajia's annoyance. "*I'm* done for the day."

"No, you're *not* you liar," Malajia contradicted, shooting him a side-glance. "Don't you have a class at four?"

"Fuck that class." Mark replied instantaneously.

Malajia shook her head in amusement as they entered the cluster gates. "Slackin' ass." She gave him a light backhand to his arm. "I'm about to get a nap in before this dry class," she announced, pairing off from him. "See you later."

"Later." Mark slowed his pace as he watched Malajia walk to her door. He found himself mesmerized by her long, sexy strides. Not to mention the way that her skinny jeans fit her, not hiding her shape. *Her legs got thicker*, he thought. *Looks good on her.*

Mark was so preoccupied that he didn't see the person walking in front of him. He snapped out of his trance when he collided with the person. "What the—? Watch where you're going," he barked.

"You bumped *me* dude," the guy shot back, continuing on his way.

"Yeah well, you saw I wasn't paying attention. You should've moved around me," Mark hurled at the guy's back. He flagged his hand in the guy's direction before looking back at the girls' house. Malajia had already disappeared inside, but he still found himself staring.

He vigorously shook his head. "I'm trippin'," he said to himself, before heading for his house.

"There is *no* way in hell that I'm gonna let her do that," Jason hissed at Malajia, shoving a piece of paper at her.

"Oh come on Jason, Don't go all 'protective boyfriend' mode on me," Malajia pleaded. "I think this will be a good thing for Chaz to do on her birthday."

"Anything involving any other guy taking shots off her damn body *isn't* gonna happen," he bit out. "Or any of that *other* shit you have on that list of yours."

Malajia rolled her eyes. She'd come over the guys' cluster to go over details with Jason for Chasity's birthday celebration. They were making progress, until Malajia showed him a list of things that she wanted Chasity to do on her birthday—that's when Jason became annoyed.

"You're being so dramatic right now," Malajia scoffed. "Everything I came up with will be funny."

Jason pointed a warning finger at Malajia and was about to lay into her, when the door opened.

"Sorry I'm late," Alex apologized, walking in and sitting her book bag on the couch. "How far did you two get?"

"We came up with a couple things to do for her," Jason informed, handing Alex a piece of paper with notes written on it.

Alex glanced at it and giggled. "Oh she's gonna hate *all* of this. I love it," she mused.

"Hold on, I got one more piece to go with that last thing and *Jason* is being a butthole about it," Malajia quibbled.

"Alex, look at the stuff that Malajia wants Chasity to do and tell me if I'm overreacting," Jason suggested, taking the paper from Malajia and handing it to Alex.

Alex grabbed the paper and began reading. When the look on her face changed from intrigued to perplexed, Jason clapped his hands together.

"Yeah, exactly," he said.

"Malajia, everything you have on here is just disrespectful," Alex chided. "I mean come on, you got down here that some random guy has to lick salt off her face?"

Malajia shrugged. "So?"

"Why would she put salt on her face in the *first* place?" Alex asked, confused. "Let *alone*, have some stranger with his nasty germs, *lick it off* her."

"That's all part of the fun," Malajia argued, putting her arms out. She was trying her best to keep from laughing. "She's supposed to do stuff that she wouldn't normally do."

Jason shook his head. "Malajia, you make my head

hurt," he griped.

"Wait, you have that she is supposed to walk over to a group of guys and give one of them a *lap dance*…and the guy that she gives it to, has to have *cornrows*?" Alex read. "Really? With her boyfriend watching her? You're out of your mind."

"That's what *I've* been saying," Jason commented.

Malajia tossed her hands up in the air. "Y'all are ruining the fun," she jeered. "Where's Mark at? *He'd* be on my side."

Alex flagged Malajia with her hand. "Don't worry Jase, Sidra and *I* will make up a list for her to do," Alex assured. "Malajia, you're banned from list duty unless you come up with something reasonable."

"Soooo, no male strippers with neon thongs on, slinging their dicks in her face then, huh?" Malajia asked.

Disgusted, Jason hopped up from the table. "I'm done," he barked, heading for his room.

"Jason I'm kidding," Malajia laughed after him. "They don't *have* to wear thongs, just boxers with a big hole in it." She laughed harder when she heard the door slam.

Alex balled up Malajia's list and tossed it, hitting her in the head with it. "You need help," she concluded.

Chasity pulled the covers over her before glancing at the clock on her nightstand. It was after midnight. She rolled her eyes and laid her head on her pillow. The sooner she fell asleep, the better. The minute that she closed her eyes, she was disturbed by a knock on her door.

"Get away from my damn door," she barked, not bothering to open her eyes.

"Come on Chaz, open up," Alex pleaded through the door.

"No," Chasity refused. "I'm tired, leave me alone."

Not hearing another word, Chasity figured that she was successful in making her late visitors leave. That was until she heard a key jiggling in her doorknob. Her eyes popped open and she bolted up in bed. "The hell?!" she exclaimed when the door swung open and in walked the girls.

"I had a copy of your room key made *just* for this occasion," Malajia revealed, holding up the key.

"Seriously?" Chasity griped. Malajia smiled, shaking the key repeatedly. "I hate all of you right now."

Emily turned the lamp on; Chasity quickly covered her face with her hands. She'd been in the dark so long that the sudden light hurt her eyes. "Just go away," she groaned.

"Somebody's twenty-one!" Malajia exclaimed, followed by loud cheers from Alex, Sidra and Emily.

"Happy Valentine's—I mean *birthday* Chasity," Sidra teased, sitting on the bed next to her.

"Very funny," Chasity ground out. "Can we do this later? I'm tired," she whined, trying to lay back down.

"Oh no you don't," Alex said, grabbing her arm and pulling her upright.

"You've got to take a shot, at least," Malajia added, revealing a bottle of pink liquor from a paper bag.

Chasity looked at it, repulsed. "Is that vodka?" she wondered. Malajia nodded. "Why the fuck is it pink?"

"Oh, I put pink food coloring in it because I know how much you *love* the color," Malajia boasted, flashing a smile.

Chasity squinted her eyes; everybody knew how much she hated the color pink. "Get out," Chasity said, pointing to the door.

"Shot first, *then* we leave," Sidra insisted, as a giggling Emily handed Chasity a Valentine's Day shot glass.

"Why is there a bear on it?" Chasity snapped, holding the glass up.

Malajia filled the small glass to capacity. "Just shut up and drink it," she ordered.

Chasity eyed the contents and frowned her face up. "I just don't want to," she whined.

"The longer you take, the more shots we're gonna give you," Malajia warned.

Realizing that she had no choice, Chasity let out a loud

sigh before reluctantly tossing back the drink. She pushed the empty glass in Malajia's hand as her friends applauded her. "That shit *tastes* cheap," Chasity complained, putting her face in her hand.

"Just for that smart-ass remark about this five-dollar bottle, you gotta take *another* shot," Malajia declared, filling the glass yet again.

Chasity's head popped up. "No, I was just playing," she laughed, putting her hand up. "I hate shots."

"Don't worry boo, you'll learn to love 'em today," Malajia shot back, handing Chasity the glass. "Say something else and Alex is gonna sit on you while I pour this whole bottle down your throat…and you know her ass is wide enough to pin you," she joked.

"It is," Alex agreed, laughing.

Chasity rolled her eyes, then took the shot without saying a word. She shivered from the nasty taste. "Get out," she commanded, laying down.

"Very well," Malajia relented, heading for the door with the others following suit. "Get a good night's sleep 'cause we're gonna bug you *all* day today."

"Fine," Chasity sighed.

"Night Chaz," Emily said, turning the lamp off.

"Malajia leave that damn key," Chasity barked.

Malajia sucked her teeth as she tossed the replicated key on Chasity's dresser. "Fine, take it," she bit out. "I have another one anyway," she joked, closing the door.

Chasity, too tired to react, just closed her eyes.

Chapter 8

Sunlight peered through the blinds, pulling Chasity out of her slumber several hours later. Grabbing the cell phone from her nightstand she turned her ringer back on and scrolled through her missed calls and birthday text messages. After reading a few, she tossed her phone on the bed and pushed the covers back.

Once she took her time showering, getting dressed, and styling her hair for the day, Chasity decided to return one of the phone calls.

"Happy Birthdaaaayyyyyy!" Trisha screeched in Chasity's ear once she answered the phone.

Chasity shook her head in amusement. "Thanks Mom."

"I can't believe my baby is twenty-one," Trisha said, feeling her emotions take over. "God, it seems like you were born just yesterday."

"Technically it would've been *today*," Chasity corrected.

"You know what I mean," Trisha replied. "You're making me feel old honey—you *better* not say it either."

Chasity snickered at Trisha's stern tone. She had to admit, her mother could always pick up when she was about to say something smart. "Anyway, thanks for calling," Chasity said, fixing a wayward curl on her hair.

"Of course," Trisha said. She paused for a moment. "I want you to have a happy birthday, I want you to *enjoy* yourself. I want you to know that you are *loved* and *appreciated*."

"I know, Mom," Chasity smiled. "Now stop being weird okay?"

Trisha laughed. "Okay, I'm finished for now. Talk to you later."

"Bye." Chasity stuck her cell phone into her jeans pocket and headed for her door.

Malajia bolted away from Chasity's door. "She's coming, she's coming," she whispered.

"You whispering all loud and shit," Mark whispered back. Malajia flipped him off as she stood in the living room.

As soon as Chasity stepped out of her room, she was startled by the loud, "Surprise! Happy birthday!" that was shouted by her friends.

After the initial shock wore off, Chasity took a few steps and scanned the space with her eyes. The first floor was decorated in everything pink. Pink helium balloons were placed around the room in bunches. Pink streamers were hanging from the ceiling and wrapped around the stair banister. The dining room table was covered in a pink table cloth; pink eatery, heart confetti and candy sat atop of it. Her round birthday cake was covered in pink buttercream flowers. A huge Valentine's Day banner hung from the wall with the words 'Valentine's Day' crossed out and 'Birthday' written in its place.

Chasity put her hands on her hips and stared at her friends, who were staring back at her, big smiles plastered to their faces. They were certainly bold, and she was amused. "I hate all of you," she said.

"Happy Valen-birthday Chaz," Josh teased, giving her a hug.

"Good one!" Alex laughed, clapping her hands together.

"Y'all had way too much time on your hands last night," Chasity commented, plucking one of the balloons.

"Sure did, and we knew those shots would knock your low-tolerance ass right out so you wouldn't hear us," Malajia chuckled, reaching for something on the couch.

Jason walked over to Chasity and gave her a kiss. "Look at the present I bought you," he said, pointing to a large object in a corner.

Chasity sucked her teeth when she saw the oversized stuffed Valentine's Day teddy bear. "You play too much, Jason," she said, tapping him on the arm, earning a laugh from him.

"Don't worry, I'll give you your real present later," he said to her.

"Jason, giving her the *D* is not a real present," Mark joked. David nearly choked on the candy that he was eating. "Don't be cheap bruh."

Jason glared at Mark while laughter erupted around him. "A girl that you tried to give *yours* to for her birthday cussed you out about it, didn't she?" Jason threw back.

Mark frowned, before lowering his head in shame. "She called me a cheap bastard and kicked me out her room when we were done," he admitted. Then snickered when the guys laughed at him. "Fuck y'all, she still *got* it though."

"It ain't about y'all *dicks* right now, it's about Chasity's birthday," Malajia hissed.

"I'd much rather hear about dicks," Chasity joked.

Malajia laughed. "Yeah me too, but it's time for your birthday breakfast," she said, walking up to Chasity. "Oh and you have to wear this all day," she said, putting a pink boa around Chasity's neck.

"I'm not wearing this bullshit," Chasity snapped, trying to remove it.

"Hey! You *wear* it or I'm gonna sneak in your room and steal all your body wash," Malajia threatened. "I still have a key and you got the *good* kind."

Before Chasity could react, Emily grabbed her arm and pulled her to the table. "Come on, you're gonna enjoy what we made you for breakfast," Emily promised as Chasity sat

down in a chair. When Emily went to get her food, Chasity
snatched the boa off of her neck.

"Put it back on," Malajia barked.

"It's making me itch," Chasity shot back, tossing it to
the floor. She rolled her eyes when Emily set the food down
in front of her. Chasity put her elbow on the table and put her
face in her hand, sighing in the process.

On the plate in front of her were heart-shaped pancakes
covered in whipped cream, strawberry pie filling, and pink
and red mini chocolate candies. Alongside the pancakes were
scrambled eggs that appeared to have a pink tint to them, and
a few strips of turkey bacon. To top it off, a glass of
strawberry milk sat in front of her.

"What's up with these pink ass eggs?"

"That was Malajia being extra with the food coloring,"
Sidra laughed.

"Yeah, we told her not to put it in there and as soon as
we turned our backs…." Alex sighed. "It's *Malajia* after all."

Malajia feigned hurt. "I think I did a good job with the
eggs," she defended.

"Yeah, I'm not eating those," Chasity refused, grabbing
a piece of bacon.

As people retreated to the kitchen to grab some
breakfast, Mark pulled something out of his pocket and
walked over to Chasity.

"Yo, you gotta share some food with my young bul,"
Mark said, much to Chasity's confusion.

"What are you talking about, boy?" she sneered.

Mark winded something up and placed it on the table in
front of Chasity. She busted out laughing, watching the little
wind up heart with feet walking towards her. "You're so
damn stupid," she laughed.

"I got her to laugh, yes!" Mark rejoiced, doing a dance.

"Where's your damn boa, Chasity?" Malajia questioned,
as the group made their way into a lounge later that evening.

"You said you would wear it after we left dinner."

"*Obviously* I lied," Chasity admitted without a qualm. "I wasn't wearing that itchy thing."

After Chasity's surprise breakfast in her decorated house earlier that morning, the group left her alone to relax for a few hours, before dragging her to indoor go-karting. After returning home and changing, the group took Chasity out to dinner at the new Italian restaurant that Josh had mentioned previously. Their final destination: a lounge.

"Yeah well, you owe me twenty dollars then," Malajia declared, folding her arms in a huff.

Sidra shot Malajia a puzzled stare. "You didn't even *buy* it," she contradicted. "You *stole* it from the drama club prop room."

"Nobody asked you!" Malajia snapped, stomping her foot on the floor. Sidra just flagged Malajia with her hand.

The group walked up to the bar and filled the empty seats. "Can we get some shots of vodka please?" Jason asked the bartender.

"Sure, ID's please?" The polite, lady bartender requested.

While everyone showed their ID's, Emily put her hand up. "I'll just have a glass of cola please," she said.

"You salty, you the only one who isn't twenty-one yet," Malajia teased, removing her coat.

"It's fine, I'm used to being the baby," Emily shrugged.

"Oh, it's *this* one's birthday today," Alex informed, pointed at Chasity who was fixing her hair in a small mirror. "She needs *two* shots."

"No, I can't do too many shots," Chasity protested as the bartender began preparing the shots. "I don't want to get too drunk."

"You're not driving, you'll be fine," Jason dismissed, taking money from his wallet. The bartender set the drinks in front of the group, then smiled when Jason handed her some money.

Chasity frowned at the two shots in front of her. "Ugh,"

she scoffed.

"Hurry up and drink these, 'cause we got some stuff that we want you to do," Malajia urged, handing Chasity one of the glasses.

Shaking her head, Chasity reluctantly downed the drink and was immediately handed the second shot. "Give me a minute!" she snapped, slapping her hand on the bar counter top.

"Nope, no breaks," Jason teased, gesturing for her to drink up.

She drank the second shot as her friends cheered. "This is so *gross*," she complained. While she was gaining her composure from the back to back shots of straight liquor, someone tapped her on the shoulder. She spun around in her seat to see who it was.

"Hey, you're Chasity right?" the short, bubbly, brown skinned girl asked.

Chasity eyed her skeptically. "Yeah."

"Oh no, I'm not a stalker or anything," she laughed, sensing Chasity's hesitation. "I'm in your Machine Assembly class…Nicole." She extended her hand.

"Oh, yeah I've seen you," Chasity remembered, shaking the girl's hand. "Hi."

"I overheard your friends mention that today is your birthday," Nicole continued. "Happy birthday… *Mine* was the other day."

"Well happy birthday to you too," Chasity said.

While Chasity was busy chatting with her classmate, Jason quickly signaled for the bartender to hand him an empty glass. As soon as the glass was placed in front of him Jason, along with the others, quickly poured their shots into the glass, snickering in the process. Emily tried her best to keep from laughing out loud as she splashed a little bit of her cola into the glass, giving it a little color.

Chasity finished talking and turned back around, just to be met by a glass with a straw in it, in her face, held by Jason.

"Here taste this," he said.

"What is it?" she questioned, trying to push his hand away.

"Just try it," Jason insisted, pushing the straw close to her mouth.

Sucking her teeth, she took a big sip and nearly spat it out.

"Don't you spit that out!" Mark yelled at her. "Drink it, driiiinnnkkk iittttt."

Jason took the cup from her, patting Chasity's back as she coughed.

"Just swallow it," Malajia goaded. "Pretend its Jason's jizz." Malajia vulgar comment took everyone by surprise, inciting glares and some laughs. Laughs mostly coming from the guys.

"Damn Malajia," Jason commented.

"You are so gross and disrespectful," Sidra chided. "Have some class."

Malajia flipped her off.

Jason took a sip of the drink, as Chasity finally gained her composure. "I don't swallow, bitch," she hissed.

Jason spat his drink out.

"Really Jase? All over the bar though?" Chasity chastised. He started laughing.

"Shit, *I* would," Malajia laughed, much to the embarrassment of some of her friends. She looked next to her and saw Mark staring at her with the biggest smile on his face. She frowned in disgust. "Boy, I'm just joking," she snapped, slapping him on the arm. "You're such a pervert."

Alex shook her head. "Amateurs," she chortled of Malajia and Chasity. "If you're gonna do it, follow through."

"Okay, I think you've had enough," Emily joked, moving a drink away from the laughing Alex.

Mark pointed to Alex. "Yo! Alex just admitted that she swallows," he exclaimed. "I knew you were a freak."

Sidra put her hand over her face. She was mortified at the conversation. "Oh my God, eww," she admonished.

Alex shot a glower Mark's way. "Why am I *not* surprised that you would say that out loud?" she said, taking a sip of her drink.

Mark just laughed as he signaled for the bartender to bring him another drink.

"Okay, birthday girl. Now that we got some more drinks in you, it's time for our little game," Sidra declared, removing a piece of paper from her purse and handing it to Alex.

Alex cleared her throat. "Okay, these are some things that you have to do before the night is over," she began. She then frowned when she read off the first item. "Rub salt on your face and ask a strange man with cornrows to lick it off?"

"The fuck?!" Chasity exclaimed, offended. Malajia busted out laughing.

"Malajia!" Jason barked, slamming his hand on the counter top. "What did I tell you?"

"This isn't the list that we came up with Chaz," Alex assured, tossing a napkin at Malajia. "Malajia's ignorant ass must've switched them."

Malajia tried to speak, but she was laughing too hard. "You should've seen your faces," she said, putting her hand on her chest.

"Where is the real list, Malajia?" Sidra hissed.

Malajia wiped a tear from her eye. "I put it in my coat pocket," she replied, then she looked at the floor. "My other coat…that's in my closet…at the house."

Alex balled up the piece of paper and tossed it on the bar counter. "Well so much for *that*," she griped. "Next time we do something like this, Malajia is not allowed to help."

"That list y'all came up with was corny any-damn-way," Malajia grumbled.

Having a thought, David pushed his glasses up on his nose. "There *is one* thing that we can have Chaz do," he suggested.

Chasity shot him a side-glance. "David, don't make me slap those glasses across the bar," she ground out, causing

Mark to nearly choke on his drink from laughter.

"You can go take a picture with that girl who came over here earlier," David said, ignoring Chasity's threat. "Nicole...that was her name, right?"

"Why would I do that?" Chasity asked, looking at David like he was stupid.

David seemed embarrassed. "Well—"

"He just wants to look at her picture later and shit," Mark commented. "He thinks she's cute but don't wanna say anything. He was staring hard as shit at her when she walked over."

"Are you through?" David sniped.

"For *now*," Mark jeered, taking a sip of his drink.

"Yeah, go do it Chaz," Malajia egged on, pointing to Nicole, who was sitting at a table with some friends. "She's right over there. Be a friend and help David get his jollys," she teased, earning an eye roll from David.

Standing from her seat, Chasity let out a huff. "This is fuckin' stupid."

"Here, drink this first," Jason laughed, handing her a shot. Chasity snatched the glass and quickly downed the drink before walking away from the bar.

Chasity's friends watched in amusement, while she put on a good act of being nice to the chatty girl. Once she got her picture, Chasity approached the bar and flipped the middle finger to her friends, who were cracking up at her.

Flopping in her seat, she clicked on the picture in her phone. "Erase this bitch out my phone." She handed the phone to David, then reached for a tissue.

"What happened?" Alex laughed.

"She touched my fuckin' face," Chasity griped, wiping her face with the tissue. "Talking about 'smile birthday girl'." She tossed the tissue on the counter. "I think she had hot sauce on her finger. I should've slapped her."

Chasity looked over to David, who was smiling at the picture in Chasity's phone. Annoyed that she had to do that in the first place, she snatched the phone and erased the picture.

"No wait!" David protested. Realizing it was too late, he sat back in his seat, sucking his teeth.

"He salty," Mark laughed.

Over the next few hours, the group migrated from the bar, to the dance floor, *back* to the bar, and finally out of the lounge and back to campus. Malajia, who was drunk, took way too long trying to stick her key in the front door of their house.

"Yo, will you come the hell on?" Mark slurred. "I gotta pee!"

"Go pee in your *own* damn bathroom," Malajia scoffed, pushing open the door. Mark tripped over her and darted up the steps. "Boy!" she hollered while the others poured into the house.

Jason carried a drunk, sleeping Chasity into the house and gently laid her down on the couch. He searched in her purse for her room key.

"Awww, she didn't even get to cut her cake," Alex said, pointing to the cake still sitting on the table. "Maybe she can do it tomorrow."

"Naw, we cutting that shit *tonight*," Malajia slurred, grabbing a knife from the utensil drawer. "I'm starving, those drinks sucked up all my food."

Sidra walked over and grabbed the knife from a wobbly Malajia. "Yeah, *you* won't be cutting *anything*," she said. "*I'll* cut it." Malajia put her hands up in surrender.

Sidra, along with David, volunteered to be designated drivers that night. Sidra had no desire to drink, just remembering how drunk she had gotten on her twenty-first birthday months ago made her sick to her stomach. "Chaz is gonna suffer so badly tomorrow," Sidra said, cutting the cake into slim triangles. "I feel bad for her already."

"Yep and I'm gonna scream right in her face as soon as she wakes up," Malajia said.

Mark bolted down the steps. "Yo, I heard somebody mention cake," he said, rubbing his toned stomach. "Break off some of that. I'm hungry," he loudly added.

"You're going to wake her," Alex frowned.

"No, she's dead to the world," Jason assured them, opening Chasity's room door.

Alex sucked her teeth at Mark, who began dancing at the sight of cake.

Sidra placed slices on the small plates. Malajia grabbed her slice and walked over to Chasity. "I gotta give her some cake," Malajia whispered, putting the cake close to Chasity's mouth.

"Malajia, chill," Jason ordered, stern.

Malajia straightened up. "Ooh, his voice got extra deep just now," she observed, amused.

Jason shook his head at Malajia, then picked Chasity up in his arms and carried her to her room.

Malajia was about to take a bite of her cake when she looked over at Mark, who was chewing and smacking his piece loudly. "This is soooo good," Mark groaned, his eyes closed.

"You want this one too?" Malajia offered, then smashed the cake on Mark's cheek. She jumped back in anticipation of his cake retaliation. Instead, Mark removed the smashed pieces from his face and stuffed them into his mouth. "Eww," she grimaced. He just shrugged.

Chapter 9

Mark pulled the knit cap down on his head as he approached the girls' front door. Before he could knock, it opened.

"Hey Chaz, still hung over from the other night?" Mark teased as Chasity and Sidra emerged.

"I *wasn't,* but seeing your face is giving me that sick feeling again," Chasity bit back.

Mark made a face at her. "Ha ha."

Sidra giggled. "You looking for Malajia?" she assumed.

Mark looked at them with confusion. "Why would you just automatically assume I'm here to see *her*?" he asked, defensive. Sure, he was there to meet Malajia so they could walk to class together. But he didn't know why they just assumed that every time he came over, it was because he wanted to see Malajia.

"Because if you're not eating our *food*, you're looking for *her*," Sidra pointed out. "Take that attitude down a notch."

Mark flagged Sidra with his hand. "Whatever," he mumbled.

Chasity sucked her teeth. This run-in with Mark was taking up too much of her time. She opened the door and stuck her head back inside. "Mel! Your loud ass dog is out here shittin' on the grass again," she yelled in the house, much to Mark's irritation.

Mark's eyes flashed as Sidra put her hand over her face to hide her laughter. "How *do* you survive in hell all day?" he sneered at Chasity, who in turn mocked him with her smile before she and a laughing Sidra walked off. "It wasn't that damn funny Sidra!" he yelled after them.

Malajia stepped out the house before Mark could go in. "What are you out here hollering about?" she asked, frowning.

"You should've been outside already," Mark snapped at her, pointing. "You left me out here with the damn ice queen and the giggling princess."

Malajia stared at him as if he was crazy for seconds. "You done?" she asked.

"Yeah, let's go to this stupid ass class," he responded, gesturing for her to walk ahead of him.

"I'm seriously considering changing my major," Emily declared, repeatedly tapping her highlighter on her textbook.

"Why is that?" Alex wondered, taking a sip of soda from her cup. Alex, who was finished with her last class of the day, and Emily, who had some time between classes, were sitting in the cafeteria having a much-needed quick bite.

Emily sighed. "I don't know. I guess I'm just nervous about some of these assignments for my education class," she admitted, highlighting some lines in her textbook. "I have to create these mock assignments and activities and… It's just hard."

"I thought you had that course last semester," Alex recalled.

"That was 301, this is *302*," Emily explained, highlighting more notes. "It's a lot harder."

"You want to teach kindergarten, right?" Alex asked, before taking a bite of her pickle.

"Preschool through third grade," Emily corrected.

"Awww, that's so cute," Alex cooed, smiling. "I can *totally* see you teaching the babies. You have that patience that's needed."

"I guess," Emily sighed yet again. She ran her hands through her straight, sandy-brown hair, which almost touched her shoulders. "I just want to make sure that whatever I do, will hold their attention and help them learn. I can only imagine the little balls of energy that'll be bouncing around in the classroom... I'm starting to wonder if I'll be able to handle it."

Alex chuckled. "If you handled the pressure of your mom, then you can handle *anything*."

Emily thought for a moment as she opened her bag of chips. "That's just the thing. I *couldn't* handle the pressure," she sulked. "I ended up drowning my stress in *alcohol* and getting placed on academic probation."

Alex eyed Emily with concern. "Maybe *so*. But you eventually stood up to her and ended up getting *off* of academic probation," she emphasized. "You busted your ass to get back to where you need to be."

Emily held a sullen gaze as Alex spoke.

"You put your mind to something and you followed through with it. Don't let fear keep you from something that you want," Alex added. "I will never let you forget what you've accomplished."

Emily let a smile come through. "Thank you."

Alex patted Emily's hand before picking up her turkey sandwich. "Speaking of your mother," she began. "Have you spoken to her at all?"

Emily shook her head. "I tried calling her recently because my grandmom's birthday is coming up and I wanted to know what I should get for her," she sucked her teeth. "Not surprisingly, my messages went unanswered."

"Wow, she's still on that silent treatment mess, huh?" Alex regretted her decision to even bring it up. She knew it was a sore spot for Emily.

"Yeah," Emily bit out, taking a chip from her bag. "I mean, fine she doesn't want to talk to me, but I'm asking about *Grandmom*."

"Sorry Em."

Emily once again shook her head, letting Alex know that she didn't want to talk about it any longer.

"Point taken," Alex assured, sincere.

Alex decided to concentrate on her sandwich. Just as she took a big bite, Eric walked over.

"Hey ladies," he greeted, then chuckled when he saw Alex cover her mouth with her hand, trying to scarf her food down her throat. "Please don't choke," he said.

Alex took a sip of her drink once she swallowed her food. "I'm fine," she smiled. "What's up?"

"I noticed you over here and just came over to see if you wanted me to walk you to work later," Eric replied.

"Sure," Alex returned. "I close tonight."

"Okay," Eric replied.

"So…you don't have to *stay* there with me," she added.

Eric placed his hand on his chest. "Now what kind of man would I be if I let you walk back to campus alone at night?" he asked. "I have no choice *but* to stay and hang out."

Alex was amused at how blatantly dramatic he was being. "Eric, one of my friends will come pick me up," she declared. "You don't have to worry, I'll be fine."

Eric thought for a moment. "Well, they can pick us *both* up," he grinned. "If they don't mind of course."

Emily smiled at the awestruck look on Alex's face when she spoke to Eric. *That is so cute*, she thought.

Alex admitted to herself that she enjoyed the times when Eric walked her to work and hung out with her. It made the time pass by and she felt it made them closer as friends. "Well okay then," she agreed. "They won't mind."

Eric's smile could have lit the building. "I'll meet you at your house in a few hours then."

Alex nodded at him as he walked away from their table. Emily held her gaze on Alex, who looked down at her sandwich, a smile on her face.

"Alex, why are you not dating him?" Emily bluntly asked, snapping Alex out of her trance.

"I'm not interested in dating anyone right now," Alex proclaimed. "Eric and I are just *friends*."

"So I've heard," Emily teased. "But he's such a sweet guy and you two have already done the…the *do*. So what's stopping you?"

Alex sighed as she pondered Emily's question. Those were the same questions that she had been asking herself lately. "I'm focused on school right now, Em."

"School is more than books Alex," Emily said. "You girls made that clear to *me*, freshman year."

Alex ran her hands through her hair. "Okay, honestly…part of it is that I'm still a bit… *scorned* from my last relationship," she revealed. "I guess as great as Eric *is*… I'm just afraid that he might hurt me like *Paul* did."

Emily gathered her belongings as she registered what Alex had said. Before she stood up, she tapped Alex's hand. "Don't let fear keep you from something that you want," she said.

Alex was impressed and it showed on her face. She picked up her drink and nodded as Emily walked away. *Touché Em, Touché*.

"Aye Mel, hurry up with those chips," Mark demanded, flipping through the pages of his notebook. He'd been at the girls' house studying with Malajia for over an hour and was starving.

Malajia walked out of the kitchen, holding a bowl of chips and a scowl on her face. "Who are you talking to?" she snapped, slamming the bowl down in the middle of the table. "You can take your freeloading ass back to your *own* damn house."

Mark chuckled. "I'm just joking, chill."

Malajia rolled her eyes as she sat down in the seat across from him. "Yeah whatever," she mumbled, picking up her highlighter.

Mark reached for the bowl, then looked around the table. "You ain't bring the dip?" he asked, face frowned up. He slowly stood from the table as Malajia shot him a piercing look. "It's cool, I'mma go ahead and just grab it," he declared, heading for the kitchen himself.

"Bring me a can of soda out the fridge while you're in there," Malajia called to him. Mark threw his head back and let out a loud, exaggerated groan at her request. "Just shut up and bring it," she demanded, slamming her hand on the table.

Mark laughed, setting the cold can of soda in front of Malajia.

"Thank you, now was that so hard?" she said, opening the can. Using the remote, she turned some music on and began to bob her head to a hip hop track.

After staring at his work for several agonizing minutes, Mark reached for more chips. Trying at first to reach the bowl without taking his eyes from the words in his book, he eventually looked up and caught a glimpse of Malajia. Forgetting about his quest for more chips, he found himself staring at her.

Malajia, unaware that he was staring, was mouthing the words to a song as she read through her textbook. Mark, completely in a daze, watched her, taking in every part of her. Her beautiful brown complexion, delicate features, long hair, which she had laying over one shoulder. He watched as her dainty hand grabbed a chip from her napkin and placed it into her mouth. He focused on her mouth as she began slowly chewing the snack. He'd never noticed how full her lips were, and the burgundy tinted gloss that she was wearing only enhanced them. It was when he imagined himself kissing those lips that he grabbed his head with both hands and began hollering at the top of his lungs, completely startling Malajia.

"What the hell is *wrong* with you?!" she yelled at him, nearly choking on her chip.

Mark's fantasy of Malajia had shaken him. But realizing that his reaction was completely uncalled for, he looked around nervously. "Um, my fault. Something bit me," he lied.

Malajia patted her chest as she picked up her can of soda and took a sip. "So you had to scream like a freakin' maniac?" she harped. "What the hell bit you?"

Mark quickly began gathering his books from the table. "A bat, listen I gotta go," he replied quickly.

Malajia looked at him as if he was crazy. Before she could respond, he walked out of the door, leaving her dumbfounded. While she was still trying to register what had just happened, the door opened and Mark walked back in and over to the table.

"Forgot these," he declared, picking up the bowl of chips and walking back out the door.

"Boy! You better bring my damn bowl back," Malajia hollered after him. "Jackass," she mumbled to herself when he didn't.

Still disturbed by his inner most thoughts, Mark stormed into his house, tossed his book bag down on the floor and kicked it across the living room. As he began pacing back and forth while cursing to himself, Jason walked out of their room.

"Hey Mark—"

Mark spun around, pointing at him. "Don't you ask me shit about no damn Malajia!" he snapped.

Jason put his hands up as he eyed Mark suspiciously. "Um...I *wasn't*," he slowly replied. "I was going to tell you that I'm on my way to the store and wanted to know if you needed me to pick up anything for you."

Feeling silly, Mark sat on the couch and rubbed his hair with his hand. "Sorry man," he sighed. "Yeah, can you pick me up some more deodorant?" he asked, taking some money out of his wallet.

Jason raised an eyebrow as Mark handed him the money. "What? You're actually giving up money without a fight?" he chortled. "Yeah, something's got you screwed up."

Mark shook his head as Jason walked out of the house. "Don't I fuckin' know it," he grunted to himself.

"I hate coming to the mailroom. I never get shit anyway," Malajia complained, slamming her mailbox shut. She folded her arms and walked over to Chasity, who was standing at a window waiting to sign for her package. "Who did you get a package from?"

"My mom," Chasity replied, tapping her nails on the counter.

Malajia let out a huff. "Can you hurry up and get your expensive *whatever* it is, so we can go to the mall please?" she fussed. "I wanna get off this dry ass campus."

"Don't rush me because your parents don't send you shit anymore," Chasity teased, handing the worker her ID.

"Yeah well, at least I can *talk* to *both* of my parents," Malajia snarled.

Chasity glared at Malajia "Goddamn it Malajia!" she exclaimed,

Malajia's eyes widened, she knew she'd crossed a line "Ooh, too far?"

"A little bit," Chasity admitted, grabbing the box from the counter.

"I'm sorry," Malajia apologized, as they proceeded out of the post office. "I'm cranky today."

"Its fine," Chasity replied, adjusting the box in her hands. "Why the hell are you so damn cranky anyway?"

"'Cause I'm bored, horny, and *hungry*," Malajia vented. "Stupid Alex ate my leftover pizza and I didn't feel like cooking anything."

"I believe that was *her* leftover pizza," Chasity pointed out.

"*And*?!" Malajia snapped, much to Chasity's amusement. "She know that whatever pizza is still in the fridge the next day is *mine*. Those are the rules. She violated them and I *don't* appreciate it."

"Yeah okay," Chasity laughed.

As the girls entered the parking lot, they noticed Josh leaning up against a car, talking to a female.

Malajia craned her neck to get a good look. "Ooh, I think Josh is talking to that January girl," she said.

"*December*," Chasity corrected, unlocking her car with her keyring.

"Yeah whatever, it's still a damn month," Malajia bit out, waving her hand dismissively at Chasity. "I don't get some of these names that these parents come up with."

"Yeah…'cause *your* name is so typical right?" Chasity sneered.

"Asks the girl who's named after a damn belt," Malajia flashed back, still watching Josh from a distance.

Chasity glared at her. "It's not even *spelled* the same," she hissed, shoving her box into the trunk of her car. "Let's just go before I change my mind."

Malajia put her hand up. "No wait," she protested. "Josh is keeping this girl from us. I think it's time we go meet her."

"I don't *want* to though," Chasity fussed, pushing some hair behind her ears.

Malajia grabbed her arm. "Sure you do. Let's go," she insisted, pulling Chasity along.

Josh was so busy smiling and laughing that he didn't notice the girls walk up to him.

"What's up with you, Josh?" Malajia cheerfully greeted, patting him on his back.

Josh looked at the girls with wide eyes. "Um…hey Malajia, Chasity. What's up?" he replied, nervously.

"Why do you look scared?" Chasity teased.

He looked back at the smiling December, before looking back at the girls. "Scared? Why would I be scared?"

Malajia eyed him, recalling Mark's comment about Josh being afraid to introduce them to December because they might scare her. "Uh huh," she mocked. She tapped him on the arm. "Come on *Joshua*, introduce us."

He leaned in close to Chasity and Malajia, so that only they could hear him. "You *better* be nice," he whispered through clenched teeth.

"Why wouldn't we be nice?" Chasity loudly asked, much to Malajia's amusement and Josh's annoyance.

"We're just messing around Josh," Malajia assured once her laughter subsided. "Stop being rude."

Josh sighed; he really wasn't ready to introduce December to all of his friends yet. He knew that if they liked her, they would press him to bring her around. He just wanted to wait until he and December were serious before he started bringing her into their crazy fold. But knowing how persistent the girls were, he had no choice but to make the introductions right then and there. "December, these are two of my friends Chasity and Malajia. Girls, this is December Harley."

"Why didn't you say *our* last names?" Malajia fussed.

"Cut it out, Mel," Josh ordered sternly.

Malajia put her hand up. "I'm playing," she giggled. "You'll learn that I play too much," she directed at December.

"It's nice to finally meet you both," December smiled. "Joshua talks about all of you a lot."

"Is that so, *Joshua*?" Chasity smirked at him.

"Stop it," Josh ordered through clenched teeth.

"We may look mean, but we're really fun to be around," Malajia assured. "You should hang out with us sometime."

"I'd love that, thank you," December cheerfully returned, pushing some of her hair over her shoulders. "And you don't look mean *at all*."

"Oh I was really talking about *her*," Malajia jeered, pointing to Chasity, who flipped Malajia the finger. Malajia pointed to December's hair. "I like that wave, what kind of hair is that?" she asked.

Josh pinched the bridge of his nose and let out a sigh as December grabbed a handful of her locks. "Umm, mine," she innocently answered.

Chasity snickered loudly while a salty look appeared on Malajia's face. "I knew that," Malajia lied. December giggled.

"That's what you get, weavie," Chasity said to Malajia, who in turn just flipped *her* off. "Anyway, we gotta go," Chasity declared. "See you around."

December waved to the girls as they walked off.

Josh turned to December and she rubbed his shoulder. "You look so nervous," she teased.

"Those two scare me sometimes," he joked.

Chapter 10

"I'm over this cold weather," Malajia complained, dipping one of her curly fries into some ketchup. "I'm sick of wearing this damn coat... Damn buttons done popped off it and shit. Spring needs to come *on*."

"I hear you," David chuckled, looking at his watch. The guys walked over to the girls' house a half hour earlier to pick up Malajia and Chasity, so that they could all go to the gym.

Josh looked at Malajia with confusion. "Why are you eating all those fries when you're about to go work out?" he questioned.

"Mind your business, Josh," Malajia spat, picking up another fry. Josh just shook his head.

"Mark, are you meeting us at the gym later?" Josh asked. "I remember you saying that you had to meet your project group at the library." When Mark didn't respond, Josh looked over at him. "Mark," he called.

Mark was so busy staring at Malajia that he did not hear his name being called. Josh, noticing that his friend was distracted, picked up a pillow from the couch and tossed it at him, hitting him in the face.

"Ouch! What the hell?!" Mark bellowed, jumping up from his seat. "Who threw that?"

"*I* did," Josh replied calmly. "You act like you couldn't hear me."

Mark ran his hand over his head as he sat back down. "My fault, what did you say?"

Josh raised an eyebrow at him. "I asked if you were gonna meet us at the gym later," he repeated.

"Oh. Yeah, I have to meet this dry ass group at the library to go over this project in my marketing class," Mark replied. "They corny. With those stupid ass ideas they be coming up with."

Jason looked at his watch as he rose from his seat. "Chaz, come on," he called. "We want to get in there before it gets too crowded."

"Alright, I'm coming," Chasity replied, walking out of her room with her gym bag. She frowned her face in disgust. "Why does the whole kitchen smell like vinegar?"

"I put it on my fries," Malajia answered, picking up another one. "I wanted to see what they would taste like with vinegar on them."

"What did you do, drown them in it?" Chasity fussed.

"Sure did," Malajia replied, putting her plate in the sink. "Okay I'm ready."

"I'm just gonna walk with y'all since the library is on the way to the gym," Mark stated, rising from his seat and grabbing his book bag from the floor.

Mark walked slightly behind the group to the campus commons area, quiet as his mind wandered. He couldn't understand why Malajia had been plaguing his thoughts lately. *What the hell is wrong with me?* he thought, rubbing his hands over his face.

Malajia stopped suddenly. "Shit!" she yelped, causing everyone to halt their progress.

"What's wrong Mel?" David wondered.

"I forgot my towel," Malajia answered, running her hands over her hair. "*And* a damn ponytail holder. I gotta go back to the room."

"Are you serious?" Jason laughed. "A towel, I can understand, but you want to walk all the way back to the room for a *ponytail holder?*"

Malajia grabbed a handful of her hair. "Hell yeah, this is *weave* sweetie. I'm not tryna get this mess all gross with sweat," she threw back. "I need this off my neck. Chaz, walk me back."

"What? No!" Chasity exclaimed. "*I* have my towel and holder. Why do *I* need to go back to the house?"

Malajia placed her hands on her hips as she shot Chasity a glare. "Because if you *don't* I'm gonna pour my vinegar all in your orange juice," she threatened.

Chasity put two fingers on the bridge of her nose. Malajia's threats were always silly and worked her nerves. "Fuck you Malajia. Guys let's go," she hissed as she proceeded to walk off.

Malajia busted out laughing. "Come on, can you please walk me?" she begged. "If I go back by myself, I'm gonna get back in my bed and I *need* to get to the gym."

You don't need to do anything, your body is perfect, Mark thought.

Chasity let out a loud sigh. "Fine," she relented, teeth clenched. "You better not take forever either."

"See y'all there," David said as the two girls walked away.

As the guys were getting ready to continue their walk to the gym, they saw that Mark's focus was on Malajia walking away. David, Josh, and Jason exchanged knowing glances and smirks.

Jason tapped Mark's shoulder, snapping him out of his daze. "You hoping to see through her clothes or something?" he teased.

"Huh?" Mark looked confused. "Whatchu' mean?"

"I'm talking about Malajia," Jason clarified. "You're staring at her like a lost dog."

Mark flagged him with his hand. "Shouldn't y'all be

getting on your damn way?" he bit out, sitting on a bench.

Not intending on stopping the subject, the guys sat down as well.

"Come on man," Mark complained, tossing his hands up in aggravation. "I don't have time for this."

"Time for *what* exactly?" Josh prodded.

"Time for whatever the hell y'all about to start running your mouths about," Mark shot back.

"You mean *Malajia*," David pressed. "And the way you keep looking at her."

Mark rolled his eyes. "I look at *plenty* of women."

Jason sucked his teeth. "You're full of shit," he hurled. "Bro, just admit that you like her."

Mark could've jumped out of his seat. Hearing the words that he'd actually been thinking himself said out loud made him uneasy.

"Fuck you Jason," he barked, earning a laugh from Jason. "Malajia is my *friend*, my buddy, homie—"

"It doesn't matter how many synonyms you use, it doesn't change the fact that you like her *more* than that," Jason threw back.

Mark looked over at Josh who snickered hard. "Something funny?"

"He played you using the word 'synonym'," Josh laughed. He looked around and saw that he was the only one amused. "*I* found it funny, that's all that matters...carry on."

"Think about it," Jason began. "She's the *first* person you call in the morning. She's the *first* person you run and share stuff with—"

"So? You do that with Chasity, and Josh *you* do that with Sidra...*used* to anyway," Mark interrupted. His comment was met with knowing looks. "What?"

"Think about what you just said," Jason pointed out.

Mark pinched the bridge of his nose. He was getting agitated.

"Let's not forget all those not-so-subtle sex

propositions," David added. "You've been making a lot of those to her lately."

"I just be *joking!*" Mark exclaimed. "Y'all always taking shit overboard."

"No, that would be *you*," Josh laughed, grabbing his gym bag from the ground. "What's wrong with you liking Malajia? She's a beautiful woman. She's smart, she's funny—"

"I mean she a'ight," Mark downplayed.

Josh shook his head. "Look, I think it's a good thing. Who *else* would put up with your shit," he joked. Jason and David nodded in agreement. "You might as well tell her how you feel."

"How did that work out for *you*?" Mark snarled, side-eyeing Josh.

Josh cut his eye at him. "That was misguided frustration and I forgive you," he quibbled, standing from his seat.

"Whatever. Y'all wasted your time on this conversation, 'cause I don't *like* no damn *Malajia*." Mark spat. "That's why I hope all the weights are gone when you get to the gym."

Jason stood up. "Denial looks sad on you brother," he chortled. "Come on guys, let's go."

"This ain't denial, this is *fact*," Mark maintained as they walked away. "Y'all swear you figured some shit out. Mel and I are *cool*, it's nothing more than that." When they ignored him, he let out a loud sigh. "They get on my nerves... I don't like her."

Mark's mind was so clouded, he knew he wasn't going to be able to concentrate on his group's project. He grabbed his bag and jumped up from the bench. "Fuck that group," he hissed, heading for the clusters.

As his pace quickened, his mind raced. "No, this *can't* be what this is," he said to himself. The more the visions of her popped in his head, the more he realized that was exactly what it was. His feelings for her had changed, and now he was forced to accept it. "Fuuuuck," he groaned aloud.

Hours later, hands in his pockets, Mark walked over to the girls' house. He raised his hand to knock, but just decided to twist the knob.

"Hey Emily," he greeted, walking in and shutting the door behind him. "Is Mel upstairs?"

"Yeah, I think she's working on a paper," Emily answered, flipping through the TV channels with the remote. "I heard her cussing a few minutes ago, so whatever she's working on has her mad...approach with caution."

"Noted," Mark said, trotting up the steps. He stood at the top of the stairs, glancing into Malajia's open door. He caught a glimpse of her, sitting at her desk, typing on her laptop.

He chuckled to himself when she smacked the screen with her hand in frustration. The amusement left his face as the reality of what he was about to attempt set in. *Nah, I can't*, he thought turning to go downstairs. He paused, tapping his fist on the banister. *Don't be like Josh. Man up.* Listening to his inner voice, he walked to the room and stuck his head in the door.

"Whatchu' doing?" he asked, startling her.

Malajia looked up at him, running a hand through her hair. "Trying to bullshit my way through this research project for my Marketing Research class," she answered. "What's up with *you*?"

Mark stepped in the room and shoved his hands in his jacket pockets. "Just chillin'," he replied, gazing at her.

Malajia caught his stare; he was fidgeting. "You good?" she chuckled. "You look like you wanna throw up."

Tell me about it. "Yeah, yeah I'm cool," Mark assured.

"You *sure*?" she pressed, spinning around in her seat. "'Cause if you *are* gonna throw up, Alex's ugly blanket is right across the hall."

Mark just shook his head. *She's so pretty... Damn it!* He

slowly sat down on her bed while trying to figure out how to feel Malajia out. "You need help with that project?" he asked.

A hopeful look appeared on her face. She raised an eyebrow at him. "Yeah, do you know how to do these?"

"Nah," he returned. His answer annoyed her and it showed.

"Why did you even *ask* me if you can't help?" she spat out, turning back to her laptop. "You just pissed me off."

"My bad," he apologized. He clapped his hands together while she went back to typing. "Yo umm, I haven't heard about you talking to anybody...like *talking* talking."

Malajia looked baffled. "You *wouldn't*, 'cause I'm *not*," she replied.

Good, Mark thought.

Malajia looked at him. "What even made you mention that?"

"Just asking," he defended.

"Do I ask about the trolls *you* talk to?"

Mark laughed. "I'm not talking to any *trolls*," he returned. "I think I've had enough of the...randoms."

"You mean *hoes*?" Malajia jeered.

Mark put his hands up. "Nope, you won't get me to say that word," he refused. "My mom would slap me all the way from Delaware."

Malajia chuckled. "Well...good you're done with them. 'Cause despite how simple you are ...you could do better," Malajia commented, reaching for her cup of water that sat on her desk.

Mark nodded. "Yeah...I know," he said under his breath. "So umm...what are you doing tomorrow?" he asked after a moment.

Malajia pondered the question. "What is tomorrow, Friday?" She tapped her finger on her chin. "Nothing that I *know* of," she answered. "Why, what's up?"

Mark nervously ran his hands over his hair. "You uh...you wanna go to dinner?"

"I don't see why not," Malajia shrugged. "If the others are cool with going, count me in."

Mark shook his head. "No, I mean…"

"Mean what?" she cut in when he hesitated. "Boy you're being weird."

"Trust me, I know," he admitted. He ran his hand over his head again, exhaling deeply. "I mean… Do you want to go to dinner…just you and me?" he clarified.

Malajia frowned slightly. She wondered if she heard correctly. "I don't get it…like to the caf?"

Mark slowly shook his head. "I mean *out* to dinner…off campus…somewhere nice." Malajia was still confused and it showed all over her face. "Just the two of us," he added.

Mark's proposition still wasn't registering with Malajia. "Soooo, you mean you wanna go out with me?... Like on a *date?*"

"Yes," Mark replied.

"Like a *date*, date?"

"Yes," he repeated.

Malajia blinked slowly. "As in *you'll* be paying for it?"

Mark sighed loudly. "*Yeah* man."

Malajia sat there for a moment, trying to register what was happening. "But…*why?*" she asked, much to Mark's frustration.

He stood up from the bed. "Come on, Malajia," he bristled. "I'm being serious."

She too rose from her seat. "So am *I*," she promised. "I just don't get it. Why would you want to go on a date with me?" Her tone was calm. She wasn't trying to be funny; she genuinely wanted to know. "I mean…we hate each other."

"I don't hate you," Mark denied. "I never *did.*"

Malajia folded her arms, fixing a skeptical gaze. "Come on now."

Mark tossed his hands up. "Okay *now*. I don't hate you *now*," he clarified. "Are you saying that you hate *me?*"

"Of *course* I don't," Malajia replied, defensively. "Okay, we may not *hate* each other, but we don't like each other like that."

Mark just looked at her. The intensity of his gaze and his lack of protest took her back.

"*Do* we?" she questioned. "Do *you?*" She pointed to herself. "Do you *like* me like me?"

Mark sucked his teeth. "You're being smart," he scoffed, moving for the door; she stopped him by grabbing his arm.

"Mark, I *promise* I'm being serious," she insisted, looking at him. "Are you saying that you like me like that?"

Mark rubbed his hands over his face, trying to keep his composure. Expressing his feelings in a serious way was never his strong suit. "*Yeah* Mel, I like you alright," he blurted out, exasperated. "I like you more than a friend... Damn! You always gotta drag shit out."

Malajia was in complete shock, standing there with her mouth open. *What...the...hell?* She never in a million years would have thought that Mark would *ever* see her as more than a friend, especially given the nature of their friendship. She didn't know why, but hearing him admit that...actually made her feel good—*really* good.

"Well..." she began finally. "When did you come to that realization?"

"What's up with all these questions?" he barked.

Malajia frowned at him. "What the hell are you so damn *mad* at?!" she snapped.

"'Cause you always tryna prolong shit," Mark shot back. "I didn't come over here to play twenty questions. Do you wanna go to dinner or *not?*"

"So you think talking to me like that is gonna make me say *yes?*" Malajia bit out.

Mark knew that his reaction was uncalled for...but it was typical of him to exaggerate. And typical of them to argue. "Either you do or you don't," Mark bit back.

Annoyed, Malajia put her hands on her hips. "*First* of all you asshole, that is *not* how you get a woman to go out with you," she scolded. "I ain't one of those trashy bitches you're used to, I deserve better than that. *Second*, you can't fault me for questioning your motives."

Mark folded his arms and stood in silence as Malajia continued to reprimand him.

"You *know* you play *entirely too* much," she ranted, waving her hands around. "So *why* would I get excited and get extra cute for a date just for you to be like 'sike, I was just playing'? Or to get to the place only for you to pull that 'I left my wallet' bullshit, leaving *me* to pay."

Mark blinked slowly.

"I'll tell you *one* goddamn thing, I'm not paying for *shit* for you," she promised. "You'll be washing the shit out of some dishes, 'cause I will straight leave your ass sitting right there—" Malajia's rant was cut short when Mark took a step forward, gently grabbed her face with his hands, and planted a passionate kiss on her lips, silencing her. The feeling of his lips on hers made her forget how annoyed she was with him. The only time they'd kissed was when they played truth or dare sophomore year. But unlike before, she welcomed it.

Mark parted from her. "Will you go to dinner with me?" he asked, once more.

"Uh huh," Malajia replied, breathless.

"Cool, pick you up tomorrow at seven."

Malajia stood there as Mark walked out of the room. She was dumbfounded. "What the fuck just happened?" she asked herself in disbelief.

Chapter 11

Mark nervously paced the living room floor. He let out a huff.

"Bro you need to calm down," Josh urged, laughter in his voice. "You're gonna burn a hole in our carpet."

"Man fuck this old ass carpet," Mark spat.

He'd spent the previous evening and all day that day anticipating his date with Malajia. He hated to admit it, but he was nervous—*more* than nervous. "This is some bullshit!" he griped, loud, flopping down on the couch. "Why am I nervous? This is *Malajia*. I've know her ass for *years*."

"That may be true, but it's the first time that you're going out with her not just as your *friend*," Jason pointed out from the dining room table. "She has now become someone who you're interested in getting to know on a different level, and trust me when I say, that's a different kind of pressure."

Mark let out a sigh and leaned back against the sofa cushions. "My stomach hurts," he grumbled.

"Drink some ginger ale and get yourself together," David suggested.

"Can somebody bring me some?" Mark asked, holding his hand out.

"No," the guys replied in unison.

Mark just sucked his teeth. "Non-supportive asses."

Jason laughed. "You want my advice?" he asked.

"I hope it's not 'be yourself,' 'cause that gets me in trouble," Mark jeered.

"*True*," Jason agreed, laughter in his voice. "Okay be yourself minus about thirty-five percent…just for the first date," he chortled. "You don't want her cussing you out the whole night because you said or did something stupid."

Mark leaned forward and groaned aloud, "That's too much pressure!"

Malajia carefully applied the finishing touches to her makeup in her mirror. The door opened and the other girls waked in while Malajia was fussing with her hair.

"Well don't you look pretty," Alex mused, taking in Malajia's hair, jewelry, makeup and form fitting, short-sleeved burgundy sweater dress; it fell close to her knees; but hugged her body at the same time. "I see you've gained some curves."

Malajia looked down at her hips. "Ugh. I gotta stop eating like a fat ass," she mumbled.

"I'm shocked that you don't have on a dress that shows your butt cheeks," Alex teased.

Malajia shook her head while placing a bobby pin in her hair, pinning some of her curls back. "I'm trying this new thing where I don't wear clothes that show all of my God given assets if you know what I mean," she replied evenly.

"Well good for you," Alex said proudly.

"Oh don't worry, I'll still show quite a bit," Malajia joked. "My body is *everything*, new curves and all."

"Nobody asked you all that," Chasity commented.

"Just making it clear," Malajia chortled, giving herself another look.

Sidra sat down on her bed as she eyed Malajia's get up. "You're way too dressed up to go anywhere on campus," she observed. "Where *are* you going?"

"On a date," Malajia answered, adjusting one of her long silver earrings.

"On a date with *who?*" Alex asked, intrigued.

"A friend," Malajia vaguely replied. She didn't know if she was ready to tell them that the 'friend' was Mark. She could only imagine what they would think or say.

"Do we *know* this friend?" Chasity asked, helping Malajia pin another of her curls back.

Damn they nosey. "Umm...*maybe*," Malajia slowly put out.

Sidra put her finger on her cheek while fixing a gaze upon Malajia. "Why does it seem like you're trying to keep this person a secret?" she pondered.

"It's not that," Malajia lied.

"Are you *embarrassed* by this person?" Sidra pressed.

Malajia fiddled with the bracelet on her wrist. "No...I wouldn't say that I was *embarrassed.*"

"That sounds like a lie," Chasity chuckled.

"Shut up Chasity," Malajia spat. "And it's *not* a lie. I'm not embarrassed by him. I just don't want to say anything yet until I see how this date goes."

"Malajia, you already know that we're gonna bug you until you tell us who this mystery man is," Alex cut in, folding her arms. "We learned this trait from *you*, so spill it."

"Can y'all just drop it?" Malajia pleaded, grabbing her stiletto pumps off the floor.

"Absolutely not," Sidra rebuffed. "You might as well tell us and get it over with."

Malajia stepped into her shoes, letting out a loud sigh in the process. She knew if the shoe was on the other foot she would badger them for information as well. She didn't know why she figured they would not do the same. She smoothed her dress down, then put her hands up. "Okay" she agreed finally. "Y'all promise not to laugh?"

"Why would we laugh?" Emily asked, curious. "We're not mean like that."

"Shit *I* am," Chasity joked. "It's not that long-headed

boy from the basketball team, is it?"

Sidra erupted with laughter. "You mean hoagie-head Stu?" she squealed. "The one whose head looks like he's nodding when he runs?"

"Wait, they really call him hoagie-head Stu?" Chasity shrieked with laughter. Sidra nodded. "Yo, that's fucked up."

"That's a shame," Emily commented, but couldn't help but find that information funny as well.

Alex shook her head at Sidra and Chasity, who were still laughing. "You two are terrible for laughing about that man's head like that," she chided; she shot a questionable look Malajia's way. "It's not *him*, is it?"

"No, it's not hoagie-head Stu, damn it," Malajia scoffed. "He smells like his head looks."

Sidra screamed as her laughter intensified. "Wait! Please, my stomach!"

Malajia folded her arms. "Are y'all finished?"

Sidra put her hand up as her laughter subsided. "I'm sorry, I'm finished," she panted, wiping a tear from her eye. "Oh my God that was hilarious." She fanned herself. "Sorry sweetie, go ahead."

"*Promise* not to laugh," Malajia stressed.

"We promise," Emily assured.

Malajia took a deep breath. "Okay here it goes..." she said. "It's Mark."

"Eww!" Chasity blurted out, then immediately covered her mouth with her hand. Malajia narrowed her eyes at her.

"Huh?" Sidra reacted, face masked with perplexity.

"Wait a minute. Mark *who*?" Alex jumped in, putting her hand up.

"Mark Johnson," Malajia clarified.

Alex's mouth dropped open. "Hold on..." she couldn't believe her ears. "*Freeloading* Mark Johnson?"

"*Plays too much* Mark Johnson?" Chasity asked.

"*Loud mouth* Mark Johnson?" Sidra added, shocked.

Malajia rolled her eyes. "Yes, *that* Mark Johnson," she sneered, annoyed by their responses. "*This* is why I didn't want to tell you."

"We're sorry Mel, but we're just um…" Alex gestured for the girls to help her out.

"Disgusted," Chasity muttered.

"*Shocked*," Alex amended, signaling for Chasity to behave.

"Chill Chasity," Malajia warned.

"You act like I'm the *only* one who said something," Chasity threw back, frowning.

"Okay wait, because I'm *still* confused," Sidra put in, waving her hands. "So you two actually *like*, like each other? *Really?*"

Malajia sucked her teeth. "Forget it," she huffed.

"I promise I'm not being a smart ass right now. I really *am* asking," Sidra assured.

Malajia tossed her arms in the air. "Well, *maybe* Sid… maybe we just want to see where it goes. *If* it goes anywhere. Is that so bad?" she wondered, exasperated.

"I'm sorry, but growing up with you two I never would've thought that this could happen," Sidra explained. "But…I will say *this*. Mark may be a jerk sometimes, but he *does* have a sweet side to him."

"Yeah, I know," Malajia agreed, voice low.

Chasity shivered. "Ugh, this conversation is making my stomach hurt," she jeered. She caught Malajia's piercing glare and laughed. "I'm joking," she amended. "I mean, if you're into—him in that way and—want to—" She looked like she was struggling in between her words.

"Bitch, you can't even get it out," Malajia observed.

"I'm *really* trying," Chasity chortled.

Malajia couldn't help but be amused. "See… disrespectful."

"Malajia, you shouldn't worry about what we have to say about this. All that matters is how *you* feel," Emily commented.

Malajia just nodded in agreement.

"And I don't know about everybody *else,* but if you two

actually end up together, I think it'll be awesome," Emily beamed, clasping her hands together. "It's like a perfect match."

"I agree with you there, Em," Alex said, pointing to Emily. "I mean come on, who *else* is gonna put up with them besides each other?" She laughed and looked at the other girls. "Am I right?" When she didn't get any laughs, her laughter stopped.

"That was a poorly executed joke and I'm highly disappointed in you," Chasity sneered, as Sidra shook her head emphatically.

Alex's mouth fell open. She was sure that she had made a good joke.

Malajia cut her eye at Alex. She didn't appreciate her attempt. "How you talkin' about who would put up with *me*, when *we* gotta put up with *you* wearing the same clothes two days in a damn row?" Malajia spat out, flinging her hand in Alex's direction.

"That's not true!" Alex exclaimed.

"Alex, you had that *same* brown ass T-shirt on *yesterday*," Malajia threw back. "We *all* saw it."

"Yeah, I wasn't gonna say nothing, but that *is* some dirty shit," Chasity agreed, running her hand through her hair.

"And she didn't even *wash* it," Malajia threw in.

Emily and Sidra snickered at the appalled look on Alex's face.

"This is *not* the same shirt!" Alex denied, tugging on it.

Malajia's lips twisted to the side. Clearly, she didn't believe Alex.

"I bought a pack of *three*," Alex explained as laughter erupted around her. "This is a new shirt from the pack."

"You're making it worse, Alex," Sidra laughed. "Stop digging that hole."

"No, she need to *keep* digging that hole and throw those ugly ass shirts in when she's done," Malajia goaded. She busted out laughing herself when Alex stomped out of the room. "That *totally* just relaxed me," Malajia said, still laughing.

Malajia took a sip of water from her glass. "This is some good ass water," she quipped, earning a chuckle from Mark. "Doesn't taste like it came from the tap at *all*."

"All water tastes the same to me," he replied, spreading some herbed butter on his roll. "But it's good to know that you like it. I guess that means I can have your margarita, huh?"

Malajia moved her mango margarita out of Mark's reach. "Back up off my drink," she playfully warned.

Mark chuckled again, reaching for his own drink of rum and soda.

Malajia took a sip of the frozen alcoholic beverage, then sat the glass down. She folded her arms on the small, intimate table, surveying the space with her eyes. "How did you find out about this restaurant?" Malajia marveled.

The quaint seafood restaurant that Mark picked out for their date was quite impressive. The candle light on the tables and soft music that played through the place certainly added a nice ambiance. A step up from the chain-restaurants that she'd been to.

"The internet," Mark returned.

"Really?" she giggled.

Mark nodded. "I figured you're from Baltimore, so why not bring you to a place where you can get some crab legs…but *nicer*."

Malajia smiled. He'd put thought into where to take her. That was also impressive.

"You like it?" he asked, hopeful

Malajia nodded. "Yes."

"Cool," Mark replied.

Silence fell over them as Malajia grabbed a roll from the basket which sat in the middle of the table. Buttering the bread, she couldn't help but feel wound up. It wasn't that she wasn't enjoying herself, she just felt awkward. Which in her mind, was weird. They'd hung out with each other plenty of times without a problem, but now that this was considered a date, they both seemed to have their guard up.

She sat her bread down and glanced up at Mark, watching him chew his.

"Mark," she called.

He looked up at her, swallowing his food. "Yeah?"

"Am I the only one who feels weird right now?" she asked.

Mark breathed a sigh of relief. "Nah, you're not," he admitted. "I'm trying hard as shit not to be myself right now," he joked.

Malajia laughed. "We *should* be ourselves, that's how we became friends in the first place," she pointed out. "Why are we trying to act different around each other? Like we weren't chillin' just the other day."

Mark sat his roll down. "I know, right?" he agreed. "We gotta shake this awkward shit off."

Malajia thought for a moment. "I got it, let's play numbers," she proposed, much to Mark's confusion.

"What the hell is *that* gonna do?"

"It'll break the ice," Malajia held her hands up in preparation for the hand game. "Come on."

Amused, Mark rubbed his hands together to remove any leftover crumbs from his bread. "A'ight now, you don't want it," he challenged, holding his hands up. "I'm a beast at this."

"You say that about every game you wind up losing in," she jeered.

They played a competitive game of numbers for moments, getting to the number five before Malajia's large crystal costume ring scratched Mark's knuckle.

He jerked his hand back. "Ouch. Damn it," he barked, examining it.

"Oh shut up, my ring barely touched you," Malajia threw back. "You're always being dramatic."

"Yeah well, I think you scratched me on purpose," Mark accused. "You knew you were about to get owned."

Malajia just laughed. "See, feel better now?"

"I do actually," he agreed, loosening his tie. "Alright, let's just be *us* from now on. Let's just pretend we're hanging out like we *normally* do. We just happen to be on a date." He glanced up at the ceiling, pondering what he just said. "Did that make sense?"

"Surprisingly, yes," she answered as the waiter approached holding the hot plates of food that they had ordered earlier.

Mark rubbed his hands together. "This looks so damn good," he smiled of his dinner, which consisted of wood-grilled shrimp and tilapia with wild rice and broccoli. Reaching for his fork, he glanced at Malajia's food.

"Those crab cakes look good," he observed, sticking his fork near her plate. "Let me get some."

Malajia used one of her arms to shield her plate, while smacking his fork away with *her* fork. "Hell no, you know I don't play about my food."

Mark shook his head. "Why didn't you get the crab legs?" he asked, cutting his fish.

"'Cause when I eat crab legs, I go *in* and it ain't cute," she answered honestly. Mark busted out laughing. "I'd be biting the shell all ugly, flinging butter everywhere and shit," she added. Laughter erupted from Malajia as the image of her doing what she described, popped in her head.

Mark never noticed how infectious her laugh was. "You're so beautiful," he blurted out, causing Malajia's laughter to come to a stop. She put her hand over her face, blushing. He tapped the table with his hand. "Hey, hey, stop that," he teased.

"What do you want me to do? That was sweet," Malajia whined. "*Especially* for *you*."

"Well...you *are*," Mark declared. "Always thought that."

Malajia smiled bright. "Yeah?" she asked. "Even when we were younger?" Mark turned away from her. She frowned when he didn't answer. "You thought I was ugly when I was younger?" she spat.

Mark put his hand up, chuckling. "I'm messing around," he said. "You may have annoyed me back then, but I never thought that you weren't pretty...despite what I actually *said* back then."

Malajia sat back in her seat. "Well...thank you," she replied. "You're not so bad your*self*...actually you're..."

"You might as well just say it," Mark goaded when she hesitated.

"Fine, you're handsome okay?" she admitted.

"*Very*...don't let that go to your head."

"Already has," he smiled, doing a dance in his seat.

Malajia shook her head in amusement. "Seriously though...I've always been attracted to you. Like you said, you may have annoyed *me* but you were still cute."

Mark smiled back. "Got me cheesin' all hard."

They took a brief pause in conversation while they tasted some of their food. But the silence didn't last long, for Malajia had a question that she needed to ask.

"Okay, so I have to ask you this," Malajia began, sipping some water. "When did you start seeing me as more than just your friend?"

Mark looked up at her.

"I'm just curious, because before *yesterday*, I had no idea that anything had changed," she added.

"You really gonna make me do this?" Mark asked, picking up his drink.

"Yes...be honest."

Mark sat his drink on the table while gathering his thoughts. He took a deep breath. "Okay, if I'm really being honest with myself..." he paused for a moment. "I started seeing you differently sometime sophomore year...like around the spring maybe."

Malajia looked surprised. "*Really?*"

Mark nodded slowly. "I swear to God, I don't even know what *happened*," he chuckled. "I just started wanting to be *around* you more. Whether it was going to eat, playing cards, going to a party, sitting around talking shit... I guess my subconscious was trying to tell me something."

"Wow...I had *no* idea," Malajia declared, then smiled. "Wow," she repeated.

"I think a turning point for me was when you started messing with that...*bitch*." His tone became stern, mentioning Tyrone. "I watched how your mood changed when he would say some ignorant shit...and I went into protective mode over you. I know you think I was being a smart ass because I didn't want to see you happy, but I *did* want to see you happy... I just—I knew then that I really cared about you."

Malajia felt a somber mood fall over her. She twirled her knife around on the table, glancing down. "Yeah well...I should have actually *listened* to you when you were telling me that he wasn't good," she said. "I should've known after he disrespected me the *first* time that he would do it again. But nope, I just kept giving him chance after chance." She pushed some hair off of her face, and sighed. "He was the biggest mistake of my life," she concluded. "I can't believe I was that stupid."

Mark held a sympathetic gaze on her. "Yeah you made mistakes...but you're not stupid," Mark consoled. "You left him and you're alive because of it."

Malajia let out another sigh. She appreciated his words, but still couldn't shake the bad feelings within herself. But, in an effort to not ruin their date, she decided to push the thoughts to the back of her mind. "I guess you're right," she said finally, looking at Mark. "I don't know if I ever told you this, but...I appreciate what you did for me after everything came out. I want you to know that your support didn't go unnoticed."

Mark smiled. "I never thought that it did," he said. "But you don't have to thank me for that... I'd do it again in a heartbeat."

Malajia grinned. She couldn't believe that this man in front of her, someone she had known most of her life, went from a child who she despised, to a man who she had grown to care for. The apprehension that she had had flown out of the window. She no longer cared about what their friends thought or said... She wanted to see where this thing with Mark could go.

"So... Are we really gonna do this?" she wondered. "This 'dating' thing? ...I mean, do you think we can jump from being just friends to being in an actual...*relationship?*"

Mark looked confused. "Who said anything about a relationship?" he questioned. He laughed at the angry look on Malajia's face. "I'm joking."

Malajia sucked her teeth as she threw her cloth napkin at him. "You play too damn much," she snarled.

"Foreal Mel, I was just joking. I'm sorry," he said, laughter subsiding. "Honestly, I don't think that it'll be as hard as we think... *I'm* willing to try if *you* are."

Malajia nodded in agreement, letting out a satisfied sigh. "I am."

Chapter 12

"Why do these nachos taste bland?" Malajia huffed, sprinkling salt on her food. "Where's the damn seasoning?" Sidra reached over, taking a nacho from Malajia's plate. "Sidra, don't touch my food," Malajia snapped.

"Girl shut up," Sidra snapped back. "You're always stealing other people's food." She took a bite of the cheese and steak covered chip. "What do you mean these taste bland?" she wondered, confused. "They're seasoned just *fine.*"

Malajia rolled her eyes, while continuing to shake the salt over her food with vigor. After spending all day trying to finish a paper that she put off doing until the last minute, Malajia was eager to get off campus with her girls and put some food in her stomach. However, the food at the mall food court wasn't up to her standards.

"Why didn't Emily come with us again?" Sidra asked, opening her small bag of chips.

"She's trying to finish one of her mock lessons for a class," Alex informed. "I think it's due on Monday." Alex reached over and snatched the salt shaker from Malajia, who was still shaking it on her food. "Girl, cut it out with all that damn salt," she scolded. "You're gonna give yourself high blood pressure."

Malajia sucked her teeth, picking up another nacho.

"I'm surprised her pressure isn't *already* high. All that damn yelling she's been doing lately," Chasity commented, putting ketchup on her chicken sandwich.

"What's *that* supposed to mean?" Malajia sneered, cutting her eye at her.

"That you've been acting crazy," Chasity flashed back. "Don't look at me like that."

"Yeah whatever," Malajia grunted, grabbing a bottle of hot sauce from the table. She poured an abundant amount of it on her food. "I blame my mood on my ignorant ass boyfriend."

Sidra rolled her eyes to the ceiling. "What did Mark do *now*?" she asked.

Malajia slammed the bottle back on the table. "That jackass had the *nerve* to change the channel while I was watching music videos," she fussed. "And do you know what he turned on? ...Fuckin' *basketball*."

The girls stared at her for several seconds. "Sooooo, that's why I heard your loud ass tell him that your relationship was over earlier?" Chasity inquired, eyeing Malajia as if she'd lost her mind.

"Yup," Malajia admitted, full of satisfaction. "You don't do shit like that. You don't change the damn channel while I'm watching TV. That's rude," she fumed.

Alex couldn't help but laugh. "So you break up with him over a *channel switch*?" she teased. "Mel, that is beyond petty."

"You two have been a couple for only three weeks and I swear you've broken up and gotten back together like five times already," Sidra added, voice laced with amusement. "I can honestly say that you have the weirdest relationship that I have ever seen."

"Nobody asked for y'all dumb ass opinions," Malajia barked. "Bottom line, he pissed me off and now he's on couple time out."

"Malajia, over a *remote* though?" Chasity laughed. "I hate to see how y'all handle *real* issues."

Malajia made a face at Chasity. "I know *you* not talking about nobody with your evil ass," she shot back. "You snap at Jason *all the time* over *nothing*."

"That's a damn lie," Chasity argued.

"Bullshit, you cussed him out over bananas the other day," Malajia maintained. "You called him an asshole for eating your banana."

Chasity's face showed exactly how puzzled and annoyed she was. "That never happened!" she exclaimed. "Jason's *allergic* to bananas and *I hate* them. So that whole scenario makes no fuckin' sense."

Malajia flagged Chasity with her hand. "Well maybe that didn't happen," she admitted without a qualm. "But the point is that you be snapping for small reasons too."

Chasity couldn't get past the fact that Malajia just concocted an entire lie out of nowhere. "You really just sat there and lied for no reason," she said, annoyed. "The fuck is *wrong* with you?"

"These chips are nasty, *that's* what's wrong with me," Malajia grumbled.

Alex picked up her milkshake. "Honestly Chaz, I haven't heard you snap at Jason or *anybody* for that matter for the past few days…" she observed. Pausing, she thought for a moment. "Well, you snapped at *Malajia* just now, but it was within good reason." Alex giggled when Malajia flipped her the finger. "I think you may be turning over a new leaf."

"Yeah I wouldn't go *that* far," Chasity replied, reaching for her bottle of water.

"Say what you want, but *I* see more of a change in you," Alex continued, proud.

"You know what, fuck Chasity and her damn leaves," Malajia snapped suddenly.

Caught off guard by Malajia's offhand insult, Chasity spat her water out as she laughed.

Alex, who was sitting next to Chasity, caught a face full of the water. She let out a scream. "Damn it Chasity!" she shrieked, waving her hands frantically.

"I'm sorry," Chasity laughed, picking up a napkin. She tried to wipe Alex's face, but Alex snatched the napkin from her; which only made her laugh more.

"Malajia, you're being extra today," Sidra commented, picking up half of her turkey club sandwich. "More than *usual.*"

"These damn chips are dry as shit," Malajia huffed, pushing her basket of nachos away from her. "Sidra, give me some of that sandwich."

"Girl no, not after you got all nasty about me tasting one of your nachos," Sidra refused, shielding her food with her arm, to keep Malajia from grabbing at it.

"Just give me a damn piece!" Malajia erupted, banging her hand on the table.

"Okay that's it. Mel, sweetie, it's time to go," Alex urged when fellow patrons stared at them.

"Holler at me like that again, hear?" Sidra warned, wrapping the rest of her sandwich up and placing it in a bag.

"I should make her loud ass *walk* home," Chasity spat, rising from her seat.

"Come on crazy, let's go," Alex chuckled, signaling for the temperamental Malajia to get up.

Malajia made a face as she stood from her seat.

Chasity opened her room door and walked in, followed by Malajia. As Chasity set her shopping bag and purse down on her desk, Malajia flopped down on her bed.

"No, go get in your *own* bed," Chasity demanded, removing items from her bag.

"Just let me lay here for a few minutes!" Malajia snapped, pounding her fist on the bed.

Irritated, Chasity pounded her fist on her desk. "Snap at

me *one* more goddamn time and it's on. I swear to God," she forewarned, pointing at her. "I've been trying *so* hard not to slap your bitch ass all damn day."

Sitting up on the bed, Malajia let out a loud groan. She was aware of her quick temper lately; she felt bad. "I'm sorry," she said, putting her head in her hands. "I've been feeling all out of whack."

Chasity calmed her temper. "Why?" she asked, leaning against her desk.

Malajia lifted her head and pushed some hair behind her shoulder. "I'm feeling...extra gross right now," she alluded. She let out a sigh. "I'm waiting for my damn period to start... It hasn't been on since late December."

"It's almost *March*," Chasity pointed out.

"Yes, I know that. I have a calendar," Malajia sneered. "Unlike *you*, I keep track."

Chasity eyed her skeptically. "Uh huh," she muttered, ignoring her dig.

Catching Chasity's accusing stare, Malajia quickly shook her head. "No, no. I'm not pregnant," she assured.

"Uh huh," Chasity repeated, folding her arms.

"No seriously," Malajia insisted, adjusting herself on the bed. "Remember I was taking the birth control pills to regulate my period?" Chasity nodded slightly. "Remember I told you that I *stopped* taking them because I was tired of taking them every day?"

"Not really, but okay," Chasity replied.

Malajia shook her head. "Anyway, ever since I did that, my cycle went back to being messed up. Coming on when the fuck it *wants* to...pissing me off." She grabbed her stomach. "I just wish it would hurry the hell up so I can get it *over* with... I got all the *PMS* symptoms, but no damn *p*."

Chasity snickered. "Well...that sucks." She pointed to her door. "Out my room."

Malajia sighed. "Fine," she relented, standing up. "I'm about to call Mark to come over and lay some pipe right quick to bring it down," she joked, walking out.

"Ugh. Malajia, I just ate," Chasity replied, disgusted.

"I'm *starving*," Malajia complained, rubbing her stomach. "My stomach was growling loud as shit in class." Class over, she, along with Chasity, Jason, and Mark walked out of the English building and ambled along the grass lined path.

"I swear I just ate like two hours ago and my stomach feels like I haven't eaten a damn thing all day," Malajia continued to gripe.

"That's shocking because you ate your Italian hoagie *and* mine," Mark jeered, adjusting the book bag on his shoulder. "*I* should be the one complaining."

Malajia rolled her eyes. "Whatever dawg, I told you to bring me two of them," she huffed. "You wanted to be cheap and bring me one, so yours got eaten."

Mark shot her a glare. "You know what? Your ass is on time out," he fumed, pointing at her. "Don't talk to me for the rest of the day."

"*Gladly*," Malajia flashed back, folding her arms.

Chasity and Jason, who were quiet spectators to this petty argument between Mark and Malajia, shot each other glances. "So Chaz, you wanna walk me home right quick?" Jason asked, quickly.

"Sure, let's go," Chasity responded with the same quickness. They made a move to depart.

"Hey, hold up a second," Mark called after them, halting their hasty retreat.

Chasity stomped her foot on the ground as she and Jason turned around. "Shit. What do y'all want?" she spat.

Jason chuckled at her response.

"What the hell is *your* problem?" Malajia bit back "What, are y'all trying to get away from us?"

"You two have been arguing since we left class," Jason explained. "You argued before we *left* the house to *go* to class," he added. Chasity nodded in agreement. "We just wanted to give y'all some alone time to sort out *whatever* y'all got going on."

Malajia flagged Mark with her hand. "We're fine, this is normal," she said dismissively.

"Yes. We *know*," Chasity and Jason replied in unison.

Mark sucked his teeth. "Well since you two are the perfect damn couple, why don't you give us some pointers?" he mocked. "Let's all go out later tonight and you can share your couple secrets."

Jason glanced at Chasity, who just stared at Mark in disbelief at his request. The last thing that they wanted to do was spend the evening refereeing those two. "So, you mean the four of us going out together…like on a double date?" Chasity questioned.

"Exactly," Mark grinned.

Malajia happily clapped her hands together. "Ooh, that's a good idea babe," she praised, grabbing hold of Mark's arm. "BFF's hanging out together as couples. Doesn't that sound fun?" she asked Chasity.

"*No*," Chasity jeered, face scrunched.

"Chasity stop being a bitch and just agree to it," Malajia snapped, stomping her foot on the ground.

"God, just fuck *off*, Malajia," Chasity fumed, flipping Malajia off.

"Come on guys, let's just do this," Mark cut in, trying to diffuse the tension between the two girls. "Mel, quit with your damn mood swings, you fuckin' shit up."

Malajia stared daggers at him. "You're not supposed to go against me in front of other people," she barked, backhanding him on the arm. "You about to be on couple time out *again*."

Chasity rolled her eyes and let out a loud sigh as Jason shook his head. Yet another quarrel had ensued. Not even ten minutes had passed since their last one.

Noticing the displeased looks on their friends' faces, Mark and Malajia stopped arguing and gave each other a hug. "We're cool, everything's cool," Mark assured, smiling. "So what do you say?"

Jason looked at Chasity, who shook her head 'no'. Jason leaned close to her. "You *know* they won't leave us alone until we agree," he mumbled.

"I don't *give* a shit," Chasity mumbled back to him. "I don't feel like dealing with that."

Though Jason did agree with Chasity about not wanting to deal with the nonsense, he had to admit that the outing could turn out to be fun. After the long week of classes that they had endured, a night out was welcomed. Jason let out a quick sigh, then looked back at Mark and Malajia. "We'll go," he concluded, much to Chasity's surprise.

"I didn't agree to that," Chasity hissed.

"Chaz—"

"No, when does 'I don't feel like it' translate into 'I'm going'?" she fussed, cutting Jason off. "Are you deaf?"

"You're *going*," Jason stood firm.

Chasity was taken back. "Did you just put your foot down with me?" she asked, pointing to herself.

"Yes," Jason answered, defiant. "Is that a problem?"

Chasity narrowed her eyes at him; her eyes burrowed through him like a laser beam...but she didn't respond. She shocked the group by just walking off.

Jason pinched the bridge of his nose. "I'm gonna pay for that later," he muttered.

"Yeah, bet she's plotting right now," Malajia chortled.

Mark gave a sympathetic pat to Jason's shoulder, smiling with satisfaction that his request was accepted. "Double date in full affect," he mused.

"Josh, you can cancel that pizza order that I just put in," Alex called to the back of the pizza kitchen. "The guy left."

Josh, who had just slid the pizza in the oven, looked up. "Seriously?" he replied, not hiding his frustration. "After he asked for all this extra bullshit to be put on his damn pizza?"

Alex chuckled as she tossed her apron down on the counter. She and Josh were just finishing up an early evening shift at the Pizza Shack. Alex was feeling a little down because Eric wasn't able to stay this time. She had gotten used to looking across the room and seeing his smiling face. "Yeah, I'm afraid so," she answered. "He suddenly realized that he no longer wanted pizza."

Josh sucked his teeth. "Jerk," he seethed, removing his apron. "Well we're just gonna have to take this home with us."

"Sounds good to *me*," Alex mused, leaning against the counter. "How does it feel being back to work here?" she asked, amusement filling her voice.

Josh shook his head. This was his first day back to work at the Pizza Shack since he'd been back on campus. Normally he would have started when Alex did, but decided to hold off for a bit while he got a handle on his new classes. "I'll say *this*, I sometimes wish my dad had money to send me so I didn't have to *do* this," he admitted. "Trying to work and maintain a good GPA is stressful."

Alex raised a hand. "You're preaching to the choir sweetie," she agreed. "I'll tell you this though, I'm sure if your dad *had* the money, he'd send it. The same with *my* parents."

"Oh, I know that," Josh assured. "That wasn't a dig at my father. He's always done the best that he could... My mom does too....*now*." He tossed some discarded toppings that were sitting on a cutting board in the trash can. "They tried to make sure that my sister and I had what we needed. But...my sister has been sucking up our family resources for years."

Alex frowned slightly; she knew that Josh had a sister three years his senior, but he rarely spoke of her. Her curiosity was peaked. "What is she doing? If you don't mind me asking."

Josh sighed. "Sarah has been in and out of rehab since she was seventeen," he revealed. "The girl is a serious drug addict."

Alex was shocked. "Oh wow," was all that she could get out.

"Yeah," Josh confirmed. "She's run away from home, stolen from them, from *me*..." he felt his anger rise at the thought of what his sister had put his family through. "My parents kept trying to help her. *I* tried to help her until a certain point... Then I got *tired* of trying. She doesn't want help. My parents don't seem to get that so...she uses them." Josh shook his head. "Anyway, I just cut her out my life and I'm better off for it."

Alex's face held a sympathetic gaze. Josh always seemed so calm, and to see him get so upset was rare. But she certainly understood his reasons. She couldn't imagine having to live with an addict, let alone it being one of her siblings. She admired him for being able to hold it together and focus on school, after coming from such a troubling environment.

"I'm sorry Josh, I didn't mean to make you relive that," she consoled.

"Don't worry about it," Josh dismissed, with a wave of his hand. "You didn't know... Only Sidra, Mark and David know about what went on, but we all grew up together so..." he touched the counter top with his fist. "I'm focusing on the positive right now."

"You're doing a good job of that," Alex smiled. She wanted to change the subject as quick as possible. "It was nice to meet your friend today. She seems really nice."

A bright smile appeared on Josh's face. "Yeah, she's pretty cool," he admitted. December came into the parlor several hours earlier with a few of her friends to grab a takeout pizza and Josh took that opportunity to finally introduce her to Alex. "She gets excited when she meets you guys," he said, checking on the pizza that was cooking in the oven. "She met Chaz and Mel a few weeks ago."

"Did they behave?" Alex joked.

"Not at all," Josh joked in return. "Naw, they were

cool." He removed the finished pizza from the oven and placed it into a box. "Is Eric coming to walk you back to campus?"

"No, not tonight," Alex pouted. "He had study group."

Josh took notice of the sullen look on Alex's face. "Sorry to hear that. You still have *me* to walk with," he proposed.

"I know," she grinned. She leaned forward, eyeing the pizza box. "Before we leave, let's eat some of this pizza because you know as soon as it gets home, it'll be gone."

"Good point," Josh decided, opening the pizza box.

Chapter 13

"Where's the damn breadsticks?" Malajia asked, craning her neck to look for the waiter. Finally seeing him approach, she smiled and clapped her hands together. "Yes," she rejoiced, eyeing the steam flowing from the basket of warm bread. She ignored the drinks that were placed on the table as she reached for the food.

"You gonna save *us* some?" Mark teased, watching Malajia place two breadsticks onto her saucer. Smiling, Malajia took another one from the basket and put it on Mark's plate. As a reward, Mark leaned over and gave her a kiss on the lips.

Chasity frowned in disgust. "Can y'all just not do that?" she jeered, picking up her raspberry margarita.

Malajia sucked her teeth. "Oh shut up," she shot back. "As many times as we had to watch you and Jason suck face, we owe you back."

Jason chuckled as he took a sip of his drink and Chasity just shook her head. The four of them had arrived at the Italian restaurant in downtown Paradise Valley nearly fifteen minutes ago. Everything seemed to go smooth during the short time; Mark and Malajia hadn't argued yet. But what Mark and Malajia *didn't* know was that Jason and Chasity secretly made a bet to see how long that would last.

"I wonder how long it's gonna take for the food to come out?" Malajia asked, grabbing another breadstick.

Chasity moved the basket away from Malajia. "Probably soon," she answered.

"Why are you moving the bread?" Malajia frowned. "You tryna call me greedy?"

"Yes," Chasity replied without a qualm. "You're about to be a fat ass."

"I don't *get* fat," Malajia boasted with a wave of her hand.

"That button that's about to pop on your shirt says *otherwise*." Chasity threw back. Malajia quickly looked down at her long-sleeved red keyhole top, which had one button to secure the fabric on her chest. The button was in place, though she did admit that her breasts seemed a bit larger than normal. But then again, that was normal around her period.

"It is *not*," Malajia muttered, biting her food.

Mark just shook his head at the banter as he picked up his drink. He took a sip and nearly spat it out. "What the hell is *this*?" he scoffed, setting the small glass of brown liquid down.

"What did you *order*?" Jason asked.

"Scotch," Mark replied, picking up the glass again and examining it.

"Then *that's* what it is," Chasity muttered, sipping her drink.

"Why did you do that?" Jason questioned Mark, confused. "Do you know how much that small glass is gonna cost you?"

Mark shrugged. "No, how much?"

Jason picked up the drink menu and pointed to the line item. "That drink is forty dollars a *glass*," he informed, much to Mark's horror.

"It costs *what*?!" Mark exclaimed, snatching the menu from Jason. "What the hell?" he admonished. "That shit ain't worth no forty bucks!"

Chasity busted out laughing. "That's what your hype ass gets," she teased.

"Naw, they gonna have to put this back in the bottle, I barely drank any," Mark protested.

"Dawg, they can't *do* that," Jason declared. "You're gonna have to eat that charge and drink that drink."

Mark slammed the menu down on the table. "This is some straight bullshit," he fumed. "I ain't got all that money. *Especially* not for no old ass scotch." He looked at Malajia, who was concentrating on eating her breadstick. "Babe let me borrow forty dollars."

"I ain't got it, cuz," Malajia replied instantaneously.

Mark sucked his teeth at her before turning to Chasity. "Hey Chaz—"

"Fuck out my face," Chasity bristled, before Mark could even finish his question.

Mark looked at Jason, smiling a hopeful smile. "Bro?"

"No?" Jason jeered, earning laughter from the girls.

Defeated, Mark sat back in his seat. "Well, there goes that printer ink money that I owe you Jase," he huffed.

"Yeah, like you were *actually* gonna pay that back," Jason sneered, reaching for a breadstick.

"Y'all are some ignorant ass friends," Mark hissed at Jason and Chasity, then turned to Malajia. "And *you*. How you gonna laugh at your man?"

Malajia scowled at him. "Don't get mad at *me* because *your* simple ass ordered that mess. You should've already known that scotch wasn't gonna be cheap," she bit back. "Tryna be sophisticated and shit."

"You're on couple time out," Mark snapped, slamming his hand on the table. "We're not together for the rest of the night."

"So?!" Malajia yelled, nudging him with her elbow. "You're still on time out from pissing me off *earlier*." She snatched the breadstick from his plate. "Gimme my damn breadstick back."

As Mark and Malajia continued their quarrel, Chasity

turned to Jason. "Less than a half hour," she observed, glancing at her watch. "You owe me an hour massage."

Jason rolled his eyes. "Fine," he agreed, remembering the terms of the bet.

"And I mean a *whole hour*," she stressed. Jason successfully concealed his amusement. "You gets *none* until you finish."

"Okay," he agreed, rubbing his eye with his hand.

"If one of them throws food, you have to type my next paper," Chasity reminded. She laughed when Malajia tossed a piece of her breadstick at Mark's face.

"Shit," Jason complained, putting his hand over his face.

"I have one due Tuesday," Chasity mocked. "Be prepared to type those ten pages on Sunday."

"Fiiiine," Jason groaned, picking up his drink. Once he took a sip and sat it back down, he slammed his hand on the table repeatedly to get Mark and Malajia's attention. "Cut it the fuck out," he barked at them. "We didn't come here to listen to all that."

"You mad as shit right now," Malajia sneered at Jason, as the waiter brought out their food.

"Y'all just made him lose a bet," Chasity chuckled.

"*What* bet?" Mark asked, confused.

"Don't *worry* about it," Jason hissed through clenched teeth.

"We're sorry. We're good now," Mark assured, putting his hand up. Once the waiter left the table, the couples began to eat their food. Mark took a bite of his lasagna and nodded. "This is pretty good," he mused. He looked over at Malajia, who was sprinkling pepper on her seafood alfredo. "Yo, let me taste that."

Malajia pushed Mark's fork away from her plate. "Mark, don't touch my damn food," she snapped. "You already know I'm hungry. I should punch you in your neck muscle."

"How you still hungry and you ate all those damn breadsticks?" Mark argued.

"Don't worry about what the hell I ate. I just don't want

you to have none of my fuckin' food," Malajia fussed, flicking her hand at him repeatedly.

"Here we go *again*," Jason mumbled, putting a piece of his stuffed rigatoni into his mouth.

"This is your fault, you know," Chasity calmly stated, voice low.

Jason rolled his eyes. "Yes baby, I know."

"Next time I say I don't want to do something, maybe you'll listen to me, huh?" Chasity jeered to him, cutting a piece of her salmon.

"Yes baby, I will," Jason agreed, picking up his glass of water.

"You know what? I don't like how you're chewing right now. You're on couple time out," Malajia fumed to Mark, pushing her plate away from her.

"What does my *chewing* have to do with anything?" Mark asked, face masked with perplexity. He knew that Malajia was a firecracker and was used to their banter, but she seemed to be going off more than usual.

"I just can't look at you right now," Malajia scoffed, pushing her chair back from the table. "I'm going to the bathroom. Chaz can you walk me?"

Chasity let out a loud sigh. "Seriously?"

"Chasity, *please* go with her, before she starts throwing more food," Jason pleaded

Chasity sucked her teeth as she pushed her chair away from the table. "I always get dragged into her bullshit," she complained, standing up.

"I love you," Jason said to her.

"Shut up," Chasity hissed at him, before signaling Malajia with her finger. "Come the hell on," she commanded of her.

Malajia folded her arms and stomped off along with Chasity.

Once they were out of sight Mark turned to Jason and put his hands up. "I don't know what the fuck just happened," he admitted. "Can you believe that shit?"

Jason nodded. "Yep, sure can," he answered honestly, much to Mark's annoyance, who just sucked his teeth.

"Jason can you hurry up and park so I can get the fuck out this car?" Malajia bristled, removing her seatbelt. "Mark has been breathing on me for the past ten minutes and I'm about to punch him."

"Yo, you trippin' Malajia," Mark seethed, snatching off his seatbelt. "You're on my damn nerves. You about to make me break up with your ass."

Malajia leaned over and got in Mark's face. "I promise on everything I love that I don't give two shits!" she hollered, clapping her hands together.

Chasity pinched the bridge of her nose with two fingers as Jason stared out the car window, unenthused. Once he pulled Chasity's car into an empty parking space in front of the girls' house, he turned the car off.

"Well, this has been fun," Jason said, voice dripping with sarcasm.

"You two get the fuck out of my car before I turn it back on and run you over with it," Chasity threatened.

"My bad y'all. It's *her*," Mark apologized, stepping out of the car along with the others. "Her damn mood swings are out of control."

"Whatever," Malajia fumed, folding her arms.

"No, he's right. Take your ass in the house," Chasity demanded, nudging Malajia in the direction of the door. Without saying a word, Malajia walked to the door and went inside.

"Chasity, talk to her please," Mark begged once the door closed. "I don't know what's wrong with her."

"Sure, why not? 'Cause that's *just* how I pictured spending the rest of my evening. Figuring out what's wrong with *your* damn girlfriend," Chasity shot back sarcastically.

"Okay, everybody just chill out," Jason cut in. "Mark go take a walk, man," he urged.

Mark sighed and walked off in the direction of their house.

Jason turned to Chasity. "I'll make this up to you," he said to her.

"Yeah, you *better*," Chasity huffed.

Jason gave her a quick kiss and sent her into the house. Once inside, Chasity saw Malajia sitting on the couch with her arms folded and a scowl on her face.

"What is your damn problem, Malajia?" Chasity spat out, sitting down on one of the accent chairs. "You're acting crazy. And if *I'm* saying that, then there's an issue."

Malajia sighed. "I know, I know," she admitted, running her hands through her hair. "I'm sorry, but it's this damn PMS. I can't *take* it anymore."

Chasity frowned. "Your period *still* hasn't come on?"

"*No* and it's pissing me off," Malajia fumed. "I need for this to come on so I can stop feeling like this—so I can stop *acting* like this." She leaned her head back against the cushions. "I swear, I'm about to take a weekend trip home just to see my doctor so he can put me back on those pills… I shouldn't have stopped taking them in the *first* place. Now I gotta deal with this bullshit."

Chasity twirled some of her hair around her finger as she fixed a gaze on Malajia. "Mel… Are you *sure* you're not pregnant?" she asked after several seconds.

"I'm *not*," Malajia answered confidently.

"Are you *sure* though?" Chasity questioned. "I kinda went through the same thing when *I* was."

"Chaz, I'm not pregnant okay," Malajia insisted, traces of annoyance in her voice. "I've gone through this before…maybe not this *extreme*, but I've gone through it."

Chasity put her hands up in surrender. "Okay."

"It'll come on," Malajia asserted, standing from the couch. "Do we have anymore cookies?"

Chasity shook her head. "You ate them all yesterday," she calmly reminded.

"What about your stash?" Malajia pressed, impatient. "I

know you got one."

Chasity stared at her.

"Is that a 'no'?" Malajia hissed. When Chasity refused to answer, Malajia flagged her with her hand. "Fine, I know where Sidra's is. I'll get hers," she muttered, heading for the steps.

Chapter 14

Malajia pushed the covers off of her. "God, just kill me now," she groaned, grabbing her stomach. After her conversation with Chasity the night before, and her failed attempt at finding Sidra's snack stash, Malajia collapsed on the bed, falling asleep. Not waking until just now, with cramping.

Hoping that her period had finally arrived, she headed to the bathroom only to find that it had not. After cursing and slamming things around in the bathroom, Malajia decided that since she had already gotten out of bed, she might as well get herself together for the day.

She took her time getting showered and dressed. If she could call what she had on, getting dressed. Malajia felt so bloated and miserable that the only thing she felt like putting on was a pair of grey sweatpants, white t-shirt and matching sweat jacket that she had purchased strictly for the gym. It had been sitting in a bag on the floor of her closet; she hadn't been to the gym in weeks.

She refused to put on any makeup and pulled her disheveled hair up into a messy bun. Giving herself a onceover in the floor length mirror, she scoffed at her appearance. "I look like a skinny Alex with a Sidra bun," she complained of herself.

Exhaling deeply, she stomped over to her bed and flopped down. Intending on going back to sleep, she closed her eyes, then snapped them open when she heard a light tap on the door.

"What?!" she barked.

Mark slowly opened the door and cautiously poked his head in. "Hey honey," he said. His presence was met with a scowl. "You still acting like a jackass? Or are you ready to be nice to me again?" he joked.

Malajia slowly sat up, keeping her angry gaze on him. "Why are you *here*?" she growled.

"I guess I have my answer," he mumbled. He walked in the room. "Look, I came to check on you." He paused for a moment. "Are you okay?"

"No," Malajia grunted. "I feel like shit. My damn period is coming on soon and it's making me crazy." She vigorously rubbed her face with her hands. "It's hot!" she bellowed.

Mark folded his arms. "Oh..." He was trying hard to proceed with caution. Malajia clearly wasn't in the mood for any nonsense. "So um, your bad mood is because your period is about to come on?" he asked, finally.

"That's what I just *said*," she huffed.

Mark scratched his head. "Sooo...do you want me to go get you some brownies or something?" he slowly put out.

"I want you to get out my damn room so I can go back to sleep," she hissed.

"That's a 'no' to the brownies, huh?"

Malajia picked up a pillow and threw it at him, hitting him in the chest with it. "Out!"

Mark looked down at the pillow, which had fallen to the floor. "I'll just come back later," he concluded, calm.

"Don't bring your ass back here at *all*," Malajia spat. "The sound of your voice is making me want to throw up."

Resolved that today with Malajia would be no different from yesterday, Mark sighed and walked out of the room.

Malajia gave no thought about how she was treating Mark. All she knew was that she felt physically horrible and wasn't sure how long the feeling would last. She sat there for a moment, touching her chest with her hand. "Ouch," she winced at the soreness of her breasts. "I need some damn aspirin."

"You're not really gonna make me type your paper tomorrow, are you?" Jason asked as he ran a hand through Chasity's hair while they sat on the couch in his house, watching a movie.

"Absolutely," Chasity replied, opening a pack of candy. "You lost the bet, stop whining."

Jason sucked his teeth. "I'm not whining, a'ight," he sternly shot back. "I just have my *own* paper to finish typing, plus I have to finish a coding assignment."

"You know what I'm about to say, right?" Chasity retorted.

Jason rolled his eyes to the ceiling. "That it sounds like whining," he grunted. She laughed at him and he playfully nudged her. "Smart ass," he commented, amused.

Chasity was about to respond when her phone's ringtone stopped her. She looked at the phone and frowned. "The hell?" she said, before declining the call and setting it on the arm of the couch.

Jason shot her a glance. She looked annoyed. "You okay?" he wondered.

"Yep," she replied, evenly.

Not satisfied with that answer, Jason pointed to her phone. "You look like that phone call just upset you," he said. "You wanna tell me who that was?"

"Nope," she replied instantaneously.

Jason sighed as Mark walked through the door.

"Hey y'all," Mark solemnly greeted, flopping on a chair. "What's up?"

"We're just watching a movie," Jason answered. "You look salty in the face, what's wrong?"

Mark pulled his hands down his face, letting out a loud groan in the process. "I just came from taking a walk." He sat back in his seat, he looked exhausted. "Mel is still acting all…all period moody snappy," he complained.

Chasity frowned in confusion. "Wait, did you just say period moody snappy?" she questioned.

Mark nodded. "Yeah, isn't that what PMS stands for?" The bad part about what he just asked, was that he appeared to be serious.

Jason put his hand over his face to hide his laughter, while Chasity stared at Mark in disbelief. "I fuckin' hate you," she spat, causing Jason to bust out with his laughter.

Mark put his hands up. "What I do?" he asked, shocked. "God, *all* y'all women trippin'. I can't do *nothing* right."

"Bro, if Mel isn't feeling well, then you need to go over there and comfort her," Jason slid in. "Give her a hug, rub her back, *something*. *Act* like a boyfriend."

"I offered her brownies, and she told me to get out," Mark griped. "She's annoyed by my voice right now, so I doubt she wants me to touch her."

"Did you say something stupid to her?" Chasity asked.

"No, actually I did *not*," Mark threw back, making a face at her. "I just *told* you I offered her brownies."

Chasity shook her head. "Men swear that brownies cures all things period related."

"Works for *your* evil ass, doesn't it?" Mark spat.

"No, *slapping* people does. Come here, let me demonstrate on you," Chasity challenged, signaling for Mark to come to her.

"Damn, that synching shit is true, huh?" Mark quibbled.

"No, I just want to slap you," Chasity cleared up.

Mark sucked his teeth as Jason put his hand up. "Alright, you two chill out," he ordered, turning the TV down with the remote.

"You got scolded," Mark hurled at Chasity.

"No, *you* did," Chasity threw back.

Jason shook his head. "I give up," he muttered.

Mark held his hand out in Chasity's direction. "Can I get some of that candy?"

Chasity sucked her teeth as she leaned forward and shook some of the candy into Mark's open hand. "I hope you choke on it," she sneered.

"I hope I do *too*. It'll put me out my damn misery," Mark grumbled, popping a piece into his mouth.

Malajia ambled through the aisle of the convenience store in search of a few items—pain medicine being *one* of them. After finding that the house was empty of anything that could make her cramps go away, Malajia mustered up the energy to walk to the store. Normally a five-minute walk, the fatigue that she felt made the walk feel so much longer.

She grabbed a box of pills and a few boxes of maxi pads, and tossed them into her basket. Eyeing something on the bottom shelf, she bent down. "Ooh, a heating pad," she said to herself, grabbing the box. As she stood up, a wave of dizziness came over her, followed by a queasy feeling. "Ugh," she groaned, adding the item to her haul.

As Malajia turned around to walk out of the aisle, she almost collided with someone.

"Ooh be careful girl," the friendly female smiled.

Recognizing her classmate, Malajia feigned a smile. "What's up Brit?" she muttered.

Brittany returned Malajia's smile with one of her own. "Girl nothing much, just here to get some things." She raised her arm up to adjust the sleeve of her jean jacket.

The smell of Brittany's perfume wafted up Malajia's nose. She knew she'd smelled that scent before, but this time it was stronger. And it was doing a number on her stomach. "Oh okay," Malajia commented trying not to concentrate on the feeling.

"Anyway, did you get the notes from Calculus the other

day?" Brittany asked, waving her other arm.

Malajia blinked slowly as another burst of scent went up her nose. *God, did she bathe in the shit?* she thought. The nauseous feeling was getting stronger, "Sorry, I have to go." Malajia quickly put out before darting pass her stunned classmate. As Malajia ran for the bathroom, she felt vomit coming up her throat. She dropped the basket by the sink, running for the stall with her hand covering her mouth.

Kneeling over the toilet, she threw up her stomachs' contents, which due to skipping breakfast, wasn't much. None the less, vomit kept coming. After expelling the last of it, Malajia flushed the toilet and stood up slowly.

She didn't know if she was more disgusted by the fact that she threw up, or by the fact that she had to do it in a public bathroom. Hand over her stomach, she went to the sink and washed her hands. She rinsed her mouth out with water several times, then turned the sink off. She wiped the tears from her eyes with a tissue, then leaned over the sink and took a few deep breaths.

I never had to throw up during my period time. "This is bullshit," she muttered to herself.

She looked at herself in the mirror. The queasy feeling returned, but luckily, she didn't throw up again. *I don't get it. I didn't eat anything bad yesterday, why am I sick to my stomach?*

Shaking the thoughts from her head, Malajia retrieved her basket from the floor. Seeing that the items had spilled to the dirty floor, she elected not to purchase them. Leaving the bathroom, she went back to the personal aisle to restock her basket. While gathering her items, she passed by something that made her stop. Standing there, she stared at the variety of pregnancy tests on the shelf. Her mind started racing. "No, no stop, that's not it," she whispered to herself. Shaking the thought from her head, she went to walk away, but stopped again. She couldn't shake the fact that pregnancy wasn't *entirely* out of the question. She did have sex a little over two months ago…with Tyrone. Feeling short of breath, she reluctantly grabbed the test and put it into her basket.

Malajia paced back and forth in her bathroom, awaiting the results of the pregnancy test that she had taken. She tried talking herself out of taking it in the first place. She didn't want to think of the possibility of Tyrone's baby being inside of her.

Please don't be positive, please don't be positive, repeated in Malajia's head as her pacing continued. "God, why is time moving so fuckin' slow?" she barked aloud. Lucky for her, the house was empty.

She sat down on the closed toilet seat and rocked back and forth as thoughts filled her head. "Stupid, stupid, stupid," she chided herself, smacking herself in the head with her hand repeatedly. *How could you sleep with him? How?* If that question didn't haunt her enough, remembering that she neglected to make Tyrone wear a condom during their last encounter certainly did.

She put her head in her hands and took several deep breaths, trying to calm herself down. The sound of the alarm going off on her phone sent a chill down her spine. Mentally coaxing herself, Malajia grabbed the test from the sink. She closed her eyes as she held it in front of her. "Please be negative, please be negative," she pleaded, worried tears filling her eyes. She opened her eyes and through a cloud of tears, zoned in on the thing that made her fear, a reality…a pink plus sign.

She was speechless as she stared at the positive stick. She felt her chest tighten; she was holding her breath. She exhaled and the tears flew nonstop from her eyes. Malajia threw the stick at the wall and collapsed to the floor in a fit of tears. "Nooooo!" she screamed out loud. "Oh my God! No, no, no," she repeated, curling into the fetal position.

When Malajia imagined what it would be like to be pregnant, she pictured it years from now, with a man that she loved and who loved *her*. She imagined being excited, happy and maybe even nervous. She never imagined being filled with fear, pain, resentment and regret. She also never imagined that the father would be a monster, who'd hurt her physically and emotionally. Someone who broke her spirit. In that moment, Malajia couldn't focus on the baby growing inside of her; she could only focus on the hatred that she had for the man who put it there. She wished that the tears would somehow cover her face and drown her.

Malajia didn't know how long she had laid on the bathroom floor. It could have been fifteen minutes; it could have been an hour. Sitting on her bed, rocking back and forth, Malajia's mind was in a daze. *I'm pregnant with Tyrone's baby*, was all she could think. *I can't have Tyrone's baby...I just can't.* She stared out in front of her, not focusing on anything. In that moment, she felt alone, scared.

Almost as if she was not in control of her movements, Malajia walked to her desk, sat down and opened her laptop. In a daze, her fingers opened an internet search engine. After hesitating for a moment, with shaking fingers, she typed the words "abortion clinics in Paradise Valley" in the search bar. After scrolling through several clinic sites, she clicked on one that was about twenty-five minutes from campus. She checked out the site before dialing the number.

Upon ending her twenty-minute information-filled phone call with a compassionate nurse, she let out a long sigh as tears spilled yet again. Her appointment was set, yet she still had one more call left to make. She dialed the number and put the phone to her ear.

"Hey Malajia," Mr. Simmons answered, cheerful.

Malajia hesitated to speak right away. She didn't need for her father to pick up on the fact that she had been crying. "Hey Dad," she answered finally, tone low.

"Something must be wrong," he joked. "You never call us just to talk."

Malajia couldn't break a smile even if she tried. "Dad...I um..." She took the phone away from her ear, trying to convince herself not to hang up.

"Seriously, is something wrong?" Mr. Simmons asked again, this time full of concern.

"Um...I need for you and Mom to—to send me some money," Malajia sputtered.

"Money for *what* Malajia?" her father barked. "We just sent you money *two weeks* ago. We paid up your tuition and room and board for the semester, plus paid for all of your damn books on *top* of the extra that we gave to you."

Malajia put her head in her hand while her father ranted. She knew that he had every right to. But she had blown through most of her money. The hundred dollars left in her checking account would not be enough to cover the procedure that she needed. Malajia had no choice but to take it.

"Dad, can you *please* not yell at me?" she pleaded, feeling herself tear up again. "I know what you gave me, I just...I just really need you to send me more." She cringed, realizing how those words sounded coming out of her mouth.

"Are you kidding me?!" Mr. Simmons boomed. "You are *not* our only child you know!"

"Yes, I *know* that Dad," Malajia answered, fighting to keep her voice from trembling.

"You're twenty-one years old, and every five minutes you're asking for something, like you're a goddamn toddler! Your three *younger* sisters don't ask for shit as much as *you* do," he fumed. "I swear, you are the *only* one out of our grown daughters that pulls this shit. At least the other three *work*."

Malajia felt herself nearing a breakdown. "Dad, can you not do this right now?!" she yelled into the phone. "We *all* know that *I'm* the one who causes you and Mom the biggest headache, but I *don't* need to be reminded of that right now!"

"Spare me the pity party Malajia," he ground out. "How much do you want *now*?"

Malajia sighed. "Five hundred," she hesitantly answered. She then closed her eyes in anticipation of her father's explosion.

"Five hun—! Five hundred dollars?!" he exploded. "Are you *kidding* me? What the hell do you need that amount for when we just gave you money?"

Malajia pinched the bridge of her nose as she tried to come up with a believable lie. If he knew the real reason, yelling would be the least of her problems. Her father would probably disown her.

"I um...." She sighed. "I need the money to buy more books because when I went off campus a few days ago, I left my book bag on the bus and now they're gone." The line went quiet for several seconds. "Dad?" she called.

"You—you are without a doubt the simplest, careless, most *irresponsible* child that I have ever dealt with," Mr. Simmons seethed.

"I know," Malajia agreed, voice trembling.

"What is *wrong* with you?" he continued. "You think that we just have money laying around to pay for your stupid mistakes?"

Malajia put her hand over her mouth to keep from crying out loud. She knew that he was talking about books, but what he was saying was speaking to her true problem. "I know, Dad, I'm sorry." she sniffled. "I'm so sorry. Just please...*please* help me."

The sound of the phone banging against a hard surface came through the line. "I'm done with you right now," Mr. Simmons said after a moment. "I'll put the money in your bank account today."

"Thank you," Malajia replied, softly. When her father didn't respond, she correctly assumed that he had hung up on her. Letting the phone drop to the floor, she put her hands over her face as the tears continued to consume her.

Chapter 15

Chasity sat on her bed folding laundry, a task that she dreaded. It was the one downside to her extensive wardrobe. Hearing her cell ring, she sat the folded towel on the bed and grabbed it. Glancing at the caller ID, she put it to her ear.

"Hi, Mom," she said, pulling another item from her basket.

"Hi sweetie, how's everything going?" Trisha answered.

"Fine, just doing laundry."

Trisha chuckled. "Ahhh, yes, the chore you hate the most," she teased.

"I have too many clothes," Chasity griped, sitting the folded item on a pile. "What's up?"

"I won't keep you, but I just wanted to ask you if you had any plans for spring break this year?" Trisha wondered. "Doing anything with your friends?"

Chasity shook her head. "No, not that I know of," she replied. "Why?"

"I was thinking that we should take a trip to New York for a few days."

Chasity grabbed some items from her bed and walked to her closet. "Okay," she said. "Is this for any reason in particular?"

There was a pause on the line. "No, no reason," Trisha replied. "Just thought it would be nice to go."

"You hesitated," Chasity pointed out, skeptical. She knew her mother well enough to know when she was leaving details out.

"Somebody walked into my office and caught me off guard," Trisha quickly explained. "Do you want to go?"

Chasity figured that she was just being paranoid. After all, there was no reason for her mother to plan a "guilt" trip. They were in a great space. "Sure, that sounds fine," she agreed, hanging clothes.

"Okay great," Trisha beamed. "I have to go, I'll get the details together and call you later. Love you."

"Love you," Chasity replied, before ending the call.

Going back to putting her clean laundry away, she heard a knock on the door. "Chaz, its Sidra. Can I come in?"

"Yeah."

Sidra walked through the door. "Hey, you busy?" she asked.

"Not with anything that I feel like doing," Chasity answered. "Why?"

Sidra ran her hand along the back of her neck. "I'm a little worried about Malajia," she said. "She's been hibernating in her bed damn near all day. And not just today, *yesterday too*."

Chasity looked at her. "That's not really surprising. I don't think she's feeling too well."

Sidra sighed, leaning against Chasity's dresser. "Yeah, when I asked her what was wrong, she *did* say something along those lines," she recalled, somber. "But she just looks so sad... I just wanted to make sure it was nothing *more* than that."

Closing her closet door, Chasity shrugged. "Well Sidra, you know how sad and ugly *you* look when *you're* sick," she reminded.

Sidra's mouth fell open. "Well screw *you* heffa," she

ground out. She folded her arms when Chasity laughed. "You're such a butthole."

"Get out your feelings Princess, I'm joking," Chasity replied, laughter subsiding.

Sidra let out a huff. "Very well," she said, unfolding her arms. "When you're finished putting your stuff away, do you want to go to lunch with me?"

"Sure, we can go *now* actually," Chasity said, kicking her basket to a corner with her foot.

Sidra pointed to the clothes left on Chasity's bed. "You don't want to finish putting your stuff away first?"

"Are they *going* somewhere?" Chasity jeered. Sidra's eyes became slits at her tone. "I'll finish when I get back, now stop blocking my door."

"That's lazy, you know that?" Sidra accused.

"Yeah?" Chasity threw back, shooting Sidra a challenging look. "And I *wasn't* joking, you *do* look ugly when you're sick."

Sidra let out a gasp, then stormed out of the room. "Lazy *and* disrespectful," she threw over her shoulder.

"That's why your ponytail is off center," Chasity hurled at Sidra's back in amusement as she walked out the door behind her.

"Oh my God, really?!" Sidra shrieked.

Mark sat on the bench outside of the library, watching his fellow students amble along. Conversing, playing, lounging, taking advantage of the weather. Spring season had not yet fully begun, however the mild temperatures let it be known that spring was fast approaching. A day like this would have excited Mark, put him in a good mood. But not today, he just sat. Thinking.

Seeing Jason walk past, Mark sat up in his seat. "Yo Jase," he called, grabbing Jason's attention.

"What's up, man?" Jason replied, walking over to the bench.

"You wanna go run some ball?" Mark asked.

Jason looked at his watch. "I can't play basketball right now. I have study group," he declined. "Don't you have a class?"

"Fuck that class," Mark ground out.

Jason chuckled. "Keep playing 'fuck that class' and watch you not graduate next year with the rest of us," he forewarned, adjusting his book bag on his shoulder.

"Oh best believe, I'm graduating on time," Mark assured.

"If you say so," Jason shrugged. "I gotta go."

"Hold up a sec," Mark said, halting Jason's departure. "Do you know if Chasity talked to Malajia lately?"

Jason once again shrugged. "They live in the same house, I'm sure she talks to her every day," he responded. "Is everything cool with you two?"

Mark shook his head. "I don't think so man," he sulked. "I haven't spoken to her since she kicked me out of her room... That was three days ago."

Jason winced. "Oooooh." In that moment, Jason realized why Mark wanted to play basketball; he needed a distraction. "Sorry bro. Did you two have a fight or something?"

Mark ran a hand over his hair. "No...at least I didn't *think* so," he vented. "I know she's not feeling good, but...to not answer my calls, the door..." he sighed. "I know I can be an asshole at times, but I swear to God, I don't know what I *did* to her... It's like I disgust her or something."

"I don't think that's the case," Jason consoled. "Maybe she just wants space until she feels better."

"Maybe she just wants space from *me*," Mark muttered.

Jason sympathized with his friend. He wished that there was something that he could say to make Mark feel better, but he really couldn't. He'd witnessed Malajia's mood lately as well, and he had to admit that even though Mark was known to get on her nerves, his behavior lately had not warranted the reactions that Malajia was giving him.

"My study group should only be about an hour," Jason said after a moment. "You want to play ball afterwards? We can grab the other guys and go out for a drink when we're done… I'll even treat you."

"Yeah, that'll be cool," Mark agreed. "Can I get a scotch?"

"Sure…if you buy it your*self*," Jason threw back. Mark let out a laugh. Jason gave him a pat on his shoulder. "Come on man, pick your face up off the ground and go to class."

Mark exhaled loudly, standing from the bench. "I'm going, I'm going."

Malajia twisted the bracelet on her wrist over and over, counting the minutes, which seemed to move in slow motion. In fact, time in general seemed to have slowed ever since she discovered that she was pregnant three days ago.

After filling out paperwork, and waiting for what seemed like forever, Malajia was now in an office, sitting in front of the doctor, moments away from doing something she never in a million years thought she would.

"So, I'm just going to take a few moments to explain the procedure to you," Doctor Carver said.

Malajia rubbed her face with her hand. "Okay," she uttered.

"We're going to do an ultrasound first, to see—"

"I can't look at it," Malajia blurted out. Her hands started shaking. "Please don't make me look at it."

The doctor's eyes were full of compassion and understanding. "No Malajia, you don't have to," she assured. "It's just to check to make sure that things are okay enough to perform the procedure."

Malajia looked down at her hands. "I'm sorry, I didn't mean to be rude," she muttered. "I just can't—"

"It's okay," Dr. Carver said, clasping her hands in front of her. "I understand that this is not an easy decision. You're emotional and that's okay."

"It's *not* okay that this is happening to me," Malajia said, voice trembling.

Dr. Carver fixed a gaze on her. "Do you need some time to—"

"No," Malajia interrupted. She didn't want to talk, she didn't want time to think; she just wanted to get this over with. "Can you please just explain what you need to explain to me?"

Malajia sat there in silence as she listened to the doctor explain what was going to be done to her in the fifteen minutes it would take to terminate her early pregnancy. She'd read about it online before even coming to her appointment, so she had an idea. But listening to the actual words made it all the more real.

"How long will the cramping last?" Malajia wondered.

"It should start to subside after about a half hour," Dr. Carver answered. "We have a recovery room where you can rest for a while... Did you bring anybody with you?"

Malajia shook her head. "I'm here alone."

Dr. Carver watched Malajia fidget with her hands. She could see that the young woman in front of her was struggling. That this was not an easy decision for her. She leaned forward. "Malajia, like I said earlier, I know that this is not an easy decision to make... It's okay to be nervous, scared or even uncertain—"

"I'm scared...but I'm not uncertain," Malajia cut in; she fought to hold her tears in. "You're right, it's not easy for me, but I know that I have to." She looked down at her hands. "It's just the wrong..."

Dr. Carver's delicate dark brown face held her gaze on Malajia when she paused. "Time?" she finished.

Malajia looked up at her. "Person," she corrected after a moment. "It's the wrong person."

The woman slowly nodded. "I understand," she said. "I'm going to check to make sure the room is ready for you. I'll be right back."

"Okay," Malajia said. She prayed for the doctor to leave the room quickly; she felt her emotions coming to a head. It was when Malajia heard the door shut that she broke down crying. She put a hand over her mouth to keep her cries silent. She prayed that she would be able to stop before the doctor returned.

Malajia knew that this was something that she should not go through alone, but she felt that she didn't have a choice. Who could she tell? Her parents? They already felt that she was a screw up. Her best friend? She miscarried her baby; how would she feel about Malajia purposely terminating *hers*? Her boyfriend? What would he think of her? How could he look at her?

No, this is your burden alone. You created this. This is your fault for being stupid, she thought. Moving a hand to her stomach, Malajia realized that this would be the last time that she would hold a hand to her baby. An overwhelming sense of guilt consumed her. "I'm sorry," she cried. "I'm so sorry."

Chapter 16

Emily hung up her phone and slammed it on her desk in anger. Then knocked it to the floor. "She gets on my nerves," she fussed.

Alex pulled a sweatshirt over her head. "Is everything okay sweetie?" she asked.

"No, I want to punch something," Emily snapped, folding her arms.

"Um…okay," Alex replied carefully, sitting on the bed. "I can offer you one of my pillows."

Emily let out a sigh as she turned around in her seat. "No… I'm sorry for snapping," she sulked. "It's just that my grandmom's birthday was the other day and I can't seem to reach her."

"Is something wrong with her phone?" Alex asked, putting a pair of socks on.

"I don't *think* so," Emily answered. "It *rings*, she just doesn't answer… I've been calling my mom to find out if *she* talked to her and of course, she's ignoring me."

Alex shook her head. As far as she was concerned, Emily's mother had reached a new level of petty. "I'm sorry to hear that, sweetie," she consoled. "I'm sure your grandmom is fine. Maybe she's out of town or something."

Emily shrugged, looking down at the pink cordless phone lying on the floor. "I know she used to turn the ringer off at night…maybe she forgot to turn it back on," she reasoned.

"Could be," Alex said. "*My* grandmother forgets to lock the door sometimes," she chuckled. "But luckily she lives with my uncle, so he always checks."

"My grandmom lives by herself," Emily said. She seemed to calm down a bit. "She's eighty-three and refuses to live with anybody." She stood up, taking a deep breath. "I guess I better get to the library. Maybe my paper will distract me."

"How many pages is it?" Alex wondered.

"Twenty."

"Oh yeah, it'll distract you all right," Alex agreed, grabbing her sneakers from a corner. "I'll walk you out. I have to go to the bookstore. Can you believe I used up all five of my notebooks already?"

"Sure *can*," Emily replied, gathering her books from her desk.

Alex shook her head. "I guess I write as much as I talk, huh?"

Emily giggled.

Sidra removed her pale grey blazer and slung it over her arm. "Something told me not to wear this out the house," she said. "It's too warm for it." The warm weather confirmed that spring was in full affect. The perfect weather for mid-March.

"Didn't check the forecast earlier, huh?" Josh chuckled, leaning against the banister of the library steps.

"Unfortunately, no," Sidra jeered, pushing some of her long straight hair behind her shoulder.

Josh looked at her and smiled; it was rare that Sidra was seen without a long ponytail or a classic up do. He had to admit, wearing her hair down was a good look on her. "I wonder what David is doing," Josh said, looking back at the library entrance. "He got us out here waiting on him."

"You know him, he's probably re-doing his entire paper," Sidra giggled. "Or helping someone do *theirs*."

"Yeah well, the movie at the student theater will start soon," Josh informed, looking at his watch. "So if he still wants to see it, he needs to come on."

Sidra just shook her head as she heard her phone ring. Looking at the caller ID, she frowned slightly. "That's weird," she said.

"What's wrong?" Josh asked, concerned at the confused look on Sidra's face.

"It's your dad," Sidra revealed, much to Josh's surprise.

"My *dad*?" he questioned. "Why would he be calling *you*?"

Sidra put one finger up, silencing him as she answered. "Hi Mr. Hampton," she greeted sweetly as Josh looked on. "Oh sure, he's right here with me... Oh no, that's no problem ...hold on, I'll hand him the phone."

Sidra handed Josh the phone. "He wants to talk to you." Josh had a questionable look. Sidra gestured for him to put it to his ear.

"What's up Dad? Is everything okay?" Josh asked, shifting his weight from one foot to the other. "...No, I didn't see that you called earlier, I had class...What's up?..." Josh frowned as his father continued to speak. "Wait *what*? ...Is that so?"

Sidra watched Josh in curiosity as he continued to speak to his father. His expression went from surprise to blank. She made sure to keep her ears perked.

"So you're just gonna let her *stay*? ...Dad, what if she— you know what, fine, no disrespect, but that's on you... Nope... No, I *don't*, good luck with that. I have to go Dad. Bye."

Sidra stared at Josh, waiting for him to say something. "You okay?" she asked finally.

He handed the phone back to her. "Dad says he's sorry for calling your phone," Josh replied; his tone was a bit short. "He tried my room, and when I didn't answer, he called David, who told him that I was with you, so...he said that's why he called."

"You don't have to explain, I don't mind," Sidra declared, putting the phone in her purse. She waited for Josh to mention what got him so rattled. When he didn't, she figured she would just ask. "So...What did your dad say? Is everything okay with your family?"

Josh ran his hand over his head. "No. No it's not," he bit out

Sidra frowned in concern. "What do you mean? What's wrong?"

"My sister showed up at my house this morning," Josh blurted out.

Sidra's eyes widened. She was all too familiar with Josh's sister Sarah and their history. "Wait *what*? I thought she was supposed to be in rehab...*again*."

"Yeah well it's always *supposed* to, when it comes to her," Josh spat. "I honestly don't know *where* the hell she was. All I know is that she showed up at the house and Dad is letting her stay there."

Sidra shot him a sympathetic look. "Well sweetie, she *is* his daughter," she carefully said. "I couldn't imagine that he would turn her away. Even after everything."

"Yeah well, he *should* have." Josh had no intentions of being sympathetic. "After all the shit she put us through, she should *never* be allowed back there."

Sidra rubbed Josh's arm. "Maybe she's different now," she pointed out. "I mean, maybe rehab helped her this time."

"Doubt it. Look, I'm gonna go ahead to the theater and find us some seats," Josh quickly dismissed.

"That's fine sweetie, I'll wait for David," Sidra calmly replied. She followed his progress as he walked off. Knowing how much animosity Josh felt for his sister, Sidra thought that he had the right idea in taking that walk alone. Maybe it would calm him down.

"I'm not ready for this damn test today," Malajia complained, glancing at her marketing textbook.

"If you wouldn't have been dancing around in the mirror all night, maybe you'd be ready," Mark teased, squirting ketchup on his hamburger. Both Mark and Malajia had some time in between their classes, and decided to stop at the cafeteria for some lunch.

Malajia looked up at Mark. "I know your slacker ass ain't talking about *nobody*," she shot back. "All that time you spent playing that damn video game yesterday."

Mark sucked his teeth. "Yeah well, *I* don't have a test today," he threw back.

"*And?*" Malajia sneered. "You do that when you *do* have a test. I'm surprised you haven't flunked out yet."

"I do just enough to get by," Mark joked, taking a bite out of his burger.

Malajia giggled. "So stupid," she commented, looking back at her book.

Mark wiped his mouth with a napkin before pointing to Malajia's uneaten french fries. "You gonna eat those?" he asked.

"No greedy, go ahead and take them," Malajia replied, eyes not leaving her book.

"Yeeessss," Mark rejoiced, dumping Malajia's plate of fries on to his.

Malajia didn't respond; she just concentrated on her studies.

Mark fixed his gaze on her as he picked up a fry "You know, I'm glad that you're finally acting like your normal self," he commented.

"Huh?" Malajia responded, looking up at him.

"I mean, you're still a pain in my ass, but you're not as *much* of a pain in my ass as you were a few weeks ago," Mark joked. "Naw, but… I'm glad you're feeling better."

Malajia's eyes shifted as she pushed some of her hair behind her ears. It had been three weeks since she had had her abortion. Physically, she felt back to normal, but mentally…she was still struggling with the guilt. The weight of the decision, and the secret of it was weighing on her. But knowing that she had put her friends and her man through enough with her bad moods, she decided to keep how she was feeling to herself.

"Uh yeah, I'm feeling a lot better," she replied finally. She sat back in her seat. "Okay, I just want to say this…"

"What's that?" Mark wondered.

"I know that I never really apologized for the way that I was acting before," she began. "I kind of just popped up at your house…with food and a better mood," she said, recalling the peace offering meal that she had made for Mark a day after her procedure.

Mark didn't harp on the fact that she hadn't spoken to him in days; he just seemed happy that she wanted to be around him again. That made her feel good and bad at the same time. Good that he missed her and cared about her, but bad because she knew that he probably thought that her behavior was his fault.

"I just want to make sure that you know that I *am* sorry for how I was treating you. I wasn't—" she took a pause; trying to figure out what explanation she should give. "I wasn't feeling well," was all that she could think of.

Mark reached out and touched her hand. "It's cool," he assured. "Like I said, I'm glad that you're okay."

Malajia smiled at him. "Okay enough of that fussy stuff," she joked, picking up her pencil. "I'll still cuss you out."

"Yes, I know," Mark chortled, biting a fry.

While Mark was still eating, and Malajia was trying to cram for her test, a girl approached the table.

"Hey Mark," the curvy brown skinned girl greeted.

Mark looked up at her. "Um, heeeeyyyy..." he slowly drew out, trying to remember who the girl was.

The girl playfully tapped Mark on his shoulder, causing Malajia to look the girl up and down. "Stop acting like you don't remember me," she laughed. When it was clear that Mark really had no idea who she was, she sucked her teeth. "It's *Angie*. You remember we used to kick it last semester?"

Noticing the fire coming from Malajia's eyes as she stared at him, Mark's eyes widened. "Oooh, yeah I remember now," he replied nervously. "H-how you been?"

"I'm good. Been chillin'," Angie replied, pushing some of her long braids over her shoulder. "So listen, my roommate went back home so I have the room to myself and—"

"Bitch, do you *not* see me sitting right here?" Malajia snapped, staring Angie down. She didn't need to hear the rest of her proposition to Mark; she already had a pretty good idea of what it was about.

"What's the problem, y'all are *just friends*, right?" Angie nastily replied.

Mark, knowing that Malajia would have no problem slapping Angie, put his hand up. "Look Angie, you may not know this, but Malajia and I are together now," he informed. "So um, you might wanna step off."

Angie looked back and forth between Malajia and Mark in disbelief. "So y'all are *together* together?"

"You know *exactly* what that means," Malajia spat.

Angie put her hands up. "Well shit, excuse me," she huffed, before walking off.

Mark let out a slight laugh. "Mel, you need to chill yo."

Malajia wasn't amused in the least and it showed on her face. "You think that's funny?" she hissed, tossing a balled-up napkin at him. "She know *damn* well she already knew the deal. The both of us are *way* too known on this campus and everybody talks *way* too much to not know that," she

fumed, slamming her textbook closed. "With her fast ass...
Nasty bitch."

"*Chill* bee," Mark chortled.

Malajia tossed another balled-up napkin at him, hitting
him on the arm.

"Babe, that had ketchup on it!" Mark bellowed, pointing
to the napkin.

"How many of these broke down bitches have you
fucked on this campus?" she barked, ignoring his complaint.

"Not as many as you think," Mark assured, examining
his soiled shirt sleeve. "Calm down, I'm not thinking about
none of them."

"Yeah well, you better *not* be. 'Cause them *and* you will
catch these hands," Malajia warned.

"That won't be necessary," Mark promised. He smiled to
himself. "You're so adorable when you get jealous."

Malajia made a face at him. "Yeah, it's all cute until
someone gets slapped," she snarled. "Just don't say nothing
else to me."

"How you mad at *me*?" He thought this whole situation
was hilarious. This was the normal banter that he was used
to.

Malajia was about to fire off a foul-mouthed reply, when
another person approached their table. "Malajia, I've been
looking for you," the familiar voice said.

Malajia turned around and smiled. "Praz!" she
exclaimed, much to Mark's annoyance. "How are you
doing?"

"I'm good, I'm good," Praz responded, adjusting his
book bag on his shoulder. "I haven't seen you at many off
campus parties lately."

"Those parties have gotten pretty old, homie," Malajia
admitted, relishing the irritation on Mark's face as he stared
at her.

Praz was about to say something else, when Mark
cleared his throat, causing Praz to look at him and smile.
"My fault man, I didn't see you sitting there," he said.

Mark stared at him in disbelief. "Really dude?" he returned, voice full of sarcasm.

Praz shrugged, "So I'm actually gonna be throwing a party at my house on Fri—"

"What are you still *doing* here dawg?" Mark hissed. "Shouldn't you have graduated by now? I mean, you were a junior when we were *freshman*." Mark's smart remark caused Malajia to snicker as she kicked him under the table.

Praz laughed off the insult. "I graduate this June," he informed. "Anyway, I guess I'll catch you later. I started making my red hurricane's again. Let me know if you want one Mel."

"Aye, her name is *Malajia* and don't nobody want those nasty ass drinks," Mark barked as Praz walked off.

Malajia busted out laughing. "Really Mark?" she laughed. "I thought you two were cool. You had a major attitude just now."

"'Cause, how he gonna stand there and say he didn't see me sitting here?" Mark fumed. "Really? I'm a tall ass black dude sitting in this small ass booth and he didn't see me?"

Malajia reached out and pinched his cheek. "Awww, you're so adorable when you get jealous," she teased, throwing his words right back in his face.

"Shut up," he hissed, going back to eating his food.

Chasity rolled her eyes as she heard her cell phone ring. Sucking her teeth, she removed the phone from her purse and frowned at the number on her caller ID. "Are you fuckin' kidding me?" she said aloud, before declining the phone call and tossing the phone back into her purse.

Emily, who had been walking alongside her as they made their way home from the library, frowned in concern. "Is everything okay?" she asked, pushing some hair out of her face.

"Yep," Chasity replied, examining the black and silver polish on her nails.

"Are you sure?" Emily asked skeptically.

"Yep," Chasity repeated. "It's just some bitch playing on my phone."

"Oh," Emily replied. "Well at least someone is *calling* you," she solemnly added.

"What are you talking about?" Chasity asked, looking at her.

Emily sighed. "Nothing really."

"No, it's *something* or you wouldn't have said that," Chasity contradicted. "What's the matter?"

"It's just that I still haven't been able to reach my grandmom, which is concerning me a little bit," Emily revealed. "So I've been calling my mom just to see if everything is okay, and she's not returning my calls."

Chasity frowned. "I totally dislike your mother Emily."

Emily kicked a twig with her sneaker. "At this point Chasity, *so* do *I*," she sulked. "I moved out of her house in August…it's *March* and she still hasn't spoken to me… She didn't even call me on my birthday."

Chasity shot her a sympathetic look. Emily tried to enjoy her birthday dinner and game night just a week ago, but couldn't help but feel hurt that her mother hadn't called. "I tried forgetting about it, but I can't. Her hating me is not okay with me." Emily felt her anger rise, thinking about how childish her mother was being. She glanced over at Chasity. "How do *you* deal with it?"

Chasity looked perplexed. "Excuse me?"

"How do you deal with…" Emily paused, realizing the words that were about to come out of her mouth. *Oh my God, don't you ask that question!* "Never mind," she quickly dismissed.

Chasity stared at her. "How do I deal with a parent *hating* me?" she finished after a moment. Her voice was calm, but Emily could still tell that Chasity was irritated.

Emily closed her eyes. *Damn it.* "Chaz I'm sorry, I didn't mean to—" she stopped walking. "I don't know how to handle this. How do I just forget about it?"

Chasity stopped walking and faced Emily. Emily's question brought back memories of what she had gone through living with Brenda. Her aunt, the woman who, until nearly three years ago, Chasity thought was her mother. She hadn't spoken to the woman, and had no desire to. After everything that Brenda had put Chasity through, she hoped that she never would.

"Honestly Emily... you *can't* forget about it," Chasity answered honestly. "The person who is supposed to love you the most is treating you like shit and it hurts."

Emily looked down at the ground as she felt a tear fill her eye. "Yeah...it does."

Chasity certainly empathized with Emily. Their situations may not have been the same, but the hurt that they felt at the hands of a parent sure was. "Em, just try to understand that you did nothing wrong. Your mother's behavior isn't your fault," she said.

Emily nodded. "Thank you," she said, grateful.

"Sure," Chasity replied.

"No matter how many times you ask me out, I'm gonna keep giving you the same answer," Alex declared into her cell phone, voice full of amusement as she walked through the front door of the house. "I appreciate your persistence Eric, but I told you I'm not trying to date right now." She waved to Malajia and Sidra, who were preparing some sandwiches in the kitchen. "No, I'm not trying to do *that* either," she laughed. "You are so bad. Anyway are you still coming to walk me to work?... Okay then, I'll see you later... Bye."

Sidra looked at Alex as she hung up her cell phone. She giggled at the big smile that was plastered on Alex's face. "Eric's still trying, huh?" she questioned.

Alex sat on the arm of the couch while watching the two girls work in the kitchen. "Girl yes," she laughed.

Malajia looked over at her. "Let's see how much *kee kee'ing* you do when he gets *tired* of trying and moves on," she commented of Alex's humor of the situation. "You gonna be a salty ass."

Alex sucked her teeth. "Just shut up and hurry up with those sandwiches so I can have one," she demanded.

"Oh, *you* wasn't getting one," Malajia spat. Catching the glower coming from Alex, she laughed. "I'm just joking, you can have the one with the two end pieces."

"I don't *like* the bread end pieces," Alex complained.

"Well then you won't eat, 'cause that's all that's left of the bread," Malajia hurled back, cutting hers with a knife. "And *somebody* gotta eat them so tag, you're it."

Alex walked over to the kitchen and pointed to a finished sandwich covered in plastic wrap. "Why can't I have *that* one?" she asked.

Malajia pushed the sandwich back with her arm. "That's *Chasity's*," Malajia ground out. "So get your big ass away from it."

Alex sucked her teeth once again, then snatched up the dreaded end piece sandwich. She mumbled something under her breath as she walked into the living room.

"Um, how about saying 'thank you Malajia'?" Malajia snarled at her. "Ungrateful ass."

Alex turned around. "Thank you—" She let out a shriek when part of the bread broke off and fell to the floor. "Come on, this should've been thrown in the trash."

"So should that hard ass piece of cheese that's on that sandwich, but we don't waste food in this house," Malajia snapped.

Sidra, who had been laughing during most of the back-and-forth between Alex and Malajia, wiped a tear from her eye. "Malajia, you really put that slice on there?"

"Who *else's* sandwich was it supposed to go on?" Malajia shrugged. Sidra laughed more, which only annoyed Alex.

Sidra's laughter subsided as the front door opened. "Hey

Chaz and Em, you're just in time, we made sandwiches for lunch," Sidra smiled as they entered the house.

"Cool, I'm starving," Emily replied. "I'll be right back, I'm just gonna take my books upstairs."

Chasity looked at Alex as Emily darted up the steps. "Why do you look all stupid in the face?" she asked.

"She mad 'cause she got the sandwich with the old cheese and the end pieces," Malajia informed, opening a bag of chips.

Chasity busted out laughing, earning a side-glance from Alex.

Emily removed some books from her book bag and placed them on her desk. Hearing her stomach growl, she giggled. "That sandwich is calling me," she said to herself.

Alex walked through the door. "Emily, remind me the next time we get bread, to throw away all the end pieces," she ground out, flopping on the bed.

Emily giggled again. "I happen to *like* the end pieces."

Alex snickered. "You're a rare kind, my friend," she teased.

The phone rang, halting Emily's departure out of the room. She headed for her desk and grabbed the cordless phone. "It's probably my dad, I called him earlier," she said aloud.

"Tell him I said 'hi'," Alex commented, removing her sneakers.

Emily nodded as she put the phone to her ear. "Hello?" she answered.

"Emily, its Jazmine," the woman on the other end replied.

Emily frowned; her older sister never called her. She didn't even *like* Emily. "Jazmine?" she questioned in disbelief.

"Yes."

The only reason Emily could think of as to why Jazmine

would even call her was that something was seriously wrong, possibly with their mother. Panic mode set in. "Umm, what's going on? Is everything okay with Mommy?"

Alex, hearing the concern in Emily's voice, turned around and looked at her, keeping her ears perked.

"It's not Mom, it's about Grandmom," Jazmine clarified. Emily once again frowned. "Um, okay. What's wrong with her?" Emily wondered. "I've been trying to call her for a while now, and she hasn't been responding. Did she lose her phone or something?" When Jazmine didn't answer right away, Emily became frustrated. "Can you just put Mommy on the phone so she can tell—"

"Emily, Grandmom passed away," Jazmine blurted out.

The blood drained from Emily's face as she tried to register what she had just heard. "Wait...she what?" she stammered. "I'm sorry, what did you say?"

"Grandmom died, Emily," Jazmine affirmed. "Aunt Deb went to her house today and found her in her bed. She died in her sleep... They think she's been gone for a few days now."

Emily began shaking as tears poured out of her eyes and down her cheeks. "But...I was trying to call her. I don't understand," Emily cried hysterically into the phone. "Her birthday just passed... I don't—I wanted to talk to her. I was trying to talk to her!"

Even though Alex didn't hear the words that Jazmine spoke to Emily, she could tell from what Emily said and how the girl reacted, that it was something bad. Alex put her hands over her mouth in shock as she resisted the urge to go over and hug her.

"I need to talk to Mommy, where is she?" Emily cried.

"Emily, Mom doesn't want to talk to you," Jazmine bluntly stated. "She wanted me to call you and tell you about Grandmom."

"Let me talk to Mommy!" Emily screamed.

"The funeral is on Monday in South Carolina," Jazmine responded, unfazed by Emily's melt down. "Dad has the information."

"Jazmine, please just—" Hearing the phone go dead, Emily dropped the phone to the floor and collapsed in a crying fit along with it.

Alex darted over and hugged Emily as she cried. "Em. Em what happened?"

Hearing the commotion, the other girls rushed upstairs. "What's going on?" Sidra charged.

"What the hell happened?" Malajia followed up.

"My—my grandmom died," Emily managed to say between sobs.

Malajia placed her hand to her chest. "Oh my God!" she reacted the same time that Chasity exclaimed. "What?"

Chasity put her hand over her mouth in complete shock. Emily just spoke of trying to contact her grandmother not even an hour ago.

Sidra kneeled down next to Emily and rubbed her shoulder. "I'm so sorry sweetie," she consoled.

Emily put her hand over her face as she continued to bawl in the presence of her friends.

Chapter 17

Alex, Malajia, Sidra, and Chasity were sitting down in Chasity's room as they tried to wrap their heads around what had happened. Emily, who had cried for a while, had fallen asleep in Alex's arms. After helping her into her bed, Alex and the other girls went downstairs. That was an hour ago.

"I can't believe that happened," Sidra said, still in shock. "Poor Emily, I feel so bad for her."

"Yeah, I know," Malajia chimed in. "I know what she's going through. I lost my granddad at thirteen. It was hard."

Alex sighed. "I'm fortunate to still have all four of my grandparents… I just can't imagine what she's going through," she said, honestly.

"I don't even know what to say to her right now," Chasity admitted. "What *do* you say? *Sorry*? Who wants to hear that?"

"You don't have to say anything," Malajia said, patting Chasity on the arm. "Just knowing that we're here for her will speak volumes."

"Yeah, I know," Chasity solemnly replied.

"I think we should go to the funeral with her," Alex suggested. "I mean, with her mother acting funny and her relationship with her sister and brothers…*especially* that damn sister of hers, she's gonna need all the support that she can get."

"I agree with you Alex, but *only* if she *wants* us there," Sidra urged. "She may feel better going alone. We don't want to force it."

"Oh, that goes without saying," Alex assured, running her hands through her hair. She glanced over at Chasity, who was staring blankly out in front of her. "Chaz? Are you okay with coming to the funeral if she wants us to?" she asked. "I know you get uncomfortable."

Chasity looked at Alex and just nodded. She felt terrible that Emily had to deal with the death in her family. She had lost her child that she'd never even seen and knew how badly that affected her; she couldn't imagine losing someone who she had a lifelong relationship with.

"Then it's settled," Alex said. "God, I feel like we should do something for her... This is so sad."

"We just have to let her grieve right now," Malajia said. "That's all we can do."

"Did you guys hear about Emily's grandmom?" Mark asked, opening a bottle of soda that he just retrieved from the refrigerator. "Malajia just told me."

"Yeah, Chaz called me not too long ago and told me," Jason revealed, running his hand over his hair. "I heard she's taking it hard. I mean who *wouldn't?*"

Josh shook his head. "I lost both sets of my grandparents when I was really young, so I don't really remember too much," he said, pushing his leftover pasta around in his bowl. "I can't imagine growing up with someone and then losing them... It's a shame."

"I know how *I* felt when I lost my mom," David stated. "I grieved for a long time."

Jason shot David a sympathetic glance. He knew that David's mother had died when he was a teenager, but David rarely talked about it. "So sorry bro," he said. "It must be hard to relive it now."

David gave Jason a nod. "Thanks man," he replied. "She was sick for a while, so I was glad that she didn't have to suffer anymore, but at the same time…"

"It was your mom," Jason finished.

David sighed. "Yeah." He removed his glasses from his face and wiped them off with his shirt. "I still remember that day all too vividly."

"Yeah, I remember that," Josh put in. "I was at the hospital with you when it happened. Your dad nearly had a heart attack."

"I know. He had a hard time accepting that," David recalled. "I mean, we all knew it was coming, but nothing actually *prepares* you for it."

Jason looked at Mark who had just sat down on the couch, not saying anything. "Were you there too when David's mom passed?" he asked.

"No, he *wasn't*," David answered before Mark had a chance to reply. His tone was bitter, something that was not missed by Mark.

Mark looked at David. "David, I told you *back then* that I just couldn't go," he genuinely replied. "It wasn't that I didn't care. I just couldn't take all of the crying and everything. I wouldn't have been any help to you, man."

"Yeah, you told me that," David spat.

Josh, put his hands up. "Okay guys, let's not rehash this," he interjected calmly. He glanced at David. "You know even though Mark wasn't there in person, he was there in spirit." he added.

"*Exactly* man," Mark added sincerely.

David just nodded.

The news of Emily's grandmother's passing brought up some deeply hidden feelings in David. Even though his mother passed away nearly six years ago and he was at peace with her being gone, he realized that deep down he still resented Mark for not being there in his hour of need.

At fifteen, he needed his friends with him to hold him up as his mother was taking her last breaths. Josh and Sidra showed up, accompanied by their parents, and even Mark's parents came to the hospital, but not Mark. And even though Mark gave him the reason why he wasn't able to be there in person, and David accepted the explanation, he still felt that as his friend, Mark should have put his feelings aside and been there.

"It's cool," David replied after a few moments. "We're good," he directed to Mark.

"So its official, Emily would like for us to go with her to her grandmother's funeral," Alex informed, setting her laundry basket full of clothes on the couch.

"Did Emily ever talk to her mother?" Sidra asked, scratching her head.

"No," Alex replied, somber. "Her father is the one who gave her all of the details... Apparently Ms. Harris wasn't too bitter with her ex-husband to invite him to the funeral."

"Yeah, but she's too bitter to talk to her damn daughter," Sidra hissed. "I swear, I want to rip her face *right* off."

"Tell me about it," Malajia said, pulling her hair back into a ponytail. "I swear, every time I see Em break down, it just tears my heart up. That's fucked up."

"Her mother is a damn bitch. Point blank period," Chasity snapped. "It's been *two* days since Emily found out about her grandmom, and you mean to tell me her mom is *that* damn mad about Em moving out that she can't pick up the fuckin' phone to see how she's *doing*? Seriously?" Chasity was so mad, she could punch something. "Emily should never want to talk to her petty ass ever again."

"I know how you feel Chaz, but keep it down okay," Alex calmly put in, folding clothes. "Emily is right upstairs."

"No, *fuck* that bitch," Chasity spat of Emily's mother.

"I'm right there with you sis," Malajia said to Chasity. "It's not just her mom; her brothers and sister haven't even called her."

"I think her brothers *did* actually," Alex corrected. "Em

was telling me that she did hear from them and they wanted to make sure she was coming to the funeral."

"Oh…Well I'm sure her ugly ass sister didn't talk to her after that initial call," Malajia replied. "*My* sisters irk my entire face, but damn, I would *never* treat them like Jazmine treats Emily."

"Something is wrong with that girl," Sidra commented, helping Alex fold some of her clothes. Alex looked at her. "I'm sorry, I need to do something," Sidra explained.

"No, trust me I appreciate the help," Alex assured. "I hate folding anyway."

Malajia sat back in her seat and put her slipper-covered foot on the coffee table. "Jazmine was probably extra damn happy when Emily moved out of her mom's house," she ground out. "She knew she was gonna have her mom's tits all to herself."

Sidra snickered as she tried not to laugh out loud at Malajia's lewd comment.

"Isn't the bitch like twenty-six? Why is her ass still home with her mom anyway?" Chasity scoffed.

"I think Jazmine is twenty-four," Alex amended.

"Same fuckin' difference," Chasity sniped, twirling some of her hair around her finger.

Alex sighed as she shook her head.

Emily had shared stories in the past about how her siblings treated her. Emily had been picked on by her siblings all her life. They felt that their mother favored her because she was the baby. Her brothers eventually moved on, but her sister Jazmine still carried disdain for Emily.

"Okay ladies, listen. I know that you all have ill-feelings towards Emily's mom and sister… *I* do *too*. But we *have* to remember that we're going to this funeral to support Emily. Not to get into an argument with her family," Alex preached. "So, we need to keep our feelings to ourselves."

Sidra sighed. "You're right. I can do that," she agreed.

Malajia rolled her eyes. "Fine… But if her sister says anything to her, I swear to God I'm shaving her eyebrows off," she fussed.

Alex flagged Malajia with her hand before looking at Chasity, who had just caught her stare. "What?" Chasity hissed. "I'm not making any promises."

"Chaz," Alex said sternly, folding her arms. "You gotta control that temper sweetie. Any sort of conflict isn't gonna help Em."

Chasity too rolled her eyes. "Fine," she said through clenched teeth.

Alex smiled. "I appreciate it and I know she will too."

"I'm bringing my eyebrow razor anyway, just in case," Malajia joked after a few seconds of silence.

"Malajia, you're about to be on time out," Alex chided, trying not to laugh.

"You sound like Mark," Malajia replied.

Alex shook her head, then looked up at the steps, "You think we should go check on her again?" she wondered.

"It's only been like forty-five minutes, Alex," Sidra said, putting folded clothes into a neat pile.

"We can at *least* take her some food," Alex pressed. "The poor thing hasn't eaten anything all day."

"There's some left over baked chicken and rice that we made last night," Sidra informed, jumping from her seat. "I'll heat it up for her." After warming the plate up, Sidra brought it into the living room.

"Chasity, *you're* the least emotional person, go take it to her," Alex ordered.

"What's that mean?" Chasity questioned.

"If one of *us* goes up there and sees her crying, *we're* gonna cry," Alex explained of Sidra, Malajia and herself. "And that'll only make her cry *more*. So we need someone who isn't affected by tears, to go."

"You calling me heartless?" Chasity bit out.

Alex gave a nervous chuckle. "More like…*impassive*," she amended.

"Same difference," Malajia muttered, examining her nails. Alex cut her eye at Malajia, before looking back at

Chasity—eyeing her, hopeful.

Chasity narrowed her eyes at Alex, then took the plate from Sidra. "Just give it to me," she grunted.

Alex smiled. "We appreciate you, honey."

"Fuck you, Alex," Chasity spat out as she walked up the steps, earning a laugh from Malajia.

Alex's mouth dropped open at the response. "And she wonders," she mumbled.

"It's open," Emily sniffled when she heard a light tap on the door.

Chasity opened the door to find Emily sitting up on her bed, clutching one of her pillows. Her face was streaked with tears; it was clear that she had just finished crying.

"Hey…I brought some food up for you," Chasity said, walking in, gesturing to the plate in her hand.

"I'm not hungry, but thank you," Emily murmured, wiping her face with the sleeve of her shirt.

"Okay," Chasity said, sitting the plate on the desk. "You might want it later, so I'll just leave it."

Emily didn't say anything, but she nodded, wiping her face again as tears spilled.

Chasity, eyeing the empty tissue box on the floor near Emily's bed, reached into the pocket of her sweat jacket and retrieved a tissue from it. "Here, don't worry it's not used… I just always carry one," she assured, handing it to Emily.

Emily grabbed it from her, grateful. "God, I just want to stop crying," she said, wiping her face with the tissue. "It's giving me a headache."

"I know," Chasity commiserated, standing by the door. She felt horrible for Emily. "Do you want us to leave you alone?" she asked. She knew how she dealt with pain and grief, but wasn't sure if Emily dealt with it the same.

Emily looked down at the floor. "No," she answered. "I need you guys."

Chasity walked over and sat on the bed next to Emily.

Without saying another word, Chasity just wrapped her arms around Emily, pulling her in.

Emily covered her face with her hand as she leaned on Chasity's shoulder. "I can't believe she's gone. I—I just want to talk to her one more time," Emily sobbed.

Chapter 18

"I swear I hate button down shirts," Malajia complained, eyeing herself in the large mirror of the funeral home bathroom. She tugged on the collar of her black short-sleeve button down blouse that she'd worn on top of a black and red dress that fell just above her knee. "And why is it so damn *tight*?"

"Look, *you're* the one who asked to borrow a shirt," Sidra reminded. "It's not *my* fault that you're uncomfortable. You used to be able to fit into my stuff just fine," she added, adjusting the pins in her bun.

Two more days had gone by, and it was the day of Emily's grandmother's funeral. The girls, who had arrived in South Carolina nearly an hour ago, were hiding out in the bathroom waiting for the funeral to begin.

"Yeah well, I put on a few damn pounds, thanks for mentioning it," Malajia spat, pulling the shirt down. Malajia realized that the extra pounds that she put on due to overeating was the result of her brief pregnancy. She was far from fat, but the gain did fill her out in certain areas. So much so that some of the clothes that she used to be able to fit in, she couldn't.

"I didn't put all that food you were eating weeks ago to your lips," Sidra nonchalantly replied, carefully putting tinted lip gloss on her lips. "Don't take it out on me."

"Nobody asked you for that smart-ass comment Sidra," Malajia hissed.

"Watch your damn tone *Malajia*," Sidra bit back.

"Hey, hey!" Alex snapped, slamming her hand on the counter top. "Don't start this mess. Emily doesn't need any added hostility from y'all. Now behave."

"What do you mean *y'all*?" Chasity sneered, running her fingers through her hair. "I haven't *done* anything."

"Oh you *will*," Malajia taunted, flicking some of her hair over her shoulder. "It's just a matter of time before Satan rears its evil head."

"Fuck you *and* your tight ass shirt," Chasity hissed, inciting a loud gasp from Malajia.

"Didn't you hear a word of what I just said?" Alex ground out, once again tapping her hand on the counter. "Stop acting like children."

"Malajia started it," Chasity returned.

"Did *not*," Malajia pouted.

Alex put two fingers on the bridge of her nose. "Girls, don't make me put you all in a damn corner," she said.

"She's talking to *you* two," Malajia mumbled to Chasity and Sidra.

Alex shook her head as she adjusted the small gold hoop earring in her ear. *What am I gonna do with these three?*

The door opened and the four girls looked at the door, wondering who was about to step foot inside. "Hey, the service is about to start," Emily informed, walking in.

"Okay sweetie, we'll be sitting in the back row," Alex replied, holding her arms outstretched.

Emily forced a slight smile as she embraced Alex. Once she parted, Emily looked in the mirror and pushed her straightened hair behind her ears. "I know that I told you girls this like five times already, but I *really* appreciate you coming here with me today," she stated sincerely. She faced the girls. "I know it's going to be awkward for you."

"It already *is*," Chasity said. "But that's okay."

"Em, don't worry about us," Sidra added, grabbing Emily's hand. "We can handle ourselves."

"Yeah, we just want to make sure *you're* good," Malajia chimed in.

Emily smiled gratefully. "I don't know why my mom can't see how good you girls are," she said.

"*Fuck* her," Chasity spat, earning a glare from Alex and a snicker from Malajia. Chasity noticed the sadness on Emily's face. "Sorry, I'll keep my thoughts to myself," she said, turning back to the mirror.

"You sure about that?" Alex sneered.

"Nope," Chasity shot back.

"Em, have you seen your mom yet?" Sidra asked, hoping that bringing the focus back to Emily would stop Alex from going off on Chasity.

Emily let out a loud sigh. "Yeah, I saw her," she replied. "She gave me a hug and said it was good to see me."

Alex looked pleasantly surprised. "Well *that's* good," she gushed.

"No, that was *fake*," Emily spat. "She's only doing that because the rest of the family are here and she doesn't want them to see how she *really* acts."

"I'm sorry sweetie," Sidra sympathized. "I know it'll be hard, but try not to let her *or* your sister get to you today."

"I'll try," Emily promised, adjusting the pink crystal charm on her necklace.

Malajia scratched her head. "Em… Can I *please* shave your sister's eyebrows? 'Cause she look like she got a caterpillar sitting on her face," she requested after a few moments of silence.

Emily couldn't help but crack a smile at Malajia's silliness. "Stop it Malajia," she chuckled.

"God Malajia, you make my head hurt," Sidra commented, pinching the bridge of her nose with two fingers.

"And you're worried about *me* saying something," Chasity ground out, rolling her eyes.

Emily felt herself tear up at the sound of the organ music

playing. "Here we go," she sullenly said, fighting the urge to cry.

Emily led the way out of the bathroom with the girls following her. Emily gave a slight wave to the girls, as she made her way up to the front of the room to sit with her family. The girls took a seat in the last row and watched as the crowd poured in.

Malajia looked at Sidra, rubbing her stomach. "Hey Sid, you still got that candy bar in your purse?" she whispered.

"No, I ate that an hour ago," Sidra whispered back. "Now will you hush up? You're being rude."

Malajia sucked her teeth. "Yo, I'm so hungry. It's not even funny," she murmured, ignoring Sidra's request. "I ain't eat no breakfast."

"Whose fault is *that*?" Alex whispered, voice traced with frustration. "We passed about *ten* fast food places on the way here from Virginia and you acted like you didn't want anything."

"I ain't have no money," Malajia whispered angrily. She sat back in her seat and folded her arms. "Fine, y'all ignorant," she huffed. She then looked around, pointing to each of the girls. "Don't say nothing when my stomach starts growling all loud back here."

"Shut the fuck *up* Malajia," Chasity whispered, completely irritated with Malajia's whining.

Malajia sat up right and turned towards Chasity. "You're going to hell for cussing all up in a church," she whispered, pointing at Chasity.

"It's not a *church*, it's a funeral home," Chasity shot back, voice low.

"Same thing you antichrist," Malajia ground out.

"I swear to Gooooood," Chasity griped, repeatedly smacking her hand on her head in exasperation.

Alex gave Malajia a hard nudge as Sidra shook her head. "Malajia, stop cutting up, turn your behind around and show some damn respect," Alex whispered loudly, giving her shoulder another nudge with her finger.

Malajia, not having anything else to say, sucked her teeth and turned around in her seat with a huff. After a few seconds, she made a soft gurgling noise with her throat. Chasity, although annoyed by Malajia's childish antics, was slightly amused and it showed on her face as she shook her head. Sidra, also slightly amused reacted by putting her face in her hand.

"That's what y'all about to hear in like two minutes," Malajia warned.

Alex, who wasn't the least bit amused, let out a frustrated sigh.

Emily let the cold water run over her hands for several seconds before filling her hands with the water and splashing it over her face. After dabbing her face dry with paper towels, she examined her red eyes in the bathroom mirror. They had mere moments before they had to head out to the burial site to lay her grandmother to rest. She wasn't looking forward to riding in the hearse with her immediate family. The tension between her mother and herself was thick. Not to mention the added tension with her sister.

"Please just let me make it through the rest of the day," Emily prayed to herself, placing her hands on the counter and bowing her head. Hearing the door swing open snapped her out of her trance. She looked up to see her mother approaching her.

Before Emily could open her mouth and say anything, Ms. Harris put her hand up in anger. "How *dare* you bring those damn girls to my mother's funeral?" she hissed.

Emily shook her head. *Unbelievable!* "Mom, I didn't ask them to come to upset you," she assured, trying to remain calm. "I brought them here because I needed support."

"That's what your *family* is for," Ms. Harris spat.

Emily frowned in confusion. "Family?" she questioned. "You mean like Jazmine? Who has barely *looked* at me since I got here? She wouldn't even *hug* me," she pointed out. "Or *you*? *You* will barely look at me."

Ms. Harris waved her hand at Emily in exasperation. "I don't have time for this. I have to bury my mother," she bit out, making a beeline for the bathroom door.

"Mom, hold on a second," Emily called after her, halting her progress. "Aside from *today*, you haven't spoken to me since I moved. It's been months... How can you be okay with that?"

Ms. Harris spun around, facing her youngest daughter. "You're really going to do this *now*?"

Emily closed her eyes to fight back tears. "I *have* to... At the rate you're going, I may not see you after this," she admitted sorrowfully. "Why are you cutting me out of your life? I'm your *daughter*."

"Yes, I *know* that Emily, I have the stretch marks to prove it," Ms. Harris sneered, putting her hands on her hips. Emily fought the urge to roll her eyes. "You're my daughter and I've done *everything* for you. I loved you, I protected you, I sheltered you—"

"And I appreciate that, but you sheltered me *too* much," Emily interrupted. "You didn't let me do *anything* for myself. I know you thought you were helping me, but you were hindering me," she argued. "God Mom, I was in college, supposed to be on my own for the first time and I was still trying to follow *your* rules. I wasn't getting anything out of my experience because I was so busy acting like a child."

"I don't want to talk about this now," Ms. Harris insisted, putting her finger up.

"You're being ridiculous," Emily spat.

"And *you're* being disrespectful."

"I'm *not* being disrespectful to you. I am simply telling you how I *feel*," Emily contradicted, putting her finger up. "And you're brushing me off just like you *always* do."

"Because you are a *child* who doesn't know what's good for her," Ms. Harris argued.

"I turned twenty almost two weeks ago, Mom," Emily

hissed.

Ms. Harris turned away briefly.

"I'm not a *child anymore*," Emily continued. "I'm changing as a person and I would hope that you would be proud of that... of *me*." She shook her head. "But you're *not* and that's a shame because I *like* who I'm becoming."

"You *like* being a *deserter*?!" Ms. Harris erupted.

Emily's eyes widened. "I'm a deserter because I *grew up*?" she flashed back, putting her hand over her heart. She no longer had remorse, only anger. "Do you realize how much sense that *doesn't* make? What? Did you want me to stay home and live up under you like *Jazmine*? Huh?"

"Say what you want about Jazmine, but at least *she* didn't run off and leave me."

Emily pinched the bridge of her nose. Her mother was truly delusional and it was sad. "You know what Mom?" she began, looking her mother in the eye. "Despite your petty and vindictive nature, I still love you. And I still want you to be a part of my life... But I'm not going to force this issue anymore. If you're upset with me because I'm *finally* becoming my own person and am no longer your puppet, then that's on *you*." Emily grabbed her purse from the counter. "You may not love me or accept me for who I am, but my friends do and *that's* why they're *here*," she spat before giving her mother a quick, hard kiss on her cheek, then walked out of the bathroom, leaving Ms. Harris standing there completely astonished.

Chapter 19

Emily held on to her father's arm as they and the rest of the mourners made their way to their cars from the gravesite. Her grandmother was laid to rest and the family was getting ready to head to the repast.

"At least the weather is nice today," Mr. Harris pointed out, glancing up at the clear sky.

"Yeah," Emily sighed.

Mr. Harris put his hand on his daughter's shoulder and smiled. "You now have an angel watching over you," he said, tone comforting, Emily smiled slightly. "She was a good woman and I know that she was proud of you."

"Thanks Daddy," Emily said, giving her father a hug. As they parted from their embrace, Emily caught a glance of her sister walking arm in arm with their mother. Jazmine was staring daggers at her.

"Don't let Jaz get to you, Emily," Mr. Harris advised, catching the interaction.

"I'm not," Emily said. Even though her tone sounded confident, on the inside she was still intimidated by her sister. Having been constantly picked on by her as a child, Emily never had the courage to stand up to her. "Um, I'm gonna go check on my friends," she said before hurrying off.

"That was a beautiful service," Sidra commented, relishing the warm weather. "I didn't know Miss Ella, but I teared up."

Sidra, and the other three girls, were standing by the cemetery gates waiting for Emily.

"Yeah, based on all those stories, her grandmom seemed pretty cool," Malajia admitted, tugging on her shirt. "God, can I take this tight ass shirt off now?" she complained.

"What type of straps do you have on that dress under there?" Sidra asked, looking at her watch.

"It's strapless," Malajia answered, fanning herself.

"Then no," Sidra spat. "Keep yourself covered. Be respectful."

Malajia rolled her eyes. "Whatever yo," she huffed. "I'm starving," she mumbled after a few seconds of silence.

"Malajia, *please* stop whining," Alex pleaded, running her hand through her hair. "We *know* you're hungry. You've been saying that for the past few hours."

"Well, *feed* me then," Malajia barked.

"I'm sure you'll get to eat at the repast," Alex replied.

"We don't really have to *go* to that, do we?" Chasity asked. Chasity had no problem attending the funeral to support Emily, but she really had no desire to sit and break bread with Emily's family.

"I know right? I'm not really down for going to that either," Malajia confessed. "I mean I love Em to death, but uh, I don't know her people and I don't eat everybody's potato salad...you know they gonna have some."

Alex rolled her eyes. "If she *wants* us to go, then we're *going*. Simple as that," she sternly stated. She then smiled as Emily approached them.

"Everybody is pulling out now," Emily informed, pushing some hair behind her ears. "They're all heading back to the repast."

Chasity forced a smile. "Uh…do *we* have to go?" she asked, through clenched teeth, still holding her smile.

Alex backhanded her on the arm as Emily chuckled.

"No, you don't have to go to that," Emily confirmed, much to the girls' relief. "I wouldn't do that to you."

"Thank God," Malajia breathed. "Sorry Em," she amended, catching the somber look on Emily's face.

"No, you're fine," Emily assured with a wave of her hand. "To be honest, I don't even know if *I* want to go… I got into an argument with my mom back at the funeral home."

"Really?" Chasity responded, a hint of surprise in her voice.

Emily nodded. "Yeah, I mean I didn't cuss her out per se, but I *did* let her know how ridiculous she was acting," she told.

"I'm proud of you for voicing your feelings to her," Alex praised. "I know that you would never disrespect your mother, but she needed to know how her behavior is affecting you."

Emily shrugged, "Anyway—" Before she could get another word out, she heard a familiar voice yell her name. She closed her eyes in fear. "Shit," she whispered to the girls.

"Wait, did you just say *shit*?" Malajia asked, shocked. She'd never heard Emily curse before.

"Emily why is your bitch ass sister walking over here like she's crazy?" Chasity asked, seeing Jazmine approach with haste.

"I think I have a pretty good idea," Emily said, still facing her friends. The last thing that she wanted to do was have a confrontation with her sister.

"She better not try nothing, or that's her ass," Malajia warned, unbuttoning her blouse.

Sidra proceeded to try to button the shirt back up. "No, you leave this on," she hissed as Malajia slapped her hands repeatedly.

Before Emily could react, Jazmine walked up behind

her. "You know you heard me calling you, Emily," Jazmine spat, folding her arms.

Emily slowly turned around to face her sister. "Jaz, I don't want to argue with you right now," she pleaded, putting her hands up.

"Oh please Emily, there'll be no *argument* 'cause you never *could* say shit to me," Jazmine spat confidently. "Is that why you have your body guards here? For your protection?"

Sidra shot Jazmine a glare as Malajia and Chasity sucked their teeth. "Bitch—" Chasity spat. Alex, put her arm out to keep Chasity from making a move towards Jazmine, interrupting her words as well.

"No, no, calm down. Let Emily deal with her," Alex softly urged.

Jazmine looked smug. "So, what did you plan on accomplishing by bringing them here when you know that Mommy hates them?" she scoffed.

"Like I told Mom earlier, they're not here to be of any trouble," Emily stammered. "I asked them here because I needed some support."

"Oh I already know what you said to her earlier. She told me," Jazmine hissed, waving her hand at Emily. "I should smack the shit outta you for upsetting my mother."

"It's not my fault that she's being unreasonable," Emily shot back. "I just wanted to know why she's treating me the way she is."

"So you decide to bring that bullshit up, the day that she had to bury her mother?" Jazmine barked.

"You don't understand—"

"I *don't* understand and I don't *care*," Jazmine interrupted. Her tone was nasty. "You need to take your spineless ass back to where you came from. Because Mommy doesn't need you. *Nobody* does."

Feeling herself tear up, Emily shook her head. The day's events took a lot out of her and the last thing that she needed was to be taunted by her sister the rest of the day. Feeling hurt, she turned around to walk away, but was blocked by the girls. Jazmine, satisfied with her ability to make Emily cower, smirked and turned away to make a departure.

"Emily, don't you let her miserable ass run you out of here," Chasity charged.

"I can't do this with her," Emily replied, voice trembling.

"If you don't stand up to her *now*, she's *always* gonna think that she can treat you this way," Sidra added.

"They're right sweetie," Alex put in. "Your sister is mean and ignorant. Stand up to her like you did your mother."

Emily looked at the ground.

Chasity grabbed Emily's chin and lifted her head up. "You want me to punch her for you? 'Cause I'll do it," she offered.

"No, that won't be necessary Chasity, calm down," Alex said.

"Em, call her back over here and tell her that that behavior is not okay," Sidra urged.

Emily ran her hands over her hair as she let out a loud sigh. "Okay," she agreed.

"And make sure you call her a bitch. An ignorant ass, bushy eyebrow having bitch," Malajia ground out. "Just throw that in your argument."

"Malajia," Emily said, shaking her head as she turned around.

Alex looked back and forth between the three girls as Emily called Jazmine's name. "Girls, let *Emily* handle this. No jumping in, got it?" she urged.

"If she *touches* Emily, I'm fucking her up," Chasity promised, folding her arms.

"I know that's right," Malajia mumbled.

"Chaz," Alex warned.

"Don't 'Chaz' me Alex," Chasity spat.

"What do you want Emily?" Jazmine hissed, walking up and standing face to face with Emily yet again. "Why the hell

are you still *here*? I said Mommy doesn't want you here."
Emily frowned in confusion as she stared Jazmine in the
eye. She was tired of running scared; she was tired of her
sister thinking that she could walk all over her. Her friends
were right—it was time to speak her mind. "Jaz, I honestly
for the life of me don't know what I ever did to you for you
to dislike me so much," she calmly stated. "I've been nothing
but nice to you and…You treat me like you hate me."
"Bitch," Malajia taunted from behind Emily, earning a
quick glance from Alex.
"What is your *point* Emily?" Jazmine snarled, folding
her arms.
"The point *is*," Emily bit back. "You're my big sister,
you're supposed to love me and protect me, and all you've
ever done is put me down."
"Bitch," Malajia repeated, smugly. Sidra pinched the
bridge of her nose.
"I can't believe that I wasted so much time wanting to
have a relationship with you, and in all honesty, I really
shouldn't give a damn," Emily continued.
"Bitch," Malajia repeated. Chasity shot Malajia a
confused side-glance as Alex gave Malajia a hard nudge,
accompanied by Sidra plucking her on the arm. Even Emily
turned around to shoot Malajia a glare. Malajia's eyes
shifted. "Sorry, I got carried away," Malajia softly admitted,
putting her hands up.
"You wanna know why I don't like you Emily?"
Jazmine asked, voice filled with disdain.
"Yes, I would *love* to know," Emily returned.
"You took Mommy's attention away from me," Jazmine
revealed, angry. "Before you came along, *I* was her baby girl.
I was the one who got her attention. Brad and Dru always
had each other to bond with as boys," she spoke of their older
brothers. "*I* was Mommy's pride. Then *your* ass came along,
and all of a sudden everything was about freakin' *Emily*."
"So, you're mad at me because I was *born*?" Emily
questioned, trying to wrap her head around the reason for her

sister's animosity.

"Pretty much," Jazmine snarled.

"It's not my fault that Mom favored me. I didn't *ask* her to do that," Emily argued. "Trust me, I would've *loved* for her to take her attention off *me* and put it on *you*." She pointed to herself. "She always handled me with kid gloves and that wasn't helping me... If you want that type of attention and control, then you can *have* it."

"Whatever Emily," Jazmine dismissed. "Frankly, I'm glad that you're gone, but I don't like seeing my mother hurt."

"I didn't *hurt* her," Emily barked, stomping her foot on the ground.

"You *did*," Jazmine maintained, stomping *her* foot. "Mommy did *everything* for you, she sacrificed her relationship with *us* for *you*. And how do you repay her? You leave her and run off to live with *Daddy*." Jazmine eyed Emily with disgust. "Now you're sucking up all *his* attention."

"No, you don't get to do that Jaz," Emily threw back, pointing at her sister. "*You* could've had a relationship with Daddy too, but you were too busy listening to all the mean stuff that Mom would say about him."

"Why am I wasting my time even *talking* to you?" Jazmine scoffed. "Like I said when I first came over here, just leave. Go back with Daddy and back to your little *college*."

"My little college, huh?" Emily sneered, folding her arms.

"Right," Jazmine bit back. "If I never have to see you again, I'll be the happiest person alive."

"That's just the thing... You're *not* happy," Emily realized. "You're twenty-four, still living up under Mommy. You have *no* job, *no* goals, and no *purpose*. You're mad because you didn't have the courage to leave home and go away to school like *I* did. You're *mad* because I followed my own mind and continued to have a relationship with Daddy, no matter how hard Mom tried to persuade us *not* to." Emily gave a smirk as she had a revelation. "You know what, maybe, just maybe, *I'm* not the weak one after all...*you* are."

Emily's words struck a nerve with Jazmine and it showed on her face. She hated that her little sister, the person who had been afraid of her her entire life, had just read her like a book. Not knowing how else to react, she balled up her fist and took a step towards Emily, looking as if she was about to swing at her.

Alex, sensing that the girls were about to react, put her arms out, halting them. She understood their need to protect Emily from her sister—she felt the same way—but she knew that Emily needed to handle her sister on her own.

Emily just stared at Jazmine, shaking her head. "So now you want to hit me because you know I'm right?" she questioned calmly. "That's sad sis."

Jazmine's jaw tightened as she fought the urge to do bodily harm to Emily. Too enraged to say another word, Jazmine turned and stormed off.

It was at that time that Emily took a deep breath.

"Bitch," Malajia spat at Jazmine's back one last time.

Emily turned around and shook her head at Malajia as she tried not to laugh. She admitted she was nervous—she had no idea if her sister was going to swing on her or not—but Emily knew that whatever happened, she wasn't going to run away scared. She wasn't doing that anymore.

"I'm so proud of the way that you handled yourself," Alex gushed, giving the smiling Emily a hug.

"You still should've let me punch her," Chasity jeered, inciting a laugh from Malajia.

"Naw, that caterpillar might've jumped from *her* face to *yours*," Malajia laughed. "You too cute for that."

"The sad thing is that as much as she hates my guts...I still love her," Emily resolved. "She's my sister, I guess I *have* to." Emily shrugged. "But thanks anyway for offering to hit her for me," she joked.

"Well, that's what we're here for," Sidra joked in return.

"So… What do you want to do now? You wanna get out of here?"

Emily thought for a moment. "You know what? You guys can go ahead without me. I think I'm gonna stay another day," she answered.

"Are you sure?" Alex asked.

Emily smiled. "Yeah. My dad will bring me back, and I want to catch up with my brothers and my cousins," she said. "I'll be fine," she added, patting Alex on the arm.

"Alright then, we'll see you tomorrow," Malajia said, giving Emily a hug. She unbuttoned her blouse as Emily hugged the other girls. "I can't take this goddamn shirt anymore," she huffed, snatching it off and handing it to Sidra.

"Uh no, you will wash that first before returning it to me," Sidra ordered, slowly pushing Malajia's hand away from her. "You've been sweating in it all day."

Malajia rolled her eyes. "How about I *burn* it? Would you like *that*?" she hissed.

"See you Em, we love you," Sidra said, before walking off.

"Love you too," Emily said.

As they walked away, Malajia raised her hand. "Can we *please* stop and get some food?"

"Somebody shut her up, or I swear I'm making her ride on the roof," Chasity spat, earning a giggle from Sidra.

"This is gonna be a long ride back to campus," Alex complained.

Emily watched with pride as her friends disappeared through the parking lot in search of their car. Feeling a breeze brush past her face, she glanced up at the sky.

She felt good. Sure, she was sad that she had to say goodbye to her grandmother, but she was finally able to shed that last ounce of fear that she had and tell those who'd hurt her feelings how she felt. That gave Emily a reason to smile.

Chapter 20

"Spring break is in a matter of weeks and I can't wait," Malajia happily declared as she and the rest of the gang ambled out of the cafeteria and down the steps. "I'm sick of these damn classes. It's like every class decided to have a test the *same* day."

"I know, it's like the professors get together and figure out the best ways to torture us," Sidra added, adjusting the books in her hand.

"With they old asses," Malajia sneered.

Mark laughed as he put his arm around her shoulder.

David pushed his glasses up his nose. "So, what is everyone doing tonight?" he asked the group.

"I have to work, and then I'm gonna hang out with Eric after that," Alex informed, smoothing some of her wayward tendrils back into her high ponytail. She caught the gaze of her friends. "No, we're not doing *that*. We are just hanging out. I told you guys we're not doing the 'benefit' thing anymore," she assured, voice filled with amusement.

"Yeah whatever," Chasity said, voice laced with sarcasm. "For the past week you've been complaining about being horny and suddenly your ass is *calm*? Yeah you got it in recently."

"Oh shut up Chasity," Alex shot back, giving her a playful nudge.

"She didn't deny it," Malajia teased. "She got that back cracked *real* good."

Alex rolled her eyes as her friends snickered and giggled at her expense. "Look, I gotta go get ready for work," she huffed, hurrying off.

"You guys want to hit the skating rink?" David asked the rest, shifting his books from one arm to another.

"Sorry bro, Chaz and I are going to drive down to the waterfront later," Jason informed as he put his arm around Chasity. "They're having some sort of festival down there,"

"Ooh, that sounds like fun, we might as well come with y'all," Mark put in of him and Malajia.

Chasity frowned. "You're not *invited*," she hissed.

"We don't *need* an invite to go to the waterfront," Mark shot back. "It's free space. So, me and Mel can go down there if we *want* to."

Chasity narrowed her eyes at Mark for several seconds. "I hope you know you're the least liked person here," she spat, earning snickers and laughs from the group.

"Oh shit," Jason laughed.

Mark stood there with a salty look on his face. He then slowly turned and looked at Malajia, who was cracking up laughing. "You laughin' kinda hard there Malajia," he spat at her.

Malajia composed her laughter. "Awww," she teased, pinching his cheek. "That's okay, we can get them back by ruining their alone time," she joked, much to Mark's amusement.

"Good idea babe," Mark approved. Then looked back at Jason and Chasity. "We're gonna follow y'all *everywhere* you go."

Jason and Chasity glanced at each other. "Run Chaz!" Jason belted out as he and Chasity took off running down the path.

"They're tryna avoid us, Mel come on!" Mark laughed,

taking off running after them.

"Boy, I got heels on!" Malajia yelled, trotting along after him. "Damn those two and their athletic asses!"

David suppressed a chuckle. "So anyway, *you* guys want to do something tonight?" he asked Sidra and Josh.

"Sorry man, I'm hanging out with December," Josh revealed.

Sidra shot David a sympathetic look. "I'm afraid you'll have to count me out too, sweetie," she chimed in, adjusting per pocket book strap on her shoulder. "James is in town for only a few hours, so we're going out for a quick bite."

David shrugged. "Oh," he said, not masking his disappointment. "Well, you guys have fun. I guess I'll just head to the library and get a head start on my paper."

"Why don't you go see a movie or something?" Sidra suggested. "It's Friday and a nice day out."

David looked at the ground as he shuffled his weight from one foot to the other. Truth was, he would love to go see a movie, but not alone. "No, I think I'm pretty settled on my library plans," he replied solemnly, approaching the library steps. "See you later," he said, before heading for the entrance.

"Later man," Josh responded, as Sidra gave a slight wave.

Sidra frowned slightly. "Is it just me or does David seem a bit sad?" she asked Josh.

"It's not just you...he does," Josh agreed. "But I'm sure he'll be okay."

Sidra just let out a small sigh as they continued their walk back to the clusters.

David looked at his books spread across the library table and sighed. "Why am I in here on a Friday afternoon?" he mumbled to himself.

He felt pathetic at that moment. All his friends had plans, and here he was, sitting in a half empty library, working on a paper that wasn't due for another few weeks. Letting out a loud sigh, he quickly began to gather his books and place them back into his book bag. Just as he was about to shove the last book into his bag, he noticed a young lady standing near a shelf, thumbing through a book.

She's so pretty, he thought as he stared, starry-eyed. He had a thing for short, curvy women and this brown skinned beauty with shoulder length locks had curves in all the right places. He must have been staring with his mouth open because when she caught sight of him, she shot him a questionable glance.

David shyly pushed his glasses up on his nose, looking down at the book in his hand. *Stupid, just go say something to her.* Even though his head was telling him to go talk to her, he couldn't. He just grabbed his belongings and made a mad dash for the exit. He was so relieved to get away from the awkward situation, that he didn't even see Emily as he headed out of the door.

"Hey David," Emily said, spinning around.

Startled, David turned around and gave a nervous chuckle. "Oh, hey Emily," he stammered. "I'm sorry, I didn't see you."

"That's okay," she smiled. "Everything okay? You seem to be in a hurry."

David scratched his head. "I'm fine. I was just…never mind," he replied with a wave of his hand. How embarrassing would it be to admit that he was trying to make a hasty get away to avoid talking with a girl? "Hey, how are you doing anyway? Coping with your grandmother's passing, I mean?" he asked, changing the subject.

Emily looked down at the floor as she smoothed her hand over her low ponytail. "I'm um…I'm doing okay," she admitted. "I mean, it's hard."

David shot her a sympathetic look, nodding. "It's only been a few weeks Emily, of *course* it's hard," he consoled. "I mean, my mom has been gone for almost six years and it *still* gets hard for me sometimes."

Emily reached out and touched David's shoulder. Emily felt for him; she couldn't imagine losing her mother, no matter how annoyed she was with her. Especially at fifteen years old.

David waved his hand. "Hey, I'm fine. Like I said, it's been almost six years," he reiterated. "I said all that to say…take all the time you need to mourn."

Emily nodded. "I will."

"And if you need to talk, you can call me anytime," he added.

Emily smiled. "Thank you, and I will," she replied. "I have to return these books, so I'll see you."

"Oh sure," David said, giving a slight wave to Emily as she hurried inside. David, alone once again, trotted down the steps.

Chasity happily clapped her hands together as she stared at her laptop. "Yeeessssss, finally got this stupid program to work," she rejoiced to herself, rising from her seat. After the successful implementation of a program that she had been working on for a week, Chasity was in a good mood. She flung open her room door and headed up the steps. "Malajia!" she yelled, banging out a rhythm on the door.

Malajia jerked open the door and frowned in confusion. "Girl, why are you making beats on my damn door?" she grunted, walking back over to her desk.

Chasity laughed. "Just paying you back for all the times you did that on *my* door," she teased.

Malajia flagged Chasity with her hand as she sat down. "What are *you* so damn happy about?" she asked, noticing Chasity's bright mood.

"I just got this hard ass computer program to *finally* work," Chasity beamed, doing a silly dance.

Malajia shook her head. "You shouldn't do that," she jeered, of her dance. "It's not cute."

Chasity quickly stopped. "No? Not even a little bit?" she

wondered, frowning slightly. Malajia quickly shook her head, earning a shrug from Chasity. "Oh well, can't win 'em all."

"True," Malajia replied evenly, staring at the screen of her laptop. "Yo, since you're the computer expert in the group, can you tell me why my laptop is running like damn molasses?" she ground out, vigorously clicking her mouse over and over before smacking the screen.

Chasity frowned. "First of all, stop abusing the damn thing," she bit out, walking over to look. "Malajia, come on!" she exclaimed, laying eyes on the image frozen on the screen.

"What?" Malajia questioned, confused.

Chasity narrowed her eyes at her. "So you're just gonna act like there isn't porn on this damn screen?" she sneered, folding her arms.

"So?!" Malajia barked. "You act like *you* never watch it."

Chasity rolled her eyes. "I never said that I *didn't*, but I don't let people in the damn room when I *do*, you fuckin' weirdo."

"Whatever," Malajia hissed. "I'm not ashamed."

"Yeah well you *should* be," Chasity shot back. "You probably have a damn virus on the thing."

"Well can you *fix* it?" Malajia asked, exasperated.

"Not with that dick on the screen," Chasity chuckled.

Malajia sucked her teeth as she tapped on the power button, shutting down the laptop. "Fuck this laptop," she scoffed, closing it and sliding it back on the desk. She then reached down to the floor and grabbed her cell phone. "I can always watch it on my phone."

Chasity shook her head. "Go get laid Malajia," she teased.

"I *would*, but I don't want my first time with him to be on some 'I-just-watched-porn-let's-get-it-in-right-quick' shit," Malajia sneered, thumbing through her phone screen.

"Still haven't crossed that line yet, huh?" Chasity asked.

"Nope, we *haven't*," Malajia answered.

"Well, don't do it until you want to. You made that mistake *last* time," Chasity pointed out.

"Yes Chasity, I *know* that," Malajia spat. The last thing she wanted to be reminded of was losing her virginity to Tyrone.

"Eww to your attitude," Chasity sneered.

"Sorry, being horny makes me cranky," Malajia shrugged, tossing her phone on the desk. "Anyway, I'm over this porn mess." She got up from her seat and stood in front of Chasity. "You wanna go do something?" she asked.

Chasity eyed her skeptically. "Malajia, get your freak ass away from me," she spat out.

Malajia's eyes widened once she realized what Chasity thought she meant. "Girl ain't nobody tryna get freaky with you. I don't swing that way!" she exclaimed, then smiled. "But if I *did*, you'd be my first choice with your sexy self."

Chasity frowned in disgust. "Gross," she scoffed, turning to walk out the room.

"No wait," Malajia laughed. "Let's go out to eat."

"Fine, come on," Chasity replied evenly.

Malajia happily bounced up and down, putting a hand on Chasity's shoulder. "Yay, best friend time," she cooed.

"Don't touch me," Chasity hissed, jerking Malajia's arm off of her, earning a giggle from Malajia.

"Oh, so you're just gonna cheat like that?" Josh laughed, tapping the keys on his game controller.

"Don't accuse me of cheating because you suck at this game," December taunted, pushing her buttons.

"Oh really?" Josh replied, before taking his hand and covering her controller.

"Josh, stop cheating!" she exclaimed, watching her car crash into a wall on the game.

Josh jumped up and tossed his arms up in victory, letting the controller slip from his lap. "Yes! I win, hoagies on you," he teased.

December adjusted the messy bun on her head. "You *so* cheated, Joshua," she pouted. "I thought you were Mr. Nice Guy."

"I *am*," he assured. "Except when it comes to this game," he laughed. December rolled her eyes as she rose from the couch. "Fine, I'll buy the hoagies," she relented. "But *you* buy the soda."

"Don't have to, already have some in the fridge," Josh boasted. As he began to wrap the cord around his controller, the front door opened.

"Playing that game again, huh?" David asked, noticing the game title on the TV screen in the living room.

"Yep and December lost," Josh taunted, pointing at her. December gasped as she playfully slapped his hand down.

"Cheater," she hurled.

David gave a slight smile as he shook his head. It was nice to see Josh spending some quality time with a nice girl like December. He deserved it after the emotional mess that he went through over his feelings for Sidra. David only wished that he could find someone to spend time with himself. "Alright, you two carry on. I'm gonna go study," he said, heading for the stair case.

"Um, do you want to hang out with us David?" December asked. "We're just going to pick up some sandwiches and watch a movie."

"Yeah, I know that we couldn't hang out with you the other day, but today we can," Josh added. "Come chill."

David forced a smile. *Great, they want me to be a third wheel.* "Thanks for the offer, but I really do need to study," he declined.

"David, you study *all the time*," Josh chortled. "You have a 4.0 GPA, you're good man."

"And studying is how I *keep* that 4.0," David chuckled. "Later guys," he said, heading up the steps.

Josh shrugged as he grabbed December's light weight jacket from the arm of the couch. "Come on, the hoagies await us," he commented.

December made a face at him as she snatched the jacket.

Malajia stood over Chasity's shoulder, watching her fix several plates of chicken and broccoli alfredo; she let out a frustrated groan. "Why do *you* get to dish out all the dinner?" she asked.

"'Cause between you and Mark's greedy asses, nobody else will get any," Chasity shot back, shoving a plate of food in her hands. "Now stop breathing on my neck and take the damn plate to your greedy ass animal."

"Hey! I heard that," Mark barked from the couch in the living room.

Chasity looked over at him. "Point *is*?" she sneered, causing Mark to loudly suck his teeth.

"Smart ass," he mumbled.

"Say *what* now?" Chasity barked.

"Nothing," Mark lied. "Aye Mel, hurry up with my plate before she throws it away," he ordered, holding a hand out.

Malajia stopped suddenly and fixed an angry gaze. "Don't get embarrassed boy," she warned. "I'll spit all on this plate."

Mark chuckled. "I'm just messing with you," he assured, holding a smile. Malajia held her gaze as she slowly walked over, then shoved the plate in his hand. "Better had," he said once the plate was out of Malajia's hand. He then laughed and hopped up from the couch when Malajia tried to snatch the plate back. "Mel, chill I'm playing."

"Stop showing off," Malajia hissed, poking him on the arm.

"I said it once and I'll say it again," Sidra began, picking up her glass of water. "You two have the weirdest relationship."

"Naw, we got the *awesomest* relationship. Right sugar face?" Mark replied, holding his hand up for Malajia to high five it.

"No, awesomest isn't a damn word and stop talking to

me," Malajia scoffed, walking away from him.

Mark shook his head as Jason laughed. "You need to stop messing with her, man," Jason advised, placing a fork full of food into his mouth.

"He just had *better*," Malajia agreed, flopping down on the couch. "Or he'll be waking up with something *missing*."

Mark looked at her. "Sugar if you want to touch me, just *do* it," he teased. "No need to use bodily harm as an excuse."

Malajia made a face at him.

Sidra grabbed her plate and stood from the dining room table. "This conversation seems like it's about to get vulgar," she muttered. "I'll just excuse myself."

"Please take me with you," Chasity jeered, spearing her food with her fork. Sidra laughed as she walked upstairs.

Jason chuckled. "You'd leave me down here with them babe?" he directed at Chasity.

"In a heartbeat," she immediately threw back. "Love you though."

Jason shook his head in amusement. "Love you too."

Malajia cut her eye at Mark. "Why can't *you* be cute like that?" she barked at him. "You always gotta be an ass."

Mark dropped his fork on his plate, a shocked look on his face. "*Me*?!" he exclaimed, pointing to himself. "*You* just threatened to cut *body parts* off me."

"Well…stop making me mad," Malajia said in a sad attempt to defend herself.

As the couple once again started to bicker, Chasity stood up. Signaling Jason, she gradually walked backwards into her bedroom. Following suit, Jason slowly rose from the couch and crept to Chasity's room, darting the rest of the way in.

"You get on my damn nerves," Malajia hissed, folding her arms.

"What the hell *else* is new?" Mark threw back. He looked around, noticing the empty seats. "Wait, where did Chaz and Jase go?"

Malajia too looked at their empty seats. Annoyed, she sucked her teeth. "See? Your black ass ran them off," she bit out, slapping her hand on the arm of the couch. Mark tossed his hands in the air in frustration.

Chapter 21

David ambled out of the science building after his last class of the day. He was relieved; that hour seemed like an eternity. As he turned the corner to head back to the clusters, he spotted Chasity talking to the girl that came up to her in the lounge the day of her birthday; the same girl that he saw in the library nearly a week ago. His eyes lit up as he watched the two girls engage in conversation.

"I swear, I have no idea what I'm doing in class," the girl chortled. "I completely froze when Professor Madison asked me to finish writing the program on the board in front of everyone."

"Yeah, he's a temperamental bastard," Chasity replied, inciting a chuckle from the girl.

"Tell me about it," she agreed. "I thought he was gonna yell at me."

Chasity was about to say something else, but she caught David staring at them out the corner of her eye. "Uh huh," she stated flatly, shooting David a side-glance.

"Anyway, thanks for helping me understand the homework assignment. I was too afraid to ask him for clarification," she said, gratefully.

"Sure," Chasity replied evenly, still looking at David. Without taking her eyes off him, she waved slightly to her classmate as she walked away. Chasity then signaled David to come over with her finger. Pushing his glasses up on his nose, he walked over to her wearing a smile.

"Hey Chaz," he greeted.

"Why were you over there looking like a stalker?" Chasity asked bluntly, much to David's embarrassment.

"What are you talking about?" he asked, feigning innocence,

Chasity slowly folded her arms and shot David a knowing look.

He gave a nervous laugh. "Oh, you mean my staring?"

"Um, *yeah.*"

"Oh, well I was just shocked to see you talking to someone other than, you know...*us*," he teased.

Chasity frowned. "What the fuck is *that* supposed to mean?" she snapped.

David's smile quickly disappeared; he looked nervous. *Oh shit!* The last thing he wanted to do was piss off Chasity or *any* girl for that matter. "I didn't mean any—"

Chasity smirked. "I'm just messing with you."

David breathed a sigh of relief. "Cool," he smiled. He scratched his head as he tried to think of the best way to ask Chasity what he wanted to ask her. "So um...you're friends with that girl that you were talking to?"

"Nicole?" she questioned. David nodded. "We're not *friends,* she's just a classmate," Chasity shrugged. "Why?"

"Oh..." David looked down at his sneakers. "Um, do you think you could get her number for....um....me?"

Chasity looked at him as if he had lost his mind. "Why would I do that, David?"

David didn't say a word as he scratched his head yet again. How could he tell his friend that he was too nervous to ask for the number himself? Sure, he had no problem talking to his friends, but when it came to any female outside of his circle, he just didn't have the confidence.

"Never mind, she probably has a boyfriend anyway," he concluded.

Chasity eyed him skeptically. "And maybe she *doesn't*," she pointed out. "Just ask the girl for her number."

David shook his head. "Forget about it," he solemnly replied. "I have to go study anyway."

"Okay then sweetie, have fun with that," Chasity jeered, flipping her hair over her shoulder. "Later," she said, walking away.

David let out a sigh before walking off in the opposite direction.

Josh ran his hand over his head while he stared at the pizza on his plate. "I swear, I'm feeling off today," he announced to his friends who were busy eating their food.

"What do you mean?" Sidra asked, spearing a tater tot with her fork.

"Are you *seriously* eating tater tots with a *fork*?" Malajia asked, pinching the bridge of her nose with two fingers. "You have taken being uppity to a whole new level."

Sidra cut her eye at Malajia, "I don't want the grease on my fingers," she hissed.

"Weirdo," Malajia sneezed. The outburst and gesture incited chuckles from their friends.

Malajia, Mark, Josh, David, and Sidra elected to grab a bite to eat at the mall food court before catching a movie that Saturday afternoon.

Ignoring Malajia, Sidra turned her attention back to Josh. "Anyway Josh, why do you feel off?" she asked.

"I don't know," Josh replied honestly. "You ever just feel like something stupid is going to happen?"

"That's because you *are* the stupid thing that happens," Mark chuckled.

Malajia rolled her eyes at the lackluster joke, but elected not to comment. She just concentrated on eating her burger.

Josh also wasn't amused. "That wasn't even funny and that would be *you*," he shot back. Josh was in no mood for Mark's foolishness. He couldn't pinpoint why he was feeling so down. His thoughts were interrupted by the sound of Mark's phone ringing. Mark removed the phone from his jeans pocket and began dancing in his seat to his loud ringtone—a sample of a poplar rap song.

Malajia covered her face in embarrassment. "Dear God," she muttered.

"You know this song is killin' it," Mark commented, putting the phone to his ear. "Yizzo," he greeted. He frowned in confusion. "Hey Mr. Hampton."

Josh's head snapped towards Mark at the mention of his father's name.

"Naw, it's cool. Yeah he's right here." Mark looked at Josh, handing him the phone.

Suspicious, Josh grabbed the phone from Mark and rose from the table. "Yeah Dad?" he solemnly answered, stepping away from the table.

"Yo, Josh's pop is a stalker," Mark joked.

"That's not funny Mark," Sidra scolded. "You know Josh doesn't have a cell phone. So *what* if his dad calls our phones to get in touch with him?"

Mark frowned. "Why you all defensive?" he questioned. "I was just making a joke."

"Because you always joke about stuff that isn't *funny*," Sidra pointed out. "You're going to say or do something to someone thinking it's a damn joke, and you're going to end up getting your feelings hurt."

Mark flagged Sidra dismissively with his hand. "Whatever," he grumbled, reaching for the remaining fries on Malajia's plate. As he stuffed one into his mouth, he laughed when he saw David approach their table. "Damn David, did you fall in the toilet?" he teased, much to David's annoyance.

"I wasn't in the bathroom all that time," he assured, sitting in his seat.

"You were gone for like fifteen minutes," Mark laughed, he then nudged Malajia who was staring at her nails. "David was in there taking a shit."

"*So?*" Malajia snapped, shooting Mark an exasperated

look. "Can you be quiet for ten damn minutes? Shit."

"Come on with all that, Mark," David barked. "I'm not in the mood for your teasing right now."

Mark loudly sucked his teeth. "I should've stayed my ass home. Y'all are being extra corny today," he griped.

Josh's presence at the table interrupted Mark's complaining. "I swear if my dad calls me *one* more time about Sarah, I'm going to snap," he griped, flopping down in his seat.

"What did he have to say about her *now*?" Sidra wondered, not hiding her concern. Josh hadn't spoken to his father since he was informed that Sarah was back home.

"He keeps trying to get me to talk to her, and I'm not interested," Josh seethed, handing the phone back to Mark.

"Well, I know you don't want to hear it, but maybe you *should* talk to her and hear what she has to say," Sidra carefully suggested.

"And I'll tell you like I told you *before*, I'm not interested in hearing *anything* she has to say," Josh nastily responded.

Sidra sighed slightly, pushing some of her hair over her shoulder. Josh being stubborn wasn't new to her. Sidra understood what he was feeling, but could only hope that he could one day get past the animosity he held.

"That explains that weird feeling that I had," Josh grumbled. "That *conversation* was the something stupid."

"Why don't we get to the movie, before the good seats are taken?" Sidra suggested, changing the subject.

"Yeah, let's get going, because if I gotta sit in the front again, I'm going home," Malajia chimed in, gathering her trash.

"That movie was dry bee," Mark complained, flopping on the couch in the girls' house.

"I told you it *would* be," Alex laughed, letting her ponytail down. She ran a hand through her natural waves.

"Eric told me that he saw it last week. Said it was horrible."

"You always gotta find a way to throw Eric's name in the mix," Malajia teased, searching through the contents of the refrigerator.

Alex laughed. "Hush up Malajia."

Malajia slammed the refrigerator door. "Which one of y'all thirsty asses drank all of the orange juice?"

"That would be me," Alex revealed, raising a hand. "And before you start running your mouth, *please* keep in mind that *you* drank the last of the apple juice the other day."

Malajia, grabbed an apple out of a bowl on the counter. "I was talking about the *orange juice*," she spat. "Nobody asked you about *apple*."

"Yeah, okay. Girl hush," Alex demanded.

Sidra turned her attention to David, who was thumbing through the channels on the television. "Are you okay David? You were pretty quiet on the way home," she observed.

David turned the TV off and gave a slight smile. "I'm fine," he replied. He wondered if anyone believed him.

"Naw, I think he's salty that he can't get that girl's number that he's been asking everybody to get for him," Mark slid in.

David's eyes widened in embarrassment as Malajia backhanded Mark on his arm.

"You are such an asshole," Malajia condemned.

"What I do *now*?" Mark replied, surprised.

"You're always embarrassing him," Sidra scolded.

"What? Malajia *you're* the one who told me that he asked you to ask the girl for her number yesterday," Mark reminded, pointing to her. "He asked Chaz before *that*."

"Yes, I *know* that dickhead, but I didn't mean for you to blab about it," Malajia snapped, nudging him. "I'mma stop telling you shit."

Mark sucked his teeth. "Look, it's not my fault that glasses boy is too damn scared to ask the chick for her number," he sneered, rubbing his arm. "She got a damn boyfriend *anyway*."

Well...so much for that, David thought, disappointed. "Whatever Mark," he hissed. "But really Sidra, I'm fine," he insisted.

Glaring at Mark, Malajia put her hands on her hips. "And how do *you* know she has a man?" she ground out. "What? Were you trying to talk to her or something?"

Mark let out a loud sigh, pulling his hands down his face. "Don't start that bullshit, Malajia," he warned. "I play ball with her dude sometimes. She comes to watch him play. Damn."

"David, there are plenty of other girls on campus who would love to give you their number," Sidra smiled to David. She hoped to cheer him up and cut Malajia and Mark's bickering short.

David shrugged. "I doubt it, but it's okay," he solemnly replied.

"Trust me, there are," Sidra assured. "You're a great guy and you deserve to have some companionship."

"In other words, you need to get laid," Mark spat. "By a *real* person. I'm sure your glasses are tired of you fondling them," he laughed.

David rolled his eyes at Mark. *Jackass*. He didn't know why, but he felt the need to come clean. "Mark's ignorant comment *aside*, I do admit, I have been feeling a bit lonely lately," he admitted after a moment.

"Oh wow, really?" Alex was curious. David was always so focused on his studies; she never suspected that he wanted a girlfriend.

David once again shrugged. He wondered if he should've even revealed his feelings about his loneliness, especially in front of Mark. "I guess I'm just seeing everyone pair off into relationships...."

Sidra tilted her head and shot him a sympathetic look as he hesitated.

"I mean, Jason and Chaz are together, Sidra you're with James, Josh has December, Mark and Mel are together...that still sounds weird to say, by the way," David continued.

"Who *you* tellin'?" Malajia mumbled, playing with strands of her hair.

"And Alex, *you're* with Eric," David added. "*Emily* will eventually end up with someone and I just…I wouldn't mind going on a date or two."

"David, Eric and I aren't together—"

"God Alex, shut the hell up," Malajia snapped, interrupting Alex. "You know what he meant, just stop it."

Alex clenched her jaw as she stared daggers at Malajia. "Make me get up from this couch, hear?" she warned, pointing at her.

Malajia feigned a shiver before waving her hand at Alex dismissively.

Mark sat up in his seat. "David, you *really* wanna go on a date?" he asked.

David let out a loud sigh; he was certain that Mark was about to say something smart. "That's what I said, Mark," he ground out.

Mark tapped his finger to his chin, thinking. "I think I got the perfect girl for you," he said finally. "I can set y'all up on a blind date."

David, as well as the rest of his friends, eyed him suspiciously.

Mark looked around. "Why are y'all staring at me?"

"You're actually going to set me up on a blind date?" David asked. "*You*, with so much to say, is actually going to help me out?"

Mark nodded happily. "I got you dawg."

"Mark, I swear she better not be ugly," Sidra spat, causing Alex to snicker. "You know you play too much, don't do that to my brother. Don't set him up with some beast."

"Sidra, that's so mean," Alex chided, trying to suppress her laughter. "Beauty is in the eyes of the beholder."

"Ugly is ugly, I don't care what nobody says," Sidra hissed, folding her arms.

"Shit, you ain't lying Sid," Malajia added before

pointing to Mark. "And how do *you* know this girl?" she hurled at him. "You better not be playing me Mark. There are *too* many of your old hoes coming out the wood works."

"Can you chill?" Mark fussed. "I'm not thinking about them."

As Mark and Malajia began to quarrel yet again, David smiled to himself; his week was looking up after all. Maybe, just maybe, the girl that Mark would set him up with would turn into a nice relationship.

Chasity grabbed her book bag, slung it over her shoulder, and made a mad dash out of the classroom. Her Technical Writing class couldn't have ended soon enough. She barely got three hours of sleep the night before. Having two reports due, a program assignment to finish, and a test to study for; Chasity was surprised she'd gotten *that* much sleep. She couldn't wait to get back to her room and rest.

Seeing Jason come out of the library, she waved to him. "Hey babe."

Jason smiled back, approaching. "Hey yourself," he said, putting his arm around her. "What time did you wind up going to sleep last night?"

She shot him a glance. "*Last night?*" she scoffed. "Try five this *morning.*"

Jason winced. "Shit," he commented. "I know you're tired."

"Tired is an understatement," she confirmed, pushing hair behind her ear. "I'm not even sure how I'm *walking.*"

"Make sure you go to sleep when you get home," Jason urged.

"Yeah," she agreed as they continued their journey along the heavily-grassed path leading back to the clusters.

"So, are you ready for midterms?" Jason asked after some silence.

"I don't even want to think about those right now," she replied.

Jason chuckled. "Yeah, tell me about it."

Chasity retrieved her ringing cell phone from her jeans pocket. She frowned at the number.

"Something wrong?" Jason asked, noticing the confused look on her face.

"I don't recognize this number," she replied, staring at the number flashing on her screen. "It's a New York area code."

"Who would be calling you from New York?" Jason inquired, adjusting his bag on his shoulder.

Chasity shrugged. "I'm supposed to be going to New York with my mom for break... Maybe someone from the hotel was trying to reach her and can't." Chasity normally did not answer unknown numbers, but throwing caution aside, she decided to answer. "Hello?"

There was silence on the line. "Hi Chasity," the male voice replied after a moment.

She stopped walking. A mask of anger covered Chasity's face; she recognized the voice. "Hell no," she blurted out. "Dad?"

Jason's ears perked as he too stopped. He knew that Chasity had not seen or spoken to her father since winter break of their sophomore year. She had shared with Jason a long time ago the relationship, or lack thereof, that she had with her father. Jason couldn't understand how a father could be okay with not having a relationship with his child.

"Yeah, it's me," Derrick Parker answered hesitantly. "How are you?"

"You've got to be kidding me," she spat. "I don't hear from you for almost a *year and a half* and suddenly you wanna call with this casual bullshit?"

"I know I'm one of the last people that you want to talk to but...I just want—"

"*Whatever* you want, I promise I'm *not* interested in," Chasity hissed into the phone before abruptly ending the call.

Jason watched her shove her phone back into her pocket. He hesitated on saying anything right away; she looked like she wanted to scream.

"What the *fuck*?" she fumed.

Jason put his hand on Chasity's arm, attempting to comfort her. "Just breathe," he urged. "Do you want to talk about it?"

"You already know I *don't*," she spat.

"Maybe you *should*," he calmly suggested. "You know how you get when you bottle stuff up, babe."

Chasity let out a loud sigh. "Why is he just calling me *now*?" she wondered aloud. "After all this fuckin' time?"

Jason tried hard to think of the right thing to say. In all honesty, he wondered the same thing. "I don't know sweetheart, maybe... Maybe he was just trying to find the right time."

Chasity shot Jason a confused look. "The right *time*?" she barked.

Jason sighed. "I'm sorry, I didn't mean that—"

"Jason, my mom told him the truth about everything *last year*..." Chasity cut in, furious. "Which means that he knew that *I* knew...*last year*. He knew I was a fuckin' mess after everything came out and he didn't bother to check on me *once*..." She folded her arms. "Fuck him."

Jason felt himself getting angry. Chasity was clearly hurting and the man who caused it was her own father. He didn't know what to do or say to make her feel better. If he was in her position, he'd doubt that anything could make him feel better.

Chasity glanced at the ground as she tried to calm herself down. "I'm not mad at you," she said to Jason.

"I know that," he assured, hugging her. "I don't know what to say right now."

"It's nothing *to* say," she said, parting from him. "I'm tired, I need to go sleep."

"Okay, I'll call you later," Jason said to her as she walked off.

Chapter 22

David gave himself a once over in the mirror. His day started off somber, as it did every year. But things were beginning to look up. He was anticipating the blind date that Mark had set him up on. He glanced at his watch. "Almost seven," David muttered to himself; he had mere minutes before he had to leave.

Removing his glasses, David cleaned his lenses with a cloth, then placed them back on his face. He adjusted the collar on his dark blue button-down shirt, then walked out of the bathroom.

Hearing the guys cheer for him as he walked down the steps, David couldn't help but smile. "Come on guys, chill out," he chuckled, reaching the bottom of the steps.

"Uh oh, David got the black slacks on," Mark teased. "He even shined his shoes and got a fresh haircut...You killin' 'em bro."

Embarrassed, David flagged Mark with his hand.

Jason shot Mark a confused look. "You act like he's never worn dress pants before," he said.

"Yeah, but *these* don't have lint on 'em," Mark joked.

Jason pinched the bridge of his nose. *This fool can't stop making jokes for one minute.*

"You nervous?" Josh asked David.

"A little bit," David admitted. "I've never been on a blind date before, or *any* date for that matter," he added. "I never had *time* to. When Mom got sick, I spent so much time helping to take care of her, and after she died I just… Just buried myself in the books, hoping to make her proud, you know."

"She's proud of you," Jason assured, giving David a pat on his shoulder.

"Yeah, I know," David smiled. "So, besides Mark, do *any* of you know what this girl looks like? Do the girls know her?"

"No, Mark is keeping her under wraps from us," Josh answered. He laughed. "Malajia tried to beat it out of him."

"For the *last* time, she didn't beat me. I tripped on a pillow and fell," Mark barked. "You always lying and shit."

Josh looked at Mark with shock. "*Me*?!" he exclaimed, pointing to himself. "You lie more than everybody combined."

"I wasn't gonna say anything, but Malajia had you shook last night," Jason slid in, amused.

"That's 'cause she screamed at me loud as shit after I ate her candy bar," Mark jeered. "Hell, I tried to run from her ass, then I slipped on that silky ass pillow."

David put his hands up. "Guys, really, I'm freaking out here," he cut in. "Mark who is this girl?"

"Chill bee, I told you I got you," Mark stated mysteriously. "You're gonna love her. She's *just* your type."

David grinned. "Cool. *Where* am I meeting her again?" he asked, glancing at his watch.

"In the Howard building, room 105," Mark informed.

"The hospitality building?" Jason questioned. "Where the hotel and restaurant major classes are?"

Mark nodded enthusiastically. "Yep, I got the hookup for one of the classrooms," he said. "I set up something nice." He looked at David. "See, you ain't even gotta spend no money, I took care of it."

David was certainly impressed and grateful. "Wow, thanks man," he beamed.

Mark grabbed a bouquet of flowers from the coffee table. "You better get going, don't want to keep the lady waiting," he urged, pushing the flowers in David's hand.

"Right, right," David breathed, reaching for the doorknob. "Oh and thanks for keeping the girls away," he said gratefully. "I love them to death, but they would've made me even more nervous."

"No problem man," Josh returned.

David waved, "Alright guys, I'm outta here," he said, hurrying out and shutting the door behind him.

"I hope he has a good time," Josh said to the guys. "He needs it. Especially today."

Mark sat on the couch, smiling from ear to ear. "Oh this will be a date that he *never* forgets, trust me."

David was glad that the weather was nice that evening; the walk to the Howard building was long. The building was pretty much at the other end of campus. Nevertheless, he didn't mind. It gave him time to mentally prepare himself for his date.

Finally approaching the building, he glanced at his watch yet again. "Man, I'm a little late," he muttered. "I hope she's not mad."

Pushing the thought to the back of his mind, David walked into the building. Looking around, he realized that despite the fact that he'd been a student for three years, he never actually stepped foot in the building. It was pretty fancy, compared to the other buildings on campus.

The entry way looked like a modest hotel lobby, which made sense because the building *did* house a few hotel rooms. He slowly made his way through the empty hallways, glancing at the doors in search of room 105. Finding it, he stood in front of the door, taking several deep breaths.

"Here goes nothing," he said to himself. He knocked on

the door and waited. When he didn't hear anything after a few seconds, he knocked again. "She should be here," he muttered. Not hearing anything yet again, David opened the door a crack. "Hello?" he called.

Slowly pushing the door open, David stuck his head in. The room was illuminated by candle light and he heard soft music playing in the background. Stepping all the way in the room, David was disappointed to find no one there. The only furniture in the room was a small round table in the middle of the room. It had two plates, a long stem rose, and several flickering LED tea light candles sitting on top of it. Chairs were facing each other from opposite sides of the table. Tucking the flowers under his arm, David let out a sigh. "Damn...stood up," he sulked.

Completely let down, David planned on walking out, but something caught his eye. Walking up to the table, his eyes widened as he spotted the other thing sitting there— something that he had missed at first sight.

Un-fuckin-believable! was the word that filled his head. Sitting on a plate across from his seat were a pair of black framed glasses; eye stickers were placed on the lenses. He zoned in on what seemed to be raisins arranged in the shape of a smile.

A joke...it was a fucking joke. David's jaw clenched as he resisted the urge to tear up. He picked up a note sitting on what was supposed to be *his* plate. He unfolded the paper, feeling his anger intensify when he saw a wrapped condom attached with a paperclip. *In case you need this later –Mark* the note read.

David threw the flowers to the floor and pushed the table over in a fit of rage, sending the contents flying. He punctuated his actions by storming out of the room.

David reached his house in record time. He stormed through the empty space, looking for Mark. When he couldn't find him, David figured he would try the next best place.

He practically ran to the girls' house. Pushing open the door, he was greeted by Mark's boisterous laughter as he and the rest of his friends were congregated in the living room talking.

"David," Sidra reacted, surprised, noticing him standing by the door. She hadn't expected to see him so soon. "What happened on your date?"

David didn't answer. His angry gaze was fixed on Mark, who snickered.

"Yeah David, what happened on your date?" Mark taunted.

David walked over and delivered a hard punch to Mark's face, sending him stumbling back into the kitchen before falling to the floor. The move stunned everyone in the room.

"Oh shit!" Malajia exclaimed, as Jason quickly grabbed David and pulled him back, before David was able to grab Mark from the floor. Josh stood in front of Mark as Malajia went to help him up.

"What's going on?" Sidra demanded, angry. "David, what happened?"

"That was fuckin' uncalled for David!" Mark hollered, wiping the blood from his mouth.

"*Was* it?!" David exploded, struggling to get out of Jason's hold. "You are the most ignorant son of a bitch that I've *ever* met!"

"What the hell *happened*?!" Alex yelled over the commotion. "Whatever it is, fighting won't solve anything!"

"Do you guys have *any* idea 'who' he set me up on that bullshit date with?" David asked his confused and stunned friends.

"David man, it was a joke," Mark cut in, putting his hand up.

"Shut up!" David's loud, deep voice boomed off the walls.

"You've got to calm down, man," Jason calmly ordered.

"Damn David, was the girl *that* ugly?" Chasity

wondered, confused.

David gritted his teeth. "This punk ass bastard set me up on a date with a pair of fuckin' glasses," he revealed, pointing to Mark who just stood there.

The room fell silent as everyone other than Mark and David looked at each other in confusion.

"Say that again," Chasity ordered, wondering if she heard him correctly.

"He set me up on a date with a pair of *glasses*," David repeated, this time slowly.

"Come on, that's not funny?" Mark asked, looking at his friends, who were eyeing him with disgust. Malajia glared at him, moving away.

Jason released David from his grip, while Josh moved away from Mark and stood back with the girls.

"Carry on," Jason told David.

David took the opportunity and charged at Mark.

"Fuck him up, David," Chasity goaded, angry.

"Whoa, David chill!" Mark exclaimed, putting his arms out to prevent David from attacking him. "I don't wanna hurt you."

David was too enraged to think; he just wanted to fight. He and Mark began to tussle.

"Beat his ass, David!" Malajia instigated as David delivered another punch to Mark's face.

Mark was trying his hardest not to fight David back, but he wasn't about to just stand there and take a beating. As Mark prepared to throw a punch, Josh jumped in between the two guys. No matter how wrong Josh thought Mark was for what he did, he could not in good conscious stand by and watch his friends fight each other any longer.

"Okay guys, that's enough," Josh ordered, struggling to part them. "Jason, help me please."

Jason walked over and hauled David away, moving him towards the door. Josh pushed Mark back against Chasity's closed door.

"Come on, he's not worth it," Jason said to David,

opening the door and nudging the fuming David outside. He walked out behind him, shutting the door.

Sidra slowly folded her arms, scowling at Mark. She was repulsed. "How could you do that to him?" she seethed. "What the hell is *wrong* with you?"

Mark held his fingers over the bridge of his bloody nose. "It was a damn *joke*," he argued.

"What the fuck would make you think that was funny?" Chasity barked. "You take shit too damn far."

"You don't know when to quit!" Alex wailed, slamming her hand on the dining room table. "You knew how excited he was for that date. You *knew* he was feeling lonely and you go and do some mess like *this*?"

"What kind of friend *are* you?" Emily asked. She felt for David; he was the butt of a lot of Mark's jokes and pranks, but this was too far.

"He's *not* a damn friend. He's a *bully*," Sidra fumed.

"Just like he *used* to be," Josh added. "I'm surprised that David has put up with your shit for *this* long. Hell, I'm surprised that we *all* have."

Mark sucked his teeth as he wiped the blood from his nose with his hand. "Can someone get me a towel or something?" he asked, ignoring the comments.

"Ain't nobody getting your ignorant ass a *damn* thing," Malajia sneered.

"Really Malajia?" Mark scoffed. "You're turning on me? I'm your damn man."

"Not *today* you're not. I'm over you right now," Malajia bit back. "Fuck you."

"Guys, it was a *joke*!" Mark insisted. "Y'all think that a joke gave him reason to attack me like he didn't know me? No fuck *him*."

"He had *every* right to attack you," Sidra ranted. "You do this to him today of *all* days? That's messed up."

"What's so special about today?" Mark asked, confused.

"If you don't know, then you really *aren't* his friend," Josh spat.

Mark held the baffled look on his face as the front door opened and Jason walked in. He immediately shook his head at Mark.

"That was fucked up man," Jason commented. "He's really hurt by that."

"This is making me want to cry. I can't even look at you right now Mark," Sidra said, voice cracking.

"Yeah, the rest of us feel the same way," Alex agreed, pointing to the door. "Mark, you need to go."

Mark was shocked. "Are y'all serious?"

"We sure are," Alex confirmed. "It's clear that you're not a real friend and I don't want to be around someone like that. You're out."

"How you gonna put me out?" Mark barked. "Y'all are overreacting."

"Get the fuck out," Chasity ordered, pointing to the door.

Mark looked at Jason and Josh. "You two agree with them?" he asked.

"Oh absolutely," Jason confirmed. "You went out of your way to hurt your friend. That's triflin'."

"It's disgusting and you need to go fix it," Josh insisted. "And fix it *now*."

Mark sucked his teeth, snatching paper towel from a roll on the counter. "Fine," he huffed, walking to the door. He glanced at Malajia, who just turned away from him.

David sat on his bed, rubbing his swollen knuckles as he examined them. He couldn't recall if he had ever punched anyone before; all he knew was that his hand was paying for it. Sighing, he stood from the bed, walked to his desk and picked up a picture of his mother. What he wouldn't give to be able to pick up the phone and talk to her. He didn't know why everything about his mom was hitting him so bad *now*. She'd been gone so long and he thought that he was at peace with it.

David's somber thoughts were interrupted by his cracked

room door slowly opening. David frowned at the sight of Mark peeking his head in. "I suggest you leave," he spat.

Mark let out a loud sigh as he opened the door and walked in. "David come on, you know how I play," he began, unremorseful. "What's the big damn deal?"

David just stared at Mark in disbelief; how could he act so nonchalant about all of this? Was he that clueless? David shook his head as he carefully placed his mother's picture back in its place.

"You know what?" he began, facing Mark. "On this day every year, I wake up, *hoping* to have a good day. *Hoping* that something good will happen to me that would make this day a little better."

Mark sighed as he rubbed his head. "David—"

"Six years," David interrupted. "My mother has been gone six years...today."

Mark felt his heart drop; this was the anniversary of David's mother's death and he had completely forgotten. He had played a cruel prank on him the same day. *Shit!* Mark didn't know what to say.

"Forgot, huh?" David asked, almost smirking. "I'm not surprised. Sidra and Josh remembered. But not *you*," he added, spiteful. "If it doesn't have anything to do with *you*, you don't care."

Mark put his hand on his chest. "Don't say that, it's not true," he defended.

"It *is*," David insisted, folding his arms. "You're inconsiderate and heartless and a lot of that is directed towards *me*."

"I play pranks on *everybody*," Mark argued. "That's just how I am, you know that. I don't mean any harm by it."

"You direct a *lot* towards *me*," David reiterated. "I guess that's what I get for being friends with someone who used to bully me."

Mark's eyes widened; how could he throw that up in his face? "That's not fair man. That was a long time ago, we were *kids*."

"That's what I told myself," David agreed. "I convinced myself that the teasing, the shoving, the pranks were all just you being a jackass of a child, and me being the new kid who wouldn't defend himself."

Mark ran his hand over his face in shame. He remembered how bad he used to tease David. David had just moved to their city and started elementary school. Mark had taken one look at the skinny, quiet boy, with the thick glasses and no name clothes, and instantly targeted him. Though the bullying didn't last that long, Mark still felt bad. But David reassured him that he was over it and everything was good between them, or so he had thought.

"Mom told me to be careful when it came to you," David revealed, much to Mark's surprise. "She saw how you treated me even *after* we became friends and she told me to watch my back, because anybody who takes pride in hurting their friends' feelings *can't* be good." He shook his head. "But I told her that she was crazy, that you were like my brother and that you would *always* have my back and that you would never intentionally hurt me... I guess she was right," David concluded, sadness filling his voice.

Mark shook his head in disbelief. "I know I'm a jackass sometimes, but to say that I take *pride* in hurting people, is just plain wrong," he argued. "I don't always think of myself."

"Why didn't you come to the hospital the night that my mom was dying?" David asked, point blank.

"What?" Mark asked. *I can't believe he's bringing this up again.*

"Why didn't you come?" David repeated. "I needed my friends and you didn't show."

"I told you that I couldn't handle sad situations well. I *still* can't," Mark replied. "You can't keep bringing up stuff that you said you forgave me for, that's not fair."

"What's not *fair* is the fact that I wasted years of friendship on someone like you," David replied with a deceptive calm. "I'm done."

Mark frowned slightly. "What do you mean you're done? With our friendship?" he asked angrily.

"Yup. Get the hell out," David confirmed.

Mark shook his head. He wasn't about to beg David for his friendship or his forgiveness, not when all he did was play a prank.

"You got it," Mark spat, turning towards the door. Before he walked out, he turned back around. "You know what? If you and the rest of 'David's pity squad' want to write me off because of some stupid prank, that's on y'all," he said. "I'm not about to defend my character to you guys when you already know how I am."

"And that reason there is why I won't miss you being my friend," David hissed. "You just can't seem to understand why you're wrong. You never *could*."

"Yeah whatever, yo," Mark grunted, before storming out of the room, leaving David to slam his door shut behind him.

Chapter 23

"Malajia why do you continue to leave empty cereal boxes in the cabinets?" Alex asked, annoyed as she tossed two empty boxes in the trash.

"I leave them so whoever goes shopping can remember which ones I like," Malajia shrugged.

Sidra looked up from her cup of coffee, perplexed. "Just write it down on the list that we keep on the fridge," she said. "Why take up room in the cabinet with empty boxes?"

"'Cause maybe I don't feel like throwing the damn boxes in the trash," Malajia snapped, moving out of the way to allow Chasity to reach for something in another cabinet.

This morning—like many others—all five girls were trying to maneuver in the small kitchen for breakfast before classes.

"Ever think about *that*?" Malajia added.

"No. I *don't*," Sidra sneered. "But I'm not surprised."

Alex let out a loud sigh, putting the lid back on the trash can. "Malajia, you *do* know it's your turn to clean the kitchen, right?" she reminded.

"No the fuck it's *not*," Malajia loudly protested. "Sidra said if I cleaned the bathroom for her this week, she would clean the kitchen for me."

"But you didn't even *clean* the damn bathroom," Sidra

hissed. "*Alex* did."

"Exactly, so like I said, *you* have to clean the kitchen," Alex added, pointing at Malajia who was visibly irritated.

"It doesn't matter if I actually cleaned the bathroom. A verbal deal is a verbal deal," Malajia argued, pointing to Sidra whose eyes widened.

"But you didn't even hold up *your* end of the verbal deal," Sidra flashed back. "You're always trying to get out of doing any damn work."

"What did *you* clean?" Malajia questioned.

"Our *entire* room, including *your* mess," Sidra answered, teeth clenched. "Do you know how much of your trash I threw out?"

Malajia sucked her teeth. "Nobody asked—"

"God, Malajia shut the hell up already," Chasity cut in. "Stop being lazy and clean the damn kitchen," she barked, frowning at Malajia. "We go through this shit every damn week."

Malajia ran her hand over her hair. "Fine," she grunted.

"You salty, you got chastised." Alex laughed at the look on Malajia's face.

"Yeah well, you did part of my work anyway you mop-headed troll," Malajia mumbled.

Alex's laugh came to an abrupt halt. She narrowed her eyes at Malajia before walking over to the trash can. She removed the empty boxes and tossed them on the floor. "Have fun," she teased, a phony smile plastered to her face.

"Bitch," Malajia scoffed, folding her arms in a huff.

Emily, who was sitting in the living room eating her toaster pastry, glanced out of the front window. She watched Mark slowly walk past the house, staring in the window with a sad look on his face.

"Mark is walking past the house again," Emily informed.

"*And?*" Sidra hissed. "He can walk past as many times as he *wants*, he's not getting in here."

It had been four days since David and Mark had had

their falling out. Neither David nor the others had any interest in associating with Mark after what he did, and were giving him the silent treatment.

"No, he needs to quit that stalker shit," Chasity sneered. "Yesterday he stared in the window for like ten minutes straight."

Emily chuckled at the thought. "Are you serious?" she asked.

"Yes, I was sitting on the couch," Chasity replied.

"What did you do?" Emily laughed.

"I stared right back at his dumb ass," Chasity said evenly.

"Josh told me that he just sits in the living room looking at the TV, waiting for one of the guys to say something to him," Alex put in, biting a bacon strip.

"That's what he gets," Sidra barked. "He has to learn that he can't treat his friends like shit and expect everybody to be okay with it." She reached for creamer from the refrigerator. "He's always acted out and he's always targeted David, ever since we were children."

"He still *is* a damn child," Malajia scoffed, wiping the counter top with a sponge.

Emily looked at Malajia. "Do you feel bad for giving him the silent treatment?" she asked. "He's your boyfriend after all."

"Fuck no," Malajia spat out. "And don't remind me about the boyfriend thing. He's on couple time out until he gets some damn act right."

"Is he still out there Emily?" Alex asked, grabbing her book bag off of the step.

Emily looked out the window. "Yes, he's staring at me right now," she said.

"Great," Alex drawled sarcastically. "Chaz, you ready?" she asked, putting the book bag on her shoulder.

"He's such a fuckin' creep," Chasity ground out, tossing her bowl in the sink.

Malajia frowned. "Bitch you better *wash* that bowl," she

ordered. "You see me trying to clean the kitchen."

"And the dishes are a *part* of it," Chasity teased. "Have fun," she added, walking to the door.

"I really hate you right now," Malajia spat at Chasity.

"I love you too," Chasity taunted, walking out the door with a laughing Alex following close behind.

"God Mark, give it a rest!" Alex barked to Mark, shutting the door behind her.

Sidra grabbed her purse and books from the arm of the couch. "He needs to take his ass to class," she said. "See you later ladies."

As Sidra darted out the door, Emily headed up the steps to grab something that she had forgotten.

From the kitchen, Malajia craned her neck to peer out of the window. Seeing Mark standing there, staring at the house looking pitiful, made her feel bad. It was clear that he was missing his friends. She wondered if she should just go talk to him, then quickly dismissed the thought.

"No, his ass needs to learn a lesson," she said to herself, going back to washing dishes.

"Why is there never any damn food in this house?" Mark complained to himself, slamming the refrigerator door. He'd just gotten back after class and was starving. As he rummaged through the cabinets, he heard the front door open. He looked up, anticipating seeing the guys walk in.

"I'll just be a second guys, let me change my shirt really quick," Josh said to Jason and David, hurrying up the steps.

"You gotta hurry up man, the game starts in like twenty minutes," Jason called up the steps, looking at his watch.

Mark slowly closed the cabinet door as he stared. "Hey guys," he said, voice hopeful. Maybe this would be the day that his friends stopped ignoring him. Jason and David looked at him briefly before going back to their conversation.

"So anyway, I heard that this team plays really good," David said. "I was talking to—"

"So y'all are about to go to the basketball game?" Mark interrupted.

"Yep," David spat.

"So um...how about I come *with* you?" he proposed, "I won't even guilt y'all into buying me any snacks."

Jason shot Mark a glare. "How about naw?" he hissed, not amused by his attempt at a joke. "You're not invited."

Mark slammed his hand on the counter. "Come on!" he barked, furious. "I can't believe you people are *still* mad."

"Believe it," Jason countered. "Josh, come on bro, we gotta go!" he yelled up the steps.

"Alright, alright," Josh said, hurrying down the steps. As the three guys headed for the door, Mark sucked his teeth.

"I hope y'all know that you're acting like a bunch of girls," Mark scoffed. "How long are you gonna keep this shit up?"

The three guys looked at each other, then looked back at Mark. He wondered what they were going to say. He was sure that he was going to get a verbal lashing.

"Hey man, you wanna come with us?" David asked, much to Mark's shock and delight.

"Yeah," Mark smiled. "I'm just gonna go grab my wallet."

As Mark made a mad dash in his room to retrieve his wallet, David looked back at the other guys who eyed him in confusion.

"What are you doing?" Josh asked.

"Let's see how *he* feels when he's played," David said, motioning the guys to hurry out the door. Mark came out just as the front door shut. Realizing that he had been pranked, his smile faded.

He tossed his wallet on the counter. "I ain't wanna go with y'all punk asses anyway," he mumbled, leaning against the counter.

"Emily, I swear if you don't come on, I'm leaving you,"

stood there, arms outstretched.

Emily swallowed hard, seeing the hopeful look on Mark's face. She then looked at Chasity, who was tapping her foot impatiently.

Chasity had no intention on restricting Emily from communicating with Mark if she wanted to. But whatever she was going to do, Chasity wished that she would just hurry up.

"We have to go Mark," Emily softly replied, much to Mark's disappointment, which showed on his face. It also didn't help Mark when Chasity busted out laughing at the look on his face.

Mark shook his head. "You are so fuckin' evil *Chasity*," he hissed.

"Yeah?" Chasity replied, nonchalant. "At least our friends still like *me*," she taunted as she and Emily walked away, leaving Mark to sulk.

Chapter 24

"A bunch of grown people looking for Easter eggs," Sidra quipped. "This should be interesting."

Josh chuckled, taking a sip of his canned soda. "Hilarious is more like it," he corrected.

Josh, Sidra, and a few others from the group had arrived at the football field nearly fifteen minutes prior. The field had been turned into a massive, colorful activities area. There were booths set up with refreshments, picnic tables and chairs, prize tables, and a DJ booth. Further down the field was a huge obstacle course, which housed thousands of hidden, colorfully painted eggs.

"This school never ceases to amaze me with the stuff that they do for us students," Alex gushed to Malajia, flyer in hand.

Malajia shot Alex an annoyed glance. "You hype as shit over some painted ass eggs," she sneered. "Easter *been* over."

"I *would* cuss you out right now, but I know that it's just misplaced anger," Alex commiserated, approaching Josh and Sidra.

"Ain't a damn thing misplaced," Malajia mumbled, pushing her hair over her shoulder. "I stand by what I said. You hype over eggs."

Sidra shook her head as she resisted the urge to giggle. "What's wrong Mel?" she asked, picking up on what Alex previously stated.

"Nothing's wr—"

"She misses Mark," Alex quickly cut in, interrupting Malajia's words.

"No, I *don't*," Malajia denied.

"Stop lying Simmons," Alex shot back. "It's okay if you miss him. No matter *how* much of an ass he is."

Malajia sucked her teeth, flagging Alex in the process. She hated to admit it, but Alex was right, she did miss Mark. "Whatever," she grumbled.

Sidra tilted her head, studying Malajia's pouty face. "Sweetie, you don't have to continue to give him the cold shoulder like the rest of us," she assured. "If you want to start being nice to him again, then do that."

"Ain't nobody thinking about no damn Mark," Malajia dismissed. "I already told y'all, I'm good with what we're doing."

Sidra looked at Josh, who was busy watching the commotion from other students in front of him. "Speaking of Mark, has he apologized to David yet?" she asked him.

Josh shook his head. "Nope," he answered. "I honestly don't believe that he feels that he's wrong."

"Well, that's a shame," Sidra sighed. "He needs to own up to his mess."

"This is *Mark* we're talking about." Josh pointed out. "Has he *ever* owned up to anything?"

Sidra thought on that for a moment. "Nope," she replied.

The side conversation was put on hold as their remaining friends showed up. "Happy egg hunt day!" Alex exclaimed, holding her arms up with excitement.

"Shut your dumb ass up," Chasity sneered, inciting a snicker from Jason and Malajia.

Alex was appalled by the attitudes around her. "Now what's *your* problem?" she directed to Chasity. Chasity in turn just made a face. "Come on guys, it's a beautiful day.

Spring break is in a week, and we're at another fun event on our beautiful campus. Stop being so damn miserable," she chastised.

Chasity stared at her for several seconds in silence. "Are you done?"

"For now," Alex relented.

"Mark was standing outside the door again," Emily informed, scratching her head. "Scared us half to death."

"I swear, all the time he spends standing around waiting for us to interact with him, he could be figuring out how to apologize to David," Sidra fussed, tying the laces on her blue sneakers.

"I don't even *want* an apology at this point," David cut in, pushing the glasses up on his nose. "I'm just over it."

"Can we talk about something *else* please?" Malajia bit out.

"I'm with that," Alex smiled, holding up the flyer in her hand. She then began to read it. "Okay so they hid *thousands* of eggs—"

"Wasting all those damn eggs," Malajia griped. "What if I wanted an omelet later at dinner? I can't have one 'cause they used all the eggs."

Alex rolled her eyes at the interruption. "Anyway," she said, going back to her reading. "They give us a half hour to find all the eggs that we can, then we have to run through an obstacle course while trying to keep all of the eggs in the basket—"

"I'm not running with a basket full of eggs," Chasity refused.

"Can I just *finish*?!" Alex erupted. "Hold your negative remarks until I'm done, cranky and whiney."

Malajia pointed to Chasity. "Is she whiney?" she teased, relishing Alex's frustration.

"No, that would be *you*," Chasity retorted.

Jason chuckled at the tight jawed look on Alex's face. "Alright you two, let Alex finish before her head explodes," he joked.

"Thanks Jason," Alex replied. "Anyway, the people who have the most eggs after the hunt go to the obstacle course round," she read, then smiled. "Ooh, the first three people to reach the finish line win a cash prize."

This revelation made Malajia perk up. "Cash?" she beamed. "Oh I'm on that. Come on, let's go get these eggs," she urged, making her way towards the registration booth.

Emily giggled. "What about your omelets?"

"Fuck those omelets," Malajia threw over her shoulder.

Malajia gripped her red basket tightly while listening for the countdown over the loud speaker. Jason laughed at the intensity on Malajia's face and in her stance.

"Mel, why are you posed like you're about to run a race?" he asked.

"'Cause, y'all think I'm playing," Malajia boasted, staring intently at a fellow contender. "I'm winning that money."

"Malajia, don't go overboard," Sidra warned, adjusting the bracelet on her wrist. "You know how you get when you're in competition mode."

Malajia shot Sidra a side-glance. "Just because you wore sneakers today doesn't mean that you can comment about my competitive nature," she spat much to Sidra's confusion.

"What does my sneakers have—"

"One! He said one. Stop talking to me!" Malajia bellowed, interrupting Sidra's question, Malajia took off sprinting, along with every other student in the area.

The field was filled with noise as students rushed to fill their colorful baskets with hidden eggs. "Shit! I stepped on one!" Chasity fumed, examining the damage done to her black and white sneakers by the broken egg.

Alex, who was close by, fought the urge to laugh as she dug through artificial shrubs to grab some eggs. Just as she got hold of one, she felt a hand close over top of hers. "What the hell?" she said, craning her neck around the shrub to see

Malajia staring at her with intensity in her eyes. "Malajia, you *clearly* saw that I grabbed it first," she hissed as both girls held on to the egg.

"That don't mean shit, I'm getting this damn egg," Malajia promised, tugging Alex's arm.

Alex frowned, pulling back and jerking Malajia's forward in the process. "Don't make me hurt you," Alex warned. "I need that money."

"It's not like you're gonna get a new *phone* with it," Malajia shot back. She then began trying to pry the egg out of Alex's grip with her other hand. "Give it to me," she demanded, teeth clenched. When Alex didn't relent, Malajia pulled Alex's hand up to her mouth and placed her teeth on it.

Alex quickly jerked away, dropping the egg in the process. "Did you really just bite me?!" she yelped, looking down at the small wet spot on her hand.

Malajia picked up the fallen egg and ran off, leaving Alex standing there in shock.

"Josh, can you just give me some of your eggs?" Sidra asked, laughter in her voice.

After searching for nearly ten minutes, Sidra had grown tired of digging around in the grass, hay, and shrubs for eggs. She'd already ruined her nails.

"No," Josh laughed back. "I almost took a few people out for these eggs." He himself knew how much he could use the prize money.

"I'm about to quit," Sidra huffed, examining the grass stains on her jeans and sneakers. "I'm too neat for this mess." She looked at Josh, who was eyeing a few eggs off to the side. "Here sweetie, you can have mine," Sidra offered, handing her pale blue basket of eggs to the smiling Josh.

"Thanks," he beamed reaching for the basket. Before he could grab it, Malajia darted pass, snatching the basket from under him. She bumped into both Sidra and Josh in the process, sending Sidra falling to the ground, along with a few eggs.

Sidra let out a little squeal. "Goddamn it, Malajia!" she screamed, rubbing her butt where she fell.

"She plays too much," Josh fumed. He thought about helping Sidra off of the ground, but then realized that Malajia was running down the field with his eggs. He took off running after her, much to Sidra's shock.

"Seriously Joshua?!" she yelled after him as she stood up.

"Sorry!" he yelled back, continued to gain on Malajia.

Malajia looked behind her and saw that she had a good enough lead on Josh. As she turned back around with a satisfied smile on her face, she bumped into Chasity who was searching nearby, knocking herself off her stride.

"Bitch," Malajia fumed, frantically trying to catch the eggs that were tumbling out of her baskets. "You fuckin' up my progress."

"Your hype ass just bumped into *me*," Chasity snarled at her, throwing some eggs into her black basket. "Idiot."

Malajia was about to fire off a smart retort, but she became nervous when she saw Josh run up to her. She quickly tried to retrieve the eggs from the ground, just as Josh kneeled down to grab them.

"No Josh! No," Malajia screamed, trying to slap his hands away.

"Sidra gave those to *me*," Josh argued, teeth clenched as he tried to move Malajia's hand out of the way.

"Your name ain't on them," Malajia shot back, trying to bite one of Josh's fingers. Horrified at what Malajia was trying to do, Josh put his hand on Malajia's face and began pushing her away from his hand.

Chasity stared at the commotion in disbelief. "You two look fuckin' stupid," she spat, folding her arms.

"Screw you and your dirty ass sneakers," Malajia shot back, grabbing a free egg.

Chasity narrowed her eyes at Malajia before lifting her foot and stepping on an egg that Malajia was reaching for. Furious, Malajia hopped up from the ground and got in

Chasity's face. "That was some ignorant shit," Malajia fumed. Chasity just stared at her, calm. "You messin' me up. I want that money."

"How much could it possibly *be*?" Chasity replied. "You're out here biting people for what, twenty dollars?"

"It's more than I have *now*, you ass," Malajia fumed. "You shouldn't even be *playing*. You don't even *want* the prize money."

Chasity just smirked, but didn't say anything.

Realizing that she was taking way too much time arguing with Chasity, Malajia spun around to see Josh running off with all of her eggs.

"Thanks for the distraction, Chaz," Josh threw over his shoulder.

Malajia stomped her foot on the ground in frustration. "Ooh I am *seriously* reevaluating your best friend status when this is over," Malajia fussed to Chasity, then tried to smack the basket from her hands. Malajia sucked her teeth when the basket didn't fall. "Firm ass grip," she huffed, then took off after Josh.

Once the half hour of egg searching was up, a quick weighing of the baskets determined who was allowed to move to the obstacle round. The hunt eliminated Sidra, David, and Emily.

"That's messed up what you did to Em, Malajia," Alex seethed, staring daggers at Malajia who was jumping up and down, getting mentally prepared for the course. "She would've made it to this round if you hadn't stepped on her foot and caused all of her eggs to fall at the last minute."

"I love Em to death, but she was in my damn way," Malajia replied, lacking remorse. "Jogging all slow and shit with that short ass ponytail."

Josh shook his head. "You're on one hundred today Mel," he commented. "You sacrificed your friends for a few bucks. I'd hate to see what you would do for *real* money."

Malajia shot him a shocked look. "How am *I* on a hundred? All I did was step on Emily's slow ass foot," she argued.

"You bit *me*," Alex reminded, voice dripping with disdain.

"You *almost* bit *me*," Josh added.

Malajia sucked her teeth, "Okay, so *maybe* that happened, but how is David and Sidra being out *my* fault?" she asked, putting her hand up. "Sid quit and David didn't have enough eggs."

When Josh and Alex fell silent, Malajia felt that her point was proven, but she rambled on as other course participants took their places in line.

"Y'all coming down on *me*, but *Jason* tackled hoagie-head Stu and stole his eggs," Malajia grumbled.

"I want y'all to stop calling that boy, hoagie-head Stu," Alex slid in, fighting to suppress her laughter.

"I didn't tackle him, I bumped *into* him," Jason clarified.

"Yeah, with that strong ass shoulder of yours," Malajia pointed out. She looked at Chasity "Chasity, did you or did you *not* give Josh's girl a bloody nose?"

"Hey, that was an *accident*," Chasity argued, smoothing some hair away from her face. "Her face collided with my wrist when she tried to grab an egg that I was reaching for."

Josh side-eyed Chasity. "Is that so?" he sneered.

"That's my story and I'm sticking to it," Chasity replied.

"She was bleeding pretty badly, Chasity," Josh pressed.

"Then leave *me* alone and go tend to her," Chasity threw back, exasperated. Josh rolled his eyes.

"Everybody shut up," Alex commanded, waving her hand. "They're doing the countdown."

Once the announcer said the word "go," the competing students took off running for the first set of obstacles. The amount of eggs that had fallen out of everyone's basket as they ran the course was insurmountable.

Josh tried to run up an inflatable slide while holding onto

a rope, but lost his footing, sending him and his eggs tumbling back down. Malajia busted out laughing in passing when she saw Josh land on several of his eggs, leaving remnants on his shirt and jeans.

"You salty!" Malajia screamed at him, laughter still filling her voice.

Chasity jumped off the slide, managing to save several of her painted eggs. She ran towards another course consisting of large plastic pipes filled with washable paint, which students had to crawl through.

Realizing that she'd had enough of this course, Chasity stopped running; getting paint in her hair wasn't something that she felt like dealing with. As she turned to walk off, she was greeted by a strong bump to her chest, sending her and her basket to the ground.

She looked up to see one of Jason's teammates standing over her. "You hype as shit, Carl!" she yelled, clutching her chest with her hand.

"My bad Chasity," the tall, muscular player apologized. "But your eggs are mine now," he taunted.

Chasity rolled her eyes, rubbing her chest in the process. As she slowly picked herself up, she saw an angry Jason, running in her direction. She had a feeling that he'd seen what happened. Knowing how protective Jason was over her, Chasity was certain that he was coming over to take a swing at his teammate.

"Carl, you better run," she calmly stated.

Carl, spinning around to see Jason's angry approach, did as she said and took off crawling into one of the pipes.

Before Jason could grab Carl's leg, Chasity grabbed his arm and gestured for him to get up. "Jase, chill, I'm fine," she assured.

"I'll kick the shit outta him," Jason promised. "Just say the word."

Chasity couldn't help but chuckle. "Yes, I know."

Jason took a deep breath. "I threw my basket when I was running over here," he sulked.

Chasity busted out laughing. "Let's get out of here," she suggested.

"Gladly," Jason agreed.

Malajia managed to beat out many opponents while still managing to hold on to several eggs. She was heading for the finish line when she looked over and saw Alex, who was neck and neck with her.

"You ain't winning this, you nappy rag doll!" Malajia taunted. Just as she was about to pass the line, she tripped over her own foot, sending her falling to the ground, screaming.

Seizing the opportunity, Alex crossed the finish line.

"Nooooo!" Malajia screamed as Alex began jumping up and down, rejoicing.

"You lost!" Alex boasted, pointing to her. "That's what your cheating butt gets."

"How the *hell* did your fat ass catch up to me?" Malajia fumed, wiping her egg and grass-soiled hand on her black tights.

Unfazed by Malajia's comments or attitude, Alex continued to celebrate her victory

Malajia, exhausted and defeated, laid flat out on the ground.

Chapter 25

Mark drummed his fingers slowly on the girls' dining room table, waiting for someone to return.

He was furious. The Easter egg hunt was the day before. He'd gone to the field alone and stood on the sidelines, watching his friends compete. He was hurt that they didn't invite him to come along.

He'd spent all night seething about it, hoping that when he awoke the next day, he'd be over it. But he wasn't. That was the last straw.

Mark walked over to the girls' house that afternoon. He walked in to find it empty. Instead of leaving, he decided to sit there, and wait. That was nearly two hours ago. The drumming stopped once he heard the door knob turn. He slowly turned his head and stared at the door, waiting for it to open.

"So, I told Dr. Foster that I wasn't taking no damn—" Malajia's words to Chasity and Sidra stopped when the three girls screamed at the sight of him sitting there.

"What are you *doing* in here, you damn creep?!" Malajia hollered, angry.

"Y'all should really learn to lock your door when nobody's home," Mark calmly advised.

Sidra folded her arms. "Noted," she bit out. "Why are you here? You're not welcome, remember?"

"Oh trust me, I remember just fine," Mark seethed. "But obviously I don't *give* a goddamn. I got a bone to pick."

"Mark, get out," Chasity ordered, fed up with his nonsense already.

"I'm not going a *damn* step," Mark refused, folding his arms.

The girls stared at him as if he had completely lost his mind.

"Now—" he paused when the door opened yet again. "Ah, the rest of the two-faced bunch are here," he scoffed, rising from his seat.

Alex and Emily walked into the house, stunned. "What the hell?" Alex commented.

"His ass was sitting in here when we got in," Chasity spat. "*Somebody* left the door unlocked when we left earlier."

The girls looked at Malajia, who was trying to avoid their gazes. "What? I was in a rush earlier and forgot to lock it," she explained.

"*Whatever* the reason, you shouldn't be here," Alex directed to Mark.

"I'll leave when I'm done," Mark spat, holding his hand out. "Where are the guys? I know they aren't far behind."

Before anyone could say anything, the three aforementioned men walked through the door. "Well, well. If it isn't the punks of Paradise Valley," Mark taunted.

"Yo, who are you calling a punk?" Jason questioned, walking aggressively towards Mark. His progress was stopped by Josh, who put his arm out to block Jason.

"Jase, don't feed into that mess," Josh urged. "He's trying to get a reaction out of you."

"Yeah well, he's damn sure about to get his wish," Jason seethed, pointing at an equally angry Mark.

"Whatever *bro*," Mark shot back nastily.

"Yeah whatever," Jason retorted.

"Okay calm down," Alex slid in, looking back and forth

between the two hostile men. "There will be no more fighting in here."

"What do you want, Mark?" David asked. He wasn't in the mood to engage in any conversation with Mark. But it was clear that Mark being there was riling everyone up; he figured that the quicker he could get to the bottom of why Mark was there, the quicker he would leave.

Mark stared at his friends in silence for several seconds. They glanced at each other.

"Are you gonna *speak*, or stand there looking like a damn fool all day?" Chasity ground out.

Mark narrowed his eyes at her. "So... Y'all just gonna stand here and pretend like you didn't go to the Easter egg thing yesterday without me?" he began.

"*That's* what this is about?" Malajia wondered, irritated. "Some damn egg hunt?"

"And we're not pretending *anything*," Jason bit out. "We went without you on *purpose*."

"That's fucked up. You already knew I would've wanted to go," Mark shot back.

"Mark, we're not liking you right now," Sidra pointed out. "Why would we have asked you to go with us? That makes no sense."

Mark shook his head. "Treating me like shit isn't cool," he seethed. "And frankly, I'm fuckin' tired of it."

"Do you know *why* though?" Josh asked.

"Yeah, because you're still mad about the fight that me and David had," Mark said. "I can't believe everybody is still girlin' about that."

"Dude, we didn't just have a *fight*. You purposely set out to *humiliate* me," David jumped in. "Then had the *audacity* to think that you weren't wrong."

"You didn't even offer a damn *apology*," Sidra added. "You basically just told him to get over it because you were just doing what you *normally* do."

Mark tossed his hands up in the air in frustration. "So this is about a fuckin' apology?" he barked. "Is David's whining affecting you *that* much?"

"You're such an asshole," Alex scoffed. Mark's blatant ability to not own up to any wrong doing disgusted her.

"You know what Mark, I don't even *want* an apology anymore," David assured, putting his hand up. "I'm good. Like I said before, we're done."

"It's clear that that's a damn lie," Mark spat. "So if that's what I have to do in order to stop being treated like a bald-headed stepchild, then fine." He directed his attention to David. "David, I'm sorry if you felt—"

"I'm sorry, repeat what you just said," David angrily commanded.

"I'm sorry if you—"

"Say that one more time," David repeated.

Mark was visibly irritated. He took a deep breath to keep himself from snapping. "I'm sorry if—"

"*That's* the issue right there," David pointed out, much to Mark's anger.

"What the fuck are you talking about?!" Mark yelled, fed up.

"You keep saying 'if'," David said. "There is no *if*. You *did*. You, someone who is supposed to be my friend, blatantly humiliated me for your own amusement. You *still* don't get that." Mark rolled his eyes as David continued to speak. "You still don't get how messed up that was."

Mark rubbed his face in frustration as he tried to register the harsh words that were being hurled at him. His character was being attacked and it was making his blood boil.

Malajia looked at him; her friends had gone in on him and their words clearly weren't getting through. She figured it was time to speak up. "Mark," she began, voice soft.

Mark's head snapped towards her. "Oh *now* you wanna talk to me, huh?" he bit out.

Malajia shot him a glare. "I'm trying to *help* your stubborn ass."

Mark just flagged her with his hand. At that point, he wasn't interested in what she had to say. As far as he was concerned, Malajia had her chance to stand up for him in the beginning and didn't.

"Look," Malajia continued. "We're not mad at you because you had a fight with David. We fight and argue all the time. That's what family does," she said. "The *problem* lies in the fact that you refuse to own up to any wrong doing... You keep using that bullshit defense of 'y'all know how I am.' That's not cool, Mark."

Mark stared at her, taking a deep breath. "All of the fights that you all have had," he began slowly. "Has never resulted in the entire group not speaking to one person," he pointed out. "How is that fair?"

"I just *told* you why we're upset with you!" Malajia snapped.

She desperately wanted to get through to him. She hated that Mark was hurting, but he needed to see where they were coming from.

"You show *no* remorse," Malajia fumed. "You can't expect people to get past something that you've done, if you can't even acknowledge the wrong that you did."

Mark was quiet as Malajia continued.

"Us girls have said some fucked up shit to each other over the years," she remembered. "I mean some straight 'cross-the-line' shit." She pointed to Chasity. "Hell, me and this girl over here came to *blows*... But we owned up to what we did and we apologized from the heart and we forgave each other... You have to own up to your wrong doing babe. You *have* to. That is the only way to fix this."

Mark refused to speak for a moment. "You know what's fucked up?" he began, rubbing the back of his neck. "You guys were so quick to dismiss *me* for a prank. But...you're so quick to forgive each other over more damaging shit."

Malajia put her hand over her forehead. He hadn't listened to a word that she'd said. Alex, sensing that Malajia was getting upset, reached out and rubbed her shoulder.

"You *still* don't get it," Josh hissed. "Even after everything that we just stood here and said to you."

"Oh I get it just *fine*," Mark assured, not hiding his disdain. "You guys weren't my friends in the *first* place if you could just cut me out without thinking twice. So fuck y'all."

"Oh really?" Sidra challenged.

"Yeah *really*," Mark shot back. "Less you forget, I've been an only child all my life, so I'm *used* to being by myself," he reminded. "I don't need y'all. So keep your damn lectures."

Malajia turned away from Mark as he made his way out of the house. She jumped when the door slammed. "God, he's so fuckin' stubborn," she ground out, putting her hands over her face.

"Wow…just wow," Emily commented. She looked at Malajia, "Are you okay?"

Malajia nodded, but didn't say anything.

Jason ran his hands over the back of his neck. This whole confrontation drained him. "Look, he's a grown man and he needs to start acting like it," he sternly said. "Once he pulls his head out his ass, I'm sure he'll see the error in his ways. Until then, he can be by himself."

"I agree," Josh said, giving a visibly upset David a pat on his shoulder.

"I feel bad for *you*, Jase," Alex sympathized. "I know things have been awkward since you and Mark are roommates."

"Trust me, I have no problem ignoring Mark," Jason assured, folding his arms.

Mark let out a loud sigh as he gathered his belongings and rose from his desk. *I'm so sick of this dumbass Advanced Accounting class*, he fumed to himself.

"Mr. Johnson," his professor called just as Mark passed his desk.

Rolling his eyes, Mark turned around. "What's good, Professor Goodman?" he asked, not hiding his impatience.

Professor Goodman looked down through his glasses at Mark. "Excuse me?" he questioned.

"Sorry. Yes sir?" Mark amended.

"Why didn't you turn in your assignment?" Professor Goodman asked, shifting papers on his desk.

"I didn't finish it and I know you don't accept incomplete assignments… I'm sorry," Mark admitted. "I um…I have a lot on my mind." Being shut out from his friends had really taken a toll on the normally vibrant and infectious Mark.

"That's no excuse, Mr. Johnson."

Mark glanced at the floor.

"You're better than that," Professor Goodman continued. "You're an excellent student and I would hate to see you mess up the grade that you have because of personal problems."

Mark sighed; Professor Goodman was right. Despite what he portrayed, Mark was excelling in class. He would hate to slack now.

"You're right sir. I'll get it together," Mark promised.

"I sure hope *so*," Professor Goodman said.

Although the commotion around him was loud and vibrant, Mark's mood was the opposite. Normally around this time, he would be meeting his friends to go to eat, watch a movie, or just hang out. Instead, he was moseying through campus alone, watching other groups laughing and playing like his group did.

Walking up a path, he saw Malajia sitting on a bench outside of the math building, looking at her phone. He stood there from a far, just watching her. He wanted to walk over and sit next to her, hug her, talk to her, laugh at whatever she was laughing at. *Naw, things are too messed up right now,* was the thought that swirled in his head. Instead of doing what he *wanted* to do, he headed off in the other direction.

His lonely journey took him to the campus post office.

Walking over to his mailbox, he came face to face with someone that he knew.

"Yo Mark, what's good man?" the guy cheerfully greeted.

Nothing. Nothing is good right now. Mark just forced a smile in an effort to hide his true feelings. "Chillin' Rus," he replied. "Did y'all play ball today?" Russel was one of the people he normally played basketball with at the gym.

"Yeah, earlier," he replied. "I'm surprised you didn't come play. Come to think of it, I haven't seen you at the gym in almost two weeks."

"Yeah well, I've been busy studying," Mark deflected.

Knowing that Mark had a reputation for slacking, Russel laughed. "Yeah, that's funny man," he teased.

Mark shook his head as he proceeded to open his mailbox. Pulling out a larger envelope, he frowned. "What the hell is *this*?" he mumbled. Seeing that it was from his mother, Mark shrugged.

"Oh, one more thing Mark," Russel said.

Mark, back towards him, rolled his eyes. *This dude talks too damn much.* "What is it?"

"Are things with you and Malajia cool?"

Mark spun around, scowling. "What would make you ask me that?"

Russel shrugged as he adjusted the book bag on his shoulder. "You know this campus is small."

"*And*?" Mark bit out.

"I haven't seen y'all hanging out lately, so I was just wondering."

"You seem to be noticing a lot of shit about me, cuz," Mark ground out, holding his frown. "What's your reason for asking me about Malajia?"

"I was thinking that if you weren't together anymore, that maybe...*I* could ask her out."

Mark stared at him in silence for several seconds. "Fool I'll kill you," he sneered, earning a chuckle from Russel.

He put his hands up in surrender. "No disrespect, always

thought she was cute, just wanted to check," he said.

"How you gonna say 'no disrespect' when you're tryna holler at my girl?" Mark bristled.

Russel shrugged. "I only asked 'cause I—"

"Get your stupid ass away from me," Mark hissed, sending him on his way. "Disrespectful mutha—" he mumbled, glaring at Russel's departing back. Shaking his head, he stuffed the envelope into his book bag and walked out of the post office.

Chapter 26

"You still sitting here?" Sidra asked Malajia as she approached her bench.

"Obviously," Malajia sneered.

Sitting next to her, Sidra sucked her teeth. "Eww, cranky."

Placing her phone in her bag, Malajia looked up at Sidra. "I didn't mean to be bitchy," she apologized.

"It's fine," Sidra said. "What's wrong?" she asked, noticing the sullen look on Malajia's face. "You still feeling bad about what's going on with Mark?"

"Yeah," Malajia sighed. "I saw him a few minutes ago," she revealed. "He was standing over there staring at me, looking like a sad puppy."

"Did he see you?"

Malajia shook her head. "I happened to look up real quick when he *wasn't* looking."

Sidra fussed with the silver hoop earring in one of her ears. "I know this is hard on you sweetie. It's hard on *me* too… On *all* of us," she assured. "Mark is like a brother to me and I love him to death. But, we can't keep allowing him to think that what he's been doing is okay. What kind of friends would we be if we didn't call him out on his bullshit?"

"I don't disagree with you Sid. Trust me, I don't," Malajia said. "But...and don't tell him this, but it's really killing me to see him this...broken," she sulked. "Contrary to what he may think, I truly care for him and I just want things to be back to normal...well, *better*."

Malajia sighed. Part of what was bothering her about this situation was that she had lectured Mark on owning up to his mistakes and making amends, yet she still wasn't owning up to hers. How could she lecture *him* when *she* was keeping a huge secret from him?

"I miss him," Malajia pouted.

Sidra put her arm around Malajia to comfort her. "I know you do. And things will get better," she promised. "I have faith in him."

Malajia just smiled slightly. "I'll tell you *one* thing," she began. "If you had told me years ago that I would actually be sitting here talking about how much I miss some damn Mark..." Sidra busted out laughing. "I would've told you to jump in traffic."

Sidra playfully tapped Malajia on the arm. "You're so silly."

"I hate these dry ass shows at this damn school," Mark complained, flipping through the channels with the remote control. After returning from the post office earlier that afternoon, Mark fixed himself a quick lunch and ate in his room. The house was quiet; he didn't like it. Not having anything to do, or anywhere to go, he elected to take a nap. But sleep just wasn't happening with all that was on his mind.

After searching through channels and not finding anything worth watching, Mark turned the TV off and tossed the remote on the floor. Remembering that he had a letter from his mother, he grabbed his book bag from the floor and pulled the piece of mail out.

I hope its money, he thought, ripping the top off the

envelope. He frowned slightly as he pulled the contents from the envelope. It was pictures: pictures of him, Sidra, Josh and David over the years.

Not sure what to think, he grabbed his cell phone from his pocket and dialed home. "Hey Mom," he said once the line picked up.

"Hey baby, did you get the mail that I sent you?" Mrs. Johnson cheerfully asked.

"Yeah," he replied. "Um…what's up with all the pictures?"

"Oh, your father and I are in the process of cleaning out the basement. And I found all of these pictures of you guys," she informed. "I thought that maybe you would want to show those to them or even give them some."

Mark was silent as he flipped through the pictures. "Oh okay," he responded flatly.

"So? How is everything?" she asked, eager to get a more vibrant reaction from her son. "I haven't spoken to you in a while."

"I know. Things are fine," he replied evenly.

"You sound funny," Mrs. Johnson observed. "Are you okay?"

"Yeah, why do you ask?"

"Because you're my child and I can sense when something is off with you," she stated. "Normally you're being loud, cracking jokes or acting like a smart ass… You sound sad right now."

Mark rubbed his eyes with his fingers. His mother always had a knack for knowing when he was hiding something. "I'm just going through something right now," he admitted. "But don't worry about it. I'll be fine."

"Mark, you can't tell me that you're going through something, then in the same breath, tell me not to worry," Mrs. Johnson replied, sternly.

Good point, Mark admitted to himself.

"You might as well tell me what's going on," she insisted. "You didn't get anybody pregnant, did you?"

"No, nothing like that," he promised.

"You flunk a class?" she pressed, sternness in her voice.

"Surprisingly *no*," he chuckled.

"Well? What's going on?"

Mark let out a long sigh. He contemplated not telling his mother about what he was dealing with, but realized that he really did want to talk to someone about it. "My friends aren't too happy with me right now," he confessed finally.

"Oh? Well what did you do?" Mrs. Johnson asked.

"Long story short, I played a really bad prank on David and I um... I embarrassed him. He's pretty hurt behind it," Mark revealed. "And everybody is attacking my character over it... It's pissing me off."

"Why would you *do* that to him?" she questioned, disappointment registering in her voice. "You always picked on that boy."

"Yeah, so I've been reminded," Mark spat. "Anyway, I don't know *why* I did it...I guess...I thought it would be funny. I mean I always do stupid stuff like that and people always found it funny."

"No, not all the time," she stated. "I've *always* told you that you take things too far sometimes. You're not stupid Mark, you *had* to know that what you did, *whatever* that was, wasn't going to sit right with David or any of the others."

Mark rolled his eyes as his mother spoke. He regretted telling her; now she was lecturing him too.

"Did you apologize?" she asked him.

Mark hesitated. "Not really... No," he stated finally.

He heard a loud sigh come through the phone. "And why *not*?" she hissed.

"I don't know," Mark muttered. "I've never been good at sentimental stuff. I just..." He let out a frustrated sigh. "Mom, they know how I am. And so do *you*."

"Just because someone knows how you are, doesn't mean that they're just supposed to sit back and take your bullshit," she chastised. His mother never hesitated in pulling any punches when it came to him.

Mark rubbed his eyes again with his fingertips. "I know," he sulked. Deep down, he knew that what his mother was saying and what his friends had said rang true, but his pride wouldn't let him admit it... Until now. "Mom, am I a bad person?"

She chuckled. "No baby, you're not," she promised. "You've always been silly and loud and *hyperactive*...and you've done some questionable things... But you were never bad."

"Yeah, that doesn't sound any better," he grunted.

His mother's soft laugh came through the phone. "Well, I wouldn't be doing you any favors if I didn't tell you the truth," she said. "And the same goes for your friends. If they continued to allow you to go through life at damn near twenty-two years old, still acting the same way you did when you were *twelve*, they wouldn't be considered real friends, now *would* they?"

Mark pondered his mother's words. He put his hand over his face as he leaned forward. "You're right," he sighed.

"You always wanted brothers and sisters and now you *have* them... Don't ruin your relationship with them because you refuse to grow up." Her words hit him like a ton of bricks, but he knew that she was right.

"Damn Mom, maybe I should call you more often," he joked.

"Yeah well, that would be nice," she joked in return. "Did you just say 'damn' to me?"

"No Ma'am." his lie was instantaneous.

She chuckled yet again. "Uh huh. Go be a man, sweetie."

"Love you," Mark replied.

"Love you too."

After disconnecting the call, Mark looked over at his desk. His eyes fixed on an eight by ten picture of him and his friends, taken after the paintball competition they'd won last semester. Remembering that fun time, and all the others,

Mark stood from his bed, grabbed his jacket off of the chair, and headed out the door.

Mark made the less than two-minute walk from his house to the girls' house. He stood on the front step and reached for the door knob, then decided to actually knock this time. Hearing voices from the inside, he patiently waited for someone to open the door. He chuckled to himself when he heard Malajia's loud voice approach the door.

She jerked the door open. "Hey," Malajia said, shock registering slightly in her voice. It'd been a few days since their intervention with Mark, and they hadn't spoken. Malajia was happy to see him, even though that feeling didn't register on her face.

"Hey," he returned. "Can I come in?"

Malajia, moved aside. "Yeah, sure," she said, allowing him room to pass her.

Mark stood at the door, looking at his friends, who had ceased their conversations. All eyes were on him. For the first time in a while, he felt nervous. "Is David here by any chance?"

"I think he's in the library," Josh informed.

Malajia took a seat at the dining room table. "He's probably gonna be in there for a while," she added. "He had to finish doing some project."

Mark nodded slightly. "Okay," he replied. "If you see him before I do, can you let him know that I'm looking for him?"

Once they confirmed that his message would be relayed, Mark turned to walk out of the door but paused suddenly, turning back around to face the group. "I just um... I just want to let you guys know that I heard what you said...and I get it," he said. By the looks that registered on their faces, he had just shocked his friends. "You're right about me and...I promise to do better." He then smiled, before walking out the door.

"Wow," Sidra replied, once the door closed. "Did he just do a grown-up thing and admit that we were *right*?"

Josh smiled. "Yep," he confirmed. Josh was proud; even though Mark didn't say it, he knew that he planned on making things right with David. He was actually being the person that Josh always knew that Mark *could* be.

Chasity glanced over at Malajia, who was sitting across from her smiling ear to ear, playing with a potato chip. "Malajia, put your cheeks down," she teased, earning that same chip that Malajia was playing with, to be thrown at her.

"Shut up," Malajia chortled, as Chasity laughed slightly.

David was focused on the words in his textbook. "Just two more chapters," he said to himself, rubbing his eyes. He'd been back from the library for nearly an hour and was tired of looking at books. Just as he turned the page, he heard a light knock on the door. "It's open," he called, not taking his eyes off his book.

"David, can I talk to you for a sec?" Mark asked, opening the door.

David glanced up. "I don't have time right now, Mark," he rebuffed.

Ignoring David's protest, Mark walked in the room. He'd heard David come in from the library earlier and decided to give him a little time before he approached him. "Just hear me out," Mark pleaded.

David sucked his teeth as he spun around in his chair. "You have five minutes."

Mark rubbed his hand over his head as he thought of how to begin. He decided to go from his heart. "David man...I'm sorry," he said point blank. "I didn't mean to hurt you. I was just being...I was being an idiot and a bad friend... I was wrong."

Hearing the sincerity in Mark's voice, David relaxed the frown. "Look, I'm not saying that you're not allowed to *ever* make a joke or play a prank." David clarified. "But you can't intentionally hurt people like that man, that's not cool."

"I get that now," Mark assured. "Trust me when I say that."

David just nodded. "Okay."

Mark paused for a few seconds before taking a deep breath. "I also want to apologize for bullying you when we were kids."

David put his hand up. "I shouldn't have brought that up," he cut in. "That was so long ago and I was just mad."

"No, you *should* have," Mark contradicted. "I never officially said that I was sorry, I kind of just *stopped*... I should've apologized *back then*," he added. "And you were also right about the fact that I should've been there for you the day that your mom died."

David just stared at Mark while he poured his heart out.

"I was being selfish and I wasn't there for you like a brother *should* be... You *are* my brother and I'm sorry man. Really."

David looked down at his book, pondering Mark's words. He smiled after moments of silence. "Apology accepted," he said, much to Mark's relief. "We're good," he confirmed, holding his hand out for Mark to shake.

"Cool," Mark breathed, shaking David's hand.

"That must've taken a lot out of you," David teased as Mark rubbed his hands on his face.

"You have *no* idea," Mark chuckled. "I'm not good with this stuff... It's a change."

"Yeah well, we *all* have to change sometimes," David said matter-of-factly.

Mark nodded. "True," he agreed. "You wanna grab a pizza? My treat."

David stood up from his chair. "Wow, *now* you're actually paying for something?" he laughed.

"Yeah well, I figured that's the *least* that I could do after everything," Mark said, as he opened the door. "You're not getting any soda though."

David laughed. "Welcome back brother," he mused,

following him out of the room.

Chapter 27

"I don't wanna go home," Malajia complained as she and Chasity walked out of the campus bookstore.

"Well, your parents are coming to pick you up tomorrow morning, so I suggest you get over it," Chasity replied, pushing hair behind her ears.

With classes over for the week, students were leaving campus for spring break. The campus was nearly desolate; the majority of the students had left the day before.

Malajia let out a long sigh as she and Chasity continued walking. "You don't understand, I *hate* being home," Malajia whined. "I swear, it's like they hold all of their yelling and criticizing in until I walk through the door." She moved hair out of her face. "I feel like they're *always* gonna see me as the problem child... Like I'm this annoying idiot with no substance."

"Maybe you *used* to be that way," Chasity began. "But—"

Malajia cut her eye at her. "You saying I was annoying?" she cut in, insulted.

Chasity looked at her. "Did I say used to be?" she quibbled. "Sorry, I meant to say still are." Malajia narrowed her eyes at Chasity. "Don't cut me off when I'm trying to be nice," Chasity ground out.

Malajia flagged Chasity with her hand. "Anyway," she dismissed. "I'm surprised my dad is actually *coming to get me*... He's still pissed at me."

The last time that Malajia had spoken to her father was when she called him, begging him for money to help pay for her abortion. Although he wasn't aware of what she really needed the money for, he was irritated with her nonetheless and had been giving her the silent treatment.

Chasity glanced over at her. "What did you do?"

"Something stupid," Malajia alluded. Having a thought, she smiled. "Hey, you know what?—"

"No," Chasity spat out, much to Malajia's surprise.

"Damn, can I get it *out* first, rude ass?" Malajia barked, frowning.

"You're not coming home with me," Chasity calmly refused.

Malajia sucked her teeth. "Fine, mind reader," she ground out. "Selfish."

Unfazed by Malajia's attitude, Chasity flagged her with her hand.

Malajia let out a huff as the girls walked into the house. "I guess I'll just suffer in that crowded house all week, even though *somebody* has like three extra rooms in *her* house," she bit out as Chasity opened her room door.

"You know I tuned you out a long time ago, right?" Chasity threw back, nonchalant.

"You just heard *that* so..." Malajia mumbled, folding her arms.

Chasity set her purse on her bed as she looked at Malajia. "Did you ever tell them about everything that you've gone through this past semester?" she asked.

Malajia shot Chasity a confused look as she sat down on a chair. That question was unexpected. "Why would I do *that*?"

Chasity returned Malajia's confused look with one of her own. "Um, maybe because they're your *family* and if they knew what you went through, they probably wouldn't be so damn hard on you," she proposed.

"*My* family wouldn't believe shit that I *say* to them," Malajia insisted. "They would just say, 'girl stop lying for attention'."

"I highly doubt that," Chasity replied.

"Yeah okay. You don't know them like I do," Malajia argued.

Chasity rolled her eyes. "Suit yourself."

"Say pumpkin, have *you* told your mom about your pregnancy?" Malajia questioned, staring at Chasity with a challenging look.

Chasity frowned at her. "Really?" she sneered.

Malajia held her same look. "Well?"

Chasity folded her arms. "No, I haven't," she answered through clenched teeth.

"And why *not*?" Malajia pressed.

Chasity sighed as she tried to think of a reason. "I don't know," she said after several seconds.

"See, now *I* don't get that," Malajia said. "Your mom is cool as shit, she's not gonna cuss you—"

"Oh, she *will*," Chasity cut in. "You think Trisha is soft when it comes to me. No, I'll hear it, trust me."

"Well…she'll do it out of love and because she only wants the best for you," Malajia reasoned.

"And you don't think *your* family wants what's best for *you*?" Chasity threw back.

Malajia looked down at her hands "I wouldn't say that, I guess," she said, voice low. "Look, I know that I should say something to them, I just…*can't*." Malajia gave a partial explanation for why she didn't want to tell her family. Sure, she felt that they might not believe her, but even if they did, Malajia truly felt that revealing her abuse to her family would make them ashamed of her. That terrified her, because she was already ashamed of her*self*.

"You okay?" Chasity asked, as Malajia sat there silent.

Malajia looked up at her. "Yeah," she lied, rising from her seat. "I'll be cool at home. I'll just call you guys all the time while I'm there and get on your nerves."

"By 'you guys' you mean just me, right?" Chasity asked, dreading the answer that she knew was going to come out of Malajia's mouth.

"Yep, exactly," Malajia confirmed, walking out of the room. Chasity just shook her head.

Sidra watched as Josh tossed a shirt into his duffle bag. "So, where are you going to stay this week?" she asked while he searched through his closet for more items.

"Probably Mark's house," Josh answered evenly. "David and his dad are going away camping for the week."

Sidra nodded silently as she looked down at her hands. "Are you going to go home at all?" she asked carefully.

Josh shot her a warning glance. "Sidra, don't start this."

"Sweetie, I'm not trying to start anything," Sidra assured. "I just—"

"Want to know if I'm gonna go home with *Sarah* being there?" Josh finished for her.

Sidra ignored Josh's nasty tone. "I just feel that you should really hear what she has to say," she persisted.

"Unless the words coming out of her mouth are 'Josh here's the tuition money that I stole from you,' I don't want to hear it," Josh spat, tossing a pair of jeans into his bag and zipping it with force.

Sidra ran her hand over her hair. She'd remembered the hurt, anger, and panic that went through Josh and his parents when Sarah stole her father's checkbook and wrote a check to herself for the money that their parents had saved up for Josh's partial tuition payment.

He had a partial first-year scholarship from his high school, but it didn't cover everything. They had saved enough so that Josh could afford to pay the rest. When Sarah ran off with the money just a month prior to Josh leaving for college, Josh and their parents did what they could to try to replace some of the funds. Josh nearly had to postpone his entry to Paradise Valley University.

"I know that your sister put you through a lot," Sidra slowly began. "I know that she hurt you Josh, but maybe...just *maybe* she's trying to make amends with you and your parents."

"I don't care," Josh hissed. "So when is the next time James is coming to see you?" he asked, changing the subject.

Sidra shook her head at Josh's efforts to avoid any conversation about his sister. Instead of pushing the issue, she allowed the new topic to take over. "Um, in a few weeks probably," she answered. "He's working on a big case."

"Oh okay," Josh said. In all honesty, he didn't want to talk about James either, but the topic was better than the alternative. "So, are things still good between you two?"

Sidra smiled. "Yeah, I guess. I don't have any complaints," she answered. "I would hope that *he* wouldn't have any."

"I doubt that he would," Josh assured. He then let out a sigh. "I'm sure he knows how lucky he is."

"Thanks," Sidra replied. "How are things with you and um...December?"

"Things are good," he replied, still packing.

Sidra just nodded slowly. "So is she considered your *girlfriend* or...."

"We're just hanging out for now," he answered. "Maybe one day, though."

Sidra once again nodded, but didn't respond. She didn't know why, but suddenly her mood changed. She felt...blah. Chalking it up to Josh's mood just rubbing off on her, Sidra held her gaze on him. "Are you going to call me while we're on break?" she asked.

"Sure, as long as you don't bring up my sister," he returned, zipping his other bag.

Sidra let out a huff. "I'm only trying—"

"Drop it," he sternly interrupted, grabbing his two bags from the floor. Sidra put her hands up in surrender. She would in fact, drop it. For now.

"Josh! Grab your shit, and come on. Let's hit the road before this nut ass traffic gets stupid," they heard Mark yell from downstairs.

"Always so damn loud," Sidra giggled of him.

Josh too laughed. "*That* part will never change," he assured, walking out of the room with Sidra following.

"Hurry up bee," Mark urged, hopping in his car. He started the engine. "I'm tryna see this campus in the rear-view mirror."

"Calm down, I'm ready," Josh chortled, nodding to David who was already in the car waiting. Once he placed his bags into the open trunk, he gave Sidra a hug. "Be safe on the road," he said.

"I will, you guys be careful too," Sidra responded, parting from their embrace.

"You know what I think, Em?" Malajia asked, leaning against Emily's room door.

"What's that?" Emily wondered, zipping her small suitcase up.

"I don't think your dad is going on a business trip. I think he has a little girlfriend and he's going to visit her," Malajia teased.

Emily giggled. "As much as I would love for my dad to have a girlfriend, he's really going on a business trip," she replied, running her hands over her head.

"Has your dad dated anybody since divorcing your mom?" Alex asked, pulling her covers up on her bed.

"I think he dated for a bit maybe a year or so after, but it was never anything serious," Emily answered, standing from the floor.

"Shit, does he like 'em young?" Malajia quipped. "Just let me know and I'll drop Mark's ass in a minute."

Emily picked up a small throw pillow from her chair and playfully tossed it at a laughing Malajia. "Cut it out."

"I'm just messing around," Malajia promised. "I'm

gonna miss you two with your boring selves," she said to Alex and Emily. "I almost wish I was going to Philly *with* y'all."

Alex, hearing that Emily would be home alone at her father's house due to him going on another one of his business trips, offered for Emily to spend spring break with her in Philadelphia.

"What? Chaz is banning you from *her* house this week?" Alex chortled.

"Girl, you already know it," Malajia confirmed.

Emily shook her head. "I'm sure you'll have a good time when you go home," she said.

"Did *you* ever enjoy going back home?" Malajia asked, voice dripping with disdain. "*Before* your dad's house."

Emily thought for a moment. "Um…no."

"Exactly," Malajia sneered.

Alex grabbed her bag from the floor. "Malajia, you need to finish getting your stuff together. You *do* remember that your dad called and told you he would be here in forty-five minutes, right?" she said. "That was an *hour* ago."

"Man fuck him," Malajia hissed, waving her hand dismissively at Alex.

Alex shook her head. "Fine, go ahead and get hollered at," she said before giving Malajia a hug. "We gotta go, Chaz is waiting for us."

"Yeah, I know," Malajia moped, walked down the steps with the girls. They made it down just in time to see Chasity walk back into the house.

"We're coming out now," Alex chuckled, putting her hand up.

"Huh?" Chasity said, confused.

"Weren't you coming back in here to get us?" Emily asked.

"Oh. No, I'm not thinking about y'all," Chasity dismissed with a wave of her hand as she headed towards her room. "I gotta pee."

"You're such a damn toddler," Malajia joked as Chasity

walked into her room. "As soon as you drink anything, you gotta pee."

"Shut up!" Chasity barked from inside her bathroom.

"Let me put this stuff in the car," Alex said, heading out the house with Emily. "I just want to get home and relax."

Malajia walked into the kitchen and rummaged through the cabinets as Chasity emerged from her room. "You all done, tinkles?" Malajia teased, opening a bag of chips that she pulled from the cabinet.

Chasity narrowed her eyes at Malajia, watching as she placed a chip into her mouth and began to chew. Chasity then craned her neck to see a familiar van pull in front of their house. "Your dad's here," she informed.

Malajia rolled her eyes, "Lyin' ass," she mumbled, glancing out the window. Her father's van was in fact out there, much to Malajia's horror. "Ooh!" Malajia exclaimed, tossing the open bag on the counter and sending several chips flying out of the bag, and onto the counter. Chasity snickered as Malajia ran up the steps, skipping two at a time. She knew that she would have to hear her father's mouth. "Bye!" Malajia yelled down the steps as Chasity opened the door.

"Bye," Chasity returned, then smiled as she saw Mr. Simmons walk to the door. "Hi. Malajia's not done packing," she told loud enough for Malajia to hear up the steps.

"Damn it Chasity! I hate you!" Malajia shrieked as Chasity laughed and walked out of the house.

"Malajia, I don't have time for this nonsense!" Mr. Simmons barked up the steps.

"Oh my Gooooood," Malajia groaned loudly, rummaging through her belongings.

Chapter 28

"Josh, it's so nice to have you staying with us for the week," Mrs. Johnson gushed, handing him a plate of breakfast food.

"I appreciate you letting me stay," Josh smiled, surveying the stack of homemade pancakes, bacon, and eggs piled on his plate.

"Mom, how you gonna serve *him* first?" Mark jeered, reaching for his glass of orange juice. He immediately regretted his question once his mother shot him a lethal look. "Um, I'm just gonna fix my own plate," he stammered, rising from his seat. "You want me to make you one?"

"Boy, sit down," Mrs. Johnson hissed, swatting Mark on the arm with a dish towel. "I'll get it."

Josh shook his head and chuckled as Mark rubbed his hands together in anticipation. "Keep messing with your mom, she's gonna choke you," Josh advised.

Mark flopped down on the chair. "You're probably right," he chortled.

As his mother sat his plate of food in front of him, Mark glanced at Josh, who was busy eating. "So um...are you gonna go see your dad anytime this week?" he asked.

Josh rolled his eyes. "Damn bro, it's only been a day. You kicking me out already?" he bit out.

"No," Mark calmly replied. "Your dad called my phone yesterday looking for you, so I was just asking."

"Look, Sidra already tried to talk me into seeing Sarah and it didn't work. So don't *you* start it," Josh hissed.

"I didn't even *mention* Sarah," Mark pointed out, cutting his pancakes into pieces. "You snappin' at me for no reason, bro."

He's right. "My bad," Josh apologized, before returning his focus to his plate.

"It's cool," Mark assured, reaching into his pocket. "Here, call your dad back," he urged, sliding his cell phone in front of Josh.

Josh looked at the phone for seconds before letting out a loud sigh. "Fine," he mumbled, grabbing the phone and pushing himself back from the table.

As Josh walked out of the kitchen, Mark looked around to see if anyone was looking before reaching over to grab some bacon from Josh's plate. "Keep your damn hands off my bacon Mark!" Josh yelled from the other room, startling Mark.

"He hype as shit," Mark grumbled to himself, dropping the two pieces of bacon back on to Josh's plate.

Josh dialed his home number and paced the living room floor, waiting for an answer. "Dad, you called?" he said, when his father picked up.

"Yes, I um…"

Josh frowned in concern when his father's voice trailed off. "Is something wrong?"

"I need you to come home tomorrow," he revealed, much to Josh's annoyance.

"And why is *that*, sir?" he asked, voice not masking his frustration.

"We got a new shipment of car parts today and I need for you to help me sort and label everything for inventory."

Josh sighed, frown leaving his face. He knew all too well about parts inventory at his father's car repairs shop. He'd helped him do it many times before. Josh knew the task was

daunting for his father, who was getting up there in age.
Lifting some of the parts would be easier handled by Josh,
who had the strength for it.

"No problem Dad. I'll be at the shop tomorrow
morning," Josh promised.

"I appreciate it," Mr. Hampton gratefully replied.

"Sure." Josh ended the call, and headed back for the
kitchen. He stepped through the entrance just in time to see
Mark holding a piece of Josh's bacon up to his mouth.
"Dude!" he exclaimed.

Mark looked at him, eyes wide. "Oh my bad, I didn't
think you was coming back," he lied.

Josh sucked his teeth as he examined his plate. "You ate
it *all?*"

"I said, I thought you left," Mark explained, fighting the
urge to laugh.

"You play too much," Josh jeered, smacking Mark on
the back of the head as he went back to his seat.

"If y'all don't leave me alone, I'm gonna lock both of
you in the basement," Malajia fumed, shoving her little
sisters away from her. "And you *know* the ghost lives down
there."

"Ghost?! Nooooo," eight-year-old Taina screamed,
running towards the kitchen.

Malajia rolled her eyes at the exaggeration. She'd come
downstairs nearly an hour ago to watch television. Not
surprisingly, her sisters started bothering her as soon as she
flopped on the couch.

"Malajia, there is no such thing as ghosts," Dana
sneered, clicking the buttons on her tablet.

Malajia cut her eye at her. "How do *you* know?"

"Because, I looked it up online, on my tablet."

Malajia sucked her teeth. "Why do you have a damn
tablet anyway?" she asked, annoyed. "Aren't you like five?"

"I'm *twelve*," Dana corrected, making a face at her big

sister.

"Okay I don't care, bored with you, go away," Malajia scoffed, flagging her hand dismissively.

Dana flipped her long braids over her shoulder before grabbing the remote and running out of the living room. "Ha ha, you gotta get up to change the channel," she teased, mid-run.

Malajia, too tired to do anything, just let out a loud sigh. "Mini heffa," she mumbled to herself. She looked up when she saw her mother walk through the front door. "And where were *you*, lady?" Malajia quipped.

Mrs. Simmons shot her daughter a warning look. "I was minding my business, *girl*," she shot back. "Where are your sisters?" she asked, sitting down on the couch next to Malajia.

"Running around here somewhere," Malajia solemnly replied. "Oh and thanks for leaving me to look after them as always," she jeered. "That four-year-old of yours screamed for like an *hour* 'cause I told her to take a nap."

A chuckle erupted from Mrs. Simmons. "Yeah well, that's what four-year-olds do," she concluded. "Like I always said, wait as long as possible before you have children," she said, unaware of the thoughts that she was stirring up.

Malajia looked down at her hands. Her mother's words triggered her thoughts about her secret abortion. As much as Malajia tried to put the thoughts about that and her relationship with Tyrone out of her mind, she couldn't seem to escape them. "Yeah," she mumbled.

Mrs. Simmons studied the sullen look on Malajia's face. "Shouldn't you be out getting on somebody's nerves?" she joked.

Malajia rolled her eyes. "Why Mom, am I getting on *yours*?"

"Malajia, don't be sensitive," Mrs. Simmons shot back. "You're always complaining that you're bored, but you never go and do anything."

"I have no car and my friends don't live near here,"

Malajia answered evenly.

"What about your boyfriend... What's his name? Tyrone or something like that?"

Malajia pinched the bridge of her nose in frustration. "Mom, I'm not dating him anymore," she ground out. "I could've *sworn* I told you that when you asked about him on New Year's."

"I don't recall," Mrs. Simmons replied, looking at the ceiling.

"Of *course* you don't," Malajia muttered.

"Okay, *sorry*," her mother replied defensively, "you have no idea how hard it is to keep up with you girls' lives. If I forget something, you can't fault me for it."

"Mom, it's always stuff about *me* that you forget," Malajia argued.

"That's not true."

Malajia just looked at her mother; she really was clueless. Arguing about this was pointless as far as Malajia was concerned. "Whatever you say, Mom," she relented.

Mrs. Simmons, unaware of what Malajia was feeling, simply patted her daughter on her knee then rose from the couch. "I'm about to make lunch. You want something?"

I want you to stop treating me like an afterthought. "No, I'm not hungry," Malajia answered as her mother disappeared into the kitchen.

Completely over the house and its occupants, Malajia stood up from the couch, grabbed her jacket from the coat rack, and walked out the front door.

Chasity stared at the number flashing on her phone screen for several seconds, before sending it to voicemail. *I thought I blocked you, bastard.* Her inner seething was interrupted by Trisha's voice.

"I'm so glad that designer shop finally got the new line in," Trisha gushed, looping her arm through Chasity's as they casually strolled through the crowded streets of New York

City. "I've been waiting for it to come out ever since I saw the fashion show."

Chasity was silent. Even though she was enjoying the trip to New York, and the time that she was spending with Trisha, she couldn't hide the fact that she had other things on her mind.

Trisha, noticing Chasity's somber mood, looked at her. "Is something the matter?"

"No, I'm fine," Chasity answered.

Trisha shook her head, unconvinced. "Chasity, don't do this," she warned. "Obviously something is bothering you. Who called you just now?"

Letting out a loud sigh, Chasity pushed some of her hair out of her face. "It doesn't matter."

Trisha was silent for a moment as she tried to keep from getting upset at her stubborn daughter. "Was it your father?" she asked.

Chasity stopped walking and looked at Trisha. "Where did *that* come from?" she bit out.

Trisha turned around and met Chasity's confused gaze. "Well? *Was* it?" she pressed, folding her arms.

"Yeah it *was*, but the bigger question is, why would you ask me that?" Chasity spat.

Trisha sighed. "He told me that he's been trying to call you," she revealed.

"Did he *also* tell you that I told him to *stop*?"

"Yes, he told me that *too*," Trisha replied. "I think you should talk to him."

Chasity looked at her mother as if she had lost her mind. "You must be crazy," she concluded.

"Just hear him out."

"You *must* be crazy," Chasity reiterated. "No. Screw him."

"He misses you, Chasity," Trisha said.

"Bullshit," Chasity bit out. "What's his *real* reason? What's wrong with him, is he dying or something? Does he need an organ from me?"

Trisha shook her head at Chasity's sarcastic tone. "Sometimes in life…you have to give people the chance to make amends," she stated.

Chasity rolled her eyes. "If you don't *hurt* people, then there would be no *need* to make amends."

Trisha glanced over at Chasity, a sympathetic look in her eyes. *I know*, she thought. "You know what, let's table this discussion for now—"

"How about we drop it all together?"

"Fine," Trisha agreed. She meant to show Chasity a good time today; the last thing she wanted to do was argue with her. "Are you mad?"

"I'm *annoyed*," Chasity stressed.

"Hopefully some damage to my credit card will remedy that," Trisha proposed, smiling.

"It might," Chasity agreed as Trisha looped her arm through her daughter's yet again. Not wanting to argue or pass up an opportunity to spend her mother's money, Chasity forced a smile as the two women continued on their journey.

Josh rolled the last of the car tires back to the designated spot. Wiping the sweat from his brow with the back of his hand, he turned and faced his father. "Is there anything else that needs to be counted?"

Mr. Hampton smiled. "No, you've done enough," he replied, rubbing the back of his neck. "I appreciate it."

"Anytime." Josh sat down on a small metal chair. "I guess I'll be heading back to Mark's house soon."

Mr. Hampton's smile faded. "Oh okay."

The sullen tone was not missed by Josh. "Listen, I know you feel some kind of way about me not staying home this week," Josh began. "But you know I can't be under the same roof with Sarah. So as long as she's there, which knowing her, won't be long, I won't come home."

His father took a deep breath. He understood why his children were not getting along, but that didn't stop him from wanting to do his part to mend their relationship. "Maybe if you would just talk—"

"Dad, that's not gonna happen," Josh hissed, cutting his father's words off. "Sorry to sound disrespectful, but I mean what I say."

Mr. Hampton gave a slight nod, before looking at his watch. "Okay, forget about it. How about I go grab us some lunch?" he offered.

"As long as it's not pizza, I'm fine with whatever you get," Josh stipulated, amusement in his voice.

"Great, just sit tight and I'll be back."

Josh nodded as his father walked out of the shop. Physically drained, Josh just grabbed the nearest magazine, which was sitting on a nearby crate, and began thumbing through it. He heard the door open and without looking up, let out a chuckle. "What's wrong Dad? You forget your wallet?" When he didn't hear a response, he looked up—his smile faded as he stared at the person in the door way. "You've *got* to be kidding me," he muttered, angry.

"Hi Josh," the young woman greeted, hesitant.

"Don't say shit to me, Sarah," he spat.

Josh couldn't believe that his estranged sister was standing in front of him. The last time he saw Sarah, she was strung out and frail. She seemed to have put on a healthy amount of weight, her brown skin had a glow to it; her brown hair was locked into twists that fell to her shoulders. He had to admit, she looked better than she had in years, but that still didn't make the pain that he felt hurt any less.

Josh slowly stood up, dropping the magazine to the floor. "What the hell are you doing here?"

Sarah, fiddled with her hands. "Um, Dad said that you would be here," she revealed. "So, since you won't come home, I figured I'd come to you."

Josh was seething, *Dad set me up.* "It doesn't matter, I have nothing to say to you."

"Listen, I know that I was taking a chance by coming here," Sarah began. "But...I miss you and I wanted to see you."

"You saw me, now get out," Josh spat.

Sarah took a deep breath; she knew this reunion with her baby brother would not go well, but she was willing to try. "I know...I know that you're angry with me, and I don't blame you." She took a small step towards him. "I've done some horrible things to this family, and I know that I don't deserve your forgiveness, but..."

Josh shot his sister a confused look. "Hold up," he began, pinching the bridge of his nose. "I know damn well, you didn't bring your junky ass here to try to ask me for forgiveness."

Sarah's face held a hurt expression. "I'm not on that stuff anymore," she assured. "I really *am* clean right now."

"Until when?" he asked, tone condescending. "Until you're able to steal more money? Well I can tell you right now that I have none."

She shook her head at his nasty tone. "Josh—"

"Do you have *any* idea what you put me through?!" he erupted. "I almost had to delay going to school because of *you*. You stole my tuition money," he reminded. "Three thousand dollars! Mom, Dad and I busted our asses to be able to get enough money for me to go to school."

"I *know* that and I'm sorry!" Sarah bellowed.

"As if that wasn't fucked up *enough*, you got me jumped and robbed!"

Sarah was shocked and it showed on her face. "I would *never* do that to you!" she hollered. "No matter *how* bad I was, I would *never* want you hurt."

"Bullshit!" his voice boomed off the walls in the shop. "The night I found out what you did, I went looking for you at your usual hideout. I told someone at the door that I was looking for you and next thing I know, two guys came out and attacked me. Then they stole what little *else* I had."

Sarah put her hands over her mouth in horror. The night that she stole Josh's money was the last time that she'd seen him until now. She had no idea that had happened to him. "I swear to you, I had no idea that happened to you J.J."

"Don't call me that," Josh sneered. Sarah was the only one who called him by his first and middle initials as a child. He always thought it was endearing when she said it, until she began treating him badly. "You were only allowed to call me that when you *actually* loved me."

"I *still* love you. Always *have*." Tears streamed down her face. "I wish I could take back everything that I've done. But since I can't, I want to do whatever it takes to make it right, *now*."

"It's too late for that," he hissed. "You're lucky that Mom and Dad still care. If it were up to *me*, your ass would be rotting in a jail cell somewhere." He grabbed his jacket from a nearby chair and stormed towards the exit. When Sarah tried to grab his arm to stop him, he jerked away and spun around to face her. Towering over her five-foot-seven frame, he warned her, "Don't ever touch me."

"Please don't leave, let me try to make things right," she begged.

Josh thought for a moment. "You want to make things right?"

"Yes, absolutely," she replied, a sliver of hope in her voice.

Josh's eyes bore through her like a laser. "Go back to whatever hole you crawled out of, and *stay* there," he advised, before turning and storming out, leaving his sister sobbing.

As Josh made his way to the curb, he saw his father standing there. "Josh—"

"Bye Dad," Josh spat, interrupting whatever explanation his father was about to give. As far as Josh was concerned, his entire family was full of liars and he had no desire to be around them.

Malajia flopped down on her bed, cradling the cell phone to her ear. "I swear, next time I'm ignoring your threats," she said into the phone. "Summer break, I'm moving in."

"Yeah, you try it and see what happens," Chasity chuckled, opening a bottle of wine that she had removed from a table in her hotel suite.

"Hey, I'm willing to face the consequences of my actions," Malajia chortled. "It's better than staying in *this* damn dismal ass house."

Chasity poured herself a glass. "Girl, you stay whining." She took a sip of the white wine.

"What are you drinking that got you gulping in my ear all hard?" Malajia wondered.

Chasity laughed. "Wine."

"You don't even *like* wine," Malajia recalled.

"I like *this* one," Chasity replied, taking another sip. "Anyway, go find something to do if you're that damn bored. Hell, take your ass to Delaware and visit Mark."

Malajia sighed as she played with the fabric from her bed spread. "I just can't be under him right now," she admitted. "I've got too much on my mind and I'll just start snappin' at him."

"Well, at least you're being considerate of his feelings…I guess."

Malajia squinted. Chasity seemed distracted. "I know you're not drunk *already*," she teased.

"No," Chasity denied, "I thought I was getting another call in."

"Did you hear a beep or something?" Malajia wondered. "No."

Malajia laughed. "Chasity—that don't make no damn sense, that expensive ass wine got you trippin'."

Chasity snickered as she sipped more wine.

"Anyway, how about my mom brought Tyrone's raggedy ass name up," Malajia began.

"*Why?*" Chasity spat out.

"It doesn't even *matter* why. I told her ass that I stopped dealing with him *months* ago," Malajia vented. "Talking about she don't recall me saying that." She sucked her teeth. "She's always brushing me off."

Chasity let out a long sigh. "Malajia, I really think you should tell her what happened."

Malajia scoffed. "Nope."

Chasity sat on the chaise lounge. "She's not gonna know how badly bringing him up affects you if you don't tell her," she pointed out.

"Hey pot, stop lecturing kettle," Malajia shot back.

Chasity rolled her eyes. "And here goes the turnaround," she sniped, taking another sip of wine.

"Yup," Malajia agreed without a doubt. "*You* haven't told *your* mom about the baby and you know you need to. You get mad at *her* when she keeps secrets from you and then you turn around and keep a secret from *her*," she pointed out.

Chasity sat her glass on the end table as she pondered Malajia's words. "My secret doesn't affect her," Chasity argued. "*Hers* affected me."

"You're pulling excuses out of your ass, Chasity," Malajia chided. "Tell you what? When you finally get up the nerve to tell your mom about *your* secret. I'll tell my mom *mine*," she propositioned.

Chasity let out a loud sigh. "Don't base your decisions off of what I do," she spat.

"Which only means that you aren't gonna say anything, so I'm off the hook," Malajia countered.

"I gotta go." Chasity huffed.

"Enjoy your dinner and don't drink that bottle of wine to yourself," Malajia chortled.

"I'm not making any promises," Chasity replied.

Malajia laughed. "Bye, sis." She tossed her phone on the pillow next to her once she ended the call and laid down.

All traces of laughter now gone, Malajia laid there, thinking. She couldn't tell her family, she just couldn't. But she needed to figure something out; this burden that rested on her shoulders was becoming too much for Malajia to bear.

Chapter 29

The white table cloth on the restaurant table seemed to have more of Chasity's attention than her mother, who was busy running off at the mouth. After getting off the phone with Malajia, Chasity sat in her hotel suite, sipping on wine and pondering her words. She didn't know if it was the guilty feeling or the lack of food in her stomach that was making her feel queasy.

"Did you hear what I said?" Trisha asked, taking a sip of her champagne.

Chasity looked up. "Huh?"

Trisha giggled at the blank look on her daughter's face. "I asked you if you heard what I said," she repeated.

"Um, no. Sorry." Chasity ran her hands through her hair. "What was it?"

Trisha titled her head. "You okay?"

"Yeah, I'm fine," Chasity assured with a wave of her hand. "Maybe a little bit drunk, but I'm fine."

"Don't tell me you drank that whole bottle of wine."

"Maybe." Chasity's response was instant, earning a warning look from Trisha.

"And you didn't eat anything *did* you?"

"Maybe not." Chasity was feeling tipsy, but it in no way clouded her thoughts. In fact, it was making them scream louder in her head. Malajia was right; she needed to come clean.

Trisha shook her head. "Anyway," she began, pushing a dinner roll that she had just buttered in Chasity's hand. "I was saying that I just bought a new—"

"I was pregnant," Chasity blurted out. Trisha immediately stopped talking; her face taking on a blank expression. Chasity frowned slightly. "Did you hear what I just said?" she asked.

Trisha titled her head, eyeing her intensely. "Yeah, I did," she answered. "Are you serious?"

"Very," Chasity replied, fighting to hold eye contact with her mother. The way that Trisha was looking at her, almost like she was completely disappointed in her, made her want to run as far away from the restaurant as she could.

"Chasity!" Trisha exclaimed, slamming her cloth napkin on the table. "How could you be so careless?"

Chasity put her head in her hands. "I know," she agreed.

"When? When did you find out?"

Chasity took a deep breath. "October," she revealed hesitantly. She then flinched when Trisha exclaimed her name again, this time accompanied by her hand slamming on the table.

"First off, I can't believe that I'm *just* hearing about this. Second, and I repeat, how can you be so careless?" Trisha chastised. "Do you *not* know how to use a damn condom?"

Chasity narrowed her eyes at her mother's snarky remark. "Yes, I know how to use them."

"Oh don't catch an attitude with *me* sweetheart. *You* were the one who messed up," Trisha scolded, putting her hand up.

Chasity checked her attitude and sighed. "I know, and I'm sorry I didn't tell you," she said.

Trisha rubbed her face in exasperation. Having a thought, she looked at Chasity. "You said *were*," she pointed out.

"I know."

"What happened?" Trisha wondered.

"I miscarried," Chasity answered with sadness.

Trisha relaxed her frown; a feeling of sorrow fell over her. "Oh…I'm so sorry that you had to go through that, honey."

"Thanks."

Trisha reached over and touched Chasity's arm, giving it a squeeze. She didn't say anything; it was comforting to Chasity.

"Anyway, it was a whole big mess and Jason and I got into a huge fight about it and…."

"Is that what he was mad at you about over winter break?" Trisha asked, anger now subsided.

Chasity nodded. "I didn't tell him when I first found out I was pregnant, then I lost it and I just figured that there was no need to say anything about it," she revealed. "I thought we were gonna break up over it."

"Wow…are you two good now?" Trisha asked, Chasity nodded again. "Look, I know you're grown and can do what you want to do," Trisha began. "But I still want to make sure you have the best life possible and that includes *not* having children before you're *ready* for them… I want better for you."

Chasity nodded slowly. "I get it," she promised.

"*Graduate* first, at least, God," Trisha huffed.

Chasity shook her head in amusement.

Trisha signaled Chasity to come closer with her finger. Confused, Chasity leaned in. Trisha then leaned forward and gave her a kiss on her cheek. "Sorry again about the miscarriage."

"Thanks," Chasity replied. "I'm okay."

Trisha gave a slight nod as she gave Chasity's cheek a soft pat. "Okay," she said, before sitting back in her seat. She folded her arms as the waiter brought their food to the table. "Thank you for telling me."

Weight now lifting from her shoulders, wine buzz almost gone and appetite restored, Chasity grabbed her knife and fork and began cutting into her chicken.

Trisha picked up her glass of champagne and took a sip as she looked at her watch. A sense of guilt fell over her. Hearing a beep on her phone, Trisha picked it up and stared at the screen. She responded to a message, then nervously drummed her finger tips on the table.

"Um, Chasity... I'm glad that you came clean with me," Trisha said, voice somber. "I can't help but feel bad, because now I need to come clean with *you* about something."

Chasity stopped eating and regarded Trisha skeptically. *What the hell is it this time?* "Um... O-kay," she answered slowly.

Trisha downed the rest of the champagne in her glass and clasped her hands together. "Okay, so first let me start by saying that this trip to New York wasn't *entirely* for general purposes."

Chasity dropped the fork on her plate and sat back in her seat. "I knew it," she ground out.

"Please, just hear me out—"

"What is it that you're trying to bribe me into doing *now*?" Chasity cut in, angry. "Talking to Dad?"

Trisha shook her head. "No, this has nothing to do with your father," she promised.

"Then what is it?" Chasity sneered.

Trisha ran her hands over the back of her neck. "Well..." she looked around.

Chasity frowned in confusion. "What are you looking for?" she asked. "Somebody after you or something?"

"No," Trisha answered, anxious. "Chasity, I—I kind of invited somebody to join us for dinner," she revealed, much to Chasity annoyance.

Chasity held a scolding gaze on Trisha. "Who?" her voice was deceptively calm.

Trisha hesitated, it looked as if she was scared to say whatever she needed to say.

"Why are you being so goddamn vague?" Chasity snapped. "Just tell me who it is."

Trisha reached out, grabbed Chasity's hand and held it. "Listen, before I tell you, I need for you to just hear me out," she pleaded.

Confusion registered on Chasity's face. She had no idea what her mother was up to, but she was sure that whatever it was, it wasn't going to be good for her. "What are you talking—" Chasity didn't get to finish her interrogation, because she froze. Her eyes widened with shock as she laid eyes on the familiar figure standing several feet behind Trisha.

Trisha, noticing the horrified look on her daughter's face, turned around to find her sister standing there, waving slightly to her. Trisha signaled Brenda to come over, before turning back to face Chasity. "I'm so sorry," she whispered, remorseful.

"What—why would—" Chasity couldn't get her words out.

"Please don't leave," Trisha begged as Brenda approached the table. She looked up and smiled slightly as Brenda pulled up a chair and sat down.

What...the...fuck...is...going...on? was the question that screamed in Chasity's head. She sat there, frozen in silence.

"H—hi Chasity," Brenda sputtered.

Chasity couldn't even look Brenda in her face. She didn't *want* to. If she didn't feel like her legs were frozen, Chasity would have made a mad dash for the exit.

Trisha clasped her hands together. "Chaz, I'm sorry that I had to go about this, this way," she apologized sincerely.

"How could you do this to me?" Chasity charged. "Why would you bring her here?"

Brenda leaned forward. "Listen Chasity, it wasn't all—"

"I was talking to my *mother, Aunt* Brenda," Chasity hissed, shooting Brenda a death stare.

Brenda looked down at the table as she ran her hands over her short hair. She wasn't at all surprised by Chasity's reaction to seeing her again. She also didn't blame her.

"Sweetie listen," Trisha pleaded. "I know that you're upset—"

"*Upset?*" Chasity hissed. "You think I'm just upset? No, I'm fuckin' *furious*."

"I know that," Trisha assured, putting her hands up, "I know it was wrong for us to ambush you like this. But if I had told you ahead of time that Brenda was going to be here, you would never have come."

"Yeah, no shit," Chasity barked.

"She tried calling you a while ago," Trisha stated.

"Yes, I know that," Chasity spat. "Which is why I blocked the bitch." She'd seen Brenda's number pop up on her phone months prior, but not having any desire to hear anything that the woman had to say, Chasity declined the calls. She finally blocked Brenda after the fifth call.

"Chasity—"

"Why the fuck are you talking to me?" Chasity fumed, interrupting Brenda. "You have nothing to say to me."

"I *do*, actually," Brenda said. She fiddled with her hands as they began to tremble. Trisha reached out and held her hand.

"Look, if you two want to be born again sisters, then do it without me," Chasity sneered at the affectionate gesture between the two.

"Chasity don't leave," Trisha urged as Chasity pushed her chair from the table. "Please, I'm begging you. Just stay and hear Brenda out. *Please*."

"No, fuck her and fuck *you* for putting me in this situation."

Desperate, Trisha slammed her hand on the table. "Sit down goddamn it!" she yelled. "Now, you can be mad all you want, but you're *going* to sit at this table and listen."

Chasity's hazel eyes bore right through Trisha, a look that Trisha returned. Although she was furious, Chasity complied. She pushed her seat back up to the table and folded her arms.

Before Trisha could say anything else, she heard her cell phone ring. Frowning at the interruption, she looked at the caller ID. "It's Mom," she announced to Brenda. She then looked at Chasity and said, "I'll be right back."

Chasity shook her head. She was so angry, she wanted to cry. To keep any tears from falling, she avoided gazes with both women.

"Just listen to her," Trisha pleaded, before rising from her seat and leaving the table.

Brenda waited several agonizing moments before she gained the courage to say anything. "So...you look pretty," she said.

Chasity just rolled her eyes; she had no intention of participating in casual chatter with the woman who had tormented her throughout her life.

"But then again you always do," she smiled. "How is school?" When Chasity once again ignored her, Brenda let out a sigh. "Okay, since you're not saying anything, then I might as well just come out with it," she began. "I've been doing a lot of thinking over the past two and a half years, and...and, I know that I hurt you."

Still saying nothing, Chasity looked off to the side.

"You didn't deserve to be treated the way that I treated you," Brenda continued. "I put you through a lot and I know that...I just...I wanted to say that I'm sorry."

Chasity looked at Brenda for the first time since she began her speech. Chasity stared at her, frown frozen on her face, saying nothing.

Brenda fiddled with the cloth napkin on the table as she tried to gather the remainder of her thoughts. "I know that won't make up for—" she sat the napkin down. "I wanted you to know that," she said. "And...I wanted to know if...you could, um...find it in your heart to—"

"To *what*?" Chasity hissed. "*Forgive* you?"

Brenda looked down at the table. "I know that I don't have a—"

"You must be out of your fuckin' mind," Chasity

4

interrupted.

Brenda put her hand up. "Listen—"

"Don't put your hand up at me," Chasity ordered. Brenda put it back down. "You know what, you've got some nerve pulling this bullshit," Chasity fumed. "What did you think I would say after that half-assed apology?" she asked, seeing the disappointment on Brenda's slim face. "You expected me to give you a hug and say 'sure, I forgive you. I forgive all the times you hit me, all the times you locked me in my room for days at a fuckin' time, all the names you called me, all the times you degraded me in front of people. Sure, let's be one big happy damn family'."

"No, of *course* I didn't expect that," Brenda said.

"You sure?" Chasity taunted.

Brenda frowned. "You think you made things any damn easier with the *attitude* that you had, and *still* have?" she bit out.

"*You* made me this way," Chasity shot back, pointing at her. "*You* made me angry. *You* made me think everybody was gonna hurt me. If I couldn't trust my own damn *mother,* or who I *thought* was my mother, how could I trust anybody *else?*"

Brenda folded her arms, letting out a heavy sigh.

"Yeah, *you* created this monster," Chasity snarled.

"You're right Chasity. You're absolutely right," Brenda admitted. "...I didn't love you like I *should* have."

"You didn't love me at *all,*" Chasity clarified.

"No, that's not true," Brenda replied, shaking her head. "I *did,* I just didn't know how to..." Brenda rubbed her hands over her face. "Look, you know the truth, you know where you came from," she said. "You're the child of my husband and my *sister.* And yes, you didn't *ask* to be here. But when I looked at you, I saw what they did. I saw your mother, someone who betrayed me beyond imagination. I was angry, I was hurt, and maybe I didn't handle it right, but even *you* have to admit that the situation was pretty fucked up."

Chasity sat there in silence for several moments as she pondered Brenda's explanation. "While I get that you were upset, that excuse doesn't fly with me," Chasity began, Brenda sighed. "See, 'cause *I* didn't fuck your husband," she spat. "*Trisha* did. And granted, I might have been the *result* of what she did, but that was no reason for you to treat me the *way* that you did." Chasity slammed her hand on the table. "If it was so damn hard for you to *look* at me then you should've A- given me *back* to her, or B- given me to someone who wouldn't have treated me like a fuckin' mistake."

"Trisha couldn't take care of you and I couldn't give you to anyone else, because at the end of the day you were my husband's child."

Chasity shook her head. "I think anything would've been better than the alternative."

Brenda placed both of her hands on the table. "Chasity, I understand that my apology is the last thing that you want to hear," she said. "And I know that forgiving me is the last thing that you want to *do*. I don't have a *right* to ask, but I *am* asking you to please find it somewhere in your heart to forgive me… If you feel *anything* for me as a daughter—" Brenda felt her emotions coming to a head. "*Please* Chasity. I am so sorry."

Chasity stared at Brenda as she grabbed her purse from the arm of her chair. She'd had enough of this conversation. "Look, what happened to you was fucked up," she said. "I told Mom that myself when I found out. That's not something that someone should put their sister through. And if you want to forgive her for that, then that's on you. But *I'm* not gonna be that damn nice to *you*."

Brenda felt that she was about to break down as Chasity pushed herself back from the table. "Please, don't leave," she begged.

"Don't call me anymore," Chasity spat, before turning to walk away.

Brenda, feeling desperate and at the end of her rope, did

the only thing that she could to stop Chasity from leaving: yell something that always seemed to strike fear in her as a child. Brenda slammed her hand on the table. "Don't walk away from me!"

Those words froze Chasity in place. She remembered all the times Brenda would shout that to her; it was always accompanied by something being thrown at her, or her being attacked. Not turning around, she just stood there as Brenda began to speak.

"Just...*please* don't leave. I need to make things right with you," Brenda pleaded. "I don't—I don't have much time...I just need to make things right."

Chasity turned around, a frown on her face. "What are you talking about?" she hissed.

Brenda looked down at the table. "I'm sick... I'm dying Chasity," she revealed.

Chasity shook her head. "No, you don't get to do that," she barked, pointing at her. "You can't lie about something like that just to get me to do what you want."

"Chasity...I'm not lying," Brenda promised.

Chasity was confused, and it showed on her face as she processed what she just heard. She didn't know what to think or how to feel. Sure, she despised the woman, but she didn't wish death on her. Even *she* couldn't do that. Not knowing how to react, Chasity went to her normal response. She walked away, leaving Brenda sitting alone, looking completely broken.

Trisha, finally finished with her phone call, approached the table. Seeing Chasity's empty seat, she looked at Brenda, who just glanced up at her with a tear-streaked face and shook her head. Trisha sighed as she sympathetically rubbed her older sister's shoulder.

Chapter 30

Malajia, slowly and meticulously folded the laundry that she had just pulled out of the dryer. Setting each neatly folded item on the bed, she couldn't remember the last time she folded that perfectly. She went to toss the basket by her bedroom door when Geri opened the door. Malajia put her hands over her face as the basket almost hit her sister. Luckily, Geri shut the door before it hit her. "My bad Geraldine," Malajia apologized as Geri opened the door again.

"Who the hell is Geraldine?" Geri chuckled. "I told your crazy self to stop expanding my damn name."

Malajia smirked. "What do you want?" she asked, placing some items into a drawer.

Geri put her hand on her hip. "Less you forget, this is *my* room too," she sneered.

"Oh my Gooooodddd, I don't caaaaarrreee," Malajia groaned, tossing her head back. "What do you want?"

Ignoring her sister's tone, Geri walked over to Malajia, holding her cell phone out. "Look whose picture I found in my phone," she said.

Concentrating on her clothes, Malajia didn't look up at the phone. "Who?" she asked, unenthused.

"Just *look* at it," Geri pressed.

Malajia let out a loud sigh as she looked up. "Girl, what the hell—" Malajia froze, seeing Tyrone's face frozen on her sister's phone screen. She couldn't speak.

"I think this is the picture that you sent me when y'all first started dating," Geri chortled, unaware of Malajia's feelings.

"Get that away from me," Malajia demanded, tone low.

Geri frowned in confusion. "Well, I was gonna delete it *anyway*. I just wanted—"

"I said, get it away from me," Malajia snapped, smacking her sister's hand, sending the phone falling to the floor.

Geri was horrified. "Malajia! What the hell is wrong with you?" she wailed, bending down to retrieve the phone.

"I'm sorry," Malajia softly said.

Geri looked at her cracked phone screen. "I can't believe you just did that!" she yelled. "You owe me a new damn phone." Geri accompanied her yells with a punch to Malajia's arm.

Although the punch didn't hurt necessarily, seeing Tyrone's picture, accompanied by being hit, just triggered something in Malajia. "Don't put your fuckin' hands on me!" she screamed, pushing her older sister with such force that it sent her stumbling into the wall. As Geri laid on the floor in shock, Malajia, realizing what she had done, walked over to her. "I'm sorry, Geri," she panicked, reaching her hand out.

"Don't touch me," Geri barked, slapping her hand away. "You're freakin' crazy!"

Malajia, not wanting to break down and cry in front of Geri, hurried out of the room and ran down stairs. Feeling the need to get out of the house, she snatched open the door only to find Sidra standing there. Seeing her there shocked Malajia and it showed on her tear streaked face. She'd forgotten that Sidra was coming down to see her today.

Sidra eyed Malajia in concern. "Mel, what's wrong?"

"I gotta get out of here," Malajia stammered, hysterical.

Sidra grabbed Malajia's hand and pulled her to her car. Once both girls were in, Sidra sped off.

After a short drive to the harbor, Sidra found a small restaurant. She hoped that some air and food would help calm Malajia down. Malajia hadn't said two words since she got in the car. Her sitting in silence much longer wasn't going to fly with Sidra. "What happened?" she asked, as a waiter sat menus in front of them.

"I don't wanna talk about it," Malajia mumbled, rubbing her arm.

"Oh no, you're *gonna* talk," Sidra demanded. "If not to *me*, then someone else." She pulled her phone out of her purse. "Do you want me to call Chasity?"

Malajia shook her head. "No, don't bother her," she said. "I'll tell you."

Sidra sat in anticipation. "What's going on with you?"

Malajia sighed, "I think I hurt Geri."

Sidra frowned. "What do you mean?"

"I mean, I just... She showed me a picture of Tyrone that she had in her phone and then she hit me—"

"She *hit* you?" Sidra charged.

"No, it wasn't hard," Malajia clarified; she'd almost forgotten how protective Sidra could be of her. Sidra, knowing Malajia's family wouldn't hesitate to cuss one of her sisters out. "I freaked out when I saw his picture and I broke her phone," she told. "She got mad and hit me and I just...I lost it and I pushed her and... I think I'm going crazy."

Sidra shook her head. "You're not going crazy," she assured. "But I *do* think that going through the abuse that you went through with that bastard has traumatized you."

"I wouldn't say that I'm traumatized," Malajia argued.

"No?" Sidra challenged, raising an eyebrow. "You snapped on your sister because seeing Tyrone triggered an anger in you."

Malajia let out a sigh and sat back in her seat.

"I don't think you've dealt with it," Sidra added.

"I'm dealing fine," Malajia ground out, rubbing her arm yet again.

Sidra too let out a sigh as she reached for a menu. "Why would Geri show you his picture anyway?" she questioned. "Doesn't she know that you're not together?"

"Like my *mother*, she obviously didn't *hear* me when I told her that things were over," Malajia spat out, spinning a fork around on the table. "It's bad enough I have the memory of him in my head, now I have to keep hearing his name in my *house*."

"You need to tell them what happened," Sidra advised, stern. Malajia rolled her eyes. "*Seriously*, Malajia."

"You sound like Chasity," Malajia grunted.

"And she's *right*," Sidra confirmed. "They obviously aren't taking you seriously when it comes to you not dealing with him anymore…They need to know what he did to you."

"For *what*?" Malajia argued. "So they can *judge* me? They do that enough."

"Sweetie, you don't know what they're gonna say or how they're gonna feel unless you stop being scared and share your truth with them," Sidra pushed back. "At the end of the day they love you."

"I'd really like to *not* talk about this anymore," Malajia huffed. "I'm sure you didn't drive all the way down here to hear my drama."

"I *came* because I didn't like how *dry* you sounded over the phone," Sidra replied. "I'm glad I *did*."

Malajia managed a small smile, she was grateful. "Well…thanks Ponytail."

Sidra giggled. "You're welcome," she replied. "You want a drink?"

"Yes, please," Malajia immediately replied.

Chasity sat in her hotel suite in silence. She had only

returned from walking an hour ago. With the table lamp dimmed slightly, she stared at the moon shining through the window. The dinner with Brenda and Trisha the night before mentally drained her.

She'd turned her phone off and avoided Trisha like the plague, which was easy since Trisha elected to stay in a separate room after her ambush.

Hearing the door knob jiggle, Chasity rolled her eyes. Trisha still having the spare copy of Chasity's room key; Chasity knew that it was only a matter of time before she used it.

Trisha opened the door slowly and walked in, taking a few steps towards Chasity. Both women were silent. Trisha was on edge. Chasity was furious with her; she was mentally preparing to be screamed at.

"Is it true?" Chasity asked evenly, shocking Trisha.

"Yes, it's true," Trisha answered. Trisha walked over and sat on a chair next to Chasity. "I found out a few weeks after Christmas."

Chasity remembered seeing Brenda at her grandmother's house during Christmas and leaving abruptly.

"When we saw each other on Christmas, we decided to sit down and talk...We *did*, for a long time. It seemed like hours...It probably *was* hours," Trisha revealed, somber. "After a lot of arguing and screaming and *tears*...I apologized for what I did to her and she apologized to *me* for what she did to *you*." Trisha sighed, "We just...we wanted to try to move past things. Maybe not all at once but we wanted to try... We figured it was time." Trisha looked down at her hands. "I saw her here in New York a few weeks later when I was here on business, and I asked her why she was here. She told me she moved here to be treated by a specialist and...that's when she told me that she was sick. That she's been sick for about a year and a half."

"How long does she have?" Chasity flatly asked after several moments of silence.

"Not long," Trisha answered honestly, "a few months at the most."

"So, it's taking her to die, to realize that she was wrong," Chasity concluded.

Trisha sighed. "She realized *before* that," she said, tone soft. "She told me that she felt remorseful after she attacked you at Mom's house your freshman year. After she sobered up, it hit her hard and… she said she would've reached out to you *then*, but she knew that you wouldn't talk to her…her dying just gave her the courage to do it now."

"After all those years, she *finally* felt bad?" Chasity hissed. "*After* she humiliated me in front of a house full of people on a fuckin' holiday? It hit her *then*?" Chasity shook her head as she stood up.

"Chasity, I understand that this is hard for you," Trisha said.

"You have no idea," Chasity ground out.

"I *do*," Trisha replied. "And I know that the idea of forgiveness is hard to even consider—"

"Did *you* forgive her?" Chasity spat out, staring Trisha down.

Trisha looked down at her hands. "I *had* to," she said, voice faltering. "She forgave *me*."

Chasity shook her head. "Well good for *you*," she bit out. "*I can't.*"

Trisha watched as Chasity headed for the door. "Chasity wait—"

Chasity paused, she looked at Trisha whose eyes were glassed over with tears. "I'm sorry that your sister is dying," she offered.

Trisha watched with sorrow as Chasity walked out of the room. She knew that she couldn't make Chasity forgive her sister, but she could only pray that she would try. Not just for Brenda, but for herself.

Chapter 31

"You know what we should do before the end of this semester?" Mark suggested, leaning back in his seat at the dining room table in his cluster house.

"What's that?" Josh asked dryly, picking at his hoagie.

"We should go camping," Mark answered enthusiastically, grabbing a few chips out of a large bowl.

Spring break now over, the gang spent the past few days back on campus trying to mentally prepare for finals, which were merely weeks away. But Mark needed a mental break. He was desperate to find something fun for the group to do.

Sidra frowned. "Are you crazy?" she scoffed, reaching for a chip. "Does it *look* like I would go camping? And you already know that your girlfriend isn't gonna go for it…Chaz neither."

"Look, I'll handle Malajia," Mark promised. "And I'm sure Jase can persuade Chaz to go. Alex and Em won't be a problem."

"Yeah, I don't see it happening," Sidra chuckled.

Mark was about to make a comment, when a flashing light on his phone caught his eye.

Looking at the screen, he let out a loud sigh. "Josh, for the love of God, *please* call your dad back," he urged, seeing a missed call from Josh's father.

"Nope," Josh muttered, looking at his plate of un-eaten food.

"Dawg, he's been calling our phones for *days*," Mark stated.

"Yeah, he's been calling the room like three times a day, man," David added. "He really wants to talk to you."

"Just block his number," Josh spat.

"I'm *about* to," Mark mumbled. "No, but seriously, you need to call him back."

Sidra watched as Josh picked at his hoagie. He'd been picking at the same turkey and cheese hoagie for the past half hour. She knew that his lack of appetite had to do with seeing his sister for the first time in almost three years.

"Josh, I know that you're still upset with your father for—"

"I don't wanna *talk* about it Sidra," Josh hissed, interrupting her words.

Sidra had no intention on scolding him for his tone. She just stared at him, full of sympathy. She remembered the anger that Josh displayed when he called her the evening after he saw Sarah. He was vague on what exactly was said between the siblings, but he made it clear that he was furious with his father *and* with Sarah.

"I'm sure he's sorry for setting you up with Sarah like that. But try to put yourself in *his* shoes," she advised, sincerely. "Both of his children are at odds with each other, and he just wants to resolve it."

"He shouldn't want to resolve *shit* with that crack-headed liar!" Josh yelled, pounding his fist on the dining room table. "She hurt *him too*…"

Sidra ran her hands over her hair and sighed as Mark put his hands up in surrender. "Chill bro," Mark urged.

"Don't tell me to chill, Mark," Josh seethed, rising from his seat. "You have *no* idea what I went through."

"You're right, we *don't*," David put in, compassionate. "But we have an *idea* because we were there for you when you were going through it."

"We just want you to get past it sweetie," Sidra added.

"How can you say that?" Josh fussed.

"Easy, we see what the resentment is doing to you," Mark put in, with a seriousness that nobody expected. "You've been *miserable* since you found out she was back... We hate seeing you like this."

"I'm not getting past it and to hell with y'all for even *suggesting* that," Josh fumed, heading for the door. "*You* never had to deal with an addict. *You* never had money stolen from you. *You* didn't have to work and watch your parents struggle to recoup what was stolen. *You* didn't have to almost delay starting school, so you don't get to tell *me* how to feel about it."

Mark, David, and Sidra were silent as Josh stormed out of the house, slamming the door behind him.

"Yo, I fuckin' *hate* 'miserable Josh'," Mark jeered, reaching for another chip.

Sidra looked at Mark. "Come on, cut him some slack," she said. "He's entitled to feel how he feels."

"I agree with you Sid, but that resentment is gonna eat him up inside," David said.

"Yeah, I know," Sidra sighed. "So...do you think we should ever tell him about where that tuition money *really* came from?"

"Naw," Mark said. "Besides, it won't change how he feels about Sarah."

"True, but it might make him feel a little better," Sidra pressed.

"I doubt it," Mark said. "You know how Josh is when he gets in his damn feelings. Nothing can change his mind."

Sidra once again ran her hands over her hair and sighed. She knew all too well. "Yeah, I guess you're right," she agreed. "We just have to be here for him and keep trying to get through to him."

"No doubt," Mark agreed. "But I don't have to like his attitude, and I reserve the right to slap him in his chin if he gets too much outta pocket."

"No, we'll have none of that," David laughed.

"Why not?" Mark frowned at David. "*You* punched me in *my* damn face when I got outta pocket."

"Damn right, and I'll do it again," David joked, earning a middle finger from Mark.

"Geri, how long are you gonna stay mad at me? I *said* that I was sorry," Malajia said into the phone as she paced back and forth in her room that evening.

Her sister Geri still had not forgiven her for breaking her phone, and more importantly for pushing her. Malajia let out a sigh, listening to the loud rambling come through the phone. "I already said that I would pay for your phone... Yes, I know that you scratched your back on a tack on the wall... Yes, I know it still hurts... Geri, I don't know what else you want me to say... Fine, go ahead but I'm just gonna call you back later." Malajia removed the phone from her ear as her sister abruptly ended the call.

"Malajia," Alex called from across the hall.

"What?" Malajia dryly responded.

"I made some spaghetti, you want any?"

"Alex, nobody wants that dry ass spaghetti," Malajia scoffed, rubbing the back of her neck. "You never get the *good* sauce."

Alex walked across the hall and stuck her head in Malajia's room. "All you had to say was 'no' smart ass," she chuckled. Noticing the sullen look on Malajia's face, Alex frowned in concern. "Are you okay, sweetie?"

"Yeah, I'm fine," Malajia said, unconvincingly. "I just got off the phone with Geri... Well, she actually hung up on me."

"Still mad at you, huh?" Alex assumed.

Malajia nodded. She'd told the other girls what had happened with Geri and her breakdown. She was hoping that talking out her problems with all the girls would make her feel better, but it hadn't.

"She'll get over it eventually," Malajia resolved. "We used to fight all the time as kids. Then we got close and started fighting our older sisters," she added at an attempt at a joke.

Alex leaned against the door. "So um…have you ever considered talking to someone about Tyrone?" she asked carefully.

"I *am* talking to someone… You guys," Malajia returned, folding her arms. "Frankly I'm *tired* of talking about him."

"That's not what I mean," Alex said, voice stern. "I mean like…a counselor." When Malajia explained what triggered her reaction against Geri, Alex felt that maybe Malajia needed some help in putting the past behind her.

Malajia frowned at her. "You think I need *therapy?*"

"Not that extreme, but I *do* feel that a counselor will help you come to terms with what happened," Alex placated. "Maybe you can talk to Ms. Smith—"

"I'm not talking to Ms. Smith's old ass okay, I'm not Emily," Malajia grunted.

Alex shook her head; Malajia was referring to the time when Emily took a meeting with the school counselor sophomore year to vent about the issues with her mother. It helped Emily. Alex only wanted the same for Malajia.

"You talkin' about coming to terms with shit, how about *you* come to terms with your fear of commitment issues," Malajia threw back, angry. "Talk to her about *that*."

Alex flipped Malajia off before turning on her heel and walking out the door.

Regretting her words, Malajia walked out the room. "Sorry Alex," she called after her.

"No, screw you, I was only trying to help," Alex fumed, before slamming her door.

"Come on, I didn't mean it," Malajia said through the closed door.

"Go away, Malajia," Alex barked.

Malajia rolled her eyes and let out a loud sigh, before

heading down the steps.

Chasity sat on the steps of the library, studying the text messages on her phone. She was so focused that she didn't hear or see Jason approach from behind.

"You're still sitting out here?" he chuckled, setting his book bag on the step next to her. When she didn't answer, he called her name.

Chasity looked up at him. "Huh?"

Jason sat down next to her. "What are you still doing out here?" he asked. "I've been in the library for like an hour."

"Shit. Has it been that long?" She glanced at her watch, before sighing. "I had every intention of going back to my room after you went in, but I started reading these damn text messages."

"Still haven't spoken to your mom since you left New York?" Jason asked, correctly assuming that the messages were from Trisha.

Chasity slowly shook her head as she stared out in front of her.

Although Chasity wasn't looking at him, Jason looked at her. He knew exactly what was going on in her mind. He recalled the frantic phone call that he had received from Chasity the night of her ambush meeting with Brenda. He heard the anger and confusion in her voice when she revealed everything that was said, as well as the news of Brenda's failing health. Although she appeared to be much calmer, he knew that the thoughts were still booming in her head.

"Are you still angry with her...your mom I mean?" he asked.

"Yes," Chasity answered honestly as she placed her phone back into her bag. "For her to try to force Brenda on me after everything, just isn't fair."

"I get that," Jason assured, moving some of her hair behind her shoulder. "You've been through a lot, I know she's aware of that. But I'm sure that being stuck between her daughter and her dying sister isn't great for her either."

"I never said that it *was*," Chasity hissed.

"I didn't say that you *did*," Jason returned, voice calm. "I'm just trying to give you another perspective on why she did what she did." Chasity rolled her eyes but didn't respond. "I'm sure she would much rather hear your voice than send you text messages. It's been almost a week."

"I don't too much care about what she wants right now," Chasity seethed. "She *wants* me to forgive Brenda, she *wants* me to talk to my dad…When is she gonna care about what *I* want? Which is to be left the fuck alone by these people."

"I'm sorry," Jason apologized. He hated seeing her so hurt. "I wish I could make all of this go away."

"I know you do," she sighed. "I'm just…tired."

Jason nodded. "I can imagine. You didn't fall asleep until late last night."

"No, I'm not talking about that," she clarified, shaking her head. "I'm tired of stupid shit happening. Every time I turn around, it's *something*. I'm either fighting or arguing, or dealing with drama—I'm *tired* of it, I don't want to go through this shit anymore. Why can't I just be happy?"

"Do you want to know what I think?"

"Sure, why not?" her tone was flat.

Jason took a second to make sure that he chose his words carefully. "I think that this is happening to you for a higher reason."

Chasity sucked her teeth. "Jason, don't give me that divine reasoning bullshit," she sneered.

"Just hear me out, baby," he pleaded, putting his hand up. "I think for you to truly be happy…you need to come to terms with your past. You need to…make peace with that before you can find peace within yourself." She rolled her eyes as he continued talking. "You may think you're okay with just leaving your past where it is, but you have to admit the fact that it still affects you. I see you trying to change, but you're still angry inside and until you make peace with what hurt you, you will *continue* to be angry."

"So you're saying that I should just let everything go?" she asked, voice not hiding her frustration. "Just forgive everything? You sound like Trisha's sentimental ass. You're supposed to be on *my* side."

"I *am*," Jason assured. "I'm not saying this to make you angry. You think I want to see you hurt? To see you upset? ...No, it's *killing* me, and honestly I hate Brenda and Derrick *for* you, but hating them isn't going to help you in the long run."

Chasity gathered her book bag from the step. "I'll make sure to say 'no' the next time you ask me if I want to hear what you think," she bit out, standing up.

Jason rose to his feet as well. "You can be upset with me all you want," he said, unfazed by her irritation with him. "It's my job to do what's best for you, and that includes telling you the truth. No matter how much you don't like it."

"Whatever," she drawled, walking off.

"Yo, this food is wack," Mark complained of the pizza in the cafeteria. "They need to get some new shit in here."

"No, you just need to stop *eating* the same stuff over and over," Sidra pointed out, flipping through her notebook. "All you eat is pizza and burgers."

Mark flagged her with his hand before sitting up in his seat to address the rest of the group. "So, about this camping trip, we should go the weekend before finals."

"Boy are you crazy?" Alex scoffed, picking up her tuna melt. "We don't have time or money to be going camping. Not to mention that finals are crucial."

"First of all, why you gotta use new words and shit?" Mark complained. "*Crucial*...nobody knows what that means."

"*I* do," Jason chuckled.

"So does *everybody*," Chasity bit out, folding her arms.

Alex stared at Mark in amazement as Malajia put her

hand over her face in embarrassment. "Are you really that stupid?" Alex drew her words out slowly.

Mark sucked his teeth. "No man, I know what 'crucial' means," he assured. "Bottom line, we know that finals are important, they are *every* damn semester. And *every* semester we get all stressed out and shit over them. I think that the camping trip will clear our minds."

"Laying out in the damn wilderness isn't gonna clear my mind," Malajia bristled, picking a pepperoni slice off of Mark's pizza. "It's gonna piss me off...I'm not going."

"Yes, you *are*," Mark promised.

"And what about the money? I don't—"

"Oh my God, we *get* it, you're broke," Mark teased, interrupting Alex. "Stop whining, camping won't cost us any money. We just pick a public spot and go."

Sidra raised an eyebrow at him. "Um... Yeah, I think you may wanna double check that," she advised.

"*I'll* check into it," David assured. "I actually think it'll be fun. I even have camping equipment...well my *dad* does. We've been a few times."

"I'm in," Emily smiled, sticking her straw into her milkshake. "I could use a getaway after the past few months I've had."

Alex sighed as she ran her hands through her hair. "I'd rather *study,* but if everyone else is in...*I'm* in." She had a sudden thought. "Ooh, can Eric come?"

"Nope. Josh, you in dawg?" Mark replied, instantaneously, earning a laugh from Alex.

"Asshole," Alex joked, tossing a balled-up napkin at him.

"I'll go," Josh put in flatly.

Jason looked at Chasity with anticipation, who returned a frown. "Do I *look* like the camping type?" she sneered.

Jason looked at Mark. "We're in," he assured, causing Chasity to let out a loud groan as she put her head in her hands. "Hush, it'll be fun," he chuckled of her reaction.

"Good. Princess, no need in whining, you're going *too*," Mark declared, before Sidra had a chance to object.

"Fine," Sidra huffed, closing her notebook. "But if I get bit, or stung, or *anything*, I'm cussing everybody out."

Mark stared at Malajia, who was busy examining her nails. She shot him a side-glance. "I don't know why you're looking at me," she hissed. "You already know I'm not doing that bullshit. You got me chopped."

"Malajia, don't be a jackass," Mark threw back, slamming his hand on the table. "I don't wanna hear your shit. You're *going*."

Malajia frowned at him. "I don't care *what* you don't wanna hear, you bastard. I'm not going camping, so you can kiss my ass."

"Oh, I'd *love* to," he teased. "And you're still going."

Malajia glared at him as he gathered up his belongings. "You can't tell me what to do," she barked. "Fuck you."

"Maybe if you did *that,* you would get more say so in this relationship," he joked. Mark laughed when he saw Malajia's eyes widen with shock. He shielded his face and head with his hands as Malajia delivered a slap to his arm. "Ow! Damn it. Use your *words* Malajia," he howled.

Mortified, Malajia delivered another stinging slap to his arm before sliding out of the booth. "You're on 'couple time out' you asshole," she seethed before storming off.

"Just wow," Chasity commented after several moments of silence, earning snickers from the group.

"You two are certified crazy," Sidra commented, shaking her head.

Mark chuckled. "She knows I'm just messing with her. That's my big-headed baby." He slung his book bag over his shoulder as he rose from his seat. "I gotta go fail this test right quick. I'll see y'all later."

Alex looked around at her remaining friends as Mark walked off. "Do we *really* want to be stuck in the wilderness with those two?" she chortled.

"Fuck no," Chasity answered.

"I second that," Sidra giggled.

Malajia tapped her pencil against her textbook, trying to concentrate on the words on the page. *I'm over this fuckin' semester*, she thought, sighing.

Mark, who was sitting next to her on his bed, looked at her. "That's like the eighth time you sighed in the last fifteen minutes," he observed.

Malajia rolled her eyes. "You always exaggerating. It was only three times," she spat, turning the page in her book.

Mark laughed a little, grabbing the can of soda from his nightstand. Since the nightstand was closer to Malajia, Mark had to lean over her to reach his soda. Malajia took a deep breath as his body brushed hers. That slight unintentional touch sent chills down her spine. *I'm so damn horny!* she screamed to herself.

"Can you move your stuff over there near *you*?" she hissed as he opened the can. "I'm tired of you climbing over me and shit."

Mark frowned at her. "You forget this is *my* room," he returned, taking a sip. "You don't like me climbing over you? Switch sides with me so I can reach my stuff."

Malajia didn't want to admit it, but she actually didn't mind the touching. In fact, she wanted it—she wanted it badly. "I'm comfortable, so I'm not moving," she bit out.

"Suit yourself," he replied nonchalantly, grabbing the TV remote.

Malajia let out another loud sigh as she tried to focus on her studies. The problem was that the things swirling around in her brain had nothing to do with what was in her textbook. Sitting with Mark, alone in his room, normally wouldn't be an issue for her. But as her feelings for him grew, so did her desire to sleep with him. And yet she just couldn't bring herself to take that step with him, even though she ached for it.

"There's never anything on," Mark complained, clicking off the TV. He looked at Malajia who was staring down at her book with a blank expression on her face. "So, Jase is staying at Chaz's tonight," he hinted.

"Huh?" Malajia answered, snapping out of her mental trance.

"I got the room to myself tonight," he smiled. "You wanna spend the night?"

Yes, she thought. "No, I don't wanna sleep over in this raggedy bed with you," Malajia barked, closing her textbook.

Mark rolled his eyes. "First of all, you got the same bed in *your* room," he ground out. "Second, why is it that every time I ask you to sleep over, you give me attitude?"

Malajia sucked her teeth. Mark had a point; this wasn't the first time that he had asked if she wanted to sleep over. And every time, she'd turned him down, and with plenty of attitude.

"'Cause the only reason why you want me to sleep over here is because you want to have sex with me," she bit out, rising from the bed. "You made it clear that us not having sex is an issue for you, today in the cafeteria."

Mark frowned in confusion. "You're not talking about that stupid joke I made, are you?"

"Oh absolutely. You think that was *funny*?" Malajia spat, folding her arms. "You think everybody needs to know our business?"

"Malajia, we *all* know each other's business in this group," he pointed out. "Hell, me and you spill *half* the damn secrets."

"Whatever Mark. Bottom line is that I don't appreciate the not-so-subtle comments about us not going there yet," she argued. "If you have a problem with waiting, then you need to tell me."

"Mel, it's no secret that I'm hoping that we'll take that next step and sleep together," he admitted. "But I don't have a problem with waiting if that is what you want... I just wish you would *tell* me point blank that that's what you want, instead of dodging every damn effort that I put in."

Malajia looked away briefly. She felt bad. She never officially told Mark that she wasn't ready to sleep with him, Malajia just gave him attitude every time he made a move on her. As much as she wanted to tell him the reason why she was avoiding his sexual advances, she just couldn't. *He won't understand*, she thought.

He stood from the bed. "Listen," he said, mistaking her silence for anger at him. "Even though we're not sleeping together, I would still like for you to spend the night with me."

"What purpose would that serve?" she snarled.

"Maybe I just want to have your ignorant ass sleeping next to me. You ever think about that?" he returned, irritated with her behavior.

Malajia rolled her eyes in an effort to keep her attitude. Aside from the "ignorant ass" part, she thought that what he said was kind of sweet. "Well, I'm not sleeping over," she maintained. "I don't trust you and your grabby hands."

Mark sighed, running a hand over his head. He was frustrated with Malajia; he needed to take a walk. "Fine," he relented, walking towards the door. "I'll be right back."

Malajia closed her eyes as Mark closed the door behind him. "What are you doing Malajia?" she asked herself, sitting back down on the bed.

Chapter 32

"I don't wanna gooooooo," Chasity complained, tossing some bug spray in an overnight bag.

Jason laughed. "Stop being such a baby," he teased. "This will be a good thing." The weekend of the camping trip was upon the group, and while a few were excited, others like Chasity weren't too thrilled.

"A good thing for *who*?" Chasity bit out, folding her arms. "You think I'm really gonna enjoy being outdoors with a bunch of dumbass animals and bugs?"

"Chasity, you're whining," Jason pointed out, zipping his book bag.

Chasity raised an eyebrow at him. "Oh *really*?" she hissed. "That's fine, how about you don't touch my *whining* ass all weekend."

Jason shrugged as he grabbed his bag off the couch and headed for the door. "Bet money when I'm laying all up on you in that tent, you'll change your mind," he mocked.

Chasity made a face at Jason's departing back as he walked out the door. "Bastard," she seethed to herself as the other girls trotted down the steps.

"Yo, this camping trip is gonna be some straight up bullshit," Malajia grumbled, dropping her overnight bag on the floor. She gave it a kick. "I hate Mark for coming up with this stupid ass idea."

"I don't even know why you let him make decisions," Alex joked, pulling her hair back into a ponytail.

"I have no idea either," Malajia ground out. She turned her attention to Chasity, who was adjusting the belt on her jeans. "Chaz, tell me you got some 'rich girl' stuff in your bag."

Chasity rolled her eyes and let out a sigh. "Like what, Malajia?" she asked tiredly, knowing full well that Malajia was about to say something stupid.

"Like a microwave, a radio, some DVD's, *something*," Malajia replied, twirling some hair around her finger.

Chasity stared at her for several seconds. After all this time she was still amazed at the stupidity that spilled from Malajia's mouth. "A *microwave*? Really?" she snapped, picking up her bag. "How the fuck could I *possibly* fit a microwave in this bag? Huh? *How*?"

Malajia shrugged. "Maybe you have a secret compartment or something," she replied, nonchalantly. She tried not to laugh at the pure agitation on Chasity's face.

"I can't," Chasity grunted. "She's not riding in the car with me," she fumed, heading for the door.

"Chaz, you know you have to ignore her," Alex chortled as Malajia busted out laughing.

"Since you wanna stick up for stupid, Alex, *you* can't ride with me either," Chasity shot back.

Alex looked at Malajia as the door slammed shut. "Malajia, why do you always have to piss her off?" she charged. "You know when she's mad, we *all* catch her attitude."

"Stop acting scared," Malajia sneered. "Besides, I'm pissed off, so I need someone to be pissed *with* me."

"So immature," Alex huffed.

"People let's make moves," Mark urged, opening his car

door. He couldn't wait to get to the camp site. "We don't wanna lose the light."

"You hype as shit," Malajia ground out, placing her bag in the trunk of Chasity's car. "It's like ten in the morning and the site is only an hour from here. I don't think we're in any danger of losing any light."

Mark stared at Malajia for several seconds. *There goes that stank ass attitude again.* "Are you on your period, sugar face?" he jeered, much to Malajia's annoyance.

Not having anything else to say, Malajia rolled her eyes at him.

"As a matter of fact, are *all* of you girls on the rag?" Mark bit out.

"Nice Mark," Josh scoffed at the vulgar assumption.

"So what? Their attitudes suck," Mark threw back.

"I didn't even say anything," Emily pointed out, looking around.

"Not you Em," Mark corrected. "Those I'm referencing know *exactly* who I'm talking about."

"And obviously we don't *care*," Malajia muttered.

"Yeah, clearly you *don't*," Mark threw back.

"That's not even a good comeback," Malajia argued.

Mark vigorously rubbed his face with his hands. "God, *please* give me the strength to deal with her mean ass," he mumbled under his breath, getting into the car.

"What did you say?" Malajia barked

"*Nothing*," Mark spat back.

"Okay, enough with the arguing," Alex put in. "This trip is happening so let's just enjoy it. Finals are next week so we might as well try to relax."

"Why is the mop talking?" Malajia wondered, feigning confusion.

"Get in the goddamn car Malajia!" Chasity demanded from the driver's seat.

Alex sucked her teeth at Malajia as she got into the passenger's seat. "Don't make me slap you this weekend,

Malajia," she threatened, pointing.

Mark stepped out of the car and stretched his legs. After an hour and a half of driving, he was relieved to reach the Virginia camp grounds. "Ahhh, can y'all smell the fresh air?" he mused, opening the trunk of his car.

"Don't talk to us about no damn air," Malajia bit out, stepping out of Chasity's car. "You got us lost."

Mark rolled his eyes. "No, I *followed* the GPS this time," he refuted, grabbing some equipment from his trunk. "*It* got us lost. Not me."

Jason stepped out of the car. "You don't remember hearing it say *recalculating* like eight times when you turned off the road back there?" he asked, rubbing the back of his neck. "Shut up," he barked, when Mark opened his mouth to protest.

Mark flagged Jason with his hand.

"We go through this every trip," David chortled. "I don't know *why* we keep letting him lead the way."

"Whatever, we're here so stop bitchin'," Mark threw back.

"Come on guys, let's set these tents up," Alex suggested, stretching.

"*I'm* not setting *shit* up," Malajia grumbled, kicking a rock with her foot. "I didn't sign on for that."

Alex sucked her teeth at Malajia's dreary behavior "Girl, can you chill with the griping for five minutes?"

"I wish she *would*," Mark added, rubbing his head. "Nobody wants to deal with her mess all weekend."

"Well, you shouldn't have planned this stupid trip and made me come along," Malajia shot back. "You already knew I was gonna talk shit all weekend."

Mark rolled his eyes and waved his hand at her dismissively.

"Guys Alex is right, let's just set these tents up," Emily put in, trying to regain everyone's focus. "Maybe we can go exploring afterwards."

"I'm gonna explore the inside of my damn tent," Chasity said. "Y'all can go get bit up if you want to." She then smacked her arm as she felt something bite her. "Shit! Damn bugs are starting already," she spat.

As the group pulled more camping equipment from the cars, Alex looked around. "Hey, how many tents did you guys pick up from the camping store?" she asked, scratching her head.

David examined the contents on top of the car. "Three, I believe," he answered, "Chaz and Jase picked theirs up separately."

"Was that not enough, Alex?" Emily asked. "I thought we were getting three so me, you and Sidra can share one, Mark and Malajia can share one—"

"Ain't nobody sharing no tent with no damn Mark," Malajia spat, interrupting Emily.

"God, will you shut the hell up?" Mark barked, pulling his hands down his face in frustration.

Emily shook her head at the byplay. "So, yeah the last one was for Josh and David."

Alex rubbed the back of her neck. "There's only *one* up there," she revealed.

"What? That *can't* be," David insisted, rifling through the equipment. "But...there were three back at the house. Who packed the car?"

Everyone slowly turned and looked at Mark, who was staring back at them in shock. "Hell no! Y'all will *not* blame this on me," he exclaimed. "*Josh* was supposed to strap the damn tents to the roof."

"No, I *wasn't*," Josh shot back. "I was responsible for packing up the coolers and *you* were supposed to pack the tents."

Mark looked off to the side as he tried to remember. *Shit! That's what those things on the living room floor was,* he thought, coming to the realization. "Naw man, David—"

"Don't start lying," David warned, pointing at Mark.

Mark scratched his head. "Well…shit, my fault y'all," he apologized. "So how we gonna do this?"

"The girls are getting the tent," Sidra said, examining her nails. "There's no question about that."

"Yes, we know Princess," Mark jeered. "But how are all four of you gonna fit in that small ass tent? Somebody gotta take the L and sleep outside in the sleeping bags with the guys."

The girls looked at Alex, who frowned. "Yeah, that's not happening," she refused.

"Y'all can have that cheap ass tent," Malajia sneered to the girls. "I'll sleep in Chasity's tent and Jason can sleep out with the guys."

"Bullshit," Chasity calmly replied.

"Damn it Chasity—" Malajia stomped her foot on the ground. "You know what, it's *happening* so you might as well shut the hell up and get over it."

Chasity shot Malajia a piercing look. "Bitch!" she snapped. "How you gonna put *my* man out in a damn sleeping bag when *yours* is the one who fucked up? …With his silly ass."

"Damn Chaz, I'm standing right *here*," Mark pointed out as Jason snickered.

"That is not the point okay," Malajia returned. "Jason is never gonna sleep in there knowing that one of us girls are sleeping outside. So like I *said*, get over it. That's what you get for dating a *man* and not a little ass *boy* who forgets to pack tents and shit."

"What?!" Chasity hollered, confused by Malajia's argument.

"Yo, I'm about to dropkick the bullshit—" Mark clasped his hands together in an effort to keep his temper in check. Malajia and her smart comments were tap dancing on his last nerve. "Malajia you're on time out. I'm sick of you," he fussed, pointing at her.

Good, then he won't try to get all cozy with me this weekend, Malajia thought. "Fine with me," she barked back.

"Look Chaz," Jason began, noticing the annoyed look on Chasity's face. "Mel may be acting crazy, but she has a point. I can't sleep in that tent while one of the girls has to sleep outside. I'll just take a sleeping bag."

Chasity rolled her eyes at Jason. Even though she commended him on being so thoughtful, she was still aggravated. She stared at Malajia, who was holding a satisfied grin on her face; then much to Malajia's shock, Chasity turned to Sidra and signaled for her to come over.

"Sidra, you can share the tent with me," she announced, much to Sidra's delight.

"What the hell?" Malajia fumed. "Why you always gotta be an asshole, Parker?"

"Because I *can* and I don't like your face right now," Chasity threw back, satisfied by Malajia's disappointment.

Alex shook her head. "*How* the hell are you two best friends again?" she chortled.

Sidra clasped her hands together in delight. "Thank you Chaz," she turned to Emily and Alex. "I love you girls, but it would've been too crowded for me."

"Yeah, yeah," Alex mocked, feigning disappointment.

Sidra grabbed her overnight bag and headed over in Chasity's direction. "Yay, it'll be just like freshman year," she beamed, clapping her hands together.

"Sidra don't start acting corny," Chasity huffed, pulling a bottle of water from her bag.

Alex looked at Malajia, whose face was fixed in a frown. "Come on Mel, it'll be just like freshman year," she teased, fighting the urge to bust out laughing.

"Screw y'all," Malajia snapped, folding her arms.

"Yo, my sleeping bag is thin as shit," Mark complained, trying to turn over in his sleeping bag. "Punk ass salesman, selling me this bullshit."

"Don't blame the salesman," David commented, sitting up. "*You* were the one who asked the man for the cheapest bag."

Mark let out a loud groan. "Nobody asked you, *David*," he barked, unzipping the bag. It was now later that evening, and the gang decided to call it an early night, in hopes of being able to rest for an early start the next morning, but at this point, nobody was getting any sleep.

Malajia unzipped the tent and stuck her head out. "Can y'all shut the hell up?" she hurled.

"Malajia, zip the tent back up, it's cold," Alex complained from inside.

Malajia snapped her head around and faced Alex. "Alex, I'm not closing it. It smells like boot in here," she shot back.

Alex, annoyed not only by Malajia's smart mouth, but by the snickers coming from the others who were in earshot, sat up and gave Malajia a hard kick to her behind.

"Damn Alex!" Malajia yelped.

"I'm sick of your shit, get out!"

"Don't get mad at me, I *told* you to wash them socks you got on," Malajia returned, rubbing her behind.

"You know what," Alex began through clenched teeth as she snatched her blanket off of her. Malajia, seeing the anger in Alex's eyes and her sudden movement, shrieked and ran out of the tent. Alex crawled over to the opening and closed it. "You sleep out there," she ordered.

"Chill Alex, I was just joking," Malajia laughed.

"Nope!" Alex yelled from inside.

Malajia sucked her teeth and let out a loud sigh. "Can you at *least* give me my damn blanket?"

"It's not yours, it's *mine*, so nope," Alex returned. "*And* I rubbed my feet on it."

"Mel, come over here and lay with me so I can use your weave as a cover," Mark quipped, gesturing for her to come over to him.

"This weave cost more than that cheap ass bag you got," Malajia bit back, stepping over Josh to get to Chasity's tent.

Chasity rolled her eyes as she heard Malajia's voice get closer to her tent. It was bad enough that she was having a hard time getting to sleep due to the fact that her mind was racing, but now Malajia's big mouth was certain to make falling asleep impossible.

"You might as well open up," Malajia commanded, scratching her nails down the front of the tent.

"Malajia, fuck off," Chasity groaned, throwing her arm over her face.

"Rude!" Malajia hollered.

"Malajia, will you *please* shut up?" Jason complained from his tightly wrapped sleeping bag.

"I wish she *would*," Sidra chimed in, pulling the cover over her head. "You always have to be the one to disturb everybody."

"Oh shut up french roll," Malajia snapped, stomping her foot on the ground. "You just showing off 'cause you're all comfortable in that damn tent."

"I don't even *wear* french roll's though," Sidra tiredly pointed out.

"It doesn't matter— You know what, if somebody don't let me in one of these tents, I'm gonna cut holes in them," Malajia threatened. When no one responded to her, she stormed over to the group's pile of essentials and began rifling through the book bags. "Y'all think I'm playing," she mumbled, retrieving a pair of scissors from a first aid kit. Malajia quickly walked over to the tent that she shared with Alex and Emily.

Emily rolled over when she saw Malajia's shadow on the tent through the moonlight. Seeing Malajia's shadow poke at the tent, Emily sat up. "Malajia, are you *seriously* doing that?!" Emily exclaimed, when she saw the metal poke through.

Alex jumped up, infuriated, "Malajia, I swear to God!" Alex hollered. She quickly darted out of the tent and began chasing Malajia, who dropped the scissors on the ground. "Why the hell would you do that?"

"You should've let me back in," Malajia argued, jumping over Mark to escape the angry Alex. As Alex went to jump, she lost her footing and tripped over Mark, who popped right up.

"OWWWWWW!" he howled, grabbing his crotch as she fell over him.

"Is all that necessary?" Josh snapped, irritated.

"Shut up Mark, I didn't even touch you there," Alex said to Mark as she stood to her feet. "Always exaggerating."

As Alex continued to chase the laughing Malajia around the camp site, she tripped over a branch and went falling into Chasity's tent, flattening one side. Malajia screamed with laughter as everyone looked over at Alex, who was struggling to stand.

"Alex, come *on*," Jason bristled, unzipping his sleeping bag. He knew he wasn't going to be getting to sleep anytime soon. "You tripped *twice*? Really?"

Chasity and Sidra pushed their way out of the mangled tent. "Come on with your fat, slow running, ass!" Chasity erupted, tossing a pillow at Alex, who was dusting herself off.

"Was calling me fat necessary?" Alex returned, placing her hands on her hips.

Chasity looked at her with shock. "Do you *not* see my fuckin' tent?"

"I see it and I'm sorry about that and all, but that was uncalled for," Alex argued.

"I don't *give* a fuck!" Chasity threw back. "I swear, don't invite me on no more goddamn trips. Y'all always doing stupid shit! I'm over it."

Sidra folded her arms and glared at Malajia, who was practically doubled over with laughter. "Are you proud of yourself?" Sidra sneered.

She was, but Malajia didn't get a chance to respond, because every time she went to speak, laughter was all that came out.

Chapter 33

"So, who's going into the city and picking up breakfast?" Sidra asked, stretching. Despite the fact that she didn't get much sleep the night before due to Malajia's antics, Sidra was feeling refreshed. She thanked the warm sun, clear skies and gentle breeze for that.

"Sid, we already have breakfast food," David pointed out, pointing to the eggs, bacon and sausage siting on a small portable table next to a cast iron pan.

Sidra turned her nose up as Malajia stood next to her. "Don't nobody want no 'made out in the wilderness' eggs." Malajia scoffed, earning a snicker from Sidra.

David narrowed his eyes. The complaining was wearing thin. "We have covers for the pans, so you don't have to worry about anything flying in," he replied.

Malajia flagged David with her hand, then looked at Chasity, who was grabbing a bag out of her car. "What you about to do?" she asked.

"About to go to the shower house," she informed, running her hand through her disheveled hair.

"I don't think there *is* one," Mark stated, hesitantly. "Not at *this* camp ground anyway."

The girls collectively looked at him with shock. "Wait, you didn't check to see if there was a place for us to shower?" Alex questioned, folding her arms. Mark just shrugged.

"Well you know what? I'll take my ass back to campus," Chasity declared. "Y'all got me chopped if you think I'm gonna go all day without taking a shower."

Mark began laughing. "I'm joking, it's one a few minutes from here, in that direction," he said, pointing towards the path.

Malajia stared at him with confusion for a few moments as Mark continued to chuckle to himself. "That wasn't even a cool joke," she bit out, causing him to abruptly halt his laugh.

Later that morning, after everyone was showered and fed, the gang decided to take a hike through the woods. "Ooh, we should collect bugs," Emily suggested, adjusting the book bag on her back.

"Emily, don't make me dropkick you," Chasity calmly warned.

Emily giggled. "I was kidding."

Alex shook her head, "Now, now cranky," she directed at Chasity.

"Alex, I suggest you not talk to me, because your goofy ass still owes me another tent," Chasity returned, fixing her ponytail.

Alex chuckled. "I apologize. Put it on my tab."

Feeling something on her arm, Sidra smacked the spot. "Eww," she whined, seeing a small black smashed insect. "Ugh, this is so *gross*. Somebody please give me a tissue."

"Em, there's your first bug right there," Alex joked, pointing to Sidra's arm.

Sidra made a face as Chasity handed her a tissue.

As the group ambled along. Malajia kicked a few rocks with her sneaker-covered feet. Her mind was racing. She hadn't had a civilized conversation with Mark in days, and it was mostly her fault... It was *all* her fault. He'd even tried to get cozy with her earlier that morning despite her erratic behavior, and she snapped at him again. *I'm going crazy, I need a distraction,* she thought. She racked her brain for a way to stir up some trouble to get her mind off her *own* troubles.

Approaching a gurgling stream, the group decided to stop and take in the peaceful scenery. "That water looks so clear," David mused, taking in the clear waters.

"If it was a teeny bit warmer, we could've gone swimming," Alex pondered.

"I don't care if it was a *hundred* degrees out, I wouldn't go swimming in that," Sidra scoffed. "There's germs and fish crap in there."

Malajia shot Sidra a side-glance. *Perfect*, she thought before giving Sidra a quick shove, sending her screaming and falling into the water.

"Malajia are you crazy?!" Alex hollered as everyone looked at the scene in shock.

"Mel, you trippin'," Mark scolded as Josh helped the shocked and fuming Sidra out of the water.

"I'm gonna kill you Malajia!" Sidra screamed, lunging for Malajia, but was held back by Josh.

"Come on, let's go take a walk," Josh urged, seeing Sidra turn red. He knew that Sidra was at her breaking point and could possibly do bodily harm to Malajia.

"No, I don't need to take a walk," Sidra fumed, trying to break out of Josh's grip. "I *need* to rip those tracks out of her fuckin' head!"

"Josh, come on, let's get her out of here," David quickly slid in, directing him to a small path. As the two guys guided the cursing and screaming Sidra away, the rest of the group looked at Malajia, who was standing there with a satisfied grin on her face.

"What?" Malajia shrugged, noticing their looks.

"What the hell did you do that for?" Chasity charged, angry. Malajia was known for doing stupid things, but this was uncalled for.

Malajia sucked her teeth. "Everybody was just standing here looking all bored, so I figured why not have some fun?" she responded in a sad attempt to defend herself.

Alex pinched the bridge of her nose in an effort to keep calm. "So…your idea of *fun*, is pushing the girl in that cold ass water?" she asked slowly. "After she said that she had *no* interest in getting in there?"

Malajia stood there, but didn't say anything. She knew that what she did was wrong, but she wasn't about to let the group know that.

"What if she couldn't swim? What if it was deeper?" Emily asked, frowning. "She could've drowned."

"Sidra has been swimming since she was *seven*, the girl wasn't gonna drown," Malajia sneered, rolling her eyes. Seeing the angry faces still fixed on her, Malajia let out a loud sigh. "Okay fine, I'll apologize."

"No, I don't think that's gonna make things better," Alex said, looking past Malajia.

"Well, that's all she's getting from me," Malajia promised, folding her arms.

Chasity smirked as she moved a few steps over to the side. "Yeah okay," she said.

Malajia frowned in confusion. "What the hell—" Before Malajia could get another word out, Sidra darted up to her and gave her a hard push into the chilly water.

"How do *you* like it, bitch?" Sidra growled.

Malajia came up for air, frantically wiping the water from her face. "Sidra! Why you always gotta go tit for tat?!" she screamed. "I was about to apologize to your ignorant ass."

"*Keep* that bullshit apology," Sidra shot back. "Have fun blow drying that hair without electricity."

"You do the same," Malajia hissed, pushing wet hair off of her face.

Sidra made a face at Malajia.

Mark shook his head as he reached his hand down for

Malajia to grab. "Come on out of the water, soggy," he teased.

Annoyed, Malajia smacked his hand out of the way. "I don't need your help," she barked at him, pulling herself out of the water. "You stood there and watched her push me in."

"You act like you didn't *deserve* that shit," Mark pointed out, trying to wrap his arms around her to keep her warm.

"That's not the point," Malajia huffed, knocking his arms away, much to Mark's irritation.

"Fine Malajia," he bit back before turning to the others. "I'm going back to the camp site," he announced before walking off.

"We'll come with you," David said, as he and everyone, except for Chasity and Malajia followed suit.

Chasity watched their progress for a few moments, before turning to Malajia, who was wringing her hair out with her hands.

Malajia caught Chasity's stare. "What is it Chasity?" she hissed.

"You're being really extra," Chasity observed, folding her arms. "What the hell is going on with you?"

"Nothing," Malajia lied. "I was just playing too much, as usual."

"No, your behavior isn't the typical 'stupid Malajia' mess," Chasity countered. "It's something else."

Malajia frowned at her. "Did you just call me stupid?"

"Stop deflecting," Chasity snapped, pointing at her. "Now, Mark isn't my favorite person, but you're treating him like shit and that's not cool. Not to mention you're messing with everybody for no reason."

Malajia put her hands on her hips. She was in no mood for one of Chasity's mean lectures. "I said I'm *fine*, baby Alex," she sniped.

"Whatever yo," Chasity dismissed, walking away. She had her own stuff going on. The last thing she needed was to get wrapped up in Malajia's drama, yet again.

Malajia pushed her hair over her shoulder, letting out a

loud, heavy sigh.

"Even though I'm glad that tonight is our *last* night out here," Alex began, holding a marshmallow to the camp fire with a stick. "It *is* peaceful."

Later that evening, the group was sitting outside, enjoying the bright moonlight while making s'mores by the fire.

"I wish we had some fishing equipment," David said, poking at the fire with a branch. "We could've gone fishing."

"No, no. That hike earlier was enough," Sidra put in, taking a bite out of her s'more.

"I make a great campfire fish," David bragged. "We could've had that for dinner instead of those sandwiches."

Mark shot him a glance. "You hype as shit 'cause you've been camping before," he teased, earning a chuckle from David. "Ol' wilderness ass."

"Yeah well, my wilderness experience built these fires, fixed the girls' tents, *and* kept the bugs away, hasn't it?" David returned.

"Touché," Mark laughed, grabbing the bag of marshmallows. He looked over at Malajia who was sitting on a large rock, holding a throw blanket around her shoulders. "Mel, you want me to make you a s'more?" he asked, placing a marshmallow on a stick. Even though he was still irritated with her, seeing her look sad and detached made him feel bad. *I wish I knew what her problem was,* he thought.

"No, I'm not hungry," Malajia mumbled.

Mark leaned closer to her. "I didn't hear you, babe, what did you say?"

"I *said* I'm not hungry!" she snapped, earning confused looks from the group.

"What the hell are you *yelling* at me for?" Mark barked, tossing his stick to the ground.

"You're *bothering* me *as always*."

"You know what Malajia?" Mark began, deceptively

calm. "I am so fed up with your shit. You've been getting on *everybody's* nerves this *entire* weekend."

Malajia let out a loud laugh. "Are you *kidding* me?!" she exclaimed, holding her arms up in the air. "The king of fuckin' *stupid*, is accusing *me* of getting on everybody's nerves? That is hilarious."

"I haven't *done* anything to anybody this entire time and you know that," Mark pointed out.

"*Sure* you did," she disagreed. "*You* came *up* with this dumb trip in the *first* place."

He rolled his eyes. "All I was trying to do was get everybody to loosen up before finals," he defended. "Excuse *me* for thinking that it would be fun."

"Yeah and like *always*, you were wrong," Malajia hissed, examining her nails. "Just like you're *always* stupid, annoying and a fuckin' joke."

The group fell quiet. It wasn't out of the ordinary for Malajia and Mark to argue in front of everyone, but the way that Malajia spoke to and insulted Mark seemed a lot more vicious than their normal banter.

Mark stared at Malajia with disgust. He was done. He reached over and took hold of her arm. "I need to talk to you," he said through clenched teeth, as he stood up and pulled her along with him.

Jason followed Mark and Malajia's progress as they disappeared through the trees, "She's trippin'," he concluded. "Mark hasn't even been messing with her like he usually does."

"She's being a jackass for no *reason*," Sidra scoffed, pushing a few wayward wavy tendrils back up into her ponytail.

Mark, after leading Malajia to a spot that was out of earshot of the others, stopped and guided her in front of him. "What's your deal, yo?" he asked point blank.

Malajia frowned at him. "I have no idea what you're talking about?" she lied.

Mark stomped his foot on the ground. "Don't bullshit me Malajia!" he yelled, causing her to flinch.

"Don't yell at me!" she snapped back.

Mark put his hands over his face in an effort to calm down. "I don't want to yell at you," he said, tone calmer. "But I don't get why you're acting out like that."

Malajia let out a loud sigh. "Mark, ain't nobody trying to hear you talk right now," she ground out, putting her hand up. "So spare me and save it."

"No," he refused, folding his arms. "Why have you been treating me like shit?"

She rolled her eyes.

"You've been snapping at me every five minutes for *no* damn reason. Not to mention every time I try to get close to you, you brush me off," Mark added.

"Oh so we're back to the whole, 'Malajia isn't fucking Mark issue' huh?" she hissed, waving her arms in dramatic fashion.

"This isn't even about *sex*, Malajia," Mark argued. "You made it clear that you're not ready right now, and I told you that I'm good with that. But that doesn't excuse your screwed-up ass behavior."

Malajia tried to walk around him. "I don't have time for this," she sneered. Her departure was halted when Mark stood in front of her.

"Malajia, I don't want to argue with you—"

"Then *don't*," Malajia interrupted, tone nasty. "Just leave me alone."

Mark shook his head. "I *can't*," he said, honest. "You're not just some girl I can *dismiss* when she gets on my nerves…"

Malajia looked down at the ground.

"I just…I need to know what the issue is," he continued, almost pleading with her. "I know I'm not the best guy…I have shit that I need to change about myself, I know…and

I'm *trying*. But I don't feel that I deserve to be treated how you've been treating me." He stared at her. "But apparently, *you* feel differently."

Internally, Malajia felt like the scum of the earth. Mark was looking for answers as to why she was pushing him away, and all she could give him was anger and defensiveness.

When she didn't answer him, he looked down at the ground for a moment, before sighing. "Can you please just tell me what I did to you?" he pleaded.

Malajia just stared at him, trying to fight her building tears.

"I want to get close to you and I feel like I *can't*—" he paused for a moment, rubbing his face with his hand. "I care about you *so* much. I want this to *work* babe... I just need to know how to fix us. *Tell* me how to fix us."

Malajia put her hand over her face as the tears built. Mark was standing before her, sincere, vulnerable. He was telling her how much he cared for her—how much he wanted to be with her. The feelings that she had for him were like nothing she'd ever felt before; she wanted them to work too.

But despite how deep her feelings for Mark ran, she kept fighting herself and their relationship. *Just tell him what's been bothering you stupid!* she screamed to herself.

She desperately wanted to tell Mark the reason she couldn't sleep with him: she felt guilty that she had given her virginity to someone who didn't deserve it. Malajia wished she had saved it for someone who cared for her...she wished she had it to give to *him*.

She felt like she had robbed him of yet another first by getting pregnant by her abuser and getting an abortion. She wished that she could just tell him the reason that she kept pushing him away was that she was afraid that he would grow to see her how Malajia saw herself—ruined.

"Mark I..." Malajia put her hands on her head as she searched for something to say. She knew that she had to say something...but it couldn't be the truth. It just couldn't. "I just… I don't think this relationship is going to work out," she said slowly.

She closed her eyes in an effort to shut out the pained look on Mark's face. "What?" he muttered, confused.

"I don't want to be with you anymore," she added, plunging the verbal knife deeper into him. "I thought that I could cross that friendship line and be in a relationship with you, but I *can't*... Mark, I just don't see you any different than I used to…you're just not boyfriend material."

Mark stood there absorbing what she had just said to him. He was devastated. "So…you're telling me that after all these months of us being a couple, you can't see me as anything more than stupid, jackass Mark? Seriously?" he asked, voice dangerously low.

As the tears started flowing freely, she shook her head. She was deliberately hurting him because she was too much of a coward to be honest. "I'm sorry, Mark."

"You're sorry?" he scoffed. "You're *sorry*? You could've told me this a long *time* ago. Hell five *minutes* ago, before I *played* myself and told you how I felt about you and this damn relationship," he was livid. "You had me out here looking fuckin' *stupid*. Thinking that we were building something. Thinking that you had feelings for me and all this time you were *disgusted* by me?"

"You don't *disgust* me, that's not what I said," Malajia sniffled.

"You might as *well* had," Mark bit out. "I can't believe you're pulling this shit." Malajia tried to reach out and touch Mark's arm, but he moved it out of her reach. "Don't touch me, yo," he sneered.

"You're a *great friend* Mark," she said, voice cracking, "And that's why I thought it would be no issue with us being in a relationship, but I just…I'm sorry Mark. I tried, I really *did*."

"You're a lair, you *didn't* try," Mark threw back. "*I* did."

Malajia wiped the tears from her face. "I care about you—"

"Save that shit," Mark barked, putting his hand up; he wasn't interested in hearing anything else that Malajia had to say. "I put myself out there for you and you played me." He shook his head in disgust. "And here I thought *I* was the fucked up person, when in reality, it's *you*." He walked off, leaving Malajia standing there alone.

"Mark, I'm sorry!" she yelled after him. When he ignored her and continued to walk away, she busted out crying.

Chapter 34

Chasity stared at the scenery outside of her bedroom window. The muffled sound of her mother could be heard in the background as she concentrated on the leaves blowing on the trees. It was when she heard her name being called that she snapped out of her daze and looked at Trisha, standing in her doorway.

"Did you hear a word of what I just said?" Trisha asked, face frowned in concern. She had been talking to Chasity for the last ten minutes without any response.

"No, sorry," Chasity answered, running her hand along the back of her beck. "What did you say?"

"I said that I'll be over Mom's house, helping Brenda get settled," Trisha replied, hesitantly.

Chasity frowned slightly. "Brenda is getting settled for *what*?" she asked, confused.

Trisha shook her head, folding her arms. *She really wasn't listening to me.* "You *seriously* blocked out everything that I just said?" she ground out.

"What do you want from me?" Chasity snapped back. "As soon as you said 'Brenda' I tuned you out."

Trisha put her hands over her face in an effort to retain her cool. She was beyond stressed out and Chasity's attitude wasn't helping. "Look, Brenda doesn't have much longer, okay," she reminded, clasping her hands together. "She's moving in with Mom to be close to the family, and I'm going over there to help her get settled... Did you hear *that*?"

Chasity stared at Trisha, a blank expression on her face. She lied. She heard what Trisha had said the first time, but she was just trying to block the words out. Chasity had been home for summer break for nearly a week, and Brenda had been the topic of every conversation. Trisha couldn't stop talking about her and Chasity was tired of hearing about her.

"I heard you," Chasity answered finally, some bite to her voice.

Trisha turned to walk out, but paused and looked back at Chasity. "Will you at least *consider* talking—"

"Can you just not press me about this right now?" Chasity angrily interrupted, slamming her hand on the arm of her chaise. "I told you no the *first eighty* times."

"She just wants to talk to you one more time," Trisha sighed. "She has more that she needs to say."

"Tell her to say it to *you* since y'all are friends now," Chasity spat out.

Trisha ran her hand over her face. "She only has a few weeks to *live*, Chasity," she stressed.

Chasity rolled her eyes. "Don't pull this guilt trip on me," she bit out. When Trisha too rolled her eyes, Chasity rose from her seat. "Stop trying to force me to feel something for her that I *don't*."

Trisha slowly shook her head. "I'm not trying to force you," she assured.

"No? Could've fooled me."

"I just want... I just want you to really think about what you're doing by refusing to talk to her...to possibly *resolve* things with her," Trisha said, voice calm. "When she goes...*you* will still be here holding on to anger."

"That's my choice," Chasity replied, defiantly.

Trisha let out a long sigh. "You're right," she stated solemnly. "I'll probably spend the night tonight, so if you need me just call me."

Chasity simply nodded as Trisha walked out of her room. Once her mother was out of sight, Chasity sighed. Running her hands through her hair, she began to pace back and forth. "I gotta get out of this damn house," she huffed to herself before heading for the door.

"What time is Mark supposed to be coming over?" David asked Sidra, retrieving a large bowl of potato salad from her.

"I don't even know *if* he's coming," Sidra replied, grabbing a plate of fresh fruit from the kitchen counter. She signaled for David to follow her to her backyard. Sidra's family was taking advantage of the beautiful summer weather by having a cookout, and of course her parents insisted that Sidra invite her friends. "He's barely left the house since break started."

David exchanged pleasantries with Sidra's family as he set the bowl of salad on a cloth-covered table in the Howards' large backyard. "Yeah, I know. He just hasn't been himself since..." he took off his baseball cap and rubbed his head. "Since Malajia broke up with him."

Sidra shook her head. "I *swear* I don't get her," she said, "There was *no* good reason for her to do that." Sidra was certain that Malajia was not in her right frame of mind when she called things off with Mark during their camping trip. She'd been trying to talk some sense into Malajia since that night...along with the other girls. "Trust me, I'm not done cussing her out about it either... She thinks she's slick not answering my phone calls. She forgets I know where her butt lives."

David shook his head and chuckled. He glanced at a table full of people. "Uh Sid, I think that girl is trying to get your attention," he observed.

Sidra craned her neck to see. Eyeing a young woman sitting on her brother Marcus's lap, she rolled her eyes and went back to tending to the food on the table. "She better leave me alone," she muttered.

"What's wrong?" David wondered.

"That's Marcus's stupid girlfriend," Sidra sneered. "*India*," she mocked, making a face.

David looked back at them. "Ooooh, the one he breaks up with every two weeks, huh?" he chortled.

"I hate that bitch," Sidra spat out.

David chuckled at Sidra's outburst, then gave her a comforting pat on the shoulder. He smiled when he saw Josh step through the glass sliding door into the backyard. Josh was another one of his troubled friends he'd barely spoken to since school let out.

"Good to see you man," David said, patting Josh on his shoulder.

"You too, thanks for the invite Sid," Josh replied, giving Sidra a hug.

"Oh please boy, you don't have to thank me," she insisted, giving him a playful backhand on his chest. "How has it been at your mom's?"

Josh shrugged. "It's been okay," he replied. Josh decided that since Sarah was still staying with their father, that he'd go spend the summer with his mother in New Jersey. "She meditates...a *lot*."

"Well, I hear it's very calming," David pointed out.

"I guess." Josh shrugged yet again.

Sidra opened a container filled with corn on the cob. "So have you talked to your dad?" she asked, drawing her words out slowly.

"No. Are any burgers ready?" he quickly answered, changing the subject.

Sidra resisted the urge to roll her eyes at Josh. "Yeah, some should be done. Check with Daddy," she replied, pointing him in the direction of her father, who was manning the grill.

"Thanks," Josh threw over his shoulder, hurrying off.

"What are we going to do with him and Mark?" Sidra asked David once Josh was out of ear shot.

"Your guess is as good as mine," he sighed, reaching for a plate.

An hour had passed, and the Howard household was filled with family and friends. Sidra smiled, watching Josh and David play spades with her father and her brother Marcus. She was pleased that Josh seemed to be enjoying himself, but Sidra couldn't help but wonder where her other guests were.

"Yo, is that food done?" Mark asked, interrupting her thoughts.

She spun around to see Mark standing in her doorway, and smiled a bright smile. "You came," she beamed, hugging him. "I didn't think you would ever leave your house again."

"Yeah well, you know I couldn't miss an opportunity to eat Mother Howard's potato salad," he quipped.

Sidra chuckled. "Well, *whatever* got your greedy butt out of the house, I'm happy that you're here." Sidra decided not to press him about Malajia or his feelings at that moment; she wanted him to enjoy himself. "Go play cards with the guys and I'll fix you a plate," she said, pointing to where the guys were.

"Ooh is that spades?" he belted out, heading over. "Y'all might as well start the game over, 'cause you know I'm playing."

"Naw, you gotta wait," Josh laughed.

Sidra piled barbeque chicken, potato salad, baked macaroni and cheese, corn, a hamburger, hot dog, and ribs on Mark's plate before walking over and handing it to him.

As she turned to walk away, Mark looked at her. "Hey Sid, can you throw one more rib on here?" he asked, holding up his plate.

"Boy—"

"Mark, you already have damn near the whole menu on your plate already," Mr. Howard scolded, before Sidra got to finish *her* scolding. Mark shot him a salty look. "Eat *that* first and then see if you're still hungry."

"You already know I'm *gonna* be," Mark muttered, picking up a drumstick.

"Just greedy," David teased.

Sidra shook her head at the banter, then headed into the house. As she passed some conversing relatives, she grabbed her cell phone off the coffee table and looked at it.

Hmm, no missed calls from the girls, she thought. Especially one in particular. Letting out a quick sigh, Sidra dialed a number.

"Hello," the person on the other end answered, voice dry.

"Simmons. Why are you not at my cookout?" Sidra barked into the phone.

Malajia rolled over in her bed, the same place she'd been for the past two days. "Sidra, as you can tell by the sound of my dry ass voice, I am in no mood to socialize," she grumbled.

"And as *you* can tell by the sound of *my* voice, I don't give a damn about your funky mood," Sidra bit back. "I don't know what your problem is, but I don't appreciate you not returning my calls."

"Why you stalking me Sidra?" Malajia spat into the phone. "Damn, when *you* don't feel like being bothered, *you* don't return calls either. Remember?"

"And you *fussed* at me about doing that, so now I'm returning the favor," Sidra countered, walking into the kitchen. "You need to just get up and come on up to Delaware," she urged, picking up a piece of cantaloupe from a fruit tray. "Besides, Mark is here."

Malajia sat right up in bed. Her heart pounded and she felt butterflies in her stomach. She hadn't seen or spoken to Mark since she abruptly ended things with him weeks ago. She ducked and dodged him the last few weeks of school, and he basically did the same. "So?" she sneered, voice opposite how she was actually feeling.

Sidra rolled her eyes. "Whatever Malajia, play cute if

you want," she hissed. "Just get out that damn bed, 'cause I know you're in it. Take a damn shower, throw on something cute, and get your behind here," she ordered.

Malajia pulled the phone away from her ear and frowned at it. She had every intention of cursing Sidra out, but then realized she was right; Malajia needed to get out of the bed and do something with herself. "Fine," she huffed. "Put me up some of your mom's potato salad."

"Fine, but if you don't show up, I'm gonna let Marcus eat it and I'm gonna send you a picture of him doing it," Sidra promised.

"Tell his big ass not to touch my damn salad," Malajia grunted.

"Just *get* here," Sidra ordered before hanging up.

Setting the phone down on the counter, she took a bite of the cantaloupe in her hand. The sound of the front door opening, accompanied by a familiar voice greeting other guests, made her turn around. She smiled as Chasity headed into the kitchen. "Hey beautiful," she gushed, giving Chasity a hug.

Chasity frowned slightly at Sidra's wide smile. "Come on with all that cheesin'," she mocked.

"Oh hush," Sidra giggled. "I thought you weren't coming."

"I wasn't *going* to, but the walls in my house were starting to close in on me," Chasity replied, adjusting the silver bracelets on her wrist. "So I figured an hour on the highway was a better alternative."

After Trisha left to go to her grandmother's house earlier that day, Chasity decided that she couldn't just sit in the house by herself alone with her thoughts. With Jason out of town with his family, she figured she would take Sidra up on her cookout invite.

"Well, I'm glad that you're here," Sidra smiled, heading over to the refrigerator. "Do you want something to drink?"

"Is it alcohol?" Chasity asked.

"It's a wine cooler," Sidra answered, pulling a bottle

from the refrigerator.

Chasity turned her lip up as Sidra walked over with the bottle. "*And* it's pink," she jeered. "You mean to tell me you're having a cookout and this is the *strongest* thing you have? I should've stayed my ass home."

Sidra stared at her. "Are you finished?"

"Yeah," Chasity muttered.

Sidra pushed the bottle in Chasity's hand. "Now hush up and just drink it, you picky heffa," she demanded.

Chasity snickered.

"Have you talked to Malajia lately?" Sidra asked after several seconds of silence.

"Not for more than a few minutes," Chasity replied, taking a sip of her drink. "Why?"

"I was hoping that you could shed some light on what's been going on with her," Sidra replied, opening her own wine cooler.

Chasity sighed. "As much as I would love to engross myself in Malajia's issues, I don't have the energy for it," she sneered. "I have my own shit to deal with."

"Really? Like what?"

Chasity ran her hand through her hair. "You don't wanna know."

"I asked, so that means that I *do*," Sidra assured, leaning on the counter. "So tell me, what's been going on with you? You seem preoccupied lately."

Chasity looked down at the counter for a brief second, before taking a deep breath. "Brenda is dying," she blurted out.

A stunned look crossed Sidra's face. "Wait what?" she asked, confused. "Brenda who?"

"*Brenda,* Brenda."

Sidra's eyes widened. "Oh my God! You mean your mo—aunt—other—aunt-mother?"

Chasity narrowed her eyes at her. "Really Sidra?" she bit out.

Sidra put her hands up. "No sweetie, I promise I'm not

trying to be smart. I just get confused when it comes to Brenda and what she is to you."

"She's my *aunt*," Chasity hissed. "And yeah, that's what's going on."

"I'm so sorry to hear that sweetie," Sidra sympathized, holding her hand over her heart. When she noticed that Chasity wasn't looking at her, Sidra frowned slightly. "*Should* I be sorry?" she slowly drew out. "I mean...how are you feeling about this?"

"I don't like the fact that she's *dying* if that's what you're asking me," Chasity hissed.

"I wasn't asking that, Chasity," Sidra said, calm.

"I mean, I don't *like* the woman but I don't wish death on her. I'm not *that* much of a heartless bitch."

"I didn't say that you *were*," Sidra assured, putting her hand out. "I'm sorry, I just don't know what to say."

"You don't have to say anything," Chasity muttered. She paused for a moment. "Everybody wants me to react a certain way and I *can't*," she vented. "Brenda wants me to forgive her, my *family* wants me to forgive her, Trisha is in my face every freakin' five minutes pressuring me to talk to her again. She moved in to my grandmom's house so she's like *three blocks* from me, they're saying that she only has a few weeks left. It's...it's too much at once, I can't take this pressure. I'm ready to punch a freakin' wall—are you *sure* you don't have anything stronger than this?" Chasity fumed, pointing to her half drunken wine cooler.

Sidra shook her head. "No, not for you," she said. "The last thing you need with your stress level right now is to be hammered."

"That's *exactly* what I need right now," Chasity countered, setting her bottle on the counter.

"No," Sidra maintained. "You need to be clear-headed."

Chasity shot Sidra a death stare. "Don't get all 'Alex' on me right now," she fussed. "I'm on edge and could possibly smack you."

Sidra sucked her teeth. As she opened her mouth to

verbally retaliate, she heard Alex ask, "Who's getting 'Alex' on you Chasity?" She smiled, hugging Sidra. "And *whoever* it is, I'm sure they're awesome."

"Boooo," Chasity jeered, then backed away when Alex moved to embrace her.

"Nice to see you *too*, Chaz," Alex sarcastically drawled at her reaction.

"Yeah, yeah good to see you," Chasity dismissed, waving her hand.

"How was the train ride?" Sidra asked Alex, handing her a bottle of water. "Where's Em? I thought that she was spending a few weeks in Philly with you."

Alex opened the bottle and took a long sip. "The train was *hot*," she complained. "The damn air conditioning was broken. Not a good look on a ninety-degree day."

Sidra winced as Chasity frowned her face up. "Is that why you look like somebody poured a bucket of water on you?" Chasity asked smartly, eyeing Alex's glistening face and sweat stained t-shirt. "*That's* why I didn't hug you."

Alex looked down at her shirt. "Dear God," she grumbled, tugging at the damp fabric. "Anyway Sid, Emily postponed her Philly visit," she informed. "She's spending time with her brothers in Jersey."

Sidra smiled. "Oh wow, that's good," she beamed. "I'm glad that they're embracing her." Knowing Emily's history with her siblings, it made Sidra happy to know that she was beginning to get along with some of them. "So…what about the sister?"

Alex shook her head. "No progress on the Jazmine front, *or* the mother front," she revealed.

"A damn shame," Sidra bit out. "Alex, the bathroom is upstairs to the left if you want to freshen up."

Alex adjusted her large satchel on her shoulder. "Thanks girl, 'cause you know I brought a backup T-shirt," she laughed, heading in the direction of the stairs.

"I hope you got backup *deodorant* too," Chasity joked.

"Shut it up, Chasity!" Alex barked, earning a laugh from

both Chasity and Sidra.

Mark took a swig of his soda before slamming a card on the table. "What's up with these sorry cards bee?" he complained to Mr. Howard, who was busy glaring at him.

They had been playing cards for the last hour, and Mr. Howard was beginning to get fed up with Mark's complaining.

"Mark, *you're* the one who shuffled, so blame yourself," David grumbled, grabbing a handful of chips out of a wooden bowl.

"Man, how you gonna touch all the chips?" Mark griped, loud, pointing to the bowl.

"Mark, for the love of God, shut up," Josh barked.

Mark sucked his teeth, examining his cards. He couldn't figure out if it was the cards, Mr. Howard being his partner, or his overly full stomach affecting his enjoyment of this spades game. He was about to say something, when Mr. Howard stood up.

"Guys, I'm calling it quits," he announced, sitting his cards on the table.

Mark let out a sigh of relief as Mr. Howard walked off. "Good, he sucked as a partner," he said, inciting laugher from Josh and David. He glanced and saw Chasity standing by the food table with Alex and Sidra. "Aye Chaz, can you come here for a second?" he called.

Rolling her eyes, Chasity tried to ignore him. It was when he yelled her name louder and drawled out the ending of her name, that she sucked her teeth and walked over, much to the amusement of the other girls. "What, boy?" she huffed.

"Come be my spades partner," he smiled.

"No, I already told you that I'm not playing spades with you anymore," Chasity refused, turning to walk away.

Mark gently grabbed her arm, halting her departure. "Please?" he begged. "Jason isn't here and Malajia—" He rubbed his head with his hand and sighed. "Look, I'm tired of

David and Josh kicking my ass, so I need someone who knows how to play," he stated, trying to mask the hurt he was feeling at the mere mention of Malajia's name.

Chasity stared at him for a moment. She had every intention of denying his request but knowing what he was dealing with, she decided to grant him his wish. Reluctantly, she sat down in the seat across from him. "Fine," she relented. "But I swear to God, you yell at me *one* time and not only will I throw these cards at you, I'll leave this damn table," she warned.

Mark put his hands up. "Got it," he promised.

By night fall, the cookout was still in full swing. More guests had arrived, which was no problem for the Howards; they had prepared more than enough food. Sidra was standing in the kitchen with Alex, when the front door opened.

"Y'all can stop being dry, I'm here now," Malajia announced, walking into the kitchen.

Sidra glanced at the silver watch on her slender wrist.

"Don't even say nothin'," Malajia sneered before Sidra could say anything about her lateness. "It took me all damn day to persuade my dad to let me borrow the van. There was no way I was getting on that hot ass train."

Sidra chuckled, noticing the taut look on Alex's face. "Don't even *mention* that terrible train," Alex scoffed, taking a bite out of a rib.

Malajia rubbed her hands together in anticipation. "Sid, you got that potato salad for me?" she asked, a smile plastered to her face.

Sidra grabbed a foil covered plate from the refrigerator and handed it to Malajia who bobbed the plate up and down in her hand.

"This feels too damn light," Malajia charged. When she removed the foil, she frowned at the small amount of salad on the plate. "Sidra, I know this ain't all you put up for me," she barked.

Sidra put her hands up as she tried not to laugh. "Mel, listen—"

"Naw, you hit me with the flim flam," Malajia interrupted, shaking her hand in Sidra's face. "You already knew this wasn't gonna be enough."

"Malajia listen, I tried to put up more for you, but Marcus got to it before I could," Sidra assured, voice filled with amusement.

Malajia slammed her plate down, sending bits of salad flying on the counter. Sidra eyed the mess before shooting Malajia a glance, all traces of amusement gone.

Catching Sidra's piercing stare, Malajia pointed to the mess. "I'mma clean that up, but I'm *still* not pleased about the amount of salad," she declared, tearing some paper towels off of a nearby roll. When Alex began laughing, Malajia sucked her teeth. "Why do you smell like sweat and bus seats?" she mocked.

Alex stopped laughing and regarded Malajia with anger. "*First* of all, I don't smell like *anything* but deodorant and dryer sheets," she corrected. "Second, why do you always have to start?"

"'Cause you act like dryer sheets is a cool thing to *smell* like," Malajia laughed, and was soon joined by Sidra. "Sid, she said that hype as shit."

Alex slowly placed her hands on her hips as she continued to stare daggers at Malajia.

"She was rubbing dryer sheets on her clothes 'cause she's too cheap to buy perfume and shit," Malajia continued, pointing to the visibly angry Alex.

Sidra laughed harder as she wrapped her arms around Malajia. She was glad that she was acting like her normal self, no matter how simple she could be. "I'm glad you came, crazy."

"Ha, take that!" Mark boasted, throwing down a card.

"Chaz, we make a good team," he happily declared, scooped up a book from Marcus's team.

"I told you not to talk to me while I'm in the zone," Chasity hissed, putting her hand up. As spades partners, Mark and Chasity had beaten Josh and David, Mr. Howard who decided to get back in on the action with his wife, as well as Sidra's other two brothers. Mark, who had gotten his groove back, couldn't have been happier.

"Sorry, my-favorite-person-in-the-world-right-now," Mark chortled.

Chasity was about to throw down another card, when she heard Alex call her name, loudly. "Not now, Alex," she threw back. Before Chasity knew it, Alex was right next to her. Annoyed, Chasity loudly sucked her teeth. "What girl? I said not now, I'm trying to win this game."

"Yo, get outta here Alex, you messin' up my partner's concentration," Mark added, gesturing for Alex to move.

"No, stay, *please*," Marcus joked, flipping through his cards. "She's *killing* me in this game."

Ignoring Mark, Alex folded her arms. "First off, I don't care for your tone," Alex spat at Chasity.

"And I don't like that shirt you got on, what's your point?" Chasity returned, concentrating on her cards.

"Malajia's here," Alex blurted out.

"So?" Chasity barked, irritated that she was being disturbed. Then she and Alex glanced at Mark, who nearly choked on the water that he was drinking.

He glanced over and saw Malajia standing near the back door. She caught his eye and stared back at him. Shaking his head, Mark sat his cards down. "Chaz, sorry you gotta find a new partner sweetie. I'm gonna take a break," he sulked, standing from the table and walking off.

Mark walked over to the cooler on the other side of the yard and searched through it. He was in desperate need of some sort of alcohol.

"You seriously just walked by me and didn't say anything?" Malajia questioned, walking over to him.

"There's nothing to say," he replied calmly, not making eye contact with her.

Malajia let out a sigh. She was questioning her choice to come to the cookout at that moment. "Look Mark, I'm sorry."

"*What* are you sorry about exactly, Malajia?" Mark ground out, folding his arms, scowling at her. "Is it the fact that you wasted my time? That you led me on? That you dropped me like a bad habit out of *nowhere*? ...Which is it?"

Malajia took a deep breath. "*All* of it, okay?" she admitted, running her hands through her straightened hair. She'd spent the past few weeks beating herself up for what she did to Mark. She missed him. "I know that I didn't treat you right, and I probably don't deserve it but...I still would like us to be friends."

"You *don't*. Not interested," Mark hissed, walking off.

Malajia followed his progress into the house, trying to force back the tears that were starting to form in her eyes. Just as the tears were about to spill out, she heard her name being called.

"Mel, come sit out front with us," Sidra urged from the door way. Wiping her eyes with the back of her hand, Malajia made a beeline for Sidra.

When she and Sidra arrived to the front of the house, they found Chasity and Alex sitting on the steps.

"What are y'all doing out here when everyone else is in the backyard?" Malajia asked, wiping her eyes yet again.

"We saw you talking to Mark and figured that you needed to talk to us without everyone being around," Alex bluntly stated, before taking a bite out of her burger.

Malajia shook her head at Alex's honesty. "While I appreciate it, I don't need to talk. I'm fine," she assured, sitting down on the step.

"Those tears in your big ass eyes say otherwise," Chasity bit out, examining the contents of her wine cooler bottle.

Malajia shot her a glance. "How many of those did you have?" she spat.

"Not enough," Chasity returned, setting the bottle on the step next to her.

"Okay, no need to get snippy," Alex interjected. "Malajia, we know you're upset over what happened with Mark."

"Speaking of that, what exactly *happened* with Mark?" Chasity asked, looking at Malajia.

"What are you talking about?" Malajia grunted.

"Girl, you broke up with him out of nowhere," Chasity pointed out. "Now, he gets on my last nerve, but even *he* didn't deserve that."

Malajia put her head in her hands. *Tell me something I don't know*, she thought.

"Mel, Chaz is right," Sidra added. "That *was* out of nowhere. What's been going on with you?"

"Look, I'm just dealing with some stuff right now," Malajia answered, exasperated. "Stuff that I *don't* want to talk about."

"Well you need to talk to *somebody* because you're trippin'," Chasity ground out, pushing some hair behind her shoulders.

"I tried suggesting that," Alex muttered, chewing.

Malajia rolled her eyes. "Alex, you smackin' all loud, I'm sure that burger ain't that good," she scoffed.

"It *is*," Alex calmly replied. "Now stop trying to change the subject."

Malajia let out a quick sigh. "Look, like I said, I'm fine," she grumbled. "Can we talk about something else please?"

"Sure…Brenda is dying," Chasity blurted out, much to the shock of Alex and Malajia.

"Wait, *what*?!" Malajia exclaimed. She sensed that something was going on with Chasity, but she never suspected that that would be it. *Damn, I've been so wrapped up in my mess that I didn't even try to find out what was wrong with her.*

"Are you for real?" Alex questioned, still in shock.

"Yep," Chasity confirmed.

Malajia put her hand up. "Wait a minute. When did you find *this* out?"

"Over spring break," Chasity revealed. "It's a long story that I don't want to get into again, but basically she's been sick for a while now and she doesn't have much longer."

Alex put her hand on Chasity's shoulder. "Sweetie, I'm so sorry," she sympathized. "I mean, I know that you don't care for her because of what she did to you, but I know it still has to affect you. She *was* the only mother that you knew for eighteen years."

"She's about to punch you in the face for that comment," Malajia predicted.

"I'm *not*," Chasity assured. "I'm fine. It isn't affecting me like everyone *thinks* it should... Everyone including my *mother*."

"Well, it may not affect you *now*...but eventually it *will*," Alex said. Chasity just shot her a side-glance. "And when it *does*, we'll be here for you." Alex then turned to Malajia. "And Mel, whenever you decide to tell us what's going on in *your* head, we'll be here to listen."

"Yes, I know your nosey asses *will*," Malajia joked, trying to bring some light to the somber atmosphere.

"Don't be a smart ass," Alex chided, playfully backhanding Malajia on the arm, making her giggle.

Chapter 35

Sidra yawned and stretched, pulling her blue satin robe closed and tying it. She'd woken up hours ago, but decided after a long night of entertaining at her family's cookout the night before, all she wanted to do was relax. Sitting down on the couch, she grabbed the cup of tea that she had made from the glass coffee table and was just about to take a sip, when she heard a knock at the door.

She frowned slightly, rising from her seat. She walked to the door and peered out of the peephole. Shaking her head, Sidra let out a chuckle. "Why am I not surprised?" she said, opening the door. "You came over here to eat up the rest of the barbeque food?" she asked Mark, who stepped inside.

"You know me so well," Mark chortled, rubbing his hands together. "You don't even gotta fix me a plate—I know where everything is," he added, making his way to the kitchen with Sidra in tow.

"Of *course* you do," Sidra laughed, sitting at the kitchen table while Mark proceeded to go into the refrigerator and remove several foil-covered containers.

"Nice robe," he teased, eyeing Sidra's attire. "I don't think I've ever seen you not fully dressed after nine in the morning."

She giggled in return. "Yeah well, after walking around all day and night in that darn outfit I had on, I think I deserve to not have on any real clothes this morning."

"I hear you," Mark mused. "It's quiet in here. Where's the rest of the family?"

"The guys went to work, and my parents went to the Harbor in Baltimore for the day." Mark simply nodded as he fixed himself a plate. Sidra studied him; she noticed how his eyes shifted when she mentioned Baltimore. "Are you okay?" she asked, voice soft and caring.

Mark stopped what he was doing and sighed. "Naw Sid," he admitted, which shocked Sidra. The old Mark would have made some joke or deflected, but him admitting that he wasn't okay told her that he was really messed up over this Malajia situation.

"I tried talking to her to get to the bottom of why she's acting the way that she is," Sidra informed, removing the clip from her hair, sending her locks tumbling past her shoulders. "She's being vague."

"I appreciate you trying," he replied, picking his plate up. "But it is what it is. She doesn't want me, so...that's that."

"I just don't get her," Sidra seethed. "She never mentioned to me or any of the other girls that she was having second thoughts about being in a relationship with you... She seems to genuinely care for you."

Mark rubbed the back of his neck as Sidra kept talking. While he appreciated her concern, the topic of his ex-girlfriend wasn't something that he really wanted to talk about. "Sid, can we talk about something else?"

"Oh...sure, I'm sorry," she said. "I don't mean to keep talking about it, I know you're upset... I just hate that you two can't make it work."

"It's not me, it's *her*," Mark spat.

"I know," Sidra mumbled. She frowned as she heard a knock. "I'll bet you anything that this is David or Josh coming for leftovers too," she chortled, heading for the door.

Neglecting to look out the peephole this time around, Sidra smiled as she jerked the door open. Her eyes widened once she saw who was standing on the other side. "Whoa," was all that she could say.

Sarah smiled slightly at Sidra's reaction. "How are you Sidra?" she asked, remembering her brother's best friend all too well. She'd always liked her.

Sidra was practically speechless. Josh's sister was the last person she expected to see on her doorstep. The last she'd seen Sarah was before Josh left for Paradise Valley University...before Sarah stole her brother's money.

"Um...I'm fine, uh..." Sidra was desperately searching for the words to say, and the reason why Sarah was at her house. Before she could say anything else, she heard Mark's voice.

"Yo Sid, is that the guys?" he asked, walking to the door with his plate in hand. "Tell 'em that I ate the rest of the mac and—whoa," he said, coming face to face with Sarah, who smiled at him.

"Hey Mark."

Mark and Sidra shared a glance. "H—hey Sarah," he stammered. "Uh Sid, I'll leave you to your company." Sidra's eyes widened as Mark proceeded to head out the door.

"No, that's okay you can stay," she said, grabbing hold of his arm. She had no desire to talk to Sarah alone.

Mark pried Sidra's hand off of his arm. "Sidra don't be rude, I'll call you later," he said. "I'll return the plate tomorrow," he promised, holding the glass plate full of food.

Sidra put her hands on her hips. "Are you *really* taking my mama's china plate?" she barked at his back as he made a hasty retreat to his car. Shaking her head, she signaled for Sarah to come inside.

As Sidra and Sarah made themselves comfortable on the cushy sofa in the living room, Sidra looked at her. Sarah looked great, no longer like the strung-out person that she used to be. "So...what brings you to my house Sarah?" Sidra asked.

Sarah looked down at her hands. "Well…I haven't seen Josh since he was home on spring break…neither has our father," she answered.

Sidra rested her arm on the back of the couch. "He didn't tell your dad that he was spending the summer with your mother?"

"He did tell Dad," she admitted.

Sidra nodded slightly. "Sarah, *again* why are you here?" she bluntly asked.

Sarah let out a long sigh. "I was wondering if you can persuade Josh into letting me talk to him again," she said.

Sidra quickly shook her head. "No, I don't want to get in the middle of your family issues," she declined. Even though she had tried to get Josh to talk to his sister again for his sake, that wasn't something that she wanted to share with Sarah. As far as Sidra was concerned, what she and Josh spoke about wasn't any of Sarah's business.

"Sidra, please," Sarah begged. "You're his closest friend, I know he'll listen to you."

That's what you think, Sidra thought.

"I know that I haven't been the best sister. I know that I hurt him—"

"You did more than just *hurt* him Sarah," Sidra interrupted. "You almost ruined his life."

"I know that," she admitted sorrowfully. "I know what I did was wrong… I stole from our parents, I stole from *him*… He got jumped because of me—"

"Wait, he got *what*?" Sidra asked, putting her hand up.

Sarah looked at Sidra, eyes wide. "He didn't tell you?"

"No," Sidra hissed.

"Apparently the night that I ran off with his money, he went looking for me at the um…crack house, and some guys that I used to roll with jumped and robbed him."

Sidra was fuming. Josh never mentioned that part to her. She remembered talking to him after Sarah ran off and he sounded pained, but she thought it was just because he was angry. Sidra had no idea that he had been physically hurt. "How could you let that happen?!" Sidra wailed. "Drugs or no drugs, that's still your damn brother."

"I didn't know that had happened," Sarah assured, putting her hand over her own heart. "He told me that *recently*."

Sidra shook her head; she couldn't tell if the woman sitting before her was lying or not.

"I love J.J. and I just want him to know how sorry I am for everything."

"He hates you Sarah," Sidra bit out. "You put him through too much."

"I know I did," Sarah admitted. "I want to make it right."

"You need to pay back what you took, first of all," Sidra stated.

"I know and I'm working on it… But I don't want to just pay him back the money…I want to rebuild our relationship…" Sidra ran her hands through her hair as tears began to form in Sarah's bright brown eyes. "Can you please just talk to him for me?" she asked, voice cracking.

Sidra threw her head back and sighed loudly. She hated being put in this position. Sarah was in tears and begging her to convince Josh to talk to her again, and Sidra had already told herself that she wasn't going to keep pressing Josh about the situation because she saw how angry it was making him… But, she also knew, deep down, that resolving the anger with his sister would ultimately help Josh in the end. "I'll try Sarah," she promised after a long pause.

Grateful, Sarah threw her arms around Sidra. It may have been years since she'd had a real conversation with her, but Sarah always appreciated how much Sidra cared about her brother and had his back, even when they were children. She only hoped that Josh kept that in mind whenever Sidra spoke to him.

Trisha, seeing Chasity's car pull into the driveway,

stepped out the front door. When Chasity got out of the car, Trisha walked over to her. "Chasity, can you do me a favor sweetie?"

Chasity frowned slightly at the urgency in her mother's voice. "What's up?"

"I need for you to go to the grocery store for your grandmother," Trisha requested, much to Chasity's annoyance, which showed on her face.

"Are you serious?" she sniped, pushing hair over her shoulder. "I just spent all morning at the car shop, getting this thing inspected and detailed, and now you want me to go *back* out?" Seeing the somber look on Trisha's face made Chasity let out a loud sigh. "Fine, text me a list and I'll pick the stuff up. I guess you can drop it off later."

"No, I need for you to go shopping *and* drop it off," Trisha revealed hesitantly.

Chasity's face took on an angry expression. "I'm *not* going over there," she refused, making her way towards the house.

Trisha caught up to her and stood in front of her, blocking her way. "Chasity, *I* can't do it. I have an important client to meet now."

"*Now*? It's Sunday," Chasity bit out.

"You already know that I meet my clients at any time," Trisha argued. "Now, I know why you don't want to go over there—"

"And yet, you're asking me to go *anyway*," Chasity fussed.

Trisha ran her hands through her hair. It had been a little over two weeks since Brenda moved into their mother's home to live out the rest of her days. Chasity had avoided her grandmother's home at all costs and even though it annoyed Trisha, she'd succeeded in not pressuring her to go…until now.

"Just do this for her, you already know she hurt her ankle the other day and can't go, and I just told you that I have a meeting."

"Melina's big ass can't go?" Chasity spat of her most hated cousin. "I heard she's been living there ever since she lost her apartment."

Trisha rolled her eyes. "She's not there...she took Brenda out for some air," Trisha looked down at her hands. "She was getting tired of being cooped up in the house... Anyway, she's not there, so if you go *now,* you can get it over with and you won't run the risk of running in to *either* of them."

Chasity stared at her mother, clenching her jaw. She was annoyed and had every intention of refusing, but thinking of her grandmother's hurt ankle made her relent. "Fine, whatever," she huffed, walking back to the car. Trisha gave a slight grateful smile as she watched Chasity pull off in a hurry.

If the excessive summer heat didn't irritate Chasity, the hour in the crowded grocery store certainly did. Relieved to have reached her destination, she grabbed the four grocery bags from the trunk of her car and headed up to her grandmother's front step. She knocked on the door and let out a sigh as she waited for her grandmother to answer.

"Chasity, is that you darlin'?" the frail voice called from inside.

"Oh my God, just come on," she mumbled to herself angrily. "Yes, it's me," she answered, tone opposite of how she was really feeling. Chasity plastered a phony smile on her face as the front door opened. Returning Chasity's smile with a warm one of her own, Grandmother Duvall gestured for her to come in.

"Is it hot out there?" she asked, shutting the door behind Chasity once she stepped inside.

No, it's snowing out. Chasity was in no mood for small talk; she was hot, tired and irritated that she had to step foot in that house in the first place. "Yes, it's hot out. Do you want me to put these away for you?"

"I'd appreciate it if you *could*," Grandmother Duvall smiled.

Chasity spent the next ten minutes putting the groceries away, while her grandmother milled about the massive home in silence. Tossing the empty plastic bags in a broom closet, Chasity gave her grandmother a hug, then made her way towards the door. "Okay, I'll see you later," she quickly said.

"Chasity, wait a minute," Grandmother Duvall called, halting her progress. "Can you do me one more favor?" Chasity just looked at her, not saying a word. "Can you run upstairs and look in my bathroom and get my prescription bottles for me?"

Chasity rubbed the back of her neck. "*Which* bathroom?" she sighed.

"The one in my bedroom."

"Yeah," Chasity huffed, before taking the steps two at a time.

Chasity rummaged through the cabinet in the private bathroom, letting out a loud groan. "There's no damn pill bottles in here," she seethed to herself. "I don't have time for this nonsense." Stalking out of the bedroom, she came face to face with Melina, which startled her.

"Well, well, guess who decided to grace this house with her stuck-up presence," Melina sneered, tying a satin scarf around her head.

Chasity glared at her plump cousin. It was apparent that the girl had gained a few more pounds since Chasity last saw her over Christmas. "What the fuck are you doing here?" she hissed. "Aren't you supposed to be out with Brenda somewhere?"

Melina pointed an un-manicured finger at her younger cousin. "First of all, it's *Aunt* Brenda," she corrected, tone nasty. "You need to show some damn respect for her, you—"

"Melina, on everything I love, you don't want to take it there with me on the subject of Brenda and what I address her as, okay?" Chasity warned abruptly.

Melina rolled her eyes. Even though they were civil to

each other over the holidays, Melina still felt disdain for Chasity. She hated the fact that Trisha, the family's breadwinner, spoiled her, and she resented the way that Chasity was treating Brenda, knowing that she was sick. Brenda had always been Melina's favorite aunt.

"Whatever, *Pebbles*," Melina hissed, placing her hands on her hips. Chasity narrowed her eyes; everybody in their family knew how much Chasity hated her childhood nickname. "Who told you I was out with Aunt Brenda?"

"My mom did, you fuckin' whale," Chasity bit back.

"Well, she's as much a liar as you are an evil bitch," Melina retuned before turning on her heel and storming towards her bedroom.

Chasity frowned at Melina's back. Why Trisha felt the need to lie about Melina not being at the house was beyond her. It wasn't like Chasity was afraid of the girl; she just didn't like her. It wasn't until she heard a familiar voice behind her that everything clicked. Chasity slowly turned around to find a frail Brenda standing there in a long pink robe, her short hair tucked underneath a scarf.

Brenda stared at the young woman who used to call her Mom. She wanted more than anything to wrap her arms around Chasity and tell her a million times how sorry she was for everything, but the piercing gaze in Chasity's eyes told her not to make a move. Brenda just managed a small smile.

Chasity was furious. *She lied to me again*, she fumed internally of Trisha. Feeling ambushed yet again, Chasity stormed away from Brenda and down the steps, leaving Brenda standing there, defeated. As Chasity made a dash towards the front door, her grandmother rose from her seat.

"Sweetheart—"

"You helped set me up too?" Chasity hissed at the elderly woman.

Grandmother Duvall looked down at her hands. "We didn't mean to upset you Chasity—"

Chasity snatched open the door. "No disrespect

Grandmom, but save it," she ground out before walking out and slamming the door behind her.

Shaking her head sorrowfully, Grandmother Duvall glanced up at the top of the stairs and saw Brenda staring down at her. She regarded her sick daughter sadly.

Chasity barely pulled off when she dialed Trisha's phone number. Turning on the car speaker, she waited for her to pick up.

"Chasity, I know you're angry with me," was the first thing that Trisha said when she answered.

"Why do you *keep* doing shit like this to me?!" Chasity yelled.

"I'm sorry, but I didn't know any other way to get you to see her." Trisha reasoned. "I just…Chaz I just feel that you need to talk to her again."

"I don't *give* a f—" Chasity pinched the bridge of her nose in a failed attempt to calm herself down. She was livid. "I don't care about what you feel, because it's clear that you don't give a damn about what *I* feel."

"That's not true."

"It *is* true!" Chasity wailed. "You constantly do shit like this behind my back. You keep breaking my trust and I'm *tired* of it!"

"Please just calm down, I know you're driving," Trisha pleaded through the car's speaker system. "I'll be home in about an hour and we can talk face to face."

"Screw you Patrisha," Chasity hissed. "I won't be there when you get back." Chasity abruptly ended the call. As Chasity pulled into her driveway, she felt like screaming at the top of her lungs. Instead, she punched the steering wheel before putting her face in her hands.

Chapter 36

"Next time we decide to go to the movies, I'm picking which one we see," Mark declared, tossing his empty popcorn container in the trash can. "That movie sucked."

David chuckled. *"You're* the one who picked *this* movie for us to see," he reminded.

"Exactly and it was *ass*, so I get to pick the *next* one," Mark replied, voice laced with amusement.

To cope with the overwhelming heatwave, Mark, David, Sidra, and Josh decided to take an excursion to the movie theater inside the air-conditioned mall.

"What do you guys wanna do *now*?" Josh asked as the group meandered through the crowded mall.

"I don't know about *you* guys, but I'm starving. How about we head to that burger joint on the other side of the mall?" Mark suggested.

The group agreed and made their way to the small burger place. Sidra slid in to a booth and proceeded to fan herself. "I swear, after we eat, I'm going home and taking a nap," she declared. "This heat has me worn out."

Josh fiddled with the salt and pepper shaker on the table. "David and Sid, do you guys mind if I chill at one of your houses for the rest of the day?" he asked.

"Which house?" David asked.

"Doesn't matter," Josh shrugged. "I just don't feel like taking the train back to Jersey."

"What's wrong with *my* house?" Mark asked sounding offended. "You just left my name out completely."

Josh chuckled. "Naw man, I just figured that you were sick of me staying at your house," he said. "Hell, I spent the past few days there."

"Shit, I don't mind. My parents been taking trips every five minutes and I have no woman, so I just be bored anyway," Mark returned, scratching his head.

Sidra shook her head at Mark's casual brush over of his ended relationship. She picked up a menu as she turned her attention to Josh. "You can come over my house" she offered.

Josh smiled slightly. "You sure? You don't have plans or anything?"

"Nope, none," she assured with a wave of her hand. "I just bought the DVD box set of that TV show that we used to watch in high school. We can watch it."

Josh turned his nose up. "You mean that show about those high school girls?" he asked. Sidra nodded enthusiastically, and Josh groaned as he put his head on the table.

"Sid, stop acting like we were *all* hype about that show," Mark scoffed, much to Sidra's amusement.

"Oh please Mark, you guys used to watch it with me all the time," she reminded.

"Only because the girls on the show were cute," Mark argued, pointing at her. "We weren't in to those corny story lines or no shit like that… Especially the one about the drug dealing boyfriend and the pregnancy scare." Mark looked around the table to find three pair of eyes staring at him.

"Oh you weren't into the story lines, huh?" David mocked.

Mark sucked his teeth. "Okay fine, it was a good ass show," he admitted. When his friends laughed at him, he waved his hand dismissively at them. "I'm secure with my shit," he bit out.

Sidra signaled for the server to come over. She was glad that Josh was going to come over her house; she'd been wanting to spend some alone time with him. She hadn't yet figured out how to talk to Josh about his sister visiting her house over two weeks ago. Between his job and her being on vacation with her family for a week, she'd barely spoken to him.

"Don't worry Josh, I won't make you watch *all* of the episodes," she promised.

Once the orders were placed and the food arrived, the group began to devour their meals. "So when is the last time that you've been to your house Josh?" David asked, causing Josh to shoot him a glare.

"Can we not start this topic of conversation?" Josh ground out, dipping a few french fries into some ketchup.

David put his hands up in surrender. "Just asking because your father called mine the other day," he revealed. "And I knew they were talking about you."

"I don't care," Josh returned nonchalantly.

Mark picked up his soda and prepared to take a sip. "I tell you one thing, Josh," he began. "Your peoples are some stalkers. If it's not your dad calling around the world looking for you, it's Sarah going to people's houses and shit."

Shit! Sidra looked at Mark with shock at the same time that Josh shot him a confused look.

"What are you talking about Sarah going to people's houses?" Josh asked.

Mark pointed at Sidra, who was shaking her head 'no' in a frantic manner. "Sid didn't tell you?" he asked, oblivious.

Josh's head snapped toward Sidra, who rested her elbow on the table and put her head in her hand. "What did you not tell me?" he hissed.

Sidra stared daggers at Mark. "Thanks a lot, Johnson," she sneered.

Mark's eyes widened. "My bad sis, I thought you would've told him by now," he justified.

"Sidra, what do you have to tell me?" Josh asked, voice stern.

Sidra let out a sigh as she turned in her seat to face Josh, who was sitting right next to her. She could've choked Mark. "Okay Josh…Sarah came by my house two weeks ago," she drew out slowly. She put her hands up when she saw the enraged look on Josh's face.

"How could you not tell me that?" he seethed.

"It wasn't a big deal," she calmly replied. "She just wanted to talk to me about you."

Josh was furious. "She had *no* right to involve you in her bullshit," he fumed, pointing to Sidra. "And *you* had no right keeping this from me."

Sidra frowned at him. "You want to talk about *keeping* stuff?" she hissed. Josh looked perplexed. "Yeah, I didn't tell you that your sister came by my house, but *you* never told *me* or anybody *else*, that you got jumped the night that Sarah stole your money," she hurled.

Mark nearly choked on his soda as David dropped his burger on his plate. "You were *what*?" David frowned.

"Yo, who we gotta roll on dawg?" Mark jumped up, tossing a balled-up napkin on his plate. "Let's go find 'em."

Josh rolled his eyes. "It was three years ago and they were on that shit," he sneered. "I'm sure they're either in jail or dead by now."

Mark sucked his teeth as he sat back down. "Shit, I'll stomp on a mu-fucka's grave in a minute. They got me chopped," he mumbled.

Josh shook his head at Mark and turned his attention back to Sidra. "Whatever. You should've called me as soon as she got there."

"First off, I was in shock," Sidra explained. "Second, what would you have done if I *had*?"

"I would've told her to leave you the hell alone."

"Josh, she only came to me because she felt like she had no other choice," Sidra said, voice calm and sincere. "She just wants a chance to talk to you again…and to be honest with you, I think you should let her."

Josh pushed his plate away and proceeded to slide out of the booth but was stopped when Mark put his foot on the seat. "You better move, Mark," Josh warned.

"You need to chill," Mark shot back, unfazed by Josh's anger toward him.

"Josh, don't leave," Sidra begged.

"No, I'm *sick* of everybody getting on my damn nerves about this Sarah situation," he fumed, knocking Mark's leg down. "When are you guys gonna get it through your heads that I don't want anything to *do* with her?"

"Josh man, we're only trying to look out for you," David placated. "We know how your relationship with Sarah affects you and we just want you to make peace...not for her, but for *you*."

Josh rolled his eyes. "That's some bullshit," he scoffed. "If I make peace with her and she starts using again...and then starts *stealing* again, *then* what?"

"Josh, we understand how you feel," Mark said. "We went through it *with* you."

Josh slammed his hand on the table. "No you *didn't!*" he yelled, ignoring the stares of other patrons.

Sidra put her hand over her face in embarrassment. "Can you keep your voice down?"

"It's no need to get all swole up in the chest at *us*," Mark argued. "And we *did* go through that whole tuition situation with you."

"You may have been there in spirit, but you weren't affected by that," Josh shot back. "You have no idea the stress that I went through because of *her*. My life could've been ruined because of *her*. If I do as everybody suggests and let her back in my life and she does that again, *then* what? Huh? She's smart, I'm sure she'll figure out how to steal my financial aid," he sneered. "What? You guys will be fine with me dropping out of school, all because you begged me to forgive her?"

"Josh, I honestly believe that Sarah has changed," Sidra

said. "I don't think that she would ever do something like that to you again."

"And *if* she did, you wouldn't have to drop out of school," Mark added, voice more stern. "We didn't let it happen *then* and we wouldn't let it happen *now*."

Josh was confused and it showed on his face. "What are you talking about?"

David removed his glasses and rubbed his eyes. "Mark, maybe you shouldn't do this," he urged.

"Mark, not now," Sidra added.

Mark put his hand up. "Naw, you were right before Sid. It's time he knew," he decided.

"Knew *what*?" Josh barked, slamming his hand on the table. "What's *with* you guys and all the secret shit?"

Mark let out a loud sigh. "Your parents didn't come up with the money for your tuition," he blurted out.

"Oh yeah?" Josh mocked. "Then who *did*?"

Mark exchanged glances with Sidra and David. "*We* did," Mark revealed.

Josh shook his head in disbelief. "No, my *parents* did."

"No man…*we* did," David admitted, hesitantly. "Your parents tried, but they couldn't get up the money in time so…Sidra, Mark and myself, we…we went to our parents and asked them to take some money out of our college funds in order to replace the money that Sarah stole."

Josh looked down at the table and rubbed his face with his hands. *There's no way*, he thought. "Y'all are lying," he denied.

"Why would we lie about something like that?" Mark asked. "Man...we weren't gonna tell you, but we need you to understand that we got your back no matter *what* happens."

"Yeah Josh, always," David chimed in. "So you see? You *can* make peace with your sister and not have to worry."

Sidra gave Josh a long, sympathetic look. It was as if he was struggling to find the words to say to them at that moment. "Josh...please say something," she begged.

Josh couldn't find the words to express what he was

feeling. He didn't know whether to feel angry for being deceived, or grateful that they loved him enough to sacrifice their own money to make sure that he didn't have to postpone going to college. Not knowing what to do or say, he rose from the booth and walked off.

Sidra jumped up and jogged after him, leaving Mark and David at the table.

"Shit," Mark complained, rubbing the top of his head.

"He'll be okay," David assured.

Mark just shook his head, not convinced that David was right.

Sidra tailed behind Josh out of the restaurant and towards the exit door of the mall. "Josh!" she called after him, before he could walk out of the door. Josh stopped and turned around to face her, a stony expression on his face. "Please don't hate us," she pleaded, taking careful steps towards him. "We didn't do that because we felt sorry for you. We did it because we love you and we just wanted to help."

Josh stared at Sidra for a long moment, one of three people who've had his back as long as he could remember. Thinking of the sacrifice that they had made for him, he felt a well up of emotion. Not saying a word, Josh stepped forward and embraced Sidra.

Once the initial shock of Josh's reaction wore off, Sidra squeezed him tightly as he held on to her. Once they parted, Josh gave a slight smile before walking out of the mall, leaving Sidra standing there watching his progress for several moments, before running her hand through her hair and heading back to the restaurant.

Chapter 37

Chasity darted for the door of her hotel room and snatched it open. A bright smile appeared across her face as Jason stepped foot inside of the massive suite. He returned her smile with one of his own, and accompanied that by a hug and kiss.

"I missed you," he said, dropping his overnight bag on the floor.

"Missed you too," Chasity returned, closing the door. She hadn't seen much of Jason in the past few weeks. His family had dragged him on every trip possible, but they made it a point to talk to each other every day.

Jason looked around the room and nodded. "Well, you certainly know how to hide out in style," he mused.

Chasity chuckled as she pushed hair over her shoulder. "Yeah well, I'm spoiled, what can I say," she returned. It'd been days since Chasity was tricked into coming face to face with Brenda yet again by Trisha. Chasity had made good on her promise to not be home when her mother returned; she'd checked into a luxury hotel in Philadelphia.

"When is the last time that you talked to your mom?" Jason asked, fully aware of everything that transpired.

"Not since the day I left," she admitted, sitting on the

chaise lounge. "She's been blowing up my phone."

"I'm sure she *has*," Jason said, pulling up a desk chair and sitting across from her.

"I'll call her back eventually," she promised. "I'm just trying to wait until my urge to dropkick her ass goes away."

Jason shook his head. "I wish I could've been here. I hated hearing you upset like that." He had to admit, he was getting tired of Chasity's family pushing on her about Brenda. He understood why they wanted her to make peace, but it was obvious that being pressured wasn't doing anything but hurting her more.

"I know," she assured. "How was your trip?" she asked, trying to change the subject. She was tired of reliving the entire situation.

Jason ran his hand over his head. "You mean *trips*?" he corrected, voice laced with amusement. "I swear my parents must really be tired of West Chester, because we've been to Florida, North Carolina, *and* California over the past few weeks... I kept telling them that I could sit one of the trips out," he chuckled. "But they dragged me along."

"Well, maybe they just want to spend as much time with you this summer as possible, since it'll be your last summer at home," Chasity pointed out.

Jason nodded as he came to that realization. "Ohhhh, that would make sense," he chortled. "But I'm not doing another one, I am tripped out...unless *you* come with me," he smiled.

"Yeah, your mother wouldn't go for it," she scoffed.

"If she wants me to *go* she'll go for it," he assured confidently. "She knows I'll always choose you."

Chasity gave a small smile. She knew that a trip with Jason's family was never going to happen. But she thought it was cute of him to hope.

"I appreciate it," she said, reaching out and touching his face. She stared at him; she wasn't lying when she said that she missed him, she did...every single part of him. Before Jason could react, Chasity got up from her seat and straddled him.

"Well damn," he teased as she began lifting his t-shirt over his head. "I guess you really *did* miss me huh?"

"Stop talking," she commanded before kissing him. A knock at the door interrupted their heavy make out session.

"Goddamn it," Jason complained as Chasity let out a loud frustrated groan. The last thing he wanted was an interruption when he hadn't seen his girlfriend in weeks.

"I'm cussing those room service people out," Chasity fussed, standing up from Jason's lap. "I ordered that damn food an hour ago."

Jason, pulled his shirt over his head and zipped his jeans as he headed for the door. He snatched it open, prepared to meet the visitor with an icy stare, but was shocked to see Trisha standing there. "Uh, hi Ms. Trisha," he sputtered, moving aside to let her in. Upon hearing Trisha's name, Chasity turned around and her eyes widened with shock.

Trisha glanced at Jason and smirked. "I *would* hug you, but I don't think you *or* my daughter would want me to, with that hard-on you have," she commented.

"Oh shit!" he blurted out, quickly covering his bulge with his hands and turning away, embarrassed.

Chasity, who was equally embarrassed, put her hand over her face.

"Sorry about that," Jason stammered. "I'm just gonna go down to the lobby and let you two talk."

"With a hard-on?" Chasity questioned, raising an eyebrow.

"Um yeah, it's gone now," he replied. The embarrassment of Chasity's mother showing up, accompanied by her pointing out his bulging manhood, trumped desire.

Chasity shook her head as Jason scurried out of the room, leaving the two women alone. Trisha folded her arms and stared at Chasity, all traces of amusement gone. Not being able to see or even speak to her daughter in days had her seething.

"*First* off," Trisha began, tossing her purse on the king-sized bed. "I know you're angry with me, but you do *not* get to just run off and not so much as answer my phone calls."

"I didn't want to talk to you," Chasity flashed back, staring at Trisha defiantly.

"I don't give a damn *what* you didn't want to do," Trisha returned, pointing at her. "I still had the right to know where you were and that you were okay. You might be grown, but you're *still* my child and I deserve to know that you're safe," she chastised. "Luckily, I checked your credit card statements and was able to see your hotel transaction."

Chasity frowned. "*And* you invaded my privacy," she mocked. "Nice."

"I pay the damn bills, I can check what the hell I *want*," Trisha threw back. "I needed to find out where you were and you blocked my damn calls… Don't ever do that again, you hear me?"

Chasity rolled her eyes as she folded her arms. "Fine," she huffed.

Trisha relaxed the frown from her face as she slowly looked around. She had to admit, her daughter had good taste in hideout spots. "Look Chasity…I know what I did was wrong—"

"And yet you *still* did it," Chasity sneered, cutting Trisha off. "Just like you *always* do."

Trisha put her hand up. "I know…but please let me explain."

"I don't need to hear another explanation," Chasity barked. "You keep putting me into situations that hurt me. You don't need to *explain*. You *need* to stop *doing* that."

"Just *listen* to me, please," she insisted, before taking a long pause. "You know that Brenda doesn't have long…and the one thing that she wants before she dies is the chance to talk to you again…face to face…so I'm asking you—no, I'm *begging* you…to please honor her request and go see her."

Chasity clasped her hands together in an effort to keep her rising temper in check. "Why is it that *I* always have to do something that I don't *want* to do in order to please other people?" she asked, voice dangerously calm. "Why do *I* always have to bend for the sake of someone else's damn feelings?"

"I know this is hard for you and that you—"

"You think *this* is hard for me?" she hissed. "No this is *irritating* to me," she clarified. "You want to know what was *hard* for me?" Chasity spat. "Growing up how I did. Having to go through what I did, at the hands of *her*. *That* was hard for me. And now *you* want me to sit down and play *nice*."

Trisha put her hands over her face. "I know—"

"It was hard enough for me to forgive *you* for leaving me with her in the first place," Chasity hissed, much to Trisha's surprise. "Now you want me to forgive *her*? ...Whose next? My ever disappearing daddy?"

Trisha felt tears well in her eyes as she put her hand over her heart. She'd come to a realization. "This is all my fault," she said. "Everything that happened, that you've *been* through, is my fault."

Chasity sighed. "I didn't say that," she said. She felt bad seeing Trisha's tears.

"You didn't *have* to," Trisha said, voice faltering. "But it's true...*I'm* the one who slept with my sister's husband. *I'm* the one who got pregnant... *I'm* the one who let her raise you, when it should've been *me* who raised you."

Chasity stared as her mother continued to pour out her feelings.

"Yes, her husband owed it to her to stay faithful, but *I* owed it to my sister to not betray her... She was hurt and angry. Rightfully *so*..." She broke down crying, "I let her take you from me. I let her *take* you and—she took her hatred for *me* out on *you* and...that's *my* fault."

Chasity felt herself tear up as Trisha cried. "Mom, you don't have—"

"No, I have to say this," Trisha cried. "You were right to ask me why I didn't come get you…I know I gave you my reasons, but the fact is that I *should've*. I should've taken you as soon as I found out how she was treating you. But I didn't and…you had to grow up feeling like you weren't wanted. And I have to live with the fact that *my* child's upbringing was miserable. That no matter how many trips I took you on, how many things I bought you, your childhood was hell… So don't be mad at her, be mad at me…take it out on *me*."

"I can't do that," Chasity said, trying to fight back her tears. "I can't hate you."

"You *have* to. Especially if that is the only way you can bring yourself to talk to Brenda again," Trisha insisted. "I've done wrong by so many people in my life, and I've tried to make amends as best I could… My dying sister said that she's forgiven me and wants only one thing before she leaves this earth and I just…I just want to give it to her… I *have* to. I owe her that much, for what I've done." Trisha walked up to Chasity, standing face to face with her. "Please Chasity. Please help me grant her last wish…please."

Chasity wiped her eyes as she sat down on the bed. She looked at the floor as Trisha's words played over and over in her head. She didn't care what she said, Chasity could never hate her birth mother, and she still couldn't find it inside of her to forgive the mother who raised her—nor did she want to be in the same room with her.

But seeing Trisha pour her heart out made Chasity want to help relieve some of the guilt that Trisha was feeling. "I'll do it," she answered after moments of silence.

Even though Chasity's voice was low and somber, Trisha heard it loud and clear. She bent down and gave Chasity a long hug. "Thank you," she sniffled. "I love you and I'm sorry."

"I know," Chasity responded. She parted from the embrace and looked away.

Trisha, feeling like she had said enough, decided to

leave. Once the door closed, Chasity, relieved to be alone, put her head in her hands and sighed.

"Damn it!" Malajia barked, feeling the knife in her hand cut through the skin on her finger.

Mrs. Simmons walked over and examined Malajia's finger. "Girl, that is the second time in five minutes that you've cut yourself while trying to chop those onions," she pointed out, handing Malajia a wet paper towel. "Maybe you should switch tasks with Geri."

Malajia rolled her eyes as she glanced back at Geri, who was sitting at the table, peeling potatoes.

"No thanks Mom, she'll probably cut herself on the peeler *too* with her clumsy self," Geri spat, putting the peeled spuds into a large bowl.

Malajia was in no mood for Geri's smart comments that Saturday afternoon…or ever. It was bad enough that she was forced to have brunch with her family; she was also being forced to help prepare it.

"Look, I keep telling you that you need knives with better handles," Malajia sneered, showing her mother the worn, jiggly handle of the sharp knife.

Mrs. Simmons snatched the knife. "When we stop sending *you* money every five minutes while you're at school, maybe we can afford new knives," she bit back.

Malajia sucked her teeth, examining her bloody finger.

Mrs. Simmons grabbed a bandage from a box in a nearby closet, and handed it to Malajia. "Is your finger okay?"

"Sure, sure," Malajia sniped. "I'll probably need a blood transfusion, but I'm sure I'll live."

Her mother rolled her eyes. "So damn dramatic," she huffed.

"I'm *not*, but okay," Malajia mumbled, putting the bandage around her finger. She sat at the kitchen table across from Geri, who was shooting her a death stare. "What Geri, what did I do to you *now?*" Malajia hissed, catching the look.

"I'm sick of that nasty attitude of yours," Geri answered. "All you do is walk around with that same sour look on your damn face."

Malajia clenched her jaw as she tried to resist the urge to curse her sister out. But she knew that Geri was right. Ever since she came home on break, Malajia's mood had been foul, but she didn't think anybody noticed.

"Don't pay her any mind Geri, she always looks like that when she's bored," Mrs. Simmons joked. "Mel, why don't you go spend a few days with one of the girls if you don't want to be home?"

Malajia shook her head. "Am I bothering you mother?" she asked, voice dripping with disdain. "I thought that I've been staying out of everybody's way. *Clearly* I was mistaken."

"Malajia, why is it that whenever I ask you if you're going out, you act like I'm telling you that I don't want you around?" Mrs. Simmons asked.

Because, clearly you don't, Malajia thought. "Forget it," she mumbled. "Maybe I'll just go to Delaware or Chester today then."

"Good," Geri grumbled. She and Malajia's normally playful relationship had been strained ever since Malajia took her anger out on Geri during spring break. As far as she was concerned, Malajia could spend the rest of the summer being someone else's problem.

"Seriously Malajia, the attitude has to go," Mrs. Simmons chimed in. "I don't know what's got you acting all depressed, but you need to fix it."

Malajia couldn't hold her tongue anymore. "If everybody noticed that I was acting depressed—which by the way, I'm not *acting*," she hissed. "Why the hell has *nobody* in this goddamn house asked me what was wrong?"

Mrs. Simmons spun around to face Malajia, "Who are you talking to like that?" she barked. "Don't get slapped."

Malajia let out a loud huff. "I'm just saying, I would

think that *somebody* in my family would care that I wasn't acting like myself. You have *no* idea what's going on with me or even care."

Her mother walked over to her. "What's going on Malajia?" she asked.

Malajia looked up at her mother and frowned. Her tone wasn't caring, it was more condescending. She stood up and maneuvered around her. "Forget it," she repeated.

"I don't get you!" Mrs. Simmons wailed, tossing her hands up. "You want me to ask what's wrong, but when I *do,* you catch an attitude *and* you still don't say anything."

"It doesn't even matter," Malajia threw over her shoulder as she made her way towards the stairs.

She went into her room, slammed her door and flopped down on her bed. Before she knew it, she started bawling. She felt neglected and alone. Nobody in her house made any effort to care about what was wrong with her, she missed spending time with her friends, she missed Mark... Malajia missed the way she *used* to be, before she started dealing with Tyrone.

She sat up, reached over and grabbed her cell phone from her nightstand. Malajia wiped her eyes as she began to text. She typed one sentence *"I need you,"* before laying back down.

Josh unlocked the door to his mother's apartment and tossed the keys on the coffee table. Cradling his new cell phone between his ear and shoulder, he reached for the remote.

"I know I haven't talked to you in a while December and I'm sorry for that," he spoke into the phone. "I've just been dealing with some stuff, but I promise to do better with our communication in the future," he assured, flopping down on the couch. Ever since Josh left Sidra and the guys at the restaurant in Delaware days ago, he went back to Jersey with his mom and occupied himself with working double shifts at the diner.

Between dodging his father and sister and dealing with the revelation that his friends sacrificed for him, Josh had barely spoken to the woman he was supposed to be dating. He flipped through the TV channels, while December continued to vent her frustrations with him over the phone. "I know…I'm sorry, I'll make it up to you, I promise…yeah, I'll think of something." As Josh began smiling at December's suggestions of ways that he could make up for being non-existent to her over the past few weeks, his mother walked in, turned the TV off and sat down on the loveseat across from him.

Noticing the troubled look on his mother's face, Josh frowned. "Uh December, can I call you back?" He ended the call once she agreed and sat the phone down. "Everything good Mom?" he asked, concerned.

"No, not really," Norma Johnson answered honestly.

"What's the matter?"

Josh's mother looked at the floor for a moment. "Before I get into that, can I have a hug?" she asked.

Josh was confused by her behavior, but didn't show it as he rose from his seat to give his mother a strong hug. It was always awkward hugging her; she was so much shorter than him. "Now what's on your mind, Mom?" he asked, returning to his seat.

"Well…" she began, pushing her shoulder length braids back with her hand. "I talked to your father today," she revealed.

Josh rolled his eyes slightly. "Mom, if you're ready for me to go back to Dad's house, you could've just told me."

She quickly put her hand up. "No, no, I'm not ready for you to leave," she assured. "I *love* having you here, I'm just glad that you're at a place where you *want* to be here with me."

Josh smiled. "Why *wouldn't* I want to be here with you?"

"Because of what I put the family through in the past,"

she stated regretfully.

"Mom, stop." Josh shook his head as he spoke in a comforting tone. "You've been clean for years now, and I'm proud that you're continuing to stay that way."

She smiled gratefully. "I am blessed to have a family that has forgiven me for the wrong that I've done," she said, putting her hand over her chest. "Which brings me to the point of this conversation... Why can't you forgive your sister?"

Josh's easy smile, disappeared, leaving a frown frozen on his face. "So now you join the bandwagon," he spat.

"Look, all I'm saying is that you found it in your heart to forgive *me*... Why not Sarah?"

"Mom, just drop it," he warned.

"Son, we *both* did drugs," she pointed out. "I used to leave you for days at a time while I was out getting high."

"Yeah, I remember," Josh sighed, rubbing his hand over his hair.

He remembered the many nights as a young boy, looking for his mother while she was on one of her benders. He remembered the stress that her drug use put on his father, who was basically acting as a single parent, and the way that Sarah acted out due to not having a stable mother in her life. Josh remembered and had held a grudge for a long time. But after his mother had gotten clean and showed that she intended to stay that way, Josh allowed her back into his life.

"But you've worked so hard to stay clean and stable," he continued.

"And so has *she*," she pointed out. "I know that you wonder why I haven't turned my back on her—it's because I know what she's going through. It's a struggle to stay sober and I know you think that she's going to fall off the wagon again, but I believe that *this* time she will stay clean..." She clasped her hands together. "Josh at the end of the day she's still my daughter...just like at the end of the day, she's still your big sister and she loves you and she's sorry for hurting you." She studied the tortured expression on her son's face as she rose from her seat and walked over to him. "Just talk to her, okay?"

Josh sighed loudly before nodding. His mother smiled and gave him a kiss on his forehead.

As she walked away, he followed her progress. "Mom?" he called, causing her to turn around. "Why didn't you and Dad tell me that Sidra, Mark, and David are the ones who paid my tuition freshman year?"

She smiled at him. "Because they didn't *want* us to," she answered. "They just wanted to help you without taking credit for it... Your father and I struggled to make the money back and when we couldn't, we panicked. Sidra overheard your father venting to her parents. She talked to Mark and David, and they went to *their* parents for permission before making the offer to us."

"Wow," was all that Josh could say.

"Yeah, you have some amazing friends baby," she mused before heading towards her bedroom. Josh sat there in silence for a moment, before picking up his phone and dialing a number.

Chapter 38

Chasity sat on the lounge chair in her grandmother's backyard, overlooking the lush, green grass-covered grounds for what seemed like forever. It had only been fifteen minutes. She'd come to the house to fulfill a promise that she made to Trisha days ago.

She was waiting outside for Brenda. She had called Jason on the ride over to get him to talk her out of backing out, which he succeeded in doing. But the anticipation made Chasity wish that he hadn't.

Her leg bounced up and down in quick rhythm as she heard voices from inside. She let out a sigh as the back door slid open and Brenda stepped out with the help of Trisha. The woman had gotten frailer, looking weaker than she did when Chasity last laid eyes on her. Once Trisha guided Brenda down into the seat next to Chasity, she shot Chasity a grateful glance before heading back inside.

Brenda let a few strained coughs out as she looked over at Chasity, who was staring out at the grounds while continuing to bounce her leg up and down. Brenda managed a chuckle. "I see you still do that nervous tap with your leg," she observed, causing Chasity to immediately stop. "You used to do that all the time when you lived with me," she reminisced between strained breaths. "...It was usually when I was in the same room with you."

"Yeah," was all that Chasity could say, in a voice that did not hide her displeasure.

Brenda looked down at her shaking hands and rubbed one with the other as she looked back at Chasity, who was avoiding eye contact with her. "I appreciate you coming here today," she said. "I know how hard this is for you."

"Uh huh," Chasity mumbled.

Brenda sighed. "Can you look at me please?"

Chasity rolled her eyes as she spun around in her seat to face Brenda.

"I appreciate you being here."

"You said that already," Chasity spat.

"Well, thank you," Brenda said, ignoring Chasity's nasty tone.

Chasity took a deep breath, then nodded slightly.

Brenda smiled, then glanced at the lush grounds herself. "It's nice out," she commented. "The heat wave seems to have passed."

"Do you really want to talk about the weather?" Chasity questioned, tone even.

Brenda shook her head. "No, no I don't," she confirmed, looking back at Chasity. She didn't want to talk about the weather; that was the furthest thing from her mind. But she didn't know how to begin to address any of the things that she wanted to say to Chasity. *She* was the one who was nervous.

She rubbed her hands yet again. "You know, I was pregnant myself the same time Trisha was with *you*," Brenda began.

Chasity looked confused. "I know, she told me."

"Shortly before I miscarr—" she glanced down. "I found out that it was a girl... I was gonna name her Taj. Just thought that was an interesting name."

Chasity just looked at her. "Is that where my one of *two* middle names came from?" she wondered, unenthused.

Brenda gave a slight nod. "I believe that Trisha thought it would somehow honor the memory, I guess... I didn't even know that she'd given you that middle name until I got the copy of your birth certificate."

Chasity let out a sigh. She was trying her best to remain seated. Sitting around, listening to the origins of her unusual middle name, wasn't something that she felt like hearing.

"When I lost my daughter, it was the most devastating thing that had ever happened to me," Brenda continued. "Being pregnant gave me hope. It made me forget about what had been done to me...all I could focus on was the baby that I was about to have." A sadness fell over Brenda. "Then in a moment, she was gone and—losing a baby is *truly* a painful experience and it's something that I would *never* wish on *anybody*." She held her sorrowful gaze on Chasity, who just stared back at her. "I feel for *anybody* who has had to go through that."

Chasity wasn't sure why Brenda was looking at her the way that she was. Like she wanted her to say something. Chasity had no desire to share her own experience with Brenda. As far as she was concerned, it was none of Brenda's business. However, her going through her own miscarriage, made her at least empathize with Brenda for that part alone.

"Sorry," was all that Chasity had it in her to say.

Brenda took a deep breath, holding her gaze on Chasity. "Me too," she replied. Her tone was full of sympathy. After a brief pause, Brenda began to speak once again. "You were the prettiest little baby," she smiled to herself. "With the *loudest* cry. Your voice would get so high... I noticed when you thought something was really funny, your laugh would get that same high pitch." She chuckled at the memory.

Chasity sat there in silence while Brenda reminisced. Her face was void of any humor or any trace of a smile. She just listened.

"When I decided to bring you home with me, I did so with the intention to raise you like you were mine," Brenda said. "Despite how I felt about what happened, I still loved my husband and you were a part of him, so in my mind you were a part of *me*. And I intended on treating you like you were... For the first few years, things were great. You were the sweetest little girl; everything that I imagined my *own* daughter to be... I *saw* you as mine." She glanced down. "Then somewhere down the line...something changed in me... When I looked at you, I no longer saw *my* child...I saw *Trisha*. And the reality came back to me. I had to face that fact that you were *Trisha's* child. A child that was conceived with *my* husband and I just—the love that I felt for you, changed to resentment. I tried drinking to numb my feelings, but it made them worse..."

"I was five," Chasity spoke, finally. Brenda looked at her. "I was *five* when you called me a whining little bitch because I cried when you threw the box that I made for your birthday in the trash... Then when I tried to get it out, you tore it up in my face. And that was *before* you locked me in my room for the first time." Hurt showed on Chasity's face, "I was *five*. I didn't do anything wrong, and I was degraded and punished. And I had to *deal* with that for thirteen *more* freakin' years. Never knowing what I did wrong to deserve it."

Brenda was ashamed and regretful and it showed on her face. "God, I'm so sor—"

Chasity's hand jerked up. "Just don—don't," she protested through clenched teeth. "It means nothing."

Tears fell from Brenda's eyes. "If I could take it all back, I—"

"You *can't*," Chasity fumed. "You *can't* change anything, you *can't* make up for it. It just is what it is... I don't know what you want from me."

Brenda covered her mouth to cough, then let out a long sigh. "You have every right to hate me Chasity," she stated. "I did wrong by you, and I'm fully aware of it. And I know that no matter how many 'I'm sorry's' that I say, it won't change what you've been through."

"So why the hell would you ask me to forgive you?"

Chasity wondered. "When you know I *can't*."

Brenda opened her mouth to speak again, but all that came out was coughs. Brenda grabbed a tissue and kept coughing. When she moved her hand, Chasity saw blood on the tissue. She didn't want to admit it, but it shook her.

Chasity went to stand. "I'm gonna go get you some water or something," she offered.

Brenda reached out and grabbed Chasity's arm, halting her. "No, I'm okay," she insisted, breathing labored. She had a feeling that if Chasity walked into that house, that she wouldn't come back. And Brenda needed her to stay.

Chasity sat back down, folding her arms.

"I don't expect you to forgive me," Brenda stated after gaining her composure.

"Then what do you *want* from me Brenda?" Chasity questioned, frustrated.

"I just...I want you to be okay," Brenda declared.

"Okay with *what*?" Chasity bit out.

"You're angry and you're bitter and resentful...and that's not your fault, but you *are*," Brenda explained. "I don't want you to go through life being that way... I don't want you to end up like me."

"I will *never* be you," Chasity promised, voice laced with anger.

"I didn't think I could turn out the way that I did either," Brenda replied. "But I did. It's amazing what anger will do... It has a way of consuming you until that's all you feel."

Chasity was taken back by the words coming out of Brenda's mouth. It showed on her face in the form of a frown, but she couldn't bring herself to say anything.

"I don't want that for you, Chasity," Brenda continued. "I don't want you to go through life being angry. I want you to know that you are capable of loving and of *being* loved, and that you are a blessing to those around you." Brenda sniffled. "I want you to let that angry part of you die...let it die with *me*." She wiped her eyes with her hand.

Chasity just stared at Brenda.

"I want you to be happy," Brenda added. "I *need* for you to be. And if I can take your resentment with me, in order for that to happen…then my death has a purpose."

For the first time since Chasity arrived at the house, the anger left her face. She didn't know how to deal with what Brenda had just said or what to say.

Before Chasity could even figure out what to say, Brenda began coughing hysterically. Freaked out by another coughing spell, Chasity rose from her seat as Trisha rushed outside to her sister's side. "I'm okay, I'm okay," Brenda insisted as Trisha fussed over her.

Chasity headed inside without another word as Brenda's nurse rushed outside. Feeling a desperate need to get out of the house, Chasity quickened her steps to the front door, but was stopped by the sound of Trisha's voice calling her. She spun around and faced her.

"Are you okay?" Trisha asked, voice both panicked and sympathetic.

Chasity simply nodded, retrieving her phone from her jeans pocket.

"You want to talk?"

Chasity shook her head, reading a message. Trisha glanced at the back door to see what the nurses were doing, before looking back at Chasity. As she went to say something, Chasity immediately cut her off.

"I'm going to Philly for a few hours," Chasity declared.

"Okay," Trisha answered, as Chasity turned and left without so much as a goodbye. Once the door was closed, Trisha want back outside.

"Malajia, you have to eat *something* other than candy," Alex insisted, pushing a pack of crackers in Malajia's face.

Annoyed, Malajia nudged Alex's hand away as she stuffed a piece of fruit-flavored candy into her mouth. "Alex, stop trying to feed me those dry ass crackers," she barked, "I already told you I don't want those."

Alex sighed loudly as she tossed the crackers on the coffee table in her family's living room.

When Malajia texted her earlier that day, upset, Alex suggested the girls meet at her house for a gathering in an effort to cheer Malajia up. But being there with her by herself for the past two hours, Alex was growing tired of Malajia and her nasty attitude.

"Look child, I already *told* you that I'm not gonna start cooking dinner until everybody gets here, so put something other than that damn candy in your stomach before I slap you."

Malajia rolled her eyes as she picked up the crackers from the table. "I'll eat 'em…but I won't like 'em," she muttered.

Alex shook her head, then heard a knock at the door. She let out a sigh of relief when she opened the door and saw Chasity standing there. "Thank God, come get your girl before I choke her."

Chasity simply chuckled, stepping foot inside Alex's home. "Working your nerves already, huh?"

"*Yes*, for the past two damn hours," Alex complained.

Malajia looked up at Chasity and smiled, holding her arms out for a hug. "My boo, come hug me you sexy thing, you," she gushed.

"Malajia don't be weird," Chasity sneered, giving Malajia her requested hug before sitting down next to her on the couch. "What's going on with you?"

"I'm fine," Malajia replied with a wave of her hand.

"The group text that you sent saying 'I need you' says otherwise," Chasity pointed out. Chasity saw Malajia's text message, then Alex's message about them meeting at her house, when she was leaving her grandmother's house after her meeting with Brenda. She drove straight there.

"Fine, I'll talk when Sid and Em get here," Malajia promised. "And what took your ass so long?" she directed at Chasity.

"I was…never mind." Chasity quickly dismissed. With

College Life 302; Advanced Placement

Malajia needing to get whatever was on her chest off, the last thing that she wanted to do was bring the focus to herself with her own issues.

"Chasity, you want something to drink?" Alex offered, leaning over the couch.

"Yeah, thanks," Chasity replied.

Malajia chuckled. "She don't have nothing to drink but water to go with these dry ass crackers," she mocked.

Alex put her hand up at Malajia as she looked at Chasity. "Alcoholic or non?" she asked.

"Whatever you think it'll take to get me through the next few hours with *this*," Chasity jeered, gesturing to Malajia.

"Wine it is," Alex laughed, heading towards the kitchen.

"Hey!" Malajia called after her. "You didn't offer *me* any wine."

"That's because you stepped right in here starting your nonsense," Alex threw out from the kitchen.

Malajia sucked her teeth as she looked at Chasity "Can you believe—"

"Don't look over here. I already told you, you play too much," Chasity said, cutting her off.

No alcoholic beverage aside, Malajia's mood had improved since earlier that day. And it only got better with the arrival of Sidra and Emily not even twenty minutes later.

"Now that we're all here, let's cook," Alex suggested.

"I didn't sign on for all that," Chasity ground out.

"I'm too depressed to cook," Malajia chimed in, raising her hand.

Alex stomped her foot on the floor, "Look damn it, I set up everything so that we can make this new pasta dish that I saw on the cooking channel today and I got wine and everything, so get up, get your asses in the kitchen, and let's get to cooking," she barked, pointing to the kitchen. She was met with challenging stares, but the group relented and made their way to the kitchen.

378

"You *would* be the one to watch a damn cooking channel," Malajia mumbled, walking past Alex, much to the amusement of the other girls, who snickered.

"Shut it up and get in there," Alex demanded.

As Sidra opened the bottle of wine and began pouring some into the glasses, she looked at Emily. "How was your time spent with your brothers?" she asked. "I feel like I haven't talked to you in ages."

Emily grabbed a bottle of water from the counter. "It was nice. I'm glad that I decided to stay longer," she answered. Emily had planned on staying with her brothers in Jersey for only a week, but ended up staying the past few weeks with them, just arriving in Philly that day. "They really embraced me for the first time in a *long* time."

"What about that dusty sister of yours?" Malajia grunted, earning a glare from Alex.

"I still haven't spoken to *Jazmine*," Emily chortled. "I guess it's for the best. She stressed me out and I don't need stress in my life anymore. Last time I had stress, I drank like a fish."

"Yes, we remember," Chasity said, taking a sip of her wine. She frowned her face up at the taste. "Yeah, this is the cheap kind."

"Yup, a whole eight dollars and you better not waste it," Alex threw back, gesturing to Chasity's glass.

"It's *nasty*," Chasity bristled, opening a bottle of water.

"Chaz, how did your meeting with Brenda go today?" Sidra asked, causing Chasity to nearly choke on her water. She'd nearly forgotten that she'd spoken to Sidra that previous evening to vent.

"Wait what? You saw her *again*? Today?" Malajia charged.

"Can we not talk about this right now?" Chasity asked, looking around.

"I'm sorry, I thought everybody knew," Sidra apologized.

Chasity waved her hand slightly. "Its fine, Sidra."

"How are you feeling Chaz? What did she say?" Alex pressed, ignoring Chasity's request not to talk about it.

"Not *now* Alex," Chasity insisted.

"Damn the *rest* of these bitches, why didn't *I* know about any of this?" Malajia bit out, pointing to Chasity.

"Don't call us bitches," Alex demanded.

"Shut up Alex. Chaz, so is *that* what we're doing now? Not telling each other shit anymore?" Malajia fumed.

"If you would answer your fuckin' *phone*, then *maybe* I could *tell* you shit," Chasity threw back.

Malajia sucked her teeth. "I haven't been charging my phone. But whatever, I'll deal with you later," she mumbled, grabbing her glass off the counter top, then taking a sip.

The girls engaged in casual conversation as they prepared their meal of pasta made from scratch, with grilled shrimp and spinach along with a tossed salad with homemade dressing and homemade biscuits. Alex opened another bottle of wine as the girls sat down at the table.

"What's up with the candle light, Alex?" Chasity joked as Alex dimmed the overhead light in the kitchen, leaving only the candles on the kitchen table and a dim light over the stove to provide light.

Alex chuckled. "This visit is supposed to be relaxing so candles will *help* us relax."

"Candle light don't do nothing for me but make me horny," Malajia mocked. "So unless you want me to rub one out under this table, you better turn a damn light on."

Sidra shook her head as Alex flagged Malajia with her hand. Alex then looked at Chasity's full glass of wine from earlier. She pointed to it. "Girl, I said don't waste my wine."

"Alex, I'm just not drinking that," Chasity refused. "It taste like it was made with rotten grapes."

Sidra nearly spat hers out as she tried to hold in her laugh. "It's not that bad once you get used to it," she said after a moment. "Hell, *Malajia* likes it. She drank almost all of the last bottle."

"No this shit is gross, but it's numbing me so I'm tolerating it," Malajia said, sipping hers.

Alex rolled her eyes at the comments. "Let's just eat," she suggested.

While the girls began to prepare their plates, Sidra looked at Malajia. "So sweetie, what's going on with you?" she asked. "That 'I need you' text that you sent us sounded desperate... Like you really need to get something off your chest."

Malajia gave a quick laugh. "Oh girl please, I just did that so I could get everybody together," she said dismissively. "You know we haven't hung out in a while." Malajia's confession was met with angry and confused glares.

Chasity nonchalantly picked up the now empty wine bottle and pointed it in Malajia's direction. "Mel, don't make me slap you in the face with this," she warned. Chasity was in no mood for Malajia's foolishness. She'd come to Philly because she thought that Malajia really needed her, not just to hang out.

"Stop it Malajia," Alex chided, Malajia's smile faded as she looked down at the table. Alex reached over and rubbed Malajia's arm. "Come on girl, you look sad. No matter *how* much you try to crack jokes, we can see that something is bothering you... What's going on sis?"

Malajia, feeling everything that she was dealing with come to the surface, put her hands over her face as tears flowed from her eyes.

Emily pushed her chair next to Malajia's, putting her arm around Malajia to comfort her.

"I'm sorry," Malajia sniffled, wiping her eyes. "I've been holding those in since I got here," she admitted.

"Talk to us," Alex pressed, voice caring.

"I just...I'm not happy," Malajia admitted, grabbing her napkin from the table. "...I miss Mark."

"If you didn't break up with him, you wouldn't be

missing him right now," Sidra bit out.

Emily cut her eye at Sidra. "Sidra, don't be mean."

"I'm *not*, but I just don't get it," Sidra replied, looking at Malajia. "You told me that you cared for him—"

"I *do*," Malajia promised.

"Then why hurt him like that?" Sidra threw back.

Malajia looked down at her hand as more tears fell. "I just felt like…I needed to let him go," she muttered.

"But *why* though?" Alex asked, sincere. "It's clear that that's not really what you *want*."

"Exactly," Sidra agreed.

"It's what I *felt*…" Malajia shook her head. "I wanna fix it."

"Malajia, you can't fix anything with Mark until you deal with why you did what you did in the *first* place," Chasity said. "You talking to him don't mean shit if you're gonna do the same mess later."

Alex slammed her hand on the table. "Yes," she approved.

Chasity looked at her, bewildered.

Alex, looked back at her. "Sorry, I get excited when y'all are on point," she explained. "Carry on."

Sidra shook her head at Alex, then turned back to Malajia. "Why did you feel like you needed to let Mark go?" she asked. "The truth, sweetie."

Malajia grabbed her glass of wine and took a sip. She hoped that it would give her the courage to share her feelings. "I…um…"

Emily rubbed Malajia's shoulder. "The sooner you get it out, the better you'll feel."

"I feel like I won't be any good for Mark because…I'm still dealing with all these feelings about Tyrone," Malajia revealed hesitantly.

"Feelings like *what*, exactly?" Chasity asked, raising her eyebrow. "If you say out your mouth that you still care about him, I really *am* gonna slap you."

"No, it's not *that*," Malajia reassured her friends. She

rubbed her face with her hands; she was feeling much too vulnerable for her liking. "I just—I feel damaged…like Tyrone *ruined* me…."

"Malajia, you're not ruined," Chasity assured her.

"That's how I *feel*," Malajia explained, upset. "And I can't *escape* this feeling…too much has happened… I don't feel good about myself right now and I feel like he deserves someone better."

"There's nobody better for Mark, than *you*," Emily consoled. "We see how he looks at you." Malajia wiped her eyes.

"Did you *tell* him any of this?" Alex wondered.

Malajia shook her head in sorrow. "I can't even tell my own family…how could I tell *him*?"

"So *tell* your family," Alex advised. "I think that you unloading your burden on *all* those who love you, will make you feel a lot better Malajia. The more people you have supporting you…the faster you can heal."

Malajia looked at the table. Deep down, she knew that what they'd been saying was right. She just couldn't bring herself to do it. "I'm scared," she admitted.

"I know…but you have to," Sidra urged, reaching over and grabbing Malajia's hand. "Do you want one of us to be there with you when you tell them?" she asked. "For support."

Malajia glanced up at her. "I'll let you know." Sidra just nodded. "Thank you," Malajia added, looking around at her friends. "For being here for me."

"Anytime, that's what friends do," Emily smiled. Malajia smiled back. She felt a little better, for now anyway.

After a few moments of silence while the girls ate more of their food, Alex looked at Chasity. "And *you*," she charged, pointing.

Chasity looked at her. "Me, what?"

"You're not exempt from sharing," Alex answered, sipping her wine. "What's going on with Brenda?"

"No, I'm not doing this today," Chasity refused, waving

her hand at Alex. "This visit isn't about me."

"This visit is about sharing things you're dealing with," Alex clarified. "Malajia shared, and now it's *your* turn."

Chasity let out a loud huff. She realized that she wasn't going to get out of that house without giving them something. "Fine," she relented, looking at Alex. "You get to ask me one question."

"*One?*" Alex repeated, in disbelief.

"Yes," Chasity confirmed. "*Just* one, and I promise to answer truthfully."

Alex looked to the other girls for help. "Don't look at *us*, you better think of a question," Malajia threw back.

Alex sucked her teeth as she looked back at Chasity, who was staring at her, arms folded in anticipation. "Chaz are you serious?"

"Is that your question?" Chasity jeered.

Alex made a face at her. "No," she said. Alex racked her brain for her one question. She had so many that she wanted to ask. How did Chasity feel seeing Brenda after all these years? What type of illness does she have? Can she ever forgive her? But rather bog her down with those, she just thought of a simple one. "How are you feeling?" she asked finally.

Chasity shrugged. "I don't know," she answered abruptly.

Alex was annoyed and it showed on her face. "You said that you would answer *honestly*," she ground out.

"That *is* an honest answer," Chasity insisted.

"Whatever Chasity," Alex argued. "That couldn't *possibly* be your answer. You could've said *anything* else. *Really*? You don't know? How can you *not* know?"

"You asked your damn question already, Alexandra," Chasity hissed. When Alex tossed her hands up in the air out of frustration, Chasity snapped. "Look, 'I don't know' *is* a legitimate answer because in all honesty, I really *don't know* how I'm feeling or how I'm *supposed* to feel," she revealed, agitated. "I spent most of my life hating Brenda, then she shows up out of nowhere a few months ago, with the news that she's dying, and even though it's a shame, I *still* hated her… Then she said some shit to me today that has completely *fucked* me up, so now I don't know *how* to feel about her or this *entire* situation."

Alex sat in silence as Chasity vented.

"Someone that I've known my *entire* life is *dying* and *everybody* in my damn family is sad about it. My mom cries like five times a day and I can't bring myself to shed *one* fuckin' tear over it and I can't decide if that's justified because of how she *was* to me, or if it's completely *heartless*. I. Don't. Know."

Alex looked down at the table briefly; she felt bad for pressing Chasity. She couldn't imagine going through any of that. "I'm sorry," she said sincerely.

"It's okay," Chasity replied, face still frowning, bite still in her voice.

Alex sighed as she reached for her glass of wine. *I should probably learn to back off when people tell me to*, she pondered.

Chapter 39

Josh looked at his watch for the fifth time that hour as he paced his mother's living room. "Why did I agree to this?" he asked himself, flopping down on the couch.

The knock on the door sent his heart into the pit of his stomach. Sighing, he rose from the couch and hesitantly walked to the door. He took a deep breath and opened it, coming face to face with the person on the other side.

"Hey J.J.," Sarah smiled.

Not returning her smile, Josh signaled for Sarah to come inside. "I've asked you not to call me that," he bit out.

Sarah sat on the accent chair across from the couch. "I'm sorry, it's a force of habit," she sputtered. Josh sat down on the couch and folded his arms.

"I know that you went to see Sidra a few weeks ago," he blurted out.

Sarah looked down at her hands. "I didn't know what else to do," she reasoned. "I'm sorry, I didn't mean to overstep."

Josh just shook his head, scratching it in the process. The siblings sat in awkward silence, until Sarah reached in to her pocket and pulled out an envelope.

"I brought this for you," she offered, handing it to him.

Josh raised his eyebrow. "What's this?"

"My paycheck," Sarah answered. Josh looked at her. "It's not much, but I want you to have it."

"You can't give me your *entire* paycheck, you need that to live off of," Josh replied. Sure, he needed the money, but as much as he resented her, he didn't want to leave her with nothing.

"I'm staying with Dad, so I don't have to pay rent just yet... I want to pay you back. I'm not making much, so it'll take some time," she explained. Josh held his gaze on her. "Keep it...please," she insisted.

Josh sighed as he reluctantly pocketed the envelope. "Thanks," he mumbled.

"You're welcome," Sarah said, running her hands down her jeans. "I wasn't lying when I said that I wanted to make things right."

"I gotta ask you," Josh began, voice stern. Sarah looked at him, anticipating the question. "You knew what doing drugs did... You knew how it affected those around you by witnessing *Mom* use," he said, Sarah sighed. "You *saw* it...why would *you* go and do drugs after *everything*? I don't get it."

Sarah pushed some of her twists off of her face, thinking of a way to answer Josh's valid question. "When Mom ran off that last time, it really messed me up," she began. "I was angry at her, but I missed her at the same time. I didn't know how to deal with those feelings." She pointed at Josh. "You occupied yourself with school and your friends... *I* didn't have friends and I *damn* sure didn't care about school." Sarah adjusted her position on the chair. "I became depressed and I wanted something to make it stop...if just for a little while... I tried drinking, but I never could take the taste so I tried...something *else*." Tears filled Sarah's eyes as she relived her downward spiral. "And it *worked*...for a little while, I was fine... I couldn't *feel*. So every once in a while when things in my head got bad, I'd do it... And before I knew it, it had taken over my entire life."

Sarah wiped her eyes with her hand. Josh stared at her, expression still hardened. Though on the inside, seeing her break down in front of him while telling her story, made his heart soften a bit.

"I *tried* to stop, I really did," Sarah promised. "I went to rehab *five* times," she said, putting five fingers up.

"You just said that you tried and failed, five times before," Josh put in. "What makes you think that *this* time will be any different, Sarah?"

"Because I *want* it to be," Sarah insisted. "I want my *life* back. I want my *family* back. And I know the only way for me to accomplish that…is to stay clean. So that's what I'm going to do," she promised. "I've been six months sober so far. That's the longest that I've been since I started using."

Josh looked at the floor, but didn't say anything. He wanted for what she was saying to be true; he missed the relationship that they had before things spiraled out of control. But given everything that transpired, he found it hard to believe her.

"After the last time I got high, I remember waking up in this *disgusting* room," Sarah began, as Josh was still deep in his thoughts. "I sat there just staring out of that little dingy window, wondering how I ended up there… I used to carry around this one bag. I took it *everywhere* and I'm surprised that nobody ever took it," she shook her head. "Anyway, I grabbed the bag as I got ready to leave and a bunch of stuff fell out… A few coins, some costume jewelry that I tried to sell…and probably the most *important* thing that I had: a special piece of paper."

Sarah reached into her wallet and pulled out a small, folded piece of paper. She handed it to Josh.

Josh unfolded the tattered paper, looking at it. Recognizing the crayon drawing of him and Sarah that he had given to her when he was little, he became emotional. "You *kept* this?" he asked, voice cracking.

Sarah nodded. "I always loved that picture," she smiled, looking at him. Josh wiped his eyes and Sarah felt tears fill hers again. "I'm so sorry Josh," she apologized, sincere. "I wasn't the sister that you deserved then, but I want to be that *now*."

Josh clutched the paper in his hand. "I *want* to believe you, Sarah," he stammered. "I really do. I just don't know how to trust you again."

"I know… Let me earn it," she replied.

Josh looked back at the paper and rubbed his face with his hand. Sarah rose from her seat and walked over to Josh. She wanted to hug him, but didn't know how he would react. And then she decided that she didn't care…she *needed* to embrace him. Throwing caution aside, Sarah wrapped her arms around Josh. Much to her surprise, he didn't push her away. He even, just for a brief moment, hugged her back.

Jason made his way towards the door, eyeing the television screen. "Oh come on!" he yelled at the television. Opening the door, he was startled and pleasantly surprised to see Chasity standing there, staring at him. "Hey beautiful," he smiled.

"You okay?" she asked, voice low and stern.

Jason chuckled. "Oh, you heard me huh?" he said, moving aside to let her in. "This movie is getting on my nerves," he said, turning the TV off with the remote.

Chasity slowly walked to the couch. "What are you up to?" she asked, tone even.

"Nothing much, I just made some dinner," he answered. "You want some?"

Chasity shook her head. "Your parents here?"

"No, they went to visit my aunt for a few days," Jason replied. He noticed the blank stare on Chasity's face. "Is everything okay?"

Chasity sighed. "I know I should've called first."

Jason took a step towards her. "You didn't have to. I'm glad you're here," he assured. "What's wrong?"

Chasity took a deep breath, rubbing the back of her neck. "Brenda was taken to the hospital this morning," she revealed. "She...they're saying she could go at any time now."

Jason shot Chasity a sympathetic look as he stood in front of her. "I'm sorry baby," he said, pulling her into an embrace.

Chasity stared out ahead of her as Jason hugged her. She'd been feeling like she was having an out-of-body experience ever since she received the phone call from Trisha earlier that morning, informing her that Brenda had taken a turn for the worst.

It'd been a little over a week since she'd sat down with Brenda in her grandmother's backyard and ever since then, Chasity had been feeling conflicted.

"At this point, they're just making her comfortable," Chasity said, parting from Jason's embrace. "They want me to come to the hospital but I just...I can't," she said, sitting down.

Jason sat next to her and rubbed her back as she put her head in her hands. "Is there anything that you need me to do?"

Chasity looked at him. "Can I stay with you tonight?"

"Of *course* you can," he replied.

"I can't be in that house by myself right now."

"You don't have to explain," Jason said, putting a hand up. "You want me to go to your house to pick some stuff up for you?"

She shook her head. "I have a bag in the car. I was gonna go to a hotel, but when you said that your parents weren't here, I figured I'd ask."

Jason leaned over and gave Chasity a kiss on the cheek. "I'll go get your bag," he said, standing from the couch and heading for the door.

As the door closed, Chasity let out a long sigh and leaned her head against the back of the couch, closing her

Malajia flipped her breeze-blown hair over her shoulder as she looked at her phone screen. She was enjoying the new updates on her phone; it allowed her to do video calling. "How's everything going with Brenda?" Malajia asked Chasity.

"It's going," Chasity sighed. "They said she's still hanging on."

"Malajia shook her head. "This whole thing is crazy and it's happening so fast."

"Tell me about it," Chasity mumbled, fussing with her hair.

"What are you doing?" Malajia chuckled at the scene.

"Why didn't you tell me that my hair is looking all crazy?" Chasity hissed, pushing some hair over her shoulders.

"Because it *doesn't*," Malajia assured. "It just looks like your curls fell. You probably sweated them out with all that banging you're doing in Jason's empty house," she teased. "How long have you been there now? Two days?"

"Yeah," Chasity answered, tone dry.

Malajia's smile faded. "Have you gone to the hospital to see her yet?" she asked with seriousness. Chasity rolled her eyes. "You know I can see you, right?"

"So?"

Malajia sucked her teeth at her tone. "Look, I get why you don't want to go there, but—"

"I gotta go," Chasity cut in.

"*Now* who's deflecting?" Malajia ground out.

"I'll call you later," Chasity replied.

Malajia sighed. "Okay...I'll say a prayer for you."

"Use it for yourself sis, I'm okay," Chasity returned. "Bye."

"Bye," Malajia muttered as Chasity hung up. Malajia looked up at the moon lit sky. Chasity was right, she did need to pray for herself. Especially if she was going to accomplish what she needed to do. After much thought, Malajia decided that it was time to come clean to her family.

After giving herself a pep talk, Malajia stood and walked into her house. Her parents were sitting on the couch, accompanied by Geri and her other older sister Maria. Malajia slowly walked over and stood in front of the television.

"Girl, will you move?" Mrs. Simmons barked, signaling for her to move with her hand.

"Can I talk to you guys for a minute?" Malajia asked, ignoring her mother's request and the complaining from her father and sisters.

"Can it *wait*? This movie is just getting to the good part," Mr. Simmons added, reaching for his beer.

"No, it *can't*," Malajia insisted. "And this is on DVR, so you can watch it later."

"Malajia, that's not the point," Geri hissed. "Why do you have to bother us *now*? You had *all* day to talk to us and you didn't. You never *do*."

Malajia rolled her eyes and walked away. "Forget it," she fumed.

Mr. Simmons turned the TV off. "No, you got the attention that you wanted, so what is it Malajia?" he sneered.

"Yeah, what is it? What pointless nonsense do you wanna whine about *now*?" Maria added, tone nasty.

Malajia clenched her jaw as she spun around. "Maria, I swear to God, don't start with me or I'll come across this room and choke the shit out of you," she threatened.

"Did you just curse in my house?!" Mrs. Simmons wailed, hopping up from her seat. "Have you lost your damn mind?"

"Mom, I'm sorry, but I'm tired of her and everybody *else* in this house, treating me like a freakin' joke," Malajia argued.

"You better check that attitude Malajia," Mrs. Simmons warned, pointing at her daughter.

"Nobody treats you like a joke, you're exaggerating," Mr. Simmons mocked.

Malajia let out a loud sigh. "I'm *not* exaggerating," she insisted. "I really need to talk to you about something serious and you're making it seem that it's not important."

"Malajia, you *never* talk to us about anything important," her mother pointed out.

"Because I feel like I *can't!*" Malajia erupted. "No matter *what* I say, you just brush it off like it's nothing."

"God, you're being dramatic Malajia," Mr. Simmons grunted.

"I'm *not*, Dad," she argued.

"You *are!*" Mr. Simmons boomed, standing up. Malajia's behavior over the past few months had been irritating him and it was now brought to a head, "Just like you've *always* been."

Malajia wanted to cry as her father yelled at her.

"You're dramatic, irresponsible, unfocused, an attention seeker, and *spoiled*," he fumed.

Malajia shook her head.

"Like *now*, you're standing here getting everybody in an uproar because you just *need* the attention on *you*," her father ranted. "If what you had to tell us was so damn important as you so *claim*, you could've done so without pissing everybody off."

Malajia stood there in silence as she looked at her family. "I'm not *trying* to piss anybody off," she assured, voice faltering.

Mr. Simmons threw his hands up in the air in frustration as Mrs. Simmons rolled her eyes.

"Then why are you *doing* it, Malajia?" Geri spat. "This is what Mom and Dad are *talking* about."

"Nice Geri, just go ahead and join them in bashing me," Malajia mocked, wiping her eyes with her hand.

"Girl, take that crying stuff somewhere else," Maria jumped in. "Nobody's falling for it."

Malajia looked at her. "Do you even *like* me, Maria?"

she asked, angry. "'Cause you damn sure find *any* reason to throw your unwanted, uncalled for, *stupid* ass digs in about me."

Maria folded her arms in a huff. "I'm not gonna do this with you right now."

"Malajia, cuss one more time and you're getting out," Mrs. Simmons warned.

Malajia rolled her eyes. She wished she'd never walked through that door. "Y'all are making this *really* hard for me," she slowly put out, trying to keep her temper and her tears in check.

"Just say what you need to say," Maria spat. "It's probably a lie anyway."

"Maria, you might want to watch what you say because you have *no* idea what I've been through." Malajia was furious. "*None* of you do."

"What could you have *possibly* gone through?" Mr. Simmons mocked. "All you do is play around in school and spend our money like it's going out of style."

"Or you're wasting time on those stupid boys," Mrs. Simmons added. "What was the last one that we heard about?" She put her finger on her chin. "*What* was his name? Tyrone."

"I have *asked* you to *stop* bringing him up," Malajia snapped. "I have asked you *repeatedly* not to do that. Why don't you people fuckin' listen?!"

"That's it, get out!" her mother screamed at her, pointing to the door.

"Gladly!" Malajia yelled back, storming out of the house.

She stormed down the front steps and made it to the end of the driveway before she broke down crying. She pulled her cell phone out of her shorts pocket and dialed a number.

"What?" Chasity answered.

"I can't do it Chasity," Malajia cried into the phone.

"You can't do *what*?" Chasity frowned, hearing the panic in Malajia's voice.

"I'm sorry, I know you're dealing with your own mess, I shouldn't have called you."

Chasity shook her head. "Don't worry about that," she dismissed. "What can't you do?"

Malajia took several deep breaths to try to calm herself down. "I'm trying to tell my family and...I just can't," she cried.

"Calm down," Chasity urged. "You want me to come down there?"

Malajia wiped her eyes. "No," she sniffled. "Just...talk me into going back in that house."

"Go back in that house," Chasity immediately threw back.

Malajia managed a slight chuckle through her tears.

"Don't let them run you out of there Malajia, you're tougher than that," Chasity advised. "Make them listen to you."

Malajia sniffled again. "Okay," she agreed after a moment. "I'll call you back."

"Okay."

Malajia took a deep breath and ended the call. She contemplated walking off, to where she had no idea; she just knew that she didn't want to go back into that house but Chasity was right—she had to.

Wiping the rest of the tears from her face, Malajia entered the house to be greeted by her mother pointing at her. "Malajia, I swear—"

Malajia put her hand up. "I'm sorry that I was disrespectful," she apologized, voice low. "I...I just feel like I don't have a voice in this house unless I get that way... But I shouldn't have done it and I'm sorry."

"Malajia, I'm not going to tolerate your nonsense," Mrs. Simmons argued. "You're too old to be acting out like this."

"I know," Malajia replied, fiddling with her hands. "I need to tell you something important and I just need for you to listen to me."

Mrs. Simmons let out a deep sigh; she was already

mentally drained by her daughter's antics. "Malajia—"

"Mommy, *please*," Malajia begged staring at her mother.

Mrs. Simmons, seeing the tortured expression on her daughter's face, relaxed her frown. Malajia hadn't called her "Mommy" since she was a little girl; she only did so when she was sick or in some kind of pain.

"What do you need to say, Malajia?" Mr. Simmons asked with agitation; Mrs. Simmons shot him a side-glance.

"First off, I need for you guys to stop bringing up Tyrone to me," Malajia began. "I don't want to hear his name anymore. I'm not *with* him anymore and I can't get past the thought of him if you keep bringing him up."

"What *happened* between you two?" her mother asked, voice soft. Malajia had her full attention. "Did he hurt you?"

Before Malajia could open her mouth, Maria laughed. "Oh please, she probably broke up with him because he did something small like forget to notice her manicure or something like that."

Malajia shot a piercing look Maria's way. She'd had enough of her mouth. "No, that's *not* why I broke up with him you ignorant bitch," she seethed, halting Maria's laughter. "I broke up with him because he used to beat my ass, *that's* why," she revealed, voice tortured as she tried to fight back tears.

"Wait, he *what*?!" Mrs. Simmons wailed as Mr. Simmons held a mask of anger on his face.

"Did she just call me a bitch?" Maria questioned, pointing to herself.

"Maria, shut up!" Geri snapped, before looking at Malajia. "Tyrone did *what*?"

The looks of horror on her family's faces made Malajia almost wish she hadn't said anything. But it was out now so she had no choice but to continue. She put her hand over her face as the memories and tears flooded. "He...he abused me," she confirmed after a few seconds of hesitation.

Mrs. Simmons put her hand over her mouth in shock. "Oh my God," she uttered.

Her father was in disbelief. "There's no way," he denied.

"Dad, it's true," Malajia cried, walking over to him. "It was just mental at first...he'd talk down to me, disrespect me, degrade me...then one day he slapped me and—I shouldn't have taken him back after that but—I *did* and it just got worse. The one slap turned into kicks, pushes, *punches.*" She wiped her eyes. "It *happened.*"

Her father shook his head as he placed his hands on his head. "No, no that didn't happen," he refused to believe.

Malajia grabbed his arm as he went to walk away. "I know that I haven't been the best daughter. I know that I've made you question me on *many* occasions, but you have to trust me, I'm telling you the truth," she pleaded. "I would never lie about something like that."

Mr. Simmons stared into Malajia's tear filled eyes for seconds before closing his eyes and retreating for the stairs without saying a word, leaving Malajia feeling broken.

"Daddy, please don't walk away from me, I need you," Malajia called after him and was about to follow him, when her mother grabbed her and hugged her.

Geri began to tear up as she watched her sister nearly collapse in her mother's arms. She felt terrible; she felt guilty. Geri thought that if she hadn't been so dismissive of Malajia's feelings, then maybe she would have felt comfortable enough to tell her.

"I don't get it," Maria said, slowly sitting on the couch. "No man in our life *ever* abused us. How could you fall for someone who does something like that, Malajia?"

"Maria are you *serious* right now?" Geri barked. "Are you seriously *judging* her? After what you just heard?" She was disgusted. "*This* is why Malajia didn't say anything to us."

Mrs. Simmons ignored the arguing around her and only focused her attention on the daughter in her arms. "I'm so sorry baby," she repeated over and over, holding on to Malajia. She glanced up and saw her husband run down the stairs. "Where are you *going?*" she asked, furious; seeing him head for the door.

"Malajia, where is he? Where can I find him?" he asked Malajia, completely ignoring his wife's question.

Malajia looked up at her father. "I don't know," she sniffled.

"I'll find him," he fumed, grabbing is car keys from an end table. "I'll fuckin' find him and I'll—"

"You're not going to do *anything* right now except hug your daughter," Mrs. Simmons ordered.

"No, I need—"

"You *need* to hold your daughter!" Mrs. Simmons yelled. "You can deal with him *later*, Malajia needs you *now*. Come hold your daughter." Mr. Simmons looked as if he was fighting back tears as he stared at Malajia, who was clinging to his wife for dear life. "Richard," Mrs. Simmons softly called. "Come hold your daughter."

Mr. Simmons dropped his keys to the floor before walking over and putting his big arms around Malajia and his wife, burying his face in Malajia's hair. Geri and Maria looked on, somber as they watched their parents comfort their sister.

Chapter 40

Chasity stared at the TV, resting her head on Jason's chest. Having finished dinner just a half hour ago, the couple relaxed on the couch in the living room to watch TV, relishing the quiet in Jason's house. His parents weren't set to return for another day, and Chasity was dreading going back to her house. Having spoken to Trisha earlier, there was no change in Brenda; she was comatose but was still holding on.

Jason ran his hand up and down Chasity's back as the scenes played out on the screen in front of them. "Jason," she said.

"Yeah?" he answered, turning the TV down.

"Do you think I'm a bad person for not going to the hospital?"

"No, I *don't*."

"Are you lying?" she questioned.

"No, I'm *not*."

Chasity raised her head up and stared him in his eyes. "Jason, seriously," she said.

Jason turned the TV off. "I don't think you're wrong *or* bad for not going," he assured. "It's a decision that you have a right to make. But on the same token… I'm sure that your mother probably wishes that you were there. I'm sure she needs you right now."

Chasity sighed as the guilty feeling swept over her. She was about to respond, when the sound of her phone ringing startled her. Grabbing the phone off the cushion next to her, she sat up and answered it. "Yeah Mom...okay... Okay...yeah... Yes, I promise...Okay."

Jason sat up and studied the blank expression on Chasity's face as she hung up the phone. "What is it, baby?"

"Um...they don't think that she's gonna make it through the night," Chasity revealed, voice low, staring at the blank screen on her phone. "I um...I'm gonna go to the hospital."

Jason stood from the couch the same time that she did. "I'll drive you," he offered, reaching for his wallet on the coffee table.

"Okay," Chasity said. She was grateful for the offer; she was in no state of mind to drive herself.

Jason pulled in front of the hospital, letting Chasity out of the car. Not wanting to wait for one of the crowded elevators, Chasity ran up the steps. Reaching the designated floor, she ran down the hall and rounded a corner to find her family stationed outside of Brenda's hospital room. Chasity slowed her pace to a walk as she approached her somber uncle, cousins and grandmother, who were consoling each other.

Grandmother Duvall managed a slight smile through her tear streaked face as she locked eyes with Chasity. She walked over and gave Chasity a long hug. "I'm glad you're here," she whispered.

Chasity just nodded as the two women parted from their embrace. Chasity looked around the area in search of Trisha.

"She's in there with Brenda," her grandmother informed, sensing who Chasity was looking for. She directed Chasity's gaze to the small window.

Chasity slowly approached the window and through it, saw Trisha sitting next to Brenda's bed holding her hand. Her face was buried on Brenda's chest.

It was almost as if Chasity was in a daze. Her grandmother's touch to her shoulder startled her.

"Go in," Grandmother Duvall softly urged.

Chasity looked at her. "I don't know if I should," she admitted.

Grandmother Duvall touched Chasity's smooth face with her hand. "Go," she insisted, voice soft and caring as she guided Chasity in the direction of the door with her arm.

Chasity hesitated for moments, before turning the knob and walking inside. She was greeted by the beeps of the heart monitor that Brenda was hooked up to and by the sound of Trisha's sniffles. Chasity was fighting the urge to turn around and walk out of the room.

Trisha, hearing the door close, looked up and her eyes met with Chasity. She rose from her seat. "Thank you for coming," she said, wiping her eye with one hand, cradling Brenda's hand with the other.

"Uh huh," Chasity managed to say as her eyes fixed on Brenda's motionless body, laying in the hospital bed. She was staring so hard from the door that she didn't hear her mother call her name. It wasn't until Trisha called her a second time that she snapped out of it. "Yes?"

"I have to check on your grandmother," Trisha said, voice cracking. It was obvious that she was trying not to break down in front of Chasity. "Can you please sit with her for me?"

Chasity shook her head. She didn't know if she could handle being in the room alone with a dying Brenda. "*I'll* check on Grandmom," she quickly declared, turning to walk out.

"Chasity, please," Trisha pleaded, voice tortured. "Just sit with her. You don't have to say anything to her... I don't think she even knows we're here...just sit with her."

Chasity fought the urge to roll her eyes, curse, or sigh, as she walked over to Brenda's bedside to take Trisha's place.

Chasity watched Trisha walk out of the room, closing the door behind her. She sat in the chair and rubbed her face with her hand, before leaning back and staring at the bouquets of flowers which sat on the table across from her. The whole room looked like a funeral home with all of the flowers and cards. The sound of Brenda's breathing seemed like it became louder to her. Chasity slowly turned and looked at her. She sat up and looked at Brenda's face; it looked like she was trying to sleep but something was keeping her from resting. Her face looked pained.

Chasity slowly shook her head. *Damn Brenda,* she thought. She hated the fact that Brenda's life was ending this way. That she had to leave this young, and in this much pain. Chasity felt for the woman, as much as she didn't want to. She looked down at Brenda's hand, which was lying open, resting on her side. Chasity reached out and gently grabbed her hand, holding it while she watched her chest slowly rise and fall with each breath that she took.

After a few seconds, Chasity felt Brenda squeeze her hand. She frowned slightly and looked down. Sure enough, Brenda's fingers were closed over her own. Chasity looked back at Brenda's face which now looked peaceful; it even looked like she had a small smile. Before Chasity knew it, Brenda's chest rose and fell one last time, accompanied by the sound of the heart monitor flat lining.

Chasity closed her eyes and sighed as the nurses rushed in to check on Brenda. Seeing that she in fact had passed away, the nurse turned the heart monitor off and patted Chasity on her shoulder.

"I'm sorry for your loss," the nurse apologized, sincerely.

Chasity just nodded as she stood from the seat. She carefully removed Brenda's hand from hers and placed it on Brenda's lifeless chest. As the nurses moved about the room to tend to Brenda, Chasity slowly walked towards the door. She took one last look at Brenda before walking out of the room, only to be greeted by her mourning relatives. Chasity watched as the family cried and consoled one another. Melina was crouched on the floor, screaming while her uncle tried to hold her. Trisha cried as she walked up to Chasity and wrapped her arms around her, holding on to her.

Chasity held on to her mother as she gazed around at her family and realized, she was the only one not crying. Her grandmother nearly collapsed from grief, sending Trisha flying over to her. Taking the opportunity, Chasity silently slipped away and walked down the hall and into the waiting room, where she found Jason sitting.

Jason, noticing her, stood up and looked at her, eyes filed with anticipation. Chasity just slowly shook her head, silently telling him that Brenda had in fact passed. Jason crossed the floor and embraced her, offering his apologies before kissing her on the cheek. They parted and walked back over to the chairs and sat down.

"I couldn't stay back there," Chasity said, voice somber. "Everybody is hysterical. I can't deal with all that."

Jason studied her. Other than her voice, she seemed emotionless to him. "Are you okay?" he asked.

Chasity slowly shook her head. "I don't know," she answered. "I feel like I should be crying right now but...I *can't*," she admitted. "I mean...she's *dead* and I can't feel—I think there's something wrong with me."

"There's *nothing* wrong with you," Jason assured. "I just don't think that all of this has hit you yet."

"Maybe," Chasity mumbled. "I gotta go call the girls and let them know," she said before standing up and walking off.

Jason followed her progress. He was afraid for her. He knew that eventually everything that had happened in the past few months would hit Chasity like a ton of bricks, and when it did, he didn't know how she would handle it. Or if she could.

Chasity was on her way to find an isolated area to make her phone call, when she noticed Trisha standing against a wall, with her hands over her face. Chasity walked over to her and gave her another hug.

"I knew this was coming and I still wasn't prepared for it," Trisha sniffled.

"I know," Chasity said as they parted.

Trisha fumbled in her purse for a tissue. "I have to make all these phone calls. I have to start planning her funeral," she sputtered, as she pulled a pack of tissues out. "I have to call the funeral home, I have to pick out a casket, and flowers. Lilies, lilies were her favorite flower...."

Chasity stared as Trisha rambled and nervously fumbled with the tissue pack. Seeing that Trisha was beginning to get frustrated with the pack, Chasity took it and opened the tissues for her.

Trisha gave a grateful nod, taking a tissue. "I couldn't watch them take her body out of the room," Trisha said, voice cracking. "I couldn't watch them do that. I have to go clean out her room at Mom's house. She won't be able to do that...Mom, I mean... I have to plan her funeral. Brenda's funeral...my only sister's funeral."

Chasity sighed as she ran her hand along the back of her neck. Cleary, Trisha was emotional and dazed. At that moment, Chasity wanted to relieve Trisha's pressure and heartache any way that she could. "I'll do it for you," she announced, hesitantly. Trisha stared out in front of her, obviously not hearing what was just said. "Mom," Chasity called.

Trisha looked at her. "Huh?"

"I'll handle the arrangements for you," Chasity proposed.

Trisha shook her head. "No, I can't ask you to do that," she refused.

"You're not asking me. I'm offering," Chasity pointed out.

"I still have to call your father and tell him," Trisha added. Chasity fought the urge to frown. "He wanted to be here, but he got stuck on a flight."

Chasity sighed. "I'll call him," she said after a few

moments.

Tears spilled out of Trisha's eyes, she was grateful. "Are you sure?" she asked.

"No," Chasity admitted. "But I'll be fine."

"Chasity, this is a lot to handle...*I* can do it, I just need a minute to get myself together... I can call your father, I just need a minute."

"You're not going to be *okay* in a minute," Chasity argued. "I said I'll take care of it... I won't do her wrong if that's what you're thinking."

"That thought never once crossed my mind," Trisha promised.

The last thing that Trisha wanted was to put this pressure on Chasity; she'd put enough on her. But Trisha admitted to herself that she wasn't in the right frame of mind to make any phone calls or pick out flowers... Being the most stable child that her mother had, she knew that her brother wouldn't be able to handle it either. She had no choice but to relinquish her duties to Chasity. Trisha patted Chasity's face, before moving some hair off of her shoulder. "I love you. Thank you," she sniffled, before hugging her again and slowly walking off. Chasity stood there, wondering what she'd just gotten herself into.

"You're welcome," she said to herself before making her way back to Jason.

Chapter 41

Chasity checked her appearance in the large mirror inside her grandmother's private bathroom. She'd been in the bathroom for the past fifteen minutes in an attempt to hide out from the houseful of guests. *Why they wanted to have the repast here, I'll never know. These people won't be leaving anytime soon,* she seethed to herself.

The past week went quickly for Chasity; between trying to console her mother, plan her aunt's funeral and constantly reassuring her friends that she was okay, she was drained. Seeing the bathroom door open, she glanced behind her through the mirror and was relieved to see that it was Jason. "Hey," she said.

"Hey, people are looking for you," Jason informed, walking over to her.

Chasity sighed. "I just need a few more minutes to myself," she fussed. "If *one* more fuckin' person asks me why I didn't put 'Brenda is survived by her daughter, Chasity' on the obituary, I'm gonna slap 'em."

Jason shook his head as he wrapped his arms around her from behind. "You only have a few more hours to go and then I can take you home," he said.

"I'm over *all* of this," she complained, resting her head back against his chest.

"I know, but for what it's worth, you did a really good job with the funeral," he complimented.

"Thanks...she'd already started making arrangements before she died, so I really didn't do that much extra."

"Stop down playing what you did," Jason chastised. "You did a lot, even though I know you didn't want to."

"I guess you're right," she sighed.

Jason released her from his embrace and grabbed her hand. "Come on," he said to her as he pulled her out of the bathroom.

Chasity followed Jason down the steps and over to the couch, where she flopped down.

"You hungry?" Jason asked.

Chasity ran her hands through her hair and nodded.

That gesture sent Jason on a mission to get her something to eat. While she waited, Chasity grabbed her cell phone, which was sitting on one of the end tables, and started looking through it. She had several missed calls, all of them from Alex. *Why am I not surprised that Alex is the only one not to listen when I said not to bother me today.* Rolling her eyes, Chasity continued to scroll through the phone. She was so preoccupied that she didn't see that a person had approached and stood in front of her.

"Looking at anything interesting?" The deep male voice asked.

"No, not really," Chasity blindly answered, before looking up and coming face to face with the man. She frowned. "Dad," she spat.

Derrick Parker managed a small smile, even though it was clear by the way that Chasity was looking at him that she didn't plan on returning it with a smile of her own.

She shook her head. "I don't have time for this shit," she mumbled, standing from her seat.

As she tried to walk away, Derrick stood in front of her. "Listen, don't think I haven't noticed that you went out of your way to avoid me the entire day," he pointed out, calm.

Chasity folded her arms. "And?" she hissed, staring at

him defiantly.

He sighed. He'd tried countless times to talk to Chasity for *days*. He was surprised when she called him to curtly inform him of Brenda's passing for Trisha, and promptly hung up when he tried to make small talk. He didn't intend on upsetting his only child on the day of his ex-wife's funeral by trying to strike up a conversation, but he figured that he had no choice. This may be the only chance that he had to see her.

"I know that this isn't a good time to try to have this conversation, but—"

"*No* time is a good time to have this conversation," Chasity cut off. "I already told you that I don't want to talk to you."

"I know that I haven't been the best father to you—"

"You haven't been a father to me at *all*," Chasity argued. Derrick rubbed his forehead with his hand. "You detached yourself from me for most of my life and now that I'm a grown woman you want to talk to me? It's too late."

He reached out to try to touch Chasity's arm and she jerked away from him.

"Don't touch me," she hissed.

"Everything okay?" Jason frowned, appearing beside Chasity, plate of food in hand. Having witnessed the angry look on her face, accompanied by this strange man trying to touch her, he instantly went into protective mode.

"I'm fine," Chasity assured, looking at Jason. "My father was just leaving," she said.

Jason held the sternness on his face as he sized up the man in front of him. He'd never even seen a picture of Chasity's father. Looking at the tall, brown-skinned, solid man, with dark, low cut hair and beard, he could see that although Chasity looked more like Trisha, she favored him more so around the eyes. *So that's where she gets those hazel eyes from?* he thought to himself.

Derrick extended his hand. "Derrick Parker, Chasity's father," he greeted.

Jason shifted the plate that he had made for Chasity from one hand to the other. "Jason Adams, Chasity's boyfriend," he returned, shaking the man's hand with a firm grip.

Derrick smiled and nodded. *So, this is the Jason that Trisha told me about, huh?* he mused.

"Are y'all done with this exchanging of pleasantries?" Chasity bit out.

"Chasity listen—"

"Bye Dad," she sneered, before walking away leaving Jason standing there, feeling awkward. This was not what Jason had in mind when he imagined meeting Chasity's father for the first time.

"She's a stubborn one, huh?" Derrick said, at an attempt to a joke.

Jason set the plate on a nearby accent table and stared Derrick in the eye. He was not amused. Sure he was Chasity's father, and Jason would respect him as such, but knowing Chasity's history with him, he already had pre-conceived feelings about him. "Yeah, she is," he replied, voice stern.

"Jason listen, I know you don't know me, or probably even *like* me for that matter," Derrick began, voice calm and humbled.

Jason just continued to stare at him.

"I'm pretty sure she told you everything."

"She did," Jason confirmed.

"Well...I just want a chance to try to make things up to her."

"Honestly, I don't think that's possible," Jason stated. "You said so yourself, she's stubborn."

"I know... She's blocked all of my calls, and her mother even tried to talk her into talking to me and she shot her down..." Derrick locked eyes with Jason. "But something tells me that she will listen to *you*."

Jason frowned. "No disrespect, but I don't appreciate what you're asking of me," he protested.

Derrick resisted the urge to smirk. Jason wasn't

intimidated. He liked that. He knew that Chasity needed someone like that.

"Besides, why are you doing this *now*?" Jason continued. "After all this time?"

"Because I'm stupid and I gave up too easily," Derrick admitted, point blank. "When she shot me down the last time I saw her in New York—"

"Which was over a *year* ago," Jason spat, folding his arms.

"I know...I just figured that I'd respect her wishes and leave her alone," he admitted. "But with Brenda getting sick, it made me realize that life is short and I need to make the relationships that I damaged, right... I didn't get the chance to make it up to Brenda for what I did to her...but I can make it up to Chasity... I just want a relationship with my daughter."

Jason rolled his eyes. Not out of anger for Derrick, but because he couldn't believe that he was about to agree to something that was sure to upset Chasity. "I'll talk to her," he stated hesitantly. "But, I can't make any promises."

Derrick smiled, extending his hand yet again. "I don't expect you to, Jason," he confirmed, "I just appreciate you making an attempt for me."

Jason just nodded, shaking his hand.

Chasity, still reeling from the run in with her father, sought solace upstairs. She'd planned on escaping into one of the seldom used guestrooms, but upon walking down the hall, she noticed that the door to the room that Brenda had been staying in was open. She frowned; she had made sure that she closed it and she told everyone to stay out of it.

She pushed the door open to find Trisha sitting on the bed, cradling a throw pillow, staring out of the window.

Chasity slowly walked in. "You shouldn't be in here," she said, sitting on a chair across from her.

Trisha looked at her, face stained with tears. "I was just

um…getting some of her things. The last thing she asked me to do was make sure that I grab this box and take it to my house," she stammered, pointing to a small cardboard box, which sat on the dresser.

"Oh okay," Chasity replied, tiredly.

"Your father is here, did you see him?"

"I know…and yeah, I did," Chasity responded, trying to hold her comforting tone.

Trisha just nodded. She didn't want to press the issue. "Are you okay?" she asked. "I'm not just talking about seeing your father…but with everything."

"I'm fine," Chasity sighed.

Trisha sniffled. "You've been so strong for me through this whole thing and I appreciate you for that," she said. "I know that I put you through—"

"It's fine, Mom," Chasity cut in, handing Trisha some tissues from the nightstand.

Trisha wiped her face. "I just want to say one thing to you, and I know that you're not going to want to hear it, but I have to say it."

Chasity tilted her head. "You really want to do this now?"

"I *have* to," Trisha insisted, pushing some of her hair behind her ear. Chasity sat back in her seat, anticipating what Trisha was about to say. "I know that Brenda wasn't—"

"No, we're not doing this right now," Chasity quickly dismissed, standing up.

"I just hope that one day, even if it's *years* from now, you can think of her without being angry," Trisha said, despite Chasity's protest.

Chasity rolled her eyes. "I'm gonna go home," she said. As far as she was concerned, this conversation was over. Before Chasity said something insensitive, she needed to remove herself from the room. "You staying here?"

Trisha looked at Chasity for a moment. Realizing that she was deflecting, she just nodded. "Yeah."

"I'll take this box home for you," Chasity said, grabbing

it. Before Chasity walked out of the room, she looked back at Trisha. "I'm sorry for your loss," she said, before walking out and closing the door behind her.

Trisha let more tears fall as she cradled the pillow closer to her chest. "I'm sorry for yours too," she said to the empty room.

Jason removed the black tie from his neck and sat it on the couch. "Today was a long day," he sighed.

"Tell me about it," Chasity said, removing her jewelry.

Having just arrived back home, Chasity was desperate to relax. The hordes of relatives, outpouring of emotions, run-ins with people she had no interest in talking to, was almost too much for her to handle.

"This place is a damn mess," she fussed, eyeing the papers strewn across the couch and coffee table. With the stress of planning Brenda's funeral, Chasity hadn't had time to clean up, and neither did Trisha, who walked around in a catatonic state most of the time since Brenda's death.

Jason stretched. "I'll go take care of the kitchen," he offered, heading in that direction.

"Thanks Jase," she said tiredly. "Jason," she called, stopping him in his tracks. He turned around and looked at her. "Seriously, thanks for being here with me. Today and for this past week."

Jason smiled. "Where *else* would I be?" he said, before heading to the kitchen.

Chasity began gathering the papers and stacking them together. She came across a stack of obituaries. She sucked her teeth; she remembered that she'd accidentally ordered too many. Chasity picked up the paper and stared at the picture of Brenda that was chosen for the cover. She was smiling, but it looked forced, at least that's what Chasity thought. She couldn't remember the last time that Brenda was actually happy.

Setting the paper down, her elbow knocked against the

box that she had brought from her grandmother's house. Curious, Chasity began to go through it. She removed some cards, costume jewelry and other belongings that she didn't recognize.

Seeing something familiar, Chasity frowned in confusion. Reaching to the bottom of the box, she pulled out a small pink shoe box decorated with stickers, finger paint, glitter, crystal hearts and stars, and a sloppily crayon drawn birthday cake. The tattered box was covered in clear tape. Chasity stared at it; it was the box that she'd decorated and given to Brenda when she was five years old; the box that Brenda tore up in front of her... She had no idea that it'd been taped back together.

Opening the box, Chasity found a dried out pink lily; the one that Chasity picked and put in the box after she'd made it. It still had the pink ribbon tied around it. She stared at the flower and remembered that pink was Brenda's favorite color...and until Chasity turned five, it was *hers too.* Under the lily was an envelope with Chasity's name on it.

Setting the box down, Chasity opened the envelope and pulled a handwritten letter from it. It was clearly Brenda's handwriting. She was quiet as she began to read it.

Dear Chasity,

I know this sounds cliché, but by the time you read this letter, I'll be gone. I'm glad that I got to talk to you one last time. I'm amazed at how much you've grown and at how beautiful you are. You always have been. I saw how confused you were when I started talking about the child that I'd lost. I already knew that you knew about it. Trisha told me that she told you. She also told me about the one that you lost... Please don't be mad at her. I asked her to tell me everything about you. Me sharing that was just my way of trying to let you know that I knew what you'd been through and that I'm sorry that it happened.

Chasity, I truly hope that you took what I said to you, to heart. With me being the main person who hurt you in your life, I can only hope that with me being gone, that you can finally be happy. That is all that I want for you.

You were never the problem, I was. And I know that my words don't mean much but I am truly, deeply sorry for making you feel that everything wrong in my life, was your fault. For making you feel that you weren't worthy or deserving of anything...I'm sorry for everything. If you've learned anything from me, I hope it's how not to be. You're better than I ever was and as long as you don't let your anger consume you, I know you'll continue to thrive.

And please take care of my sister for me. She spent every day of her life that you were living with me, wishing that you were with her. I forgave her and I hope that you have too. And try not to be too hard on your father. I know he messed up, but if he's coming to you and trying to make amends, just talk to him at least...like you did for me. You may not see it now, but you will need him one day.

Take care of yourself sweet pea.

Chasity felt tears fill her eyes as she closed the letter. She remembered that nickname. Brenda called her that when she was a little girl, before her change. Chasity tried to force her tears back down. Noticing something else in the envelope, Chasity reached inside and pulled out a small worn, picture. Tears spilled out of Chasity's eyes as she stared at a picture of a smiling Brenda, holding her as a baby. She looked genuinely happy. Chasity turned the picture over and read the words on the back;

On this day, I looked into your eyes and called you mine. You may not believe me, but I do love you. I'm sorry —Mom

It was at that moment that a wave of emotions overcame Chasity. She put her hands over her face as she tried to fight the urge to cry out loud.

Jason emerged from the kitchen, sleeves rolled up. "The kitchen wasn't too bad, I just finished. Do you need me to do anything else?" he asked, completely unaware of what Chasity was feeling; her back was turned to him. When he noticed that she didn't respond, he called her. "You okay?" he asked, concerned.

"Uh huh," she replied, between sniffles.

Jason frowned, noticing the sound of her voice. He took several steps towards her. "Are you sure?" he asked.

She turned around to face him. At that point, Jason noticed that she was crying.

"No," she replied before breaking down and crying out.

Jason rushed over, hugged her and held on to Chasity as she collapsed in his arms. She wrapped her arms around him as she continued to cry out loud. She cried for Trisha losing her sister. She cried for her grandmother losing a daughter. She cried for Brenda losing her life, not knowing if she would ever be forgiven for the things that she has done. She cried for her unborn child and most of all, she cried for herself; letting out her frustrations, her anger, her resentment and her pain. Jason didn't speak, he just held her and rocked her as she finally let go.

Chapter 42

"How have you been? I swear I haven't spoken to you in a month of Sundays," Sidra gushed into her wireless earpiece as she drove down the highway.

Malajia chuckled. "Did your corny ass just say 'a month of Sundays'?" she teased, turning the car off.

"Don't be smart," Sidra chided.

"You're so dramatic," Malajia joked. "It's only been a few days since I last spoke to you."

"I know," Sidra admitted, looking out the rearview mirror. "So in all seriousness, how's it going?"

"It's been going pretty good actually," Malajia smiled.

"Your family still doting on you?"

Malajia frowned. "Doting?" she scoffed. "Sid, what's with all these corny words and phrases you keep using?"

Sidra giggled. "I've been reading a lot of old books," she rationalized. "Just answer the question."

Malajia ran her fingers through the long curls on her head. "Yes, my family is still loving on me," she beamed.

Ever since Malajia came clean about the abuse, her family had been comforting and supporting her through her healing. They'd even apologized to her for how they were making her feel, and that made Malajia happy.

"They made me go see a counselor," Malajia griped, rolling her eyes.

"Oh really?" Sidra asked, pleasantly surprised.

"Yeah, I've already had a few sessions."

"How is that going?" Sidra asked.

"I hate to admit it but… It's helping me," Malajia admitted. Malajia was reluctant to attend the sessions at first. But after talking with the woman, Malajia only wished that she would've gone sooner. "I don't feel…*ashamed* of myself anymore."

"I'm proud of you Malajia," Sidra gushed.

Malajia smiled. "Thanks."

"Well, school starts back in a few weeks," Sidra said. "Excited yet? We'll be *seniors*, can you believe it?"

"Hell *no*, I can't believe it," Malajia laughed. "Seems like only yesterday I was getting ready to enter as a freshman."

"Tell me about it," Sidra agreed. "Have you spoken to any of the other girls?"

"You know, Alex has been calling like every five damn minutes," Malajia quipped. "I hope she finally lets Eric snatch her ass up this year so she can stop focusing on *us* so much."

Sidra laughed. "Stop it, you know she means well," she said. "But yeah, she still hasn't learned when to back off. She keeps blowing Chasity's phone up too. I told Alex to give her some time. It's only been like three weeks since Brenda passed." Sidra sighed. "Have *you* spoken to her by any chance?"

Malajia shook her head, momentarily forgetting that Sidra couldn't see her. She hadn't activated her video talk, due to driving. "No… I spoke to Jason though. He said that she's pretty emotional right now," she revealed, somber. "She's not up for talking, but he said that as soon as she is he'll have her call us… I feel bad for her. That was a lot."

"I know, me too. But she's strong. She'll be okay," Sidra assured. "And so are *you*. You're stronger than most."

"If you say so," Malajia muttered.

"*Speaking* of strength, are you going to do what you said you were going to do today?"

Malajia sighed, glancing out of the window at the two-story single home across from where she was parked. "I will…as soon as I get up enough courage to get my fine ass out of this car."

"No time like the present," Sidra said. "Goddamn it! Will you *move* with your old ass?!" she screamed out of nowhere.

"What the hell is the problem?" Malajia frowned.

"I'm sorry, I hate highway driving with these idiots," Sidra fumed. "I'm meeting the guys for lunch and I'm already late. Anyway, don't worry about me. You go do what you need to do and call me later."

"Okay."

"Love you."

"Love you too," Malajia said, just before ending the call. Malajia sat in the car for several moments. She put her hands over her face and said a silent prayer.

"Come on, you got this," she said to herself with one last once over in the rearview mirror.

She emerged from the car and hesitantly made her way across the quiet, tree-lined street and up the walkway. Letting out a long sigh, Malajia knocked on the door.

"Hold on," she heard a male voice call from the other side.

Malajia smiled once a shirtless Mark opened the door. He greeted her smile with a confused look.

"Malajia?" he questioned, some bite in his voice. "What are *you* doing here?"

She focused on his bare, toned chest for a few seconds before snapping back to reality. "Um, can I come in?" she asked, voice hopeful.

Mark rolled his eyes as he debated on whether or not he should let her. "Come on," he relented, moving aside to let her through.

As Mark closed the door behind her and made his way over to the couch to grab his t-shirt, Malajia looked around. She'd forgotten how nice his house was. She hadn't been there since the second semester of freshman year. "You here by yourself?" she asked.

"Yeah, my parents are in Florida," he answered, pulling the shirt over his head.

Malajia looked confused. "Why are you putting your shirt on?"

"'Cause you lost the right to see this body," he sneered, smoothing the shirt out with his hands. "We're not together anymore."

Malajia held that same bewildered look. "But you don't care *who* sees your body. You play basketball without—"

"Look, that's not the point okay," he snapped, realizing that she was right.

His outburst startled Malajia, but more in a funny way. She fought the urge to smile; she thought that it was cute when he got flustered.

"Seriously Malajia, what are you doing here?" he hissed, folding his arms.

Malajia took a deep breath. "I need to talk to you."

"You've said *enough*," he sniped.

She shook her head. "No, I *haven't* said enough, and that's the problem," she countered. She pointed to the couch. "Sit down."

Mark, not interested in having any conversation with Malajia, sucked his teeth as he flopped down.

Malajia walked over and sat down next to him, situating herself to make sure she faced him, even though he wasn't looking at her. "Listen, I know that I'm probably the last person that you want, sitting here right now," she began.

"You got that right," he mumbled.

"I hurt your feelings and I know that…and I'm sorry," Malajia continued. She paused for a moment while she tried to gather her thoughts. "No matter what I said, I didn't break up with you because of *you*, I did it because of *me*."

"Yeah, whatever," Mark spat, looking ahead of him.

Malajia took another deep breath. "Can you look at me please?" she asked.

Mark shook his head. "Naw."

"Okay...that's fine" Malajia sighed. "In all honesty, I've been dealing with a lot of bad feelings lately..."

"Bad feelings about what?" Mark asked, tone still sharp.

"About my last relationship," Malajia replied, sullen.

Mark finally looked at her, but remained silent.

"Even though the relationship is over and I have *no* desire to deal with his ass *ever* again, I—" She sighed. "I just shouldn't have jumped in to a new relationship—"

"Then why *did* you?" Mark cut in. "If you knew you weren't ready, why didn't you just say no when I asked you."

"Because I *wanted* to be ready," Malajia stressed. "I *wanted* to be in a relationship, a *real* one... I wanted to be with *you*. But I hadn't dealt with the trauma of what I'd been through long enough to move on from it."

"I could've *helped* you move on," Mark insisted.

Malajia titled her head. "It wasn't that simple, babe." Malajia saw how frustrated Mark was and she understood why he was. She just wanted to make him understand.

"I spent months with someone who I should never have given a second chance to in the *first* place...but I did. I gave chance after chance and he hurt me more with every chance and I just—every decision I made when it came to him wasn't for me, it was for *him*... I let him use me and break me and it *changed* me..." she paused when she heard her voice falter; after calming herself, she continued. "I *hated* who I was when I was with him, and I realized that even though I *left* him, I still held a lot of resentment."

"You *should* resent him," Mark grunted.

"It wasn't the resentment for him that had a hold on me," she clarified, "I resented *myself*."

Mark's hardened expression softened at her words.

"Mark, I just...I felt like I was weak and stupid." Tears filled her eyes. "I put myself in *stupid* situations over and over—"

"Malajia, you're not stupid *or* weak," Mark assured.

"That's how I felt," Malajia replied, wiping her eyes. "I was stupid enough to give that bastard a part of me that I can't get back...and every time you tried to get close to me, I just kept thinking about it and wishing that I would've saved that experience for...you."

Mark took a few moments to process what Malajia just revealed to him. He had no idea that she felt guilty for losing her virginity. He took a deep breath.

"Mel," he began, softening his tone. "I don't want you to ever feel guilty about not being a virgin for me. I knew you weren't one *before* we started dating," he said, adjusting his position to face her. "That doesn't bother me, what *does* bother me is the fact that your experience wasn't what you wanted it to be... I'm sorry that you had to go through that."

Malajia wiped more tears from her face. Revealing her feelings to Mark, and the reaction that he was giving her, was making her feel a little lighter. He seemed to understand, and she hoped it was enough for him to forgive her and take her back. But she knew that before she could even think of asking for a reconciliation, that she had one more thing to tell him...something that she hadn't told anyone, not even her counselor.

Seeing a single tear fall on her face, Mark reached out and wiped it with his finger. "It's okay, you don't have to cry," he said, comforting. "I'm here for you, Mel, always will be. I may have been mad, but my feelings for you haven't changed."

"That might not be the case after today," Malajia alluded, sniffling. Mark looked confused. "I have one more thing that I have to tell you."

"Okay," Mark replied.

Malajia looked down at her hands as she paused for a moment. "Um...when I was with him over break, before he attacked me again...I slept with him again."

Mark rolled his eyes. "Malajia, I really don't need to

know all the times you had sex with him," he ground out.

"Please, just listen to me," she pleaded, voice cracking. Mark sat silently, just looking at her. "I didn't even want to…like the first time, I did it because I was tired of fighting." Malajia was scared to say the next words. She knew that she had to, but not knowing how Mark would take them, was torture for her. If he were to shun her, she didn't know what she would do.

"Anyway, a few months later, after you and I started dating…" Malajia let the tears flow as she took another deep breath. "I found out I was pregnant."

Mark sat there in shock. "What?"

Malajia looked down at her hands. "Yeah," she confirmed. "*That's* why my mood was all crazy…it wasn't my period like I thought. I was pregnant and didn't know it."

Mark opened his mouth to speak, but nothing would come out. He just rubbed his face with his hands. It was a lot to hear.

"I couldn't believe that was happening to me. I felt like my world was crashing in around me and the only thing that I could think about was the fact that I couldn't go through with it," Malajia cried.

Mark looked at her, then frowned. "What do you mean?"

She hesitated. "I *couldn't* go through with it," she repeated. "…I got an abortion." Seeing the look on Mark's face broke her. It was almost like he didn't know her. She broke down when he turned away from her. "I'm sorry," she sobbed, grabbing his arm. "It wasn't easy for me…I feel horrible, but I felt like it was my only option."

Mark put his head in his hands, but didn't say anything.

"I'm sorry that I'm putting you through this, but I had to tell you," she said. She moved closer to him, still clutching his arm. She buried her face in his shoulder. "I don't want to lose you, Mark."

Mark sat up and leaned back against the cushions. His eyes were red and there was a tortured expression was on his face. Malajia knew that he'd just shed tears. In her mind, she just blew it. Feeling defeated, she went to leave, but was stopped when he gently grabbed her arm. She turned around and looked at him.

Without speaking, Mark leaned over and hugged Malajia. She wrapped her arms around him tight, and they held each other.

"You haven't lost me," he breathed against her hair.

Hearing those words, Malajia gripped him tighter.

Mark pulled away and looked at her, eyes caring, loving. "It's okay," he promised. "I'm not going anywhere."

She smiled at him as he leaned in and kissed her forehead. She touched his face. His eyes were still red. "You were crying." It was more of a statement than a question.

"Yeah man," he admitted, rubbing his eye. "But don't tell nobody though."

She laughed a little through her tears.

"I don't need David and his glasses clowning me, and shit," he joked.

Malajia laughed again. "It's safe with me," she promised, staring at him. She closed her eyes as he touched her face. Malajia had gone to him to share her truth, not knowing what would come of it. All that she knew was that for them to move forward, she had to. Now that it was out, moving forward with him was what she wanted.

Opening her eyes, she fixed a hopeful gaze on him. "Will you take me back?"

"Thought I already did," Mark smiled. "But are you sure *you're* ready?"

Malajia nodded slowly. "Yes, I'm ready," she promised. It was the truth, she *was* ready—her mind, her heart, *and* her body.

Malajia leaned in and kissed Mark. What Mark initially thought to be a sweet simple kiss to confirm the rekindling of their relationship, turned into a full on make out session. He pulled her closer as their passion intensified. Next thing Mark knew, Malajia had straddled him.

He pulled back, catching his breath. She shot him a

questionable look. As turned on as Mark was and as much as he wanted her, Mark knew well of Malajia's previous experiences when it came to sex. He didn't want to take that step unless he was sure that she was ready for it.

"Maybe we should slow down," he suggested.

"I don't *want* to," Malajia breathed, grabbing a handful of his shirt. When Mark hesitated, she kissed his cheek. "Trust me," she promised, longing in her eyes.

"Okay then," Mark smiled. He stood up with her still straddling him.

Malajia was turned on by the fact that he carried her, extra pounds and all, up the flight of stairs with little to no effort. Malajia's adrenaline was on high as the couple entered Mark's bedroom; it only intensified as they undressed each other.

She relished Mark's kisses and touches. Unlike her first, Malajia wasn't filled with uncertainty. Unlike her first, she knew she wouldn't be filled with regret afterwards. Unlike her first…she knew that she *wanted* to give her body to the man who was pleasing her. The man who went from being a nuisance to a friend to her boyfriend, and now he'd become her lover. He took his time with her, getting to know every part of her on a deeper level

Malajia was lucky that Mark's parents weren't home; they would have heard her moans of pleasure. At that point, she didn't care if the *neighbors* heard her. She had no idea that Mark was so attentive, so passionate. He surprised her, in more ways than one. She was caught up in the moment, and enjoying every bit of it.

Emotionally drained and physically spent, the couple laid cuddled together in comfortable silence for what seemed like an eternity. Malajia's head rested on Mark's broad chest.

"It's a good thing I cleaned my room," he commented after a moment.

Malajia couldn't help but laugh. Leave it to Mark to crack a joke after an intense sexual encounter. "You know what, I'm not gonna lie, it was so—" she blushed as she thought about what they just shared. "I wouldn't have noticed if you *hadn't*," she finished. Feeling like Mark was smiling, she lifted her head up and pointed at him. "Don't let that go to your head."

"Already has," he smiled. Then kissed her.

Malajia laid her head back on Mark's chest. As her head rose up and down with each breath that Mark took, Malajia's mind wandered. Given what she'd gone through, what she'd *done*, Malajia knew that she would never be the same. But despite that, for the first time in months, she was allowing herself the opportunity to move on with her life. For the first time in months, she had something to look forward to.

College life 401;

Senior Experience

Book seven

The College life series

Coming soon!